Once Upon a Rose

Also by Nora Roberts, Jill Gregory, Ruth Ryan Langan, and Marianne Willman in Large Print:

Once Upon a Castle
Once Upon a Dream

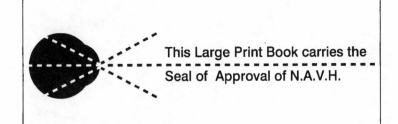

This Large Print Book carries the
Seal of Approval of N.A.V.H.

Once Upon a Rose

Nora Roberts, Jill Gregory, Ruth Ryan Langan, and Marianne Willman

Thorndike Press • Waterville, Maine

Published in 2002 by arrangement with The Berkley Publishing Group, a member of Penguin Putnam Inc.

Thorndike Press Large Print Romance Series.

The tree indicium is a trademark of Thorndike Press.

The text of this Large Print edition is unabridged. Other aspects of the book may vary from the original edition.

Set in 16 pt. Plantin by Christina S. Huff.

Printed in the United States on permanent paper.

Library of Congress Cataloging-in-Publication Data

Once upon a rose / Nora Roberts . . . [et al.].
    p. cm.
    Contents: Winter rose / Nora Roberts — The rose and the sword / Jill Gregory — The roses of Glenross / Ruth Ryan Langan — The fairest rose / Marianne Willman.
    ISBN 0-7862-4048-2 (lg. print : hc : alk. paper)
  1. Love stories, American. 2. Historical fiction, American. 3. Roses — Fiction. I. Roberts, Nora.
PS648.L6 O537 2002
813'.08508—dc21   2001058293

Contents

WINTER ROSE   7
Nora Roberts

THE ROSE AND THE SWORD   141
Jill Gregory

THE ROSES OF GLENROSS   273
Ruth Ryan Langan

THE FAIREST ROSE   383
Marianne Willman

Winter
Rose

Nora Roberts

For the three roses,
Ruth, Marianne and Jan,
who've made this so much fun

1

The world was white. And bitter, bitter cold. Exhausted, he drooped in the saddle, unable to do more than trust his horse to continue to trudge forward. Always forward. He knew that to stop, even for moments, in this cruel and keening wind would mean death.

The pain in his side was a freezing burn, and the only thing that kept him from sliding into oblivion.

He was lost in that white globe, blinded by the endless miles of it that covered hill and tree and sky, trapped in the frigid hell of vicious snow gone to icy shards in the whip of the gale. Though even the slow, monotonous movements of his horse brought him agony, he did not yield.

At first the cold had been a relief from the scorching yellow sun. It had, he thought, cooled the fever the wound had sent raging through him. The unblemished stretch of white had numbed his mind so that he'd no

longer seen the blood staining the battle-
ground. Or smelled the stench of death.

For a time, when the strength had drained
out of him along with his blood, he'd
thought he heard voices in the rising wind.
Voices that had murmured his name, had
whispered another.

Delirium, he'd told himself. For he didn't
believe the air could speak.

He'd lost track of how long he'd been traveling. Hours, days, weeks. His first hope had
been to come across a cottage, a village
where he could rest and have his wound
treated. Now he simply wanted to find a decent place to die.

Perhaps he was dead already and hell was
endless winter.

He no longer hungered, though the last
time he'd eaten had been before the battle.
The battle, he thought dimly, where he'd
emerged victorious and unscathed. It had
been foolish, carelessly foolish, of him to
ride for home alone.

The trio of enemy soldiers had, he was
sure, been trying to reach their own homes
when they met him on that path in the
forest. His first instinct was to let them go.
The battle had been won and the invasion
crushed. But war and death were still in
their eyes, and when they charged him his

sword was in his hand.

They would never see home now. Nor, he feared, would he.

As his mount plodded onward, he fought to remain conscious. And now he was in another forest, he thought dully as he struggled to focus. Though how he had come to it, how he had gotten lost when he knew his kingdom as intimately as a man knew a lover's face, was a mystery to him.

He had never traveled here before. The trees looked dead to him, brittle and gray. He heard no bird, no brook, just the steady swish of his horse's hooves in the snow.

Surely this was the land of the dead, or the dying.

When he saw the deer, it took several moments to register. It was the first living thing he'd seen since the flakes had begun to fall, and it watched him without fear.

Why not? he mused with a weak laugh. He hadn't the strength to notch an arrow. When the stag bounded away, Kylar of Mrydon, prince and warrior, slumped over the neck of his horse.

When he came to again, the forest was at his back, and he faced a white, white sea. Or so it seemed. Just as it seemed, in the center of that sea, a silver island glittered. Through his hazy vision, he made out turrets and towers. On the topmost a flag flew in the wild wind. A red rose blooming full against a field of white.

He prayed for strength. Surely where there was a flag flying there were people. There was warmth. He would have given half a kingdom to spend the last hour of his life by a fire's light and heat.

But his vision began to go dark at the edges and his head swam. Through the waves of fatigue and weakness he thought he saw the rose, red as blood, moving over that white sea toward him. Gritting his teeth, he urged his horse forward. If he couldn't have the fire, he wanted the sweet scent of the rose before he died.

He lacked even the strength to curse fate as he slid once more into unconsciousness and tumbled from the saddle into the snow.

The fall shot pain through him, pushed him back to the surface, where he clung as if under a thin veil of ice. Through it, he saw a face leaning close to his. Lovely long-lidded eyes, green as the moss in the forests of his home, smooth skin of rose and cream. A soft, full mouth. He saw those pretty lips move, but couldn't hear the words she spoke through the buzzing in his head.

The hood of her red cloak covered her hair, and he reached up to touch the cloth.

"You're not a flower after all."

"No, my lord. Only a woman."

"Well, it's better to die warmed by a kiss than a fire." He tugged on the hood, felt that soft, full mouth meet his — one sweet taste — before he passed out.

Men, Deirdre thought as she eased back, were such odd creatures. To steal a kiss at such a time was surely beyond folly. Shaking her head, she got to her feet and took in hand the horn that hung from the sash at her waist. She blew the signal for help, then removed her cloak to spread over him. Sitting again, she cradled him as best she could in her arms and waited for stronger hands to carry the unexpected guest into the castle.

The cold had saved his life, but the fever might snatch it back again. On his side of the battle were his youth and his strength. And, Deirdre thought, herself. She would do all in her power to heal him. Twice, he'd regained consciousness during his transport to the bedchamber. And both times he'd struggled, weakly to be sure, but enough to start the blood flowing from his wound again once he was warm.

In her brisk, somewhat ruthless way, she'd ordered two of her men to hold him down while she doused him with a sleeping draught. The cleaning and closing of the wound would be painful for him if he should wake again. Deirdre was a woman who brooked no nonsense, but she disliked seeing anyone in pain.

She gathered her medicines and herbs, pushed up the sleeves of the rough tunic she wore. He lay naked on the bed, in the thin light of the pale gold sun that filtered through the narrow windows. She'd seen unclothed men before, just as she'd seen what a sword could do to flesh.

"He's so handsome." Cordelia, the servant Deirdre had ordered to assist her, nearly sighed.

"What he is, is dying." Deirdre's voice was sharp with command. "Put more pressure on that cloth. I'll not have him bleed to death under my roof."

She selected her medicines and, moving to the bed, concentrated only on the wound in his side. It ranged from an inch under his armpit down to his hip in one long, vicious slice. Sweat dewed on her brow as she focused, putting her mind into his body to search for damage. Her cheeks paled as she worked, but her hands were steady and quick.

So much blood, she thought as her breath came thick and ragged. So much pain. How could he have lived with this? Even with the cold slowing the flow of blood, he should have been long dead.

She paused once to rinse the blood from her hands in a bowl, to dry them. But when she picked up the needle, Cordelia blanched. "My lady . . ."

Absently, Deirdre glanced over. She'd nearly forgotten the girl was there. "You may go. You did well enough."

Cordelia fled the room so quickly, Deirdre might have smiled. The girl never moved so fast when there was work to be done. Deirdre turned back to her patient and began carefully, skillfully, to sew the wound closed.

It would scar, she thought, but he had others. His was a warrior's body, tough and hard and bearing the marks of battle. What was it, she wondered, that made men so eager to fight, to kill? What was it that lived inside them that they could find pride in both?

This one did, she was sure of it. It had taken strength and will, and pride, to keep him mounted and alive all the miles he'd traveled to her island. But how had he come, this dark warrior? And why?

She coated the stitched wound with a balm of her own making and bandaged it with her own hands. Then with the worse

15

tended, she examined his body thoroughly for any lesser wounds.

She found a few nicks and cuts, and one more serious slice on the back of his shoulder. It had closed on its own and was already scabbed over. Whatever battle he'd fought, she calculated, had been two days ago, perhaps three.

To survive so long with such grievous hurts, to have traveled through the Forgotten to reach help, showed a strong will to live. That was good. He would need it.

When she was satisfied, she took a clean cloth and began to wash and cool the fever sweat from his skin.

He was handsome. She let herself study him now. He was tall, leanly muscled. His hair, black as midnight, spilled over the bed linens, away from a face that might have been carved from stone. It suited the warrior, she thought, that narrow face with the sharp jut of cheekbones over hollowed cheeks. His nose was long and straight, his mouth full and somewhat hard. His beard had begun to grow in, a shadow of stubble that made him appear wicked and dangerous even unconscious.

His brows were black slashes. She remembered his eyes were blue. Even dazed with pain, fever, fatigue, they had been bold and brilliantly blue.

If the gods willed it, they would open again.

She tucked him up warm, laid another log on the fire. Then she sat down to watch over him.

For two days and two nights the fever raged in him. At times he was delirious and had to be restrained lest his thrashing break open his wound again. At times he slept like a man dead, and she feared he would never rouse. Even her gifts couldn't beat back the fire that burned in him.

She slept when she could in the chair beside his bed. And once, when the chills racked him, she crawled under the bedclothes with him to soothe him with her own body.

His eyes did open again, but they were blind and wild. The pity she tried to hold back when healing stirred inside her. Once when the night was dark and the cold rattled its bones against the windows, she held his hand and grieved for him.

Life was the most precious gift, and it seemed cruel that he should come so far from home only to lose his.

To busy her mind she sewed or she sang. When she trusted him to be quiet for a time, she left him in the care of one of her women and tended to the business of her home and her people.

On the last night of his fever, despair nearly broke her. Exhausted, she mourned for his wife, for his mother, for those he'd left behind who would never know of his fate. There in the quiet of the bedchamber, she used the last of her strength and her skill. She laid hands on him.

"The first and most vital of rules is not to harm. I have not harmed you. What I do now will end this, one way or another. Kill or cure. If I knew your name"— she brushed a hand gently over his burning brow —"or your mind, or your heart, this would be easier for both of us. Be strong." She climbed onto the bed to kneel beside him. "And fight."

With one hand over the wound that she'd unbandaged, the other over his heart, she let what she was rush through her, race through her blood, her bone. Into him.

He moaned. She ignored it. It would hurt, hurt both of them. His body arched up, and hers back. There was a rush of images that stole her breath. A grand castle, blurring colors, a jeweled crown.

She felt strength — his. And kindness. A light flickered inside her, nearly made her break away. But it drew her in, deeper, and the light grew soft, warm.

For Deirdre, it was the first time, even in

healing that she had looked into another's heart and felt it brush and call her own.

Then she saw, very clearly, a woman's face, her deep-blue eyes full of pride, and perhaps fear.

Come back, my son. Come home safe.

There was music — drumbeats — the laughter and shouts of men. Then a flash that was sun striking off steel, and the smell of blood and battle choked her.

She muffled a cry as she caught a glimpse in her mind. Swords clashing, the stench of sweat and death and fear.

He fought her, thrashing, striking out as she bore down with her mind. Later, she would tend the bruises they gave each other in this final pitched battle for life.

Her muscles trembled, and part of her screamed to pull back, pull away. He was nothing to her. Still, as her muscles trembled, she pit her fire against the fever, just as the enemy sword in his mind slashed against them both.

She felt the bite of it in her side, steel into flesh. The agony ripped a scream from her throat. On its heels, she tasted death.

His heart galloped under her hand, and the wound on his side was like a flame against her palm. But she'd seen into his mind now, and she fought to rise above the pain and use what she'd been given, what she'd taken, to save him.

His eyes were open, glassy with shock in a face white as death.

"Kylar of Mrydon." She spoke clearly, though each breath she took was a misery. "Take what you need. Fire of healing. And live."

The tension went out of his body. His eyes blurred, then fluttered shut. She felt the sigh shudder through him as he slid into sleep.

But the light within her continued to glow. "What is this?" she murmured, rubbing an unsteady hand over her own heart. "No matter. No matter now. I can do no more to help you. Live," she said again, then leaned down to brush her lips over his brow. "Or die gently."

She started to climb down from the bed, but her head spun. When she fainted, her head came to rest, quite naturally, on his heart.

2

He drifted in and out. There were times when he thought himself back in battle, shouting commands to his men while his horse wheeled under him and his sword hacked through those who would dare invade his lands.

Then he was back in that strange and icy forest, so cold he feared his bones would shatter. Then the cold turned to fire, and the part of him that was still sane prayed to die.

Something cool and sweet would slide down his throat, and somehow he would sleep again.

He dreamed he was home, drifting toward morning with a willing woman in his bed. Soft and warm and smelling of summer roses.

He thought he heard music, harpsong, with a voice, low and smooth, matching pretty words to those plucked notes.

Sometimes he saw a face. Moss-green

21

eyes, a lovely, wide mouth. Hair the color of dark, rich honey that tumbled around a face both unbearably beautiful and unbearably sad. Each time the pain or the heat or the cold would become intolerable, that face, those eyes, would be there.

Once, he dreamed she had called him by name, in a voice that rang with command. And those eyes had been dark and full of pain and power. Her hair had spilled over his chest like silk, and he'd slept once more — deeply, peacefully — with the scent of her surrounding him.

He woke again to that scent, drifted into it as a man might drift into a cool stream on a hot day. There was a velvet canopy of deep purple over his head. He stared at it as he tried to clear his mind. One thought came through.

This was not home.

Then another.

He was alive.

Morning, he decided. The light through the windows was thin and very dull. Not long past dawn. He tried to sit up, and the movement made his side throb. Even as he hissed out a breath, she was there.

"Carefully." Deirdre slid a hand behind his head to lift it gently as she brought a cup to his lips. "Drink now."

She gave him no choice but to swallow before he managed to bring his hand to hers and nudge the cup aside. "What . . ." His voice felt rusty, as if it would scrape his throat. "What is this place?"

"Drink your broth, Prince Kylar. You're very weak."

He would have argued, but to his frustration he was as weak as she said. And she was not. Her hands were strong, hard from labor. He studied her as she urged more broth on him.

That honey hair fell straight as rain to the waist of a simple gray dress. She wore no jewels, no ribbons, and still managed to look beautiful and wonderfully female.

A servant, he assumed, with some skill in healing. He would find a way to repay her, and her master.

"Your name, sweetheart?"

Odd creatures indeed, she thought as she arched a brow. A man would flirt the moment he regained what passed for his senses. "I am Deirdre."

"I'm grateful, Deirdre. Would you help me up?"

"No, my lord. Tomorrow, perhaps." She set the cup aside. "But you could sit up for a time while I tend your wound."

"I dreamed of you." Weak, yes, he thought.

But he was feeling considerably better. Well enough to put some effort into flirting with a beautiful housemaid. "Did you sing to me?"

"I sang to pass the time. You've been here three days."

"Three —" He gritted his teeth as she helped him to sit up. "I've no memory of it."

"That's natural. Be still now."

He frowned at her bent head as she removed the bandage. Though a generous man by nature, he wasn't accustomed to taking orders. Certainly not from housemaids. "I would like to thank your master for his hospitality."

"There is no master here. It heals clean," she murmured, and probed gently with her fingers. "And is cool. You'll have a fine scar to add to your collection." With quick competence, she smeared on a balm. "There's pain yet, I know. But if you can tolerate it for now, I'd prefer not to give you another sleeping draught."

"Apparently I've slept enough."

She began to bandage him again, her body moving into his as she wrapped the wound. Fetching little thing, he mused, relieved that he was well enough to feel a tug of interest. He skimmed a hand through her hair as she worked, twined a lock around his finger. "I've never had a prettier physician."

"Save your strength, my lord." Her voice was cool, dismissive, and made him frown again. "I won't see my work undone because you've a yen for a snuggle."

She stepped back, eyeing him calmly. "But if you've that much energy, you may be able to take some more broth, and a bit of bread."

"I'd rather meat."

"I'm sure. But you won't get it. Do you read, Kylar of Mrydon?"

"Yes, of course I . . . You call me by name," he said cautiously. "How do you know it?"

She thought of that dip she'd taken into his mind. What she'd seen. What she'd felt. Neither of them, she was sure, was prepared to discuss it. "You told me a great many things during the fever," she said. And that was true enough. "I'll see you have books. Bed rest is tedious. Reading will help."

She picked up the empty cup of broth and started across the chamber to the door.

"Wait. What is this place?"

She turned back. "This is Rose Castle, on the Isle of Winter in the Sea of Ice."

His heart stuttered in his chest, but he kept his gaze direct on hers. "That's a fairy tale. A myth."

"It's as real as life, and as death. You, my lord Kylar, are the first to pass this way in more than twenty years. When you're rested

25

and well, we'll discuss how you came here."

"Wait." He lifted a hand as she opened the thick carved door. "You're not a servant." He wondered how he could ever have mistaken her for one. The simple dress, the lack of jewels, the undressed hair did nothing to detract from her bearing. Her breeding.

"I serve," she countered. "And have all my life. I am Deirdre, queen of the Sea of Ice."

When she closed the door behind her, he continued to stare. He'd heard of Rose Castle, the legend of it, in boyhood. The palace that stood on an island in what had once been a calm and pretty lake, edged by lush forests and rich fields. Betrayal, jealousy, vengeance, and witchcraft had doomed it all to an eternity of winter.

There was something about a rose trapped in a pillar of ice. He couldn't quite remember how it all went.

Such things were nonsense, of course. Entertaining stories to be told to a child at bedtime.

And yet . . . yet he'd traveled through that world of white and bitter cold. He'd fought and won a battle, in high summer, then somehow had become lost in winter.

Because he, in his delirium, had traveled far north. Perhaps into the Lost Mountains or even beyond them, where the wild tribes hunted giant white bear and dragons still guarded caves.

He'd talked with men who claimed to have been there, who spoke of dark blue water crowded with islands of ice, and of warriors tall as trees.

But none had ever spoken of a castle.

How much had he imagined, or dreamed? Determined to see for himself, he tossed back the bedcovers. Sweat slicked his skin, and his muscles trembled, appalling him — scoring his pride — as the simple task of shifting to sit on the side of the bed sapped his strength. He sat for several moments more, gathering it back.

When he managed to stand, his vision wavered, as if he was looking through water. He felt his knees buckle but managed to grip the bedpost and stay on his feet.

While he waited to steady, he studied the room. It was simply appointed, he noted. Tasteful, certainly, even elegant in its way unless you looked closely enough to see that the fabrics were fraying with age. Still, the chests and the chairs gleamed with polish. While the rug was faded with time, its workmanship was lovely. The candlesticks were gleaming silver, and the fire burned quietly in a hearth carved from lapis.

As creakily, as carefully, as an aged grand-father, he walked across the room to the window.

Through it, as far as he could see, the world was white. The sun was a dim haze behind the white curtain that draped the sky, but it managed to sparkle a bit on the ice that surrounded the castle. In the distance, he saw the shadows of the forest, hints of black and gray smothered in snow. In the north, far north, mountains speared up. White against white.

Closer in, at the feet of the castle, the snow spread in sheets and blankets. He saw no movement, no tracks. No life.

Were they alone here? he wondered. He and the woman who called herself a queen?

Then he saw her, a regal flash of red against the white. She walked with a long, quick stride — as a woman might, he thought, bustle off to the market. As if she sensed him there, she stopped, turned. Looked up at his window.

He couldn't see her expression clearly, but the way her chin angled told him she was displeased with him. Then she turned away again, her fiery cloak swirling, as she continued over that sea toward the forest.

He wanted to go after her, to demand answers, explanations. But he could barely make it back to the bed before he collapsed. Trembling from the effort, he buried himself under the blankets again and slept the day away.

"My lady, he's demanding to see you again."

Deirdre continued to work in the precious dirt under the wide dome. Her back ached, but she didn't mind it. In this, what she called her garden, she grew herbs and vegetables and a few precious flowers in the false spring generated by the sun through the glass.

"I have no time for him, Orna." She hoed a trench. It was a constant cycle, replenishing, tending, harvesting. The garden was life to her world. And one of her few true pleasures. "Between you and Cordelia he's tended well enough."

Orna pursed her lips. She had nursed Deirdre as a babe, had tutored her, tended her, and since the death of Queen Fiona, had stood when she could as mother. She was one of the few in Rose Castle who dared to question the young queen.

"It's been three days since he woke. The man is restless."

Deirdre straightened, rested her weight on the hoe. "Is he in pain?"

Orna's weathered face creased with what might have been impatience. "He says not, but he's a man, after all. He has pain. Despite it, and his weakness, he won't be kept to his chamber much longer. The man is a prince, my lady, and used to being obeyed."

"I rule here." Deirdre scanned her garden. The earlier plantings were satisfactory. She couldn't have the lush, but she could have the necessary. Even, she thought as she looked at her spindly, sun-starved daisies, the occasional indulgence.

"One of the kitchen boys should gather cabbages for dinner," she began. "Have the cook choose two of the hens. Our guest needs meat."

"Why do you refuse to see him?"

"I don't refuse." Annoyed, Deirdre went back to her work. She was avoiding the next meeting, and she knew it. Something had come into her during the healing, something she was unable to identify. It left her uneasy and unsettled.

"I stayed with him three days, three nights," she reminded Orna. "It's put me behind in my duties."

"He's very handsome."

"So is his horse," Deirdre said lightly. "And the horse is of more interest to me."

"And strong," Orna continued, stepping closer. "A prince from outside our world. He could be the one."

30

"There is no one." Deirdre tossed her head. Hope put no fuel in the fire nor food in the pot. It was a luxury she, above all, could ill afford. "I want no man, Orna. I will depend on no one but myself. It's woman's foolishness, woman's need, and man's deceit that have cursed us."

"Woman's pride as much as foolishness." Orna laid a hand on the staff of the hoe. "Will you let yours stop you from taking a chance for freedom?"

"I will provide for my people. When the time comes I will lie with a man until I conceive. I will make the next ruler, train the child as I was trained."

"Love the child," Orna murmured.

"My heart is so cold." Tired, Deirdre closed her eyes. "I fear there is no love in me. How can I give what isn't mine?"

"You're wrong." Gently Orna touched her cheek. "Your heart isn't cold. It's only trapped, as the rose is trapped in ice."

"Should I free it, Orna, so it could be broken as my mother's was?" She shook her head. "That solves nothing. Food must be put on the table, fuel must be gathered. Go now, tell our guest that I'll visit him in his chambers when time permits."

"This seems like a fine time." So saying, Kylar strode into the dome.

3

He'd never seen anything like the garden before. But then, Kylar had seen a great deal of
the unexpected in Rose Castle in a short
time. Such as a queen dressed in men's
clothing — trousers and a ragged tunic. The
result was odd, and strangely alluring. Her
hair was tied back, but not with anything so
female as a ribbon. She'd knotted it with a
thin leather strap, such as he did himself
when doing some quick spot of manual labor.

Her face was flushed from her work and
as lovely as the flower he'd first taken her
for. She did not look pleased to see him.
Even as he watched, her eyes chilled.

Behold the ice queen, he thought. A man
would risk freezing off important parts of
his body should he try to thaw her.

"I see you're feeling better, my lord."

"If you'd spared me five minutes of your
time, you'd have seen so before."

"Will you pardon us, Orna." She knelt and

began to plant the long eyes of potatoes harvested earlier in the year. It was a distraction, one she needed. Seeing him again stirred her, in dangerous ways. "You'll excuse me, my lord, if I continue with my task."

"Are there no servants to do such things?"

"There are fifty-two of us in Rose Castle. We all have our places and our duties."

He squatted beside her, though it caused his side to weep. Taking her hand, he turned it over and examined the ridge of callus. "Then I would say, my lady, you have too many duties."

"It's not for you to question me."

"You don't give answers, so I must continue to question. You healed me. Why do you resent me?"

"I don't know. But I do know that I require both hands for this task." When he released her, she continued to plant. "I'm unused to strangers," she began. Surely that was it. She had never seen, much less healed, a stranger before. Wouldn't that explain why, after looking into his mind, into his heart, she felt so drawn to him?

And afraid of him.

"Perhaps my manners are unpolished, so I will beg your pardon for any slight."

"They're polished diamond-bright," he corrected. "And stab at a man."

She smiled a little. "Some men, I imagine, are used to softer females. I thought Cordelia would suit your needs."

"She's biddable enough, and pretty enough, which is why you have the dragon guarding her."

Her smile warmed fractionally. "Of course."

"I wonder why I prefer you to either of them."

"I couldn't say." She moved down the row, and when he started to move with her, he gasped. She cursed. "Stubborn." She rose, reached down, and to his surprise, wrapped her arms around him. "Hold on to me. I'll help you inside."

He simply buried his face in her hair. "Your scent," he told her. "It haunts me."

"Stop it."

"I can't get your face out of my head, even when I sleep."

Her stomach fluttered, alarming her. "Sir, I will not be trifled with."

"I'm too damn weak to trifle with you." Hating the unsteadiness, he leaned heavily against her. "But you're beautiful, and I'm not dead." When he caught his breath, he eased away. "I should be. I've had time to think that through." He stared hard into her eyes. "I've seen enough battle to know when a wound is mortal. Mine was. How did I cheat death, Deirdre? Are you a witch?"

"Some would say." Because his color concerned her, she unbent enough to put an arm around his waist. "You need to sit before you fall. Come back inside."

"Not to bed. I'll go mad."

She'd tended enough of the sick and injured to know the truth of that. "To a chair. We'll have tea."

"God spare me. Brandy?"

She supposed he was entitled. She led him through a doorway, down a dim corridor away from the kitchen. She skirted the main hallway and moved down yet another corridor. The room where she took him was small, chilly, and lined floor to ceiling with books.

She eased him into a chair in front of the cold fireplace, then went over to open the shutters and let in the light.

"The days are still long," she said conversationally as she walked to the fireplace. This one was framed in smooth green marble. "Planting needs to be finished while the sun can warm the seeds."

She crouched in front of the fire, set the logs to light. "Is there grass in your world? Fields of it?"

"Yes."

She closed her eyes a moment. "And trees that go green in spring?"

He felt a wrench in his gut. For home — and for her. "Yes."

"It must be like a miracle." Then she stood, and her voice was brisk again. "I must wash, and see to your brandy. You'll be warm by the fire. I won't be long."

"My lady, have you never seen a field of grass?"

"In books. In dreams." She opened her mouth again, nearly asked him to tell her what it smelled like. But she wasn't sure she could bear to know. "I won't keep you waiting long, my lord."

She was true to her word. In ten minutes she was back, her hair loose again over the shoulders of a dark green dress. She carried the brandy herself.

"Our wine cellars were well stocked once. My grandfather, I'm told, was shrewd in that area. And in this one," she added, gesturing toward the books. "He enjoyed a glass of good wine and a good book."

"And you?"

"The books often, the wine rarely."

When she glanced toward the door, he saw her smile, fully, warmly, for the first time. He could only stare at her as his throat went dry and his heart shuddered.

"Thank you, Magda. I would have come for it."

"You've enough to do, my lady, without carting trays." The woman seemed ancient to Kylar. Her face as withered as a winter apple, her body bowed as if she carried bricks on her back. But she set the tea tray on the sideboard and curtseyed with some grace. "Should I pour for you, my lady?"

"I'll see to it. How are your hands?"

"They don't trouble me overmuch."

Deirdre took them in her own. They were knotted and swollen at the joints. "You're using the ointment I gave you?"

"Yes, my lady, twice daily. It helps considerable."

Keeping her eyes on Magda's, Deirdre rubbed her thumbs rhythmically over the gnarled knuckles. "I have a tea that will help. I'll show you how to make it, and you'll drink a cup three times a day."

"Thank you, my lady." Magda curtseyed again before she left the room.

Kylar saw Deirdre rub her own hands as if to ease a pain before she reached for the teapot. "I'll answer your questions, Prince Kylar, and hope that you'll answer some of mine in turn." She brought him a small tray of cheese and biscuits, then settled into a chair with her tea.

"How do you survive?"

To the point, she thought. "We have the garden. Some chickens and goats for eggs and milk, and meat when meat is needed. There's the forest for fuel and, if we're lucky, for game. The young are trained in necessary skills. We live simply," she said, sipping her tea. "And well enough."

"Why do you stay?"

"Because this is my home. You risked your life in battle to protect yours."

"How do you know I didn't risk it to take what belonged to someone else?"

She watched him over the rim of her cup. Yes, he was handsome. His looks were only more striking now that he'd regained some of his strength. One of the servants had shaved him, and without the stubble of beard he looked younger. But little less dangerous. "Did you?"

"You know I didn't." His gaze narrowed on her face. "You know. How is that, Deirdre of the Ice?" He reached out, clamped a hand on her arm. "What did you do to me during the fever?"

"Healed you."

"With witchcraft?"

"I have a gift for healing," she said evenly. "Should I have used it, or let you die? There was no dark in it, and you are not bound to me for payment."

"Then why do I feel bound to you?"

Her pulse jumped. His hand wasn't gripping her arm now. It caressed. "I did nothing to tie you. I have neither desire nor the skill for it." Cautiously, she moved out of reach. "You have my word. When you're well enough to travel, you're free to go."

"How?" It was bitter. "Where?"

Pity stirred in her, swam into her eyes. She remembered the face of the woman in his mind, the love she'd felt flow between them. His mother, she thought. Even now watching for his return home.

"It won't be simple, nor without risk. But you have a horse, and we'll give you provisions. One of my men will travel with you as far as possible. I can do no more than that."

He put it aside for now. When the time came, he would find his way home. "Tell me how this came to be. This place. I've heard stories — betrayal and witchcraft and cold spells over a land that was once fruitful and at peace."

"So I am told." She rose again to stir the fire. "When my grandfather was king, there were farms and fields. The land was green and rich, the lake blue and thick with fish. Have you ever seen blue water?"

"I have, yes."

"How can it be blue?" she asked as she turned. There was puzzlement on her face, and more, he thought. An eagerness he hadn't seen before. It made her look very young.

"I haven't thought about it," he admitted. "It seems to be blue, or green, or gray. It changes, as the sky changes."

"My sky never changes." The eagerness vanished as she walked to the window. "Well," she said, and straightened her shoulders. "Well. My grandfather had two daughters, twin-born. His wife died giving them life, and it's said he grieved for her the rest of his days. The babes were named Ernia, who was my aunt, and Fiona, who was my mother, and on them he doted. Most parents dote on their children, don't they, my lord?"

"Most," he agreed.

"So he did. Like their mother, they were beautiful, and like their mother, they were gifted. Ernia could call the sun, the rain, the wind. Fiona could speak to the beasts and the birds. They were, I'm told, competitive, each vying for their father's favor though he loved them both. Do you have siblings, my lord?"

"A brother and a sister, both younger."

She glanced back. He had his mother's

eyes, she thought. But her hair had been light. Perhaps his father had that ink-black hair that looked so silky.

"Do you love them, your brother and your sister?"

"Very much."

"That is as it should be. But Ernia and Fiona could not love each other. Perhaps it was because they shared the same face, and each wanted her own. Who can say? They grew from girl to woman, and my grandfather grew old and ill. He wanted them married and settled before his death. Ernia he betrothed to a king in a land beyond the Elf Hills, and my mother he promised to a king whose lands marched with ours to the east. Rose Castle was to be my mother's, and the Palace of Sighs, on the border of the Elf Hills, my aunt's. In this way he divided his wealth and lands equally between them, for he was, I'm told, a wise and fair ruler and a loving father."

She came back to sit and sip at tea gone cold. "In the weeks before the weddings, a traveler came and was welcome here as all were in those days. He was handsome and clever, quick of tongue and smooth with charm. A minstrel by trade, it's said he sang like an angel. But fair looks are no mirror of the heart, are they?"

"A pleasant face is only a face." Kylar lifted a shoulder. "Deeds make a man."

"Or woman," she added. "So I have always believed, and so, in this case, it was. In secret, this handsome man courted and seduced both twins, and both fell blindly in love with him. He came to my mother's bed, and to her sister's, bearing a single red rose and promises never meant to be kept. Why do men lie when women love?"

The question took him aback. "My lady . . . not all men are deceivers."

"Perhaps not." Though she was far from convinced. "But he was. One evening the sisters, of the same mind, wandered to the rose garden. Each wanted to pluck a red rose for her lover. It was there the lies were discovered. Instead of comforting each other, instead of raging against the man who had deceived them both, they fought over him. She-wolves over an unworthy badger. Ernia's temper called the wind and the hail, and Fiona's had the beasts stalking out of the forest to snarl and howl."

"Jealousy is both a flawed and a lethal weapon."

She angled her head. Nodded. "Well said. My grandfather heard the clamor and roused himself from his sickbed. Neither marriage could take place now, as both his daughters were disgraced. The minstrel, who had not slipped away quickly enough, was locked in the dungeon until his punishment could be decided. There was weeping and wailing from the sisters, as that punishment would surely be banishment, if not death. But he was spared when it came to be known that my mother was with child. His child, for she had lain with no other."

"You were the child."

"Yes. So, by becoming, I saved my father's life. The grief of this, the shame of this, ended my grandfather's. Before he died, he ordered Ernia to the Palace of Sighs. Because of the child, he decreed that my mother would marry the minstrel. It was this that drove Ernia mad, and on the day the marriage took place, the day her own father died in despair, she cast her spell.

"Winter, endless years of it. A sea of ice to lock Rose Castle away from the world. The rosebush where flowers had been plucked from lies would not bear bud. The child her sister carried would never feel the warmth of summer sun on her face, or walk in a meadow or see a tree bear fruit. One faithless man, three selfish hearts, destroyed a world. And so became the Isle of Winter in the Sea of Ice."

"My lady." He laid a hand on hers. Her

life, he thought, the whole of it had been spent without the simple comfort of sunlight. "A spell cast can be broken. You have power."

"My gift is of healing. I cannot heal the land." Because she wanted to turn her hand over in his, link fingers, feel that connection, she drew away. "My father left my mother before I was born. Escaped. Later, as she watched her people starve, my mother sent messengers to the Palace of Sighs to ask for a truce. To beg for one. But they never came back. Perhaps they died, or lost their way. Or simply rode on into the warmth and the sun. No one who has left here has ever come back. Why would they?"

"Ernia the Witch-Queen is dead."

"Dead?" Deirdre stared into the fire. "You're sure of this?"

"She was feared, and loathed. There was great celebration when she died. It was on the Winter Solstice, and I remember it well. She's been dead for nearly ten years."

Deirdre closed her eyes. "As her sister has. So they died together. How odd, and how apt." She rose again to walk to the window. "Ten years dead, and her spell holds like a clenched fist. How bitter her heart must have been."

And the faint and secret hope she'd kept

flickering inside that upon her aunt's death the spell would break, winked out. She drew herself up. "What we can't change, we learn to be content with." She stared out at the endless world of white. "There is beauty here."

"Yes." It was Deirdre that Kylar watched. "Yes. There is beauty here."

4

He wanted to help her. More, Kylar thought, he wanted to save her. If there had been something tangible to fight — a man, a beast, an army — he would have drawn his sword and plunged into battle for her.

She moved him, attracted him, fascinated him. Her steady composure in the face of her fate stirred in him both admiration and frustration. This was not a woman to weep on a man's shoulder. It annoyed him to find himself wishing that she would, as long as the shoulder was his.

She was an extraordinary creature. He wanted to fight for her. But how did a man wage war on magic?

He'd never had any real experience with it. He was a soldier, and though he believed in luck, even in fate, he believed more in wile and skill and muscle.

He was a prince, would one day be a king. He believed in justice, in ruling with a firm touch on one hand and a merciful one on the other.

There was no justice here, where a woman who had done no wrong should be imprisoned for the crimes and follies and wickedness of those who had come before.

She was too beautiful to be shut away from the rest of the world. Too small, he mused, too fragile to work her hands raw. She should be draped in silks and ermine rather than homespun.

Already after less than a week on the Isle of Winter, he felt a restlessness, a need for color and heat. How had she stayed sane never knowing a single summer?

He wanted to bring her the sun.

She should laugh. It troubled him that he had not once heard her laugh. A smile, surprisingly warm when it was real enough to reach her eyes. That he had seen. He would find a way to see it again.

He waded through the snow across what he supposed had once been a courtyard. Though his wound had troubled him on waking, he was feeling stronger now. He needed to be doing, to find some work or activity to keep his blood moving and his mind sharp. Surely there was some task, some bit of work he could undertake for her here. It would repay her in some small way, and serve to keep his mind and hands busy while his body healed.

He recalled the stag he'd seen in the forest. He would hunt, then, and bring her meat. The wind that had thrashed ceaselessly for days had finally quieted. Though the utter stillness that followed it played havoc with the nerves, it would make tracking through the forest possible.

He moved through a wide archway on the other side of the courtyard. And stopped to stare.

This, he realized with wonder, had been the rose garden. Gnarled and blackened stalks tangled out of the snow. Once, he imagined, it would have been magnificent, full of color and scent and humming bees.

Now it was a great field of snow cased in ice.

Bisecting that field were graceful paths of silver stone, and someone kept them clear. There were hundreds of bushes, all brittle with death, the stalks spearing out of their cold graves like blackened bones.

Benches, these, too, cleared of snow and ice, stood in graceful curves of deep jewel colors. Ruby, sapphire, emerald, they gleamed in the midst of the stark and merciless white. There was a small pond in the shape of an open rose, and its flower held a rippled sheet of ice. Dead branches with vicious thorns strangled iron arbors. More spindly corpses climbed up the silver stone of the walls as if they'd sought to escape before winter murdered them.

In the center, where all paths led, was a towering column of ice. Under the glassy sheen, he could see the arch of blackened branches studded with thorns, and hundreds of withered flowers trapped forever in their moment of death.

The rosebush, he thought, where the flowers of lies had been plucked. No, he corrected as he moved toward it. More a tree, for it was taller than he was and spread wider than the span of both his arms. He ran his fingertips over the ice, found it smooth. Experimentally, he took the dagger from his belt, dragged its tip over the ice. It left no mark.

"It cannot be reached with force."

Kylar turned and saw Orna standing in the archway. "What of the rest? Why haven't the dead branches been cleared and used for fire?" he asked her.

"To do so would be to give up hope." She had hope still, and more when she looked into Kylar's eyes.

She saw what she needed there. Truth, strength, and courage.

"She walks here."

"Why would she punish herself in such a way?" he demanded.

"It reminds her, I think, of what was. And what is." But not, Orna feared, of what might be. "Once, when my lady was but eight, and the last of the dogs died, breaking her heart, she took her grandfather's sword. In her grief and temper, she tried to hack through that ice into the bush. For nearly an hour she stabbed and sliced and beat at it, and could not so much as scratch the surface. In the end, she went to her knees there where you stand now and wept as if she'd die from it. Something in her did die that day, along with the last of the dogs. I have not heard her weep since. I wish she would."

"Why do you wish for your lady's tears?"

"For then she would know her heart is not dead but, like the rose, only waiting."

He sheathed his dagger. "If force can't reach it, what can?"

She smiled, for she knew he spoke of the heart as much as the rose. "You will make a good king in your time, Kylar of Mrydon, for you listen to what isn't said. What can't be vanquished with sword or might can be won with truth, with love, with selflessness. She is in the stables, what is left of them. She wouldn't ask for your company, but would enjoy it."

★ ★ ★

The stables lined three sides of another courtyard, but this one was crisscrossed with crooked paths dug through or trampled into the snow. Kylar saw the reason for it in the small troop of children waging a lively snow battle at the far end. Even in such a world, he thought, children found a way to be children.

As he drew closer to the stables, he heard the low cackle of hens. There were men on the roof, working on a chimney. They tipped their caps to him as he passed under the eaves and into the stables.

It was warmer, thanks to carefully banked fires, and clean as a parlor. The queen, he thought, tended her goats and chickens well. Iron kettles heated over the fires. Water for the stock, he concluded, made from melted snow. He noted barrows of manure. For use in her garden, he decided. A wise and practical woman, Queen Deirdre.

Then he saw the wise and practical woman, with her red hood tossed back, her gold hair raining down as she cooed up at his warhorse.

When the horse shook its great head and blew, she laughed. The rich female sound warmed his blood more thoroughly than the fires.

"His name is Cathmor."

Startled, embarrassed, Deirdre dropped the hands she'd lifted to stroke the horse's muzzle. She knew she shouldn't have lingered, that he would come check on his horse as it had been reported he did twice daily. But she'd so wanted to see the creature herself.

"You have a light step."

"You were distracted." He walked up beside her, and to her surprise and delight, the horse bumped his shoulder in greeting.

"Does that mean he's glad to see you?"

"It means he's hoping I have an apple."

Deirdre fingered the small carrot from her garden she'd tucked in her pocket. "Perhaps this will do." She pulled it out, started to offer it to Kylar.

"He would enjoy being fed by a lady. No, not like that." He took her hand and, opening it, laid the carrot on her palm. "Have you never fed a horse?"

"I've never seen one." She caught her breath as Cathmor dipped his head and nibbled the carrot out of her palm. "He's bigger than I imagined, and more handsome. And softer." Unable to resist, she stroked her hand down the horse's nose. "Some of the children have been keeping him company. They'd make a pet of him if they could."

"Would you like to ride him?"

"Ride?"

"He needs the exercise, and so do I. I thought I would hunt this morning. Come with me."

To ride a horse? Just the idea of it was thrilling. "I have duties."

"I might get lost alone." He brought her hand back up, ran it under his along Cathmor's silky neck. "I don't know your forest. And I'm still a bit weak."

Her lips twitched. "Your wits are strong enough. I could send a man with you."

"I prefer your company."

To ride a horse, she thought again. How could she resist? Why should she? She was no fluttery girl who would fall into stutters and blushes by being alone with a man. Even this man.

"All right. What do I do first?"

"You wait until I saddle him."

She shook her head. "No, show me how to do it."

When it was done, she sent one of the boys scurrying off to tell Orna she was riding out with the prince. She needn't have bothered, for as they walked the horse out of the stables, her people began to gather at the windows, in the courtyard.

When he vaulted into the saddle, they

cheered him like a hero.

"It's been a long time since they've seen anyone ride," she explained as Cathmor pranced in place. "Some of them, like me, never have." She let out a breath. "It's a long way up."

"Give me your hand." He reached down to her. "Trust me."

She would have to if she wanted this amazing treat. She offered her hand, then yelped in shock when he simply hauled her up in the saddle in front of him.

"You might have warned me you intended to drag me up like a sack of turnips. If you've opened your wound again —"

"Quiet," he whispered, entirely too close to her ear for comfort, and with her people cheering, he kicked Cathmor into a trot.

"Oh." Her eyes popped wide as her bottom bounced. "It's not what I expected." And hardly dignified.

With shouts and whoops, children raced after them as they trotted out of the castle.

"Match the rhythm of your body to the gait of the horse," he told her.

"Yes, I'm trying. Must you be so close?"

He grinned. "Yes. And I'm enjoying it. You shouldn't be uneasy with a man, Deirdre, when you've seen him naked."

"Seeing you naked hardly gives me cause

to relax around you," she shot back.

With a rolling laugh, he urged the horse to a gallop.

Her breath caught, but with delight rather than fear. Wind rushed by her cheeks, and snow flew up into the air like tattered lace. She closed her eyes for an instant to absorb the sensation, and the wild thrill made her dizzy.

So fast, she thought. So strong. When they charged up a hill she wanted to throw her arms in the air and shout for the sheer joy of it.

Her heart raced along with the horse, continued to pound even when they slowed at the verge of the forest that had been known as the Forgotten for the whole of her lifetime.

"It's like flying," she mused. "Oh, thank you." She leaned down to press her cheek to the horse's neck. "I'll never forget it. He's a grand horse, isn't he?"

Flushed with pleasure, she turned. His face was too close, so close she felt the warmth of his breath on her cheek. Close enough that she saw a kind of heat kindling in his eyes.

"No." He caught her chin with his hand before she could turn away again. "Don't. I kissed you before, when I thought I was dying." His lips hovered a breath from hers. "I lived."

He had to taste her again; it seemed his sanity depended on it. But because he saw her fear, he took her mouth gently, skimming his lips over ones that trembled. Soothing as well as seducing. He watched her eyes go soft before her lashes fluttered down.

"Kiss me back, Deirdre." His hand slid down until his arm could band her waist and draw her closer. "This time kiss me back."

"I don't know how." But she already was.

Her limbs went weak, wonderfully weak, even as her pulse danced madly. Warmth enveloped her, reaching places inside that had never known its comfort.

The light that had sparked inside her when their hearts had brushed in healing spread.

On the Isle of Winter in the snowy rose garden, beneath a shield of ice, a tiny bud — tender green — formed on a blackened branch.

He nibbled at her lips until she parted them. And when he deepened the kiss she felt, for the first time in her life, a true lance of heat in her belly.

Yearning for more, she eased back, then

indulged herself by letting her head rest briefly on his shoulder. "So it's this," she whispered. "It's this that makes the women sing in the kitchen in the morning."

He stroked her hair, rubbed his cheek against it. "It's a bit more than that." Sweet, he thought. Strong. She was everything a man could want. Everything, he realized, that he wanted.

"Yes, of course." She sighed once. "More than that, but it starts like this. It can't for me."

"It has." He held her close when she would have drawn away. "It did, the minute I saw you."

"If I could love, it would be you. Though I'm not sure why, it would be you. If I were free, I would choose you." She turned away again. "We came to hunt. My people need meat."

He fought the urge to yank her around, to plunder that lovely mouth until she yielded. Force wasn't the answer. So he'd been told. There were better ways to win a woman.

5

She spotted the tracks first. They moved
soundlessly through the trees, and she was
grateful for the need for silence.

How could she explain or ask him to understand, when she couldn't understand
herself? Her heart was frozen, chilled to
death by pride and duty, and the fear that
she might do her people more harm.

Her father had made her in lies, then had
run away from his obligation. Her mother
had done her duty, and she had been kind.
But her heart had been broken into so many
pieces there had been none left for her child.

And what sort of child was it who could
grieve more truly for a dead dog than for her
own dead mother?

She had nothing emotionally to give a
man, and wanted nothing from one. In that
way she would survive, and keep her people
alive.

Life, she reminded herself, mattered most.

And what she felt for him was surely no more than a churning in the blood.

But how could she have known what it was like to be held by him? To feel his heart beat so strong and fast against hers? None of the books she'd read had captured with their clever words the true thrill of lips meeting.

Now that she understood, it would be just another precious memory, like a ride on horseback, to tuck away for the endless lonely nights.

She would decide later, she thought, if the nights were longer, lonelier, with the memory than they were without it.

But today she couldn't allow herself to think like a woman softened by a man's touch. She must think like a queen with people to provide for.

She caught the scent of the stag even before the horse did, and held up a hand. "We should walk from here," she said under her breath.

He didn't question her, but dismounted, then reached up to lift her down. Then his arms were around her again, her hands on his shoulders, and her face tilted up to his. Even as she shook her head, he brushed his lips over her brow.

"Deirdre the fair," he said softly. "Such a pretty armful."

59

The male scent of him blurred the scent of the stag. "This is not the time."

Because the catch in her voice was enough to satisfy him, for now, he reached over for his bow and quiver. But when she held out her hands for them, he lifted his eyebrows.

"The bow is too heavy a draw for you." When she continued to stare, hands outstretched, he shrugged and gave them to her.

So, he thought, he would indulge her. They'd make do with more cabbage tonight.

Then he was left blinking as she tossed aside her cloak and streaked through the trees in her men's clothes like a wraith — soundless and swift. Before he could tether his horse, she'd vanished and he could do no more than follow in her tracks.

He stopped when he caught sight of her. She stood in the gloomy light, nearly hip-deep in snow. With a gesture smooth and polished as a warrior, she notched the arrow, drew back the heavy bow. The sharp *ping* of the arrow flying free echoed. Then she lowered the bow, and her head.

"Everyone misses sometimes," he said as he started toward her.

Her head came up, her face cold and set. "I did not miss. I find no pleasure in the kill. My people need meat."

She handed the bow and quiver back to him, then trudged through the snow to where the stag lay.

Kylar saw she'd taken it down, fast, mercifully fast, with a single shot.

"Deirdre," he called out. "Do you ask yourself how game, even so sparse, come to be here where there is no food for them?"

She continued walking. "My mother did what she could, leaving a call that would draw them to the forest. She hoped to teach me to do the same, but it's not my gift."

"You have more than one," he said. "I'll get the horse."

Once the deer was strapped onto the horse, Kylar cupped his hands to help Deirdre mount. "Put your right foot in my hands, swing your left leg over the saddle."

"There isn't room for both of us now. You ride, I'll walk."

"No, I'll walk."

"It's too far when you've yet to fully recover. Mount your horse." She started to move past him, but he blocked her path. Her shoulders straightened like an iron bar. "I said, mount. I am a queen, and you merely a prince. You will do as I bid."

"I'm a man, and you merely a woman." He shocked her speechless by picking her up and tossing her into the saddle. "You'll do what you're told."

However much she labored side by side with her people, no one had ever disobeyed a command. And no man had ever laid hands on her. "You . . . *dare*."

"I'm not one of your people." He gathered the reins and began to walk the horse through the forest. "Whatever our ranks, I'm as royal as you. Though that doesn't mean a damn at the moment. It's difficult to think of you as a queen when you're garbed like a man and I've seen you handle a bow that my own squire can barely manage. It's difficult to think of you as a queen, Deirdre," he added with a glance back at her furious face, "when I've held you in my arms."

"Then you'd best remember what that felt like, for you won't be allowed to do so again."

He stopped, and turning, ran his hand deliberately up her leg. When she kicked out at him, he caught her boot and laughed. "Ah, so there's a temper in there after all. Good. I prefer bedding a woman with fire in her."

Quick as a snake the dagger was out of her belt and in her hand. And its killing point at his throat. "Remove your hand."

He never flinched, but realized to his own shock that this wasn't merely a woman he could want. It was a woman he could love. "Would you do it, I wonder? I think you might while the temper's on you, but then you'd regret it." He brought his hand up slowly, gripped her knife hand by the wrist. "We'd both regret it. I tell you I want to bed you. I give you the truth. Do you want lies?"

"You can bed Cordelia, if she's willing."

"I don't want Cordelia, willing or not." He took the knife from her hand, then brushed a kiss over her palm. "But I want you, Deirdre. And I want you willing." He handed her back the dagger, hilt first. "Can you handle a sword as well as you do a dagger?"

"I can."

"You're a woman of marvels, Deirdre the fair." He began to walk again. "I understand developing skill with the bow, but what need have you for sword or dagger?"

"Ignoring training in defense is careless and lazy. The training itself is good for the body and the mind. If my people are expected to learn how to handle a blade, then so should I be."

"Agreed."

When he paused a second time, her eyes narrowed in warning. "I'm going to shorten the stirrups so you can ride properly. What happened to your horses?"

"Those who left the first year took them." She ordered herself to relax and pleased herself by stroking Cathmor's neck again. "There were cattle, too, and sheep. Those that didn't die of the cold were used as food. There were cottages and farmhouses, but people came to the castle for shelter, for food. Or wandered off hoping to find spring. Now they're under the snow and ice. Why do you want to bed me?"

"Because you're beautiful."

She frowned down at him. "Are men so simple, really?"

He laughed, shook his head, and her fingers itched to tangle in his silky black mane rather than the horse's. "Simple enough about certain matters. But I hadn't finished the answer. Your beauty would be enough to make me want you for a night. Try this now, heels down. That's fine."

He gave her foot a friendly pat, then walked back to the horse's head. "Your strength and your courage add layers to beauty. They appeal to me. Your mind's sharp and cleaves clean. That's a challenge. And a woman who can plant potatoes like a farmwife and draw a dagger like an assassin is a fascinating creature."

"I thought when a man wanted to pleasure himself with a woman, he softened her with pretty words and poetry and long looks full of pain and longing."

What a woman, Kylar mused. He'd never seen the like of her. "Would you like that?"

She considered it, and was relaxed again. It was easier to discuss the whole business as a practical matter. "I don't know."

"You wouldn't trust them."

She smiled before she could stop it. "I wouldn't, no. Have you bedded many women?"

He cleared his throat and began to walk a bit faster. "That, sweetheart, isn't a question I'm comfortable answering."

"Why not?"

"Because it's . . . it's a delicate matter," he decided.

"Would you be more comfortable telling me if you've killed many men?"

"I don't kill for sport, or for pleasure," he said, and his voice turned as frigid as the air. "Taking a man's life is no triumph, my lady. Battle is an ugly business."

"I wondered. I meant no offense."

"I would have let them go." He spoke so softly that she had to lean forward to hear clearly.

"Who?"

"The three who set upon me after the battle had been won. When I was for home.

I would have let them pass in peace. What purpose was there in more blood?"

She'd already seen this inside him, and knew it for truth. He had not killed in hate nor in some fever of dark excitement. He had killed to live. "They wouldn't let you pass in peace."

"They were tired, and one already wounded. If I'd had an escort as I should, they would have surrendered. In the end, it was their own fear and my carelessness that killed them. I'm sorry for it."

More for the waste of their lives, she realized, than for his own wounds. Understanding this, she felt something sigh inside her. "Kylar."

It was the first time she'd spoken his name, as she might to a friend. And she leaned down to touch his cheek with her fingertips, as she might touch a lover's.

"You'll rule well."

She invited him to sup with her that night. Another first. He dressed in the fresh doublet Cordelia brought him, one of soft linen that smelled lightly of lavender and rosemary. He wondered from what chest it had been unearthed for his use, but as it fit well enough, he had no cause to complain.

But when he followed the servant into the

dining hall, he wished for his court clothes.

She wore green again, but no simple dress of homespun. The velvet gown poured down her body, dipping low at the creamy rise of her breasts and sweeping out from her waist in soft, deep folds. Her hair was long and loose, but over it sparkled a crown glinting with jewels. More draped in shimmering ropes around her throat.

She stood in the glow of candlelight, beautiful as a vision, and every inch a queen.

When she offered a hand, he crossed to her, bowed deeply before touching his lips to her knuckles. "Your Majesty."

"Your Highness. The room," she said with a gesture she hoped hid the nerves and pleasure she felt upon seeing the open approval on his face, "is overlarge for two. I hope you'll be comfortable."

"I see nothing but you."

She tilted her head. Curious, this flirting, she decided. And entertaining. "Are these the pretty words and poetry?"

"They're the truth."

"They fall pleasantly on the ear. It's an indulgence to have a fire in here," she began as she let him escort her to the table. "But tonight there is wine, and venison, and a welcome guest."

At the head of the long table were two settings. Silver and crystal and linen white as the snow outside the windows. Behind them, the mammoth fire roared.

Servants slipped in to serve wine and the soup course. If he'd been able to tear his gaze away from Deirdre, he might have seen the glint in their eyes, the exchanged winks and quick grins.

She missed them as well, as she concentrated on the experience of her first formal meal with someone from outside her world. "The fare is simple," she began.

"As good as a bounty. And the company feeds me."

She studied him thoughtfully. "I do think I like pretty words, but I have no skill in holding a conversation with them."

He took her hand. "Why don't we practice?"

Her laugh bubbled out, but she shook her head. "Tell me of your home, your family. Your sister," she remembered. "Is she lovely?"

"She is. Her name is Gwenyth. She married two years ago."

"Is there love?"

"Yes. He was friend and neighbor, and they had a sweetness for each other since childhood. When I last saw her she was great with her second babe." The faintest cloud passed over his face. "I'd hoped to make my way home for the birthing."

"And your brother?"

"Riddock is young, headstrong. He can ride like the devil."

"You're proud of him."

"I am. He'd give you poetry." Kylar lifted his goblet. "He has a knack for it, and loves nothing more than luring pretty maids out to the garden in the moonlight."

She asked questions casually so he would talk. She was unsure of her conversational skills in this arena, and it was such a pleasure to just sit and listen to him speak so easily of things that were, to her, a miracle.

Summer and gardens, swimming in a pond, riding through a village where people went to market. Carts of glossy red apples — what would they taste like? Baskets of flowers whose scent she could only dream of.

She had a picture of his home now, as she had pictures in books.

She had a picture of him, and it was more than anything she'd ever found in a book.

Willing to pay whatever it cost her later, she lost herself in him, in the way his voice rose and fell, in his laugh. She thought she could sit this way for days, to talk like this with no purpose in it, no niggling worries. Just to be with him by the warmth of the fire, with wine sweet on her tongue and his eyes so intimately on hers.

She didn't object when he took her hand, when his fingers toyed with hers. If this was flirtation, it was such a lovely way to pass the time.

They spoke of faraway lands and cultures. Of paintings and of plays.

"You've put your library to good use," he commented. "I've known few scholars as well read."

"I can see the world through books, and lives through the stories. Once a year, on Midsummer, we put on a pageant. We have music and games. I choose a story, and everyone takes a part as if it were a play. Surviving isn't enough. There must be life and color."

There were times, secretly, when she pined near weeping for true color.

"All the children are taught to read," she continued, "and to do sums. If you have only a window on the world, you must look out of it. One of my men — well, he's just a boy really — he makes stories. They're quite wonderful."

She caught herself, surprised at the sound of her own voice rambling. "I've kept you long enough."

"No." His hand tightened on hers. He was

beginning to realize it would never be long enough. "Tell me more. You play music, don't you? A harp. I heard you playing, singing. It was like a dream."

"You were feverish. I play a little. Some skill inherited from my father, I suppose."

"I'd like to hear you play again. Will you play for me, Deirdre?"

"If you like."

But as she started to rise, one of the men who'd helped serve rushed in. "My lady, my lady, it's young Phelan!"

"What's happened?"

"He was playing with some of the boys on the stairs, and fell. We can't wake him. My lady, we fear he's dying."

6

Afraid to move him, they'd left the boy covered with a blanket at the base of the stairs. At first glance, Kylar thought the child, for he was hardly more, was already dead. He'd seen enough of death to recognize its face.

He judged the boy to be about ten, with fair hair and cheeks still round with youth. But those cheeks were gray, and the hair was matted with blood.

Those who circled and knelt around the boy made way when Deirdre hurried through.

"Get back now," she ordered. "Give him room."

Before Deirdre could kneel, a weeping woman broke free to fall at her feet and clutch at her skirts with bloodstained hands. "My baby. Oh, please, my lady! Help my little boy."

"I will, Ailish. Of course I will." Knowing that time was precious, Deirdre bent down and firmly loosened the terrified woman's hold on her. "You must be strong for him, and trust. Let me see to him now."

"He slipped, my lady." Another youth came forward with a jerky step. His eyes were dry, but huge, and there were tracks of tears still drying on his cheeks. "We were playing horse and rider on the stairs, and he slipped."

"All right." Too much grief, she thought, feeling waves of it pressing over her. Too much fear. "It's all right now. I'll tend to him."

"Deirdre." Kylar kept his voice low, so only she could hear over the mother's weeping. "There's nothing you can do here. I can smell death on him."

As could she, and so she knew she had little time. "What is the smell of death but the smell of fear?" She ran her hands gently over the crumpled body, feeling the hurts, finding so much broken in the little boy that her heart ached from it. Medicines would do no good here, but still her face was composed as she looked up.

"Cordelia, fetch my healing bag. Make haste. The rest, please, leave us now. Leave me with him. Ailish, go now."

"Oh, no, please, my lady. Please, I must stay with my boy."

"Do you trust me?"

73

"My lady." She gripped Deirdre's hand, wept on it. "I do."

"Then do as I bid you. Go now and pray."

"His neck," Kylar began, then broke off when Deirdre whipped her head around and stared at him.

"Be silent! Help me or go, but don't question me."

When Ailish was all but carried away, and the two of them were alone with the bleeding boy, Deirdre closed her eyes. "This will hurt him. I'm sorry for it. Hold him down, hold him as still as you can, and do nothing to interfere. Nothing, do you understand?"

"No." But Kylar shifted until he could clamp the boy's arms.

"Block thoughts of death from your mind," she ordered. "And fear, and doubt. Block them out as you would in battle. There's too much dark here already. Can you do this?"

"I can." And because she asked it of him, Kylar let the cold come into him, the cold that steeled the mind to face combat.

"Phelan," she said. "Young Phelan, the bard." Her voice was soft, almost a crooning as she traced her hands over him again. "Be strong for me."

She knew him already, had watched him grow and learn and be. She knew the sound of his voice, the quick flash of his grin, the lively turn of his mind. He had been hers, as all in Rose Castle were hers, from the moment of his first breath.

And so she merged easily with him.

While her hands worked, stroking, kneading, she slid into his mind. She felt his laughter inside her as he pranced and raced with his friends up and down the narrow stone steps. Felt his heart leap inside her own as his feet slipped. Then the fear, oh, the terror, an instant only before the horrible pain.

The snap of bone made her cry out softly, had her head rearing back. Something inside her crushed like thin clay under a stone hammer, and the sensation was beyond torment.

Her eyes were open now, Kylar saw. A deep and too brilliant green. Her breath came fast and hard, sweat pearled on her brow. And the boy screamed thinly, straining under his grip.

Both made a sound of agony as she slid a hand under the boy to cup his neck, laid her other on his heart. Both shuddered. Both went pale as death.

Kylar started to call out to her, to reach for her as she swayed. But he felt the heat, a ferocious fist of it that seemed to pump out of her, into the boy until the arms he held were like sticks of fire.

And the boy's eyes opened, stared up blindly.

"Take, young Phelan." Her voice was thick now, echoed richly off the stone. "Take what you need. Fire of healing." She leaned down, laid her lips gently on his. "Live. Stay with us. Your mother needs you."

As Kylar watched, thunderstruck, color seeped back into the boy's face. He would have sworn he felt death skitter back into the shadows.

"My lady," the boy said, almost dreamily. "I fell."

"Yes, I know. Sleep now." She brushed her hand over his eyes, and they closed on a sigh. "And heal. Let his mother in, if you will," she said to Kylar. "And Cordelia."

"Deirdre —"

"Please." The weakness threatened to drag her under, and she wanted to be away, in her own chamber before she lost herself to it. "Let them in so I can tell them what must be done for him."

She stayed kneeling when Kylar rose. The sounds of her people were like the dull roar of the ocean in her head. Even as Ailish collapsed next to her son, to gather him close to kiss Deirdre's now trembling hand, Deirdre gave clear, careful instructions for his care.

"Enough!" Alarmed by her pallor, Kylar swept her off the floor and into his arms. "Tend the boy."

"I'm not finished," Deirdre managed.

"Yes, by the blood, you are." The single glance he swept over those gathered challenged any to contradict him. "Where is your chamber?"

"This way, my lord prince." Orna led him through a doorway, down a corridor to another set of stairs. "I know what to do for her, my lord."

"Then you'll do it." He glanced down at Deirdre as he carried her up the stairs. She had swooned after all, he noted. Her skin was like glass, her eyes closed. The boy's blood was on her hands. "What did she risk by snatching the boy from death?"

"I cannot say, my lord." She opened a door, hurried across a chamber to the bed. "I will care for her now."

"I stay."

Orna pressed her lips together as he laid Deirdre on the bed. "I must undress her. Wash her."

Struggling with temper, he turned to stalk to the window. "Then do so. Is this what she did for me?"

"I cannot say." Orna met his eyes directly

when he turned back. "She did not speak of it to me. She does not speak of it with anyone. Prince Kylar, I will ask you to turn your back until my lady is suitably attired in her night garb."

"Woman, her modesty is not an issue with me." But he turned, stared out the window.

He had heard of those who could heal with the mind. But he had not believed it, not truly believed, before tonight. Nor had he considered what price the healer paid to heal.

"She will sleep," Orna said some time later.

"I won't disturb her." He came to the bed now, gazed down. There was still no color in her cheeks, but it seemed to him her breathing was steadier. "Nor will I leave her."

"My lady is strong, as valiant as ten warriors."

"If I had ten as valiant, there would never be another battle to fight."

Pleased with his response, Orna inclined her head. "And my lady has, despite what she believes, a tender heart." Orna set a bottle and goblet on the table near the bed. "See that you don't bruise it. When she wakes, give her some of this tonic. I will not be far, should you need me."

Alone, Kylar drew a chair near the bed

and watched Deirdre sleep. For an hour, and then two. She was motionless and pale as marble in the firelight, and he feared she would never wake but would sleep like the beauty in another legend, for a hundred years.

Even days before he would have deemed such things foolishness, stories for children. But now, after what he'd seen, what he'd felt, anything seemed possible.

Still, side by side with the worry inside him, anger bloomed. She had risked her life. He had seen death slide its cold fingers over her. She had bargained her life for the child's.

And, he was sure now, for his own.

When she stirred, just the slightest flutter of her lashes, he poured the tonic Orna had left into the cup.

"Drink this." He lifted her head from the pillow. "Don't speak. Just drink now."

She sipped, and sighed. The hand she lifted to his wrist slid limply away again. "Phelan?" she whispered.

"I don't know." He brought the cup to her lips a second time. "Drink more."

She obeyed, then turned her head. "Ask. Ask how young Phelan fares. Please. I must be sure."

"Drink first. Drink it all."

She did as he bade, and kept her eyes open

79

and on his now. If she'd had the strength, she would have gone to find out herself. But the weakness was still dragging at her, and she could only trust Kylar to the task. "Please. I won't be easy until I know his condition."

Kylar set the empty cup aside, then crossed the chamber to the door. Orna sat on a chair in the corridor, sewing by candlelight. She glanced up when she saw him. "Tell my lady not to fret. Young Phelan is resting. Healing." She got to her feet. "If you would like to retire, my lord, I will sit with my lady."

"Go to your bed," he said shortly. "I stay with her tonight."

Orna bowed her head and hid a smile. "As you wish."

He stepped back inside, closed the door. And turning saw that Deirdre was sitting up in bed, with her hair spilling like honey over the white lawn of her nightdress.

"Your boy is resting, and well."

At his words, he saw color return to her face, watched the dullness clear from her eyes. He came to the foot of the bed, which was draped in deep red velvet. "You recover quickly, madam."

"The tonic is potent." Indeed she now felt clear of mind, and even the echoes of pain were fading from her body. "Thank you for your help. His mother and father would have been too distraught to assist. Their worry could have distracted me. More, fear feeds death."

She glanced around the room, a little warily. Orna hadn't laid out her nightrobe. "If you'd excuse me now, I'll go see for myself."

"Not tonight."

To her shock he sat on the side of the bed near her. Only pride kept her from shifting over, or tugging up the blankets.

"I have questions."

"I've answered several of your questions already."

He lifted his brows. "Now I have more. The boy was dying. His skull crushed, his neck damaged if not broken. His left arm was shattered."

"Yes," she said calmly. "And inside his body, more was harmed. He bled inside himself. So much blood for such a little boy. But he has a strong heart, our Phelan. He is particularly precious to me."

"He would have been dead in minutes."

"He is not dead."

"Why?"

"I can't answer." Restlessly, she pushed at her hair. "I can't explain it to you."

"Won't."

"Can't."

When she would have turned her face away, he caught her chin, held it firmly. "Try."

"You overstep," she said stiffly. "Continually."

"Then you should be growing accustomed to it. I held the boy," he reminded her. "I watched, and I felt life come back into him. Tell me what you did."

She wanted to dismiss him, but he had helped her when she'd needed his help. So she would try. "It's a kind of search, and a merging. An opening of both." She lifted a hand, let it fall. "It is a kind of faith, if you will."

"It caused you pain."

"Do you think fighting death is painless? You know better. To heal, I must feel what he feels, and bring him up. . . ." She shook her head, frustrated with words. "Take him back to the pain. Then we ride it together, so that I see, feel, know."

"You rode more than pain. You rode death. I saw you."

"We were stronger."

"And if you hadn't been?"

"Then death would have won," she said simply. "And a mother would be grieving her firstborn tonight."

"And you? Deirdre of the Ice, would your people be grieving you?"

"There is a risk. Do you turn from battle, Kylar? Or do you face it knowing your life might be the price paid at end of day? Would you not stand for any one of your people if they had need? Would you expect me to do less for one of mine?"

"I was not one of yours." He took her hand before she could look away. "You rode death with me, Deirdre. I remember. I thought it a dream, but I remember. The pain, as if the sword cut into me fresh. That same pain mirrored in your eyes as you looked down at me. The heat of your body, the heat of your life pouring into me. I was nothing to you."

"You were a man. You were hurt." She reached out now, laying her hand on his cheek. "Why are you angry? Should I have let you die because my medicines weren't enough to save you? Should I have stepped back from you and my own gift because it would cause me a moment's pain to save you? Does your pride bleed now because a woman fought for your life?"

"Perhaps it does." He closed his hand over her wrist. "When I carried you in here I thought you would die, and I was helpless."

"You stayed with me. That was kind."

He made some sound, then pushed himself off the bed to pace. "When a man goes into battle, Deirdre, it's sword to sword, lance to lance, fist to fist. These are tangible things. What you've done, magic or miracle, is so much more. And you were right. I can't understand it."

"It changes how you think of me."

"Yes."

She lowered her lashes, hid the fresh pain. "There is no shame in it. Most men would not have stayed to help, certainly not have stayed to speak with me. I'm grateful. Now if you'd excuse me, I'd like to be alone."

Slowly, he turned back to her. "You misunderstand me. Before I thought of you as a woman — beautiful, strong, intelligent. Sad. Now I think of you as all of that, and so much more. You humble me. You expect me to step away from you, because of all you are. I can't. I want to be with you, and I have no right."

With her heart unsteady, she looked at him again. "Is it gratitude that draws you to me?"

"I am grateful. I owe you for every breath I take. But it isn't gratitude I feel when I look at you."

She slid out of bed to stand on her own feet. "Is it desire?"

"I desire you."

"I've never had a man's arms around me

in love. I want them to be yours."

"What right do I have when I can't stay with you? I should already be gone. Both my family and my people wait."

"You give me truth, and truth means more than pretty words and empty promises. I wondered about this, and now I know. When I healed you I felt something I've never felt before. Mixed with the pain and the cold that comes into me so bitter there was . . . light."

Watching him, she spread her hands. "I said I did nothing to bind you to me, and that is truth. But something happened in me when I was part of you. It angered me, and it frightened me. But now, just now . . ." She drew a breath and spoke without a blush. "It excites me. I've been so cold. Give me one night of warmth. You said you wanted me willing." She reached up, tugged the ribbons loose from the bodice of the nightdress. "And I am," she said as the white gown slid down to pool at her feet.

7

She was a vision. More than he could have dreamed. Slim and small, she stood in the glow of candle and firelight.

"Will you give me a night?" she asked him.

"Deirdre. My love. I would give you a lifetime."

"I want no pledges that can't be kept, no words but truth. Only give me what can be, and it will be enough," she replied somberly.

"My lady." He felt, somehow, that the step toward her was the most momentous of his life. And when he took her hands, that he was taking the world. "It is the truth. Why or how I don't know. But never have I spoken cleaner truth."

She believed he meant it, in this time. In this place. "Kylar, lifetimes are for those who are free."

So she would be, he promised himself. Whatever had to be done. But now wasn't for plans and battles. "If you won't accept that pledge, let me pledge this. That I have loved no other as I love you tonight."

"I can give that vow back to you. I thought it would be for duty." She lifted her hands to his face, traced the shape of it with her fingers. "And I thought the first time, it would be with fear." She laughed a little. "My heart jumps. Can you feel it?"

He laid a hand on her breast, felt the shiver. Felt the leap. "I won't hurt you."

"Oh, no." She laid a hand on his heart in turn. They had brushed once before, she thought. Heart to heart. Nothing had been the same for her since. Nothing would be the same for her ever again. "You won't hurt me. Warm me, Kylar, as a man warms his woman."

He drew her into his arms. Gently, gently. Laid his lips on hers. Tenderly. There once more, she thought. There. That miracle of mouth against mouth. Sighing out his name, she let herself melt into the kiss.

"The first time you kissed me, I thought you were foolish."

His lips curved on hers. "Did you?"

"Half frozen and bleeding, and you would waste your last breath flirting with a woman. Such is a man."

"Not a waste," he corrected. "But I can do

better now." With a flourish that pleased them both, he swept her into his arms. "Come to bed, my lady."

As she had once longed to do, she toyed with his silky black hair. "You must teach me what to do."

His muscles tightened, nerves and thrills, at the thought of her innocence. Tonight she would give him what she had given no other. In the candle glow he saw her face, saw that she gave him this treasure without fear, without shame.

No, he would not hurt her, but would do all in his power to bring her joy.

He laid her on the bed, rubbed his cheek against hers. "It will be my pleasure to instruct you."

"I've seen the goats mate."

His burst of laughter was muffled in her hair. "This, I can promise, will be somewhat different than the mating of goats. So pay attention," he said, grinning now as he lifted his head, "while I give you your first lesson."

He was a patient teacher, and surely, she thought as her skin began to shiver and sing under his hands, a skilled one. His mouth drank from hers, deep, then deeper until it was how she imagined it might be to slide bonelessly into a warm river.

Surrounded, floating, then submerged.

His hands roamed over her breasts, then cupped them as if he could hold her heart-beat in his palms. The sensation of those strong, hard hands on her flesh shimmered straight down to her belly. His mouth skimmed the side of her throat, nibbling.

"How lovely." She murmured it, arching a little to invite more. "How clever for breasts to give pleasure as well as milk."

"Indeed." His thumbs brushed over her nipples, and made her gasp. "I've often thought the same."

"Oh . . . but what do I . . ." Her words, her thoughts trailed off into a rainbow when that nibbling mouth found her breast.

She made a sound in her throat, half cry, half moan. It thrilled him, that sound of shocked pleasure, the sudden shudder of her body, the quick jolt of her heart under his lips. As she arched again, her fingers combed through his hair, gripped there and pressed him closer. The sweet taste of her filled him like warmed wine.

He rose over her to tug his doublet aside, but before he could satisfy himself with that glorious slide of his flesh to her flesh, she lifted her hands, ran them experimentally over his chest.

"Wait." She needed to catch her breath. It was all running through her so quickly that it nearly blurred. She wanted everything, but clearly, so that she might remember each stroke, each taste, each moment.

"I touched you when you were hurt. But this is different. I looked at your body, but didn't see it as I do now." Carefully she traced her finger along the scar running up his side. "Does this trouble you?"

He felt the line of heat, took her hand quickly. "No." Even now, he thought, she would try to heal. "There will be no pain tonight, for either of us."

He lowered to her, took her mouth again. There was a hint of urgency now, a taste of need. So much to feel, she mused dreamily. So much to know. And with the warmth of him coursing through her, she enfolded him. There was a freedom here, she discovered, in being about to touch him, stroke, explore, with no purpose other than pleasure. The hard muscles, the pucker in his smooth skin that was a scar of battle.

The strength of him excited her, challenged her own so that her hands, her mouth, her movements under him became more demanding.

This was fire, she realized. The first true licks of flame that brought nothing but delight and a bright, blinding need for more.

"I'm not fragile." Indeed she felt alive with

power, nearly frantic with a kind of raging hunger. "Show me more. Show me all."

No matter how his blood swam, he would be careful with her. But he could show her more. His hands roamed down her body, over her thighs. As if she knew what they both needed, she opened to him. Her breath came short, shivering out with quick little moans. Her nails bit into his back as she began to writhe under him.

He lifted his head and watched her fly over that first peak of pleasure.

Heat, such heat. She had never known such fire outside of healing magic. And this, somehow, this went deeper, spread wider. Her body was like a single wild flame. She cried out, the wanton sound of her own voice another shock to her system. Beyond control, beyond reason, she gripped his hips and called out his name.

When he plunged into her, the glory of it was like a shaft of lightning, bright and brilliant. There was a storm of those glorious and violent shocks as he thrust inside her. She locked herself around him, her face pressed against his neck and repeated his name as that miraculous heat consumed her.

"Sweetheart." When he could speak again, he did so lazily, with his head nuzzled between her breasts. "You are the most clever of students."

She felt golden, beautiful, and for the first time in her memory, more woman than queen. For one night, she told herself, one miraculous night, she would be a woman.

"I'm sure I could do better, my lord, with a few more lessons."

She was flushed, all but glowing, and her hair was a tangle of honeyed ropes over the white linen. "I believe you're right." He grinned and nibbled his way up her throat, lingered over her lips, then shifted so that she lay curled beside him.

"I'm so warm," she told him. "I never knew what it was like to be so warm. Tell me, Kylar, what's it like to have the sun on your face, full and bright?"

"It can burn."

"Truly?"

"Truly." He began to toy with her hair. "And the skin reddens or browns from it." He ran a fingertip down her arm. Pale as milk, soft as satin. "It can dazzle the eyes." He turned so he could look down at her. "You dazzle mine."

"There was an old man who was my tutor when I was a child. He'd been all over the world. He told me of great tombs in a desert where the sun beat like fury, of green hills where flowers bloomed wild and the rain came warm. Of wide oceans where great fish swam that could swallow a boat whole and dragons with silver wings flew. He taught me so many marvelous things, but he never taught me the wonders that you have tonight."

"There's never been another. Not like you. Not like this."

Because she read the truth in his eyes, she drew him closer. "Show me more."

As they loved, inside a case of ice, the first green bud on a blackened stalk unfurled to a single tender leaf. And a second began to form.

When he woke, she was gone. At first he was baffled, for he slept like a soldier, and a soldier slept light as a cat. But he could see she had stirred the fire for him and had left his clothes folded neatly on the chest at the foot of the bed.

It occurred to him that he'd slept only an hour or two, but obviously like the dead. The woman was tireless — bless her — and had demanded a heroic number of lessons through the night.

A pity, he mused, she hadn't lingered in bed a bit longer that morning. He believed he might have managed another.

He rose to draw back the hangings on the windows. He judged it to be well into the morning, as her people were about their chores. He couldn't tell the time by the light here, for it varied so little from dawn to dusk. It was always soft and dull, with that veil of white over sky and sun. Even now a thin snow was falling.

How did she bear it? Day after day of cold and gloom. How did she stay sane, and more — content? Why should so good and loving a queen be cursed to live her life without warmth?

He turned, studied the chamber. He'd paid little attention to it the night before. He'd seen only her. Now he noted that she lived simply. The fabrics were rich indeed, but old and growing thin.

There had been silver and crystal in the dining hall, he recalled, but here her candlestands were of simple metal, the bowl for her washing a crude clay. The bed, the chest, the wardrobe were all beautifully worked with carved roses. But there was only a single chair and table.

He saw no pretty bottles, no silks, no trinket boxes.

She'd seen to it that the appointments in his guest chamber were suited to his rank, but for herself, she lived nearly as spartanly as a peasant.

His mother's ladies had more fuss and fancy in their chambers than this queen. Then he glanced at the fire and with a clutching in his belly realized she would have used much of the furniture for fuel, and fabric for clothes for her people.

She'd worn jewels when they dined. Even now he could see how they gleamed and sparkled over her. But what good were diamonds and pearls to her? They couldn't be sold or bartered, they put no food on the table.

A diamond's fire brought no warmth to chilled bones.

He washed in the bowl of water she'd left for him, and dressed.

There on the wall he saw the single tapestry, faded with age. Her rose garden, in full bloom, and as magnificent in silk thread as he'd imagined it. Alive with color and shape, it was a lush paradise caught in a lush moment of summer.

There was a figure of a woman seated on the jeweled bench beneath the spreading branches of the great bush that bloomed wild and free. And a man knelt at her feet, offering a single red rose.

He trailed his fingers over the threads and

thought he would give his life and more to be able to offer her one red rose.

He was directed by a servant to Phelan's room, where the young bard had his quarters with a gaggle of other boys. The other boys gone, Phelan was sitting up in the bed with Deirdre for company. The chamber was small, Kylar noted, simple, but warmer by far than the queen's own.

She was urging a bowl of broth on Phelan and laughing in delight at the faces he made.

"A toad!"

"No, my lady. A monkey. Like the one in the book you lent me." He bared his teeth and made her laugh again.

"Even a monkey must eat."

"They eat the long yellow fruit."

"Then you'll pretend this is the long yellow fruit." She snuck a spoonful in his mouth.

He grimaced. "I don't like the taste."

"I know, the medicine spoils it a bit. But my favorite monkey needs to regain his strength. Eat it for me, won't you?"

"For you, my lady." On a heavy sigh, the boy took the bowl and spoon himself. "Then can I get up and play?"

"Tomorrow, you may get up for a short while."

"My lady." There was a wealth of horror and grief in the tone. Kylar could only sympathize. He'd once been a small boy and knew the tedium of being forced to stay idle in bed.

"A wounded soldier must recover to fight another day," Kylar said as he crossed to the bed. "Were you not a soldier when you rode the horse on the stairs?"

Phelan nodded, staring up at Kylar as if fascinated. To him the prince was as magnificent and foreign as every hero in every story he'd ever heard or read. "I was, my lord."

"Well, then. Do you know your lady kept me abed three full days when I came to her wounded?" He sat on the edge of the bed, leaned over and sniffed at the bowl. "And forced the same broth on me. It's a cruelty, but a soldier bears such hardships."

"Phelan will not be a soldier," Deirdre said firmly. "He is a bard."

"Ah." Kylar inclined his head in a bow. "There is no man of more import than a bard."

"More than a soldier?" Phelan asked, with eyes wide.

"A bard tells the tales and sings the songs. Without him, we would know nothing."

"I'm making a story about you, my lord."

Excited now, Phelan spooned up his broth. "About how you came from beyond, traveled the Forgotten wounded and near death, and how my lady healed you."

"I'd like to hear the story when you've finished it."

"You can make the story while you rest and recover." Pleased that the bowl was empty, Deirdre took it as she stood, then leaned over to kiss Phelan's brow.

"Will you come back, my lady?"

"I will. But now you rest, and dream your story. Later, I'll bring you a new book."

"Be well, young bard." Kylar took Deirdre's hand to lead her out.

"You rose early," he commented.

"There's much to be done."

"I find myself jealous of a ten-year-old boy."

"Nearly twelve is Phelan. He's small for his age."

"Regardless, you didn't sit and feed me broth or kiss my brow when I was well enough to sit up on my own."

"You were not so sweet-natured a patient."

"I would be now." He kissed her, surprised that she didn't flush and flutter as females were wont to do. Instead she answered his lips with a reckless passion that stirred his appetite. "Put me to bed, and I'll show you."

She laughed and nudged him back. "That will have to wait. I have duties."

"I'll help you."

Her face softened. "You have helped me already. But come. I'll give you work."

8

There was no lack of work. The prince of Mrydon found himself tending goats and chickens. Shoveling manure, hauling endless buckets of snow to a low fire, carting precious wood to a communal pile.

The first day he labored he tired so quickly that it scored his pride. On the second, muscles that had gone unused during his recovery ached continually.

But the discomfort had the benefit of Deirdre rubbing him everywhere with one of her balms. And made the ensuing loving both merry and slippery.

She was a joy in bed, and he saw none of the sadness in her eyes there. Her laughter, the sound he'd longed to hear, came often.

He grew to know her people and was surprised and impressed by the lack of bitterness in them. He thought them more like a family, and though some were lazy, some grim, they shouldered together. They knew, he realized, that the survival of the whole depended on each.

That, he thought, was another of Deirdre's gifts. Her people held the will to go on, day after day, because their lady did. He couldn't imagine his own soldiers bearing the hardships and the tedium with half as much courage.

He came upon her in her garden. Though the planting and maintenance there was divided, as all chores were in Rose Castle, he knew she often chose to work or walk there alone.

She did so now, carefully watering her plantings with snowmelt.

"Your goat herd has increased by one." He glanced down at his stained tunic. "It's the first such birthing I've attended."

Deirdre straightened, eased her back. "The kid and the she-goat are well?"

"Well and fine, yes."

"Why wasn't I called?"

"There was no need. Here, let me." He took the spouted bucket from her. "Your people work hard, Deirdre, but none as hard as their queen."

"The garden is a pleasure to me."

"So I've seen." He glanced up at the wide dome. "A clever device."

"My grandfather's doing." Since he was

watering, she knelt and began to harvest turnips. "He inherited a love for gardening from his mother, I'm told. It was she who designed and planted the rose garden. I'm named for her. When he was a young man, he traveled, and he studied with engineers and scientists and learned much. I think he was a great man."

"I've heard of him, though I thought it all legend." Kylar looked back at her as she placed turnips in a sack. "It's said he was a sorcerer."

Her lips curved a little. "Perhaps. Magic may come through the blood. I don't know. I do know he gathered many of the books in the library, and built this dome for his mother when she was very old. Here she could start seedlings before the planting time and grow the flowers she loved, even in the cold. It must have given her great pleasure to work here when her roses and other flowers were dormant with winter."

She sat back on her heels, looked over her rows and beyond to the sad and spindly daisies she prized like rubies. "I wonder if somehow he knew that his gift to his mother would one day save his people from starvation."

"You run low on fuel."

"Yes. The men will cut another tree in a

102

few days." It always pained her to order it. For each tree cut meant one fewer left. Though the forest was thick and vast, without new growth there would someday be no more.

"Deirdre, how long can you go on this way?"

"As long as we must."

"It's not enough." Temper that he hadn't realized was building inside him burst out. He cast the bucket aside and grabbed her hands.

She'd been waiting for this. Through the joy, through the sweetness, she'd known the storm would come. The storm that would end the time out of time. He was healed now, and a warrior prince, so healed, could not abide monotony.

"It's enough," she said calmly, "because it's what we have."

"For how much longer?" he demanded. "Ten years? Fifty?"

"For as long as there is."

Though she tried to pull away, he turned her hands over. "You work them raw, haul buckets like a milkmaid."

"Should I sit on my throne with soft white hands folded and let my people work?"

"There are other choices."

"Not for me."

"Come with me." He gripped her arms now, tight, firm, as if he held his own life.

Oh, she'd dreamed of it, in her most secret heart. Riding off with him, flying through the forest and away to beyond. Toward the sun, the green, the flowers.

Into summer.

"I can't. You know I can't."

"We'll find the way out. When we're home, I'll gather men, horses, provisions. I'll come back for your people. I swear it to you."

"You'll find the way out." She laid her hands on his chest, over the thunder of his heart. "I believe it. If I didn't I would have you chained before I'd allow you to leave. I won't risk your death. But the way back . . ." She shook her head, turned away from him when his grip relaxed.

"You don't believe I'll come back."

She closed her eyes because she didn't believe it, not fully. How could he turn his back on the sun and risk everything to travel here again for what he'd known for only a few weeks? "Even if you tried, there's no certainty you'd find us again. Your coming was a miracle. Your safe passage home will be another. I don't ask for three in one lifetime."

She drew herself up. "I won't ask for your

life, nor will I accept it. I will send a man with you — my best, my strongest — if you will take him. If you will give him good horses, and provisions, I will send others if the gods show him the way back again."

"But you won't leave."

"I'm bound to stay, as you are bound to go." She turned back, and though tears stung her throat, her eyes were dry. "It's said that if I leave here while winter holds this place, Rose Castle will vanish from sight, and all within will be trapped for eternity."

"That's nonsense."

"Can you say that?" She gestured to the white sky above the dome. "Can you be sure of it? I am queen of this world, and I am prisoner."

"Then bid me stay. You've only to ask it of me."

"I won't. And you can't. First, you're destined to be king. It is your fate, and I have seen the crown you'll wear inside your own mind and heart. And more, your family would grieve and your people mourn. With that on your conscience, the gift we found together would be forever tainted. One day you would go in any case."

"So little faith in me. I ask you this: Do you love me?"

Her eyes filled, sheened, but the tears did

not fall. "I care for you. You brought light inside me."

" 'Care' is a weak word. Do you love me?"

"My heart is frozen. I have no love to give."

"That is the first lie you've told me. I've seen you cuddle a fretful babe in your arms, risk your life to save a small boy."

"That is a different matter."

"I've been inside you." Frustrated fury ran over his face. "I've seen your eyes as you opened to me."

She began to tremble. "Passion is not love. Surely my father had passion for my mother, for her sister. But love he had for neither. I care for you. I desire you. That is all I have to give. The gift of a heart, woman to man, has doomed me."

"So because your father was feckless, your mother foolish, and your aunt vindictive, you close yourself off from the only true warmth there is?"

"I can't give what I don't have."

"Then take this, Deirdre of the Sea of Ice. I love you, and I will never love another. I leave tomorrow. I ask you again, come with me."

"I can't. I can't," she repeated, taking his arm. "I beg you. Our time is so short, let us not have this chill between us. I've given you

106

more than ever I gave a man. I pledge to you now there will never be another. Let it be enough."

"It isn't enough. If you loved, you'd know that." One hand gripped the hilt of his sword as if he would draw it and fight what stood between them. Instead, he stepped back from her. "You make your own prison, my lady," he said, and left her.

Alone, Deirdre nearly sank to her knees. But despair, she thought, would solve no more than Kylar's bright sword would. So she picked up the pail.

"Why didn't you tell him?"

Deirdre jolted, nearly splashing water over the rim. "You have no right to listen to private words, Orna."

Ignoring the stiff tone, Orna came forward to heft the bag of turnips. "Hasn't he the right to know what may break the spell?"

"No." She said it fiercely. "His choices, his actions must be his own. He is entitled to that. He won't be influenced by a sense of honor, for his honor runs through him like his blood. I am no damsel who needs rescuing by a man."

"You are a woman who is loved by one."

"Men love many women."

"By the blood, child! Will you let those who made you ruin you?"

"Should I give my heart, take his, at the risk of sacrificing all who depend on me?"

"It doesn't have to be that way. The curse —"

"I don't know love." When she whirled around, her face was bright with temper. "How can I trust what I don't know? She who bore me couldn't love me. He who made me never even looked on my face. I know duty, and I know the tenderness I feel for you and my people. I know joy and sadness. And I know fear."

"It's fear that traps you."

"Haven't I the right to fear?" Deirdre demanded. "When I hold lives in my hands, day and night? I cannot leave here."

"No, you cannot leave here." The undeniable truth of that broke Orna's heart. "But you can love."

"And loving, risk trapping him in this place. This cold place. Harsh payment for what he's given me. No, he leaves on the morrow, and what will be will be."

"And if you're with child?"

"I pray I am, for it is my duty." Her shoulders slumped. "I fear I am, for then I will have imprisoned his child, our child, here." She pressed a hand to her stomach. "I dreamed of a child, Orna, nursing at my breast and watching me with my lover's eyes, and what moved through me was so fierce and strong. The woman I am would ride away with him to save what grows inside me. The queen cannot. You will not speak of this to him, or anyone."

"No, my lady."

Deirdre nodded. "Send Dilys to me, and see that provisions are set aside for two men. They will have a long and difficult journey. I await Dilys in the parlor."

She set the bucket aside and walked quickly away.

Before going inside, Orna hurried through the archway and into the rose garden.

When she saw that the tiny leaf she'd watched unfurl from a single green bud was withering, she wept.

9

Even pride couldn't stop her from going to him. When time was so short there was no room for pride in her world. She brought him gifts she hoped he would accept.

And she brought him herself.

"Kylar." She waited at his chamber door until he turned from the window where he stared out at the dark night. So handsome, she thought, her dark prince. "Would you speak with me?"

"I'm trying to understand you."

That alone, that he would try, lightened her heart. "I wish you could." She came forward and laid what she carried on the chest by his bed. "I've brought you a cloak, since yours was ruined. It was my grandfather's, and with its lining of fur is warmer than what you had. It befits a prince. And this brooch that was his. Will you take it?"

He crossed to her, picked up the gold brooch with its carved rose. "Why do you give it to me?"

"Because I treasure it." She lifted a hand, closed it over his on the brooch. "You think I don't cherish what you've given me, what you've been to me. I can't let you leave believing that. I can't bear the thought of you going when there's anger and hard words between us."

There was a storm in his eyes as they met hers. "I could take you from here, whether you're willing or not. No one could stop me."

"I would not allow it, nor would my people."

He stepped closer, and circled her throat with his hand with just enough force that the pulse against his palm fluttered with fear. "No one could stop me." His free hand clamped over hers before she could draw her dagger. "Not even you."

"I would never forgive you for it. Nor lie willingly with you again. Anger makes you think of using force as an answer. You know it's not."

"How can you be so calm, and so sure, Deirdre?"

"I'm sure of nothing. And I am not calm. I want to go with you. I want to run and never look back, to live with you in the sunlight. To once smell the grass, to breathe the summer.

Once," she said in a fierce whisper. "And what would that make me?"

"My wife."

The hand under his trembled, then steadied before she drew it away. "You honor me, but I will never marry."

"Because of who made you, how you were made?" He took her by the shoulders now so that their gazes locked. "Can you be so wise, so warm, Deirdre, and at the same time so cold and closed?"

"I will never marry because my most sacred trust is to do no harm. If I were to take a husband, he would be king. I would share the welfare of all my people with him. This is a heavy burden."

"Do you think I would shirk it?"

"I don't, no. I've been inside your mind and heart. You keep your promises, Kylar, even if they harm you."

"So you spurn me to save me?"

"Spurn you? I have lain with you. I have shared with you my body, my mind, as I have never shared with another. Will never share again in my lifetime. If I take your vow and keep you here, if you keep your vow and stay, how many will be harmed? What destinies would we alter if you did not take your place as king in your own land? And if I went with you, my people would lose hope. They

112

would have no one to look to for guidance. No one to heal them. There is no one here to take my place."

She thought of the child she knew grew inside her.

"I accept that you must go, and honor you for it," she said. "Why can't you accept that I must stay?"

"You see only black and white."

"I *know* only black and white." Her voice turned desperate now, with a pleading he'd never heard from her. "My life, the whole of it, has been here. And one single purpose was taught to me. To keep my people alive and well. I've done this as best I can."

"No one could have done better."

"But it isn't finished. You want to understand me?" Now she moved to the window, pulled the hangings over the black glass to shut out the dark and the cold. "When I was a babe, my mother gave me to Orna. I never remember my mother's arms around me. She was kind, but she couldn't love me. I have my father's eyes, and looking at me caused her pain. I felt that pain."

She pressed her hands to her heart. "I felt it inside me, the hurt and the longing and the despair. So I closed myself off from it. Hadn't I the right?"

There was no room for anger in him now.

113

"She had no right to turn from you."

"She did turn from me, and that can't be changed. I was tended well, and taught. I had duties, and I had playmates. And once, when I was very young there were dogs. They died off, one by one. When the last . . . his name was Griffen — a foolish name for a dog, I suppose. He was very old, and I couldn't heal him. When he died, it broke something in me. That's foolish, too, isn't it, to be shattered by the death of a dog."

"No. You loved him."

"Oh, I did." She sat now, with a weary sigh. "So much love I had for that old hound. And so much fury when I lost him. I was mad with grief and tried to destroy the ice rose. I thought if I could chop it down, hack it to bits, all this would end. Somehow it would end, for even death could never be so bleak. But a sword is nothing against magic. My mother sent for me. There would be loss, she told me. I had to accept it. I had duties, and the most vital was to care for my people. To put their well-being above my own. She was right."

"As a queen," Kylar agreed. "But not as a mother."

"How could she give what she didn't have? I realize now, with her bond with the animals, she must have felt grief as I did for

114

the loss. She *was* grief, my mother. I watched her pine and yearn for the man who'd ruined her. Even as she died, she wept for him. His deceit, his selfishness stole the color and warmth from her life, and doomed her and her people to eternal winter. Yet she died loving him, and I vowed that nothing and no one would ever rule my heart. It is trapped inside me, as frozen as the rose in the tower of ice outside this window. If it were free, Kylar, I would give it to you."

"You trap yourself. It's not a sword that will cut through the ice. It's love."

"What I have is yours. I wish it could be more. If I were not queen, I would go with you on the morrow. I would trust you to take me to beyond, or would die fighting to get there with you. But I can't go, and you can't stay. Kylar, I saw your mother's face."

"My mother?"

"In your mind, your heart, when I healed you. I would have given anything, anything, to have seen such love and pride for me in the eyes of the one who bore me. You can't let her grieve for a son who still lives."

Guilt clawed at him. "She would want me happy."

"I believe she would. But if you stay, she will never know what became of you. Whatever you want for yourself, you have too much inside you for her to leave her not knowing. And too much honor to turn away from your duties to your family and your own land."

His fists clenched. She had, with the skill of a soldier, outflanked him. "Does it always come to duty?"

"We're born what we're born, Kylar. Neither you nor I could live well or happy if we cast off our duty."

"I would rather face a battle without sword or shield than leave you."

"We've been given these weeks. If I ask you for one more night, will you turn me away?"

"No." He reached for her hand. "I won't turn you away."

He loved her tenderly, then fiercely. And at last, when dawn trembled to life, he loved her desperately. When the night was over, she didn't cling, nor did she weep. A part of him wished she would do both. But the woman he loved was strong, and helped him prepare for his journey without tears.

"There are rations for two weeks." She prayed it would be enough. "Take whatever you need from the forest." As he cinched the saddle on his horse, Deirdre slipped a hand under his cloak, laid it on his side.

And he moved away. "No." More than once during the night, she'd tried to explore his healing wound. "If I have pain, it's mine. I won't have it be yours. Not again."

"You're stubborn."

"I bow before you, my lady. The queen of willful."

She managed a smile and laid a hand on the arm of the man she'd chosen to guide the prince. "Dilys. You are Prince Kylar's man now."

He was young, tall as a tree and broad of shoulder. "My lady, I am the queen's man."

This time she touched his face. They had grown up together, and once had romped as children. "Your queen asks that you pledge now your loyalty, your fealty, and your life to Prince Kylar."

He knelt in the deep and crusted snow. "If it is your wish, my queen, I so pledge."

She drew a ring from her finger, pressed it into his hand. "Live." She bent to kiss both his cheeks. "And if you cannot return —"

"My lady."

"If you cannot," she continued, lifting his head so their gazes met, "know you have my blessing, and my wish for your happiness. Keep the prince safe," she whispered. "Do not leave him until he's safe. It is the last I will ever ask of you."

She stepped back. "Kylar, prince of Mrydon, we wish you safe journey."

He took the hand she offered. "Deirdre, queen of the Sea of Ice, my thanks for your hospitality, and my good wishes to you and your people." But he didn't release her hand. Instead, he took a ring of his own and slid it onto her finger. "I pledge to you my heart."

"Kylar —"

"I pledge to you my life." And before the people gathered in the courtyard, he pulled her into his arms and kissed her, long and deep. "Ask me now, one thing. Anything."

"I will ask you this. When you're safe again, when you find summer, pluck the first rose you see. And think of me. I will know, and be content."

Even now, he thought, she would not ask him to come back for her. He touched a hand to the brooch pinned to his cloak. "Every rose I see is you." He vaulted onto his horse. "I will come back."

He spurred his horse toward the archway with Dilys trotting beside him. The crowd rushed after them, calling, cheering. Unable to resist, Deirdre climbed to the battlements, stood in the slow drift of snow and watched him ride away from her.

His mount's hooves rang on the ice, and his black cloak snapped in the frigid wind.

Then he whirled his horse, and reared high.

"I will come back!" he shouted.

When his voice echoed back to her, over her, she nearly believed it. She stood, her red cloak drawn tight, until he disappeared into the forest.

Alone, her legs trembling, she made her way down to the rose garden. There was a burning inside her chest, and an ache deep, deep within her belly. When her vision blurred, she stopped to catch her breath. With a kind of dull surprise she reached up to touch her cheeks and found them wet.

Tears, she thought. After so many years. The burning inside her chest became a throbbing. So. She closed her eyes and stumbled forward. So, the frozen chamber that trapped her heart could melt after all. And, melting, bring tears.

Bring a pain that was like what came with healing.

She collapsed at the foot of the great ice rose, buried her face in her hands.

"I love." She sobbed now, rocking herself for comfort. "I love him with all I am or will ever be. And it hurts. How cruel to show me this, to bring me this. How bitter your heart must have been to drape cold over what should be warmth. But you did not love. I know that now."

Steadying as best she could, she turned her face up to the dull sky. "Even my mother did not love, for she willed him back with every breath. I love, and I wish the one who has my heart safe, and whole and warm. For I would not wish this barren life on him. I'll know when he feels the sun and plucks the rose. And I will be content."

She laid a hand on her heart, on her belly. "Your cold magic can't touch what's inside me now."

And drawing herself up, turning away, she didn't see the delicate leaf struggling to live on a tiny green bud.

The world was wild, and the air itself roared like wolves. The storm sprang up like a demon, hurling ice and snow like frozen arrows. Night fell so fast that there was barely time to gather branches for fuel.

Wrapped in his cloak, Kylar brooded into the fire. The trees were thick here, tall as giants, dead as stones. They had gone beyond where Deirdre harvested trees and into what was called the Forgotten.

"When the storm passes, can you find your way back from here?" Kylar demanded. Though they sat close to warm each other, he was forced to shout to be heard over the screaming storm.

Dilys's eyes, all that showed beneath the cloak and hood, blinked once. "Yes, my lord."

"Then when travel is possible again, you'll go back to Rose Castle."

"No, my lord."

It took Kylar a moment. "You will do as I bid. You have pledged your obedience to me."

"My queen charged me to see you safe. It was the last she said to me. I will see you safe, my lord."

"I'll travel more quickly without you."

"I don't think this is so," Dilys said in his slow and thoughtful way. "I will see you home, my lord. You cannot go back to her until you have reached home. My lady needs you to come back to her."

"She doesn't believe I will. Why do you?"

"Because you are meant to. You must sleep now. The road ahead is longer than the road behind."

The storm raged for hours. It was still dark, still brutal when Kylar awoke. Snow covered him, turning his hair and cloak white, and even the fur did little to fight the canny cold.

He moved silently to his horse. It would take, he knew, minutes only to move far enough from camp that his trail would be lost. In such a hellish world, you could stand all but shoulder to shoulder with another and not see him beside you.

The man Dilys would have no choice but to return home when he woke and found himself alone.

But though he walked his horse soundlessly through the deep snow, he'd gone no more than fifty yards when Dilys was once more trudging beside him.

Brave of heart and loyal to the bone, Kylar thought. Deirdre had chosen her man well.

"You have ears like a bat," Kylar said, resigned now.

Dilys grinned. "I do."

Kylar stopped, jumped down from the horse. "Mount," he ordered. "If we're traveling through hell together, we'll take turns riding." When Dilys only stood and stared, Kylar swore. "Will you argue with me over everything or do as your lady commanded and I now bid?"

"I would not argue, my lord. But I don't know how to mount the horse."

Kylar stood in the swirling snow, cold to the marrow of his bones, and laughed until he thought he would burst from it.

10

On the fourth day of the journey, the wind rose so fierce that they walked in blindness. Hoods, cloaks, even Cathmor's dark hide were white now. Snow coated Dilys's eyebrows and the stubble of his beard, making him look like an old man rather than a youth not yet twenty.

Color, Kylar thought, was a stranger to this terrible world. Warmth was only a dim memory in the Forgotten.

When Dilys rode, Kylar waded through snow that reached his waist. At times he wondered if it would soon simply bury them both.

Fatigue stole through him and with it a driving urge just to lie down, to sleep his way to a quiet death. But each time he stumbled, he pulled himself upright again.

He had given her a pledge, and he would keep it. She had willed him to live, through pain and through magic. So he would live.

And he would go back to her.

Walking or riding, he slipped into dreams. In dreams he sat with Deirdre on a jeweled bench in a garden alive with roses, brilliant with sunlight.

Her hands were warm in his.

So they traveled a full week, step by painful step, through ice and wind, through cold and dark.

"Do you have a sweetheart, Dilys?"

"Sir?"

"A sweetheart?" Taking his turn in the saddle, Kylar rode on a tiring Cathmor with his chin on his chest. "A girl you love."

"I do. Her name is Wynne. She works in the kitchens. We'll wed when I return."

Kylar smiled, drifted. The man never lost hope, he thought, nor wavered in his steady faith. "I will give you a hundred gold coins as a marriage gift."

"My thanks, my lord. What is gold coins?"

Kylar managed a weak chuckle. "As useless just now as a bull with teats. And what is a bull, you'd ask," Kylar continued, anticipating his man. "For surely you've seen a teat in your day."

"I have, my lord, and a wonder of nature they are to a man. A bull I have heard of. It is a beast, is it not? I read a story once —" Dilys broke off, raising his head sharply at the sound overhead. With a shout, he snagged the horse's reins, dragged at them roughly. Cathmor screamed and stumbled. Only instinct and a spurt of will kept Kylar in the saddle as the great tree fell inches from Cathmor's rearing hooves.

"Ears like a bat," Kylar said a second time while his heart thundered in his ears. The tree was fully six feet across, more than a hundred in length. One more step in its path and they would have been crushed.

"It is a sign."

The shock roused Kylar enough to clear his mind. "It is a dead tree broken by the weight of snow and ice."

"It is a sign," Dilys said stubbornly. "Its branches point there." He gestured, and still holding the reins, he began to lead the horse to the left.

"You would follow the branches of a dead tree?" Kylar shook his head, shrugged. "Very well, then. How could it matter?"

He dozed and dreamed for an hour. Walked blind and stiff for another. But when they stopped for midday rations from their dwindling supply, Dilys held up a hand.

"What is that sound?"

"The bloody wind. Is it never silent?"

"No, my lord. Beneath the wind. Listen."

He closed his eyes. "It is like . . . music."

"I hear nothing, and certainly no music."

"There."

When Dilys went off at a stumbling run, Kylar shouted after him. Furious that the man would lose himself without food or horse, he mounted as quickly as he could manage and hurried after.

He found Dilys standing knee-deep in snow, one hand lifted, and trembling. "What is it? My lord, what is this thing?"

"It's only a stream." Concerned that the man's mind had snapped, Kylar leaped down from the horse. "It's just a . . . a stream," he whispered as the import raced through him. "Running water. Not ice, but running water. The snow." He turned a quick circle. "It's not so deep here. And the air. Is it warmer?"

"It's beautiful." Dilys was hypnotized by the clear water rushing and bubbling over rock. "It sings."

"Yes, by the blood, it is, and it does. Come. Quick now. We follow the stream."

The wind still blew, but the snow was thinning. He could see clearly now, the shape of the trees, and tracks from game. He had only to find the strength to draw his bow, and they would have meat.

There was life here.

Rocks, stumps, brambles began to show

themselves beneath the snow. The first call of a bird had Dilys falling to his knees in shock.

Snow had melted from their hair, their cloaks, but now it was Dilys's face that was white as ice.

"It's a magpie," Kylar told him, both amused and touched when his stalwart man trembled at the sound. "A song of summer. Rise now. We've left winter behind us."

Soon Cathmor's hooves hit ground, solid and springy, and a single beam of light streamed through trees that were thick with leaves.

"What magic is this?"

"Sun." Kylar closed his hand over the rose brooch. "We found the sun." He dismounted and on legs weak and weary walked slowly to a brilliant splash of color. Here, at the edge of the Forgotten, grew wild roses, red as blood.

He plucked one, breathed in its sweet scent, and said: "Deirdre."

And she, carrying a bucket of melted snow to her garden, swayed. She pressed a hand to her heart as it leaped with joy. "He is home."

She moved through her days now with an easy contentment. Her lover was safe, and the child they'd made warm inside her. The child would be loved, would be cherished.

Her heart would never be cold again.

If there was yearning in her, it was natural. But she would rather yearn than have him trapped in her world.

On the night she knew he was safe, she gave a celebration with wine and music and dancing. The story would be told, she decreed, of Kylar of Mrydon. Kylar the brave. And of the faithful Dilys. And all of her people, all who came after, would know of it.

On a silver chain around her neck, she wore his ring.

She hummed as she cleared the paths in her rose garden.

"You sent men out to scout for Dilys," Orna said.

"It is probably too early. But I know he'll start for home as soon as he's able."

"And Prince Kylar. You don't look for him?"

"He doesn't belong here. He has family in his world, and one day a throne. I found love with him, and it blooms in me — heart and womb. So I wish for him health and happiness. And one day, when these memories have faded from his mind, a woman who loves him as I do."

Orna glanced toward the ice rose, but said nothing of it. "Do you doubt his love for you?"

"No." Her smile was warm and sweet as she said it. "But I've learned, Orna. I believe he was sent to me to teach me what I never knew. Love can't come from cold. If it does, it's selfish, and is not love but simply desire. It gives me such joy to think of him in the sunlight. I don't wish for him as my mother wished for my father, or curse him as my aunt cursed us all. I no longer see my life here as prison or duty. Without it, I would never have known him."

"You're wiser than those who made you."

"I'm luckier," Deirdre corrected, then leaned on her shovel as Phelan rushed into the garden.

"My lady, I've finished my story. Will you hear it?"

"I will. Fetch that shovel by the wall. You can tell me while we work."

"It's a grand story." He ran for the shovel and began heaving snow with great enthusiasm. "The best I've done. And it begins like this: Once, a brave and handsome prince from a far-off land fought a great battle against men who would plunder his kingdom and kill his people. His name was Kylar, and his land was Mrydon."

"It is a good beginning, Phelan the bard."

"Yes, my lady. But it gets better. Kylar the brave defeated the invaders, but, sorely wounded, became lost in the great forest known as the Forgotten."

Deirdre continued to work, smiling as the boy's words brought her memories back so clearly. She remembered her first glimpse of those bold blue eyes, that first foolish brush of lips.

She would give Phelan precious paper and ink to scribe the story. She would bind it herself in leather tanned from deer hide. In this way, she thought with pride, her love would live forever.

One day, their child would read the story, and know what a man his father was.

She cleared the path past jeweled benches, toward the great frozen rose while the boy told his tale and labored tirelessly beside her.

"And the beautiful queen gave him a rose carved on a brooch that he wore pinned over his heart. For days and nights, with his faithful horse, Cathmor, and the valiant and true Dilys, he fought the wild storms, crossed the iced shadows of the Forgotten. It was his lady's love that sustained him."

"You have a romantic heart, young bard."

"It is a *true* story, my lady. I saw it in my head." He continued on, entertaining and delighting her with words of Dilys's stubborn loyalty, of black nights and white days, of a giant tree crashing and leading them toward a stream where water ran over rock like music.

"Sunlight struck the water and made it sparkle like diamonds."

A bit surprised by the description, she glanced toward him. "Do you think sun on water makes diamonds?"

"It makes tiny bright lights, my lady. It dazzles the eye."

Something inside her heart trembled. "Dazzles the eye," she repeated on a whisper. "Yes, I have heard of this."

"And at the edge of the Forgotten grew wild roses, fire-red. The handsome prince plucked one, as he had promised, and when its sweetness surrounded him, he said his lady's name."

"It's a lovely story."

"It is not the end." He all but danced with excitement.

"Tell me the rest, then." She started to smile, to rest on her shovel. Then there came the sound of wild cheering and shouts from without the garden.

"This is the end!" The boy threw his shovel carelessly aside and raced to the archway. "He is come!"

"Who?" she began, but couldn't hear her own voice over the shouts, over the pounding of her blood.

Suddenly the light went brilliant, searing into her eyes so that with a little cry of shock, she threw a hand up to shield them. Wild wind turned to breeze soft as silk. And she heard her name spoken.

Her hand trembled as she lowered it, and her eyes blinked against a light she'd never known. She saw him in the archway of the garden, surrounded by a kind of shimmering halo that gleamed like melted gold.

"Kylar." Her heart, every chamber filled with joy, bounded in her breast. Her shovel clattered on the path as she ran to him.

He caught her up, spinning her in circles as she clung to him. "Oh, my love, my heart. How can this be?" Her tears fell on his neck, her kisses on his face. "You should not be here. You should never have come back. How can I let you go again?"

"Look at me. Sweetheart, look at me." He tipped up her chin. "So there are tears now. I'd hoped there would be. I ask you again. Do you love me, Deirdre?"

"So much I could live on nothing else my whole life. I would not have had to risk yours to come back." She laid her palms on his cheeks. Then her lips trembled open, her fingers shook. "You came back," she whispered.

"I would have crossed hell for you. Perhaps I did."

She closed her eyes. "That light. What is that light?"

"It is the sun. Unveiled. Here, take off your cloak. Feel the sun, Deirdre."

"I'm not cold."

"You'll never be cold again. Open your eyes, my love, and look. Winter is over."

Gripping his hand, she turned to watch the snow melting away, vanishing before her staring eyes. Blackened stalks began to crackle, break out green and at their feet soft, tender blades of grass spread in a shimmering carpet.

"The sky." Dazed, she reached up as if she could touch it. "It's blue. Like your eyes. Feel it, feel the sun." She held her hands out to cup the warmth.

On a cry of wonder, she knelt, ran her hands over the soft grass, brought her hands to her face to breathe in the scent. Though tears continued to fall, she laughed and held those hands out to him. "Is it grass?"

"It is."

"Oh." She covered her face with her hands again, as if she could drink it. "Such perfume."

He knelt with her, and would remember, he knew, the rapture on her face the first time she touched a simple blade of grass. "Your roses are blooming, my lady."

Speechless, she watched buds spear, blooms unfold. Yellows, pinks, reds, whites in petals that flowed from bud to flower, and flowers so heavy they bent the graceful green branches. The fragrance all but made her drunk.

"Roses." Her voice quivered as she reached out to touch, felt the silky texture. "Flowers." And buried her face in blooms.

She squealed like a girl when a butterfly fluttered by her face and landed on a tender bud to drink.

"Oh!" There was so much, almost too much, and she was dizzy from it. "See how it moves! It's so beautiful."

In turn, she tipped her face back and drank in the sunlight.

"What is that across the blue of the sky? That curve of colors?"

"It's a rainbow." Watching her was like watching something be born. And once again, he thought, she humbled him. "Your first rainbow, my love."

"It's lovelier than in the books. In them it seemed false and impossible. But it's soft and it's real."

"I brought you a gift."

"You brought me summer," she murmured.

"And this." He snapped his fingers, and

through the arch, down the path raced a fat brown puppy. Barking cheerfully, it leaped into Deirdre's lap. "His name is Griffen."

Drowned in emotion, she cradled the pup as she might a child, pressed her face into its warm fur. She felt its heartbeat, and the quick, wet lash of its tongue on her cheek.

"I'm sorry," she managed, and broke down and sobbed.

"Weep, then." Kylar bent to touch his lips to her hair. "As long as it's for joy."

"How can this be? How can you bring me so much? I turned you away, without love."

"No, you let me go, with love. It took me time to understand that — and you. To understand what it cost you. There would have been no summer if I hadn't left you, and returned."

He lifted her damp face now, and the puppy wiggled free and began to race joyfully through the garden. "Is that not so?"

"It is so. Only the greatest and truest love, freely given, could break the spell and turn away winter."

"I knew. When I plucked the rose, I understood. I watched summer bloom. It came with me through the forest. As I rode, the trees behind me went into leaf, brooks and streams sprang free of ice. With every mile I put behind me, every mile I came closer to

135

you, the world awoke. Others will come to-morrow. I couldn't wait."

"But how? How did you come back so quickly?"

"My land is only a day's journey from here. It was magic that kept you hidden. It's love that frees you."

"It's more." Phelan wiggled his way through the crowd of people who gathered in the archway. He gave a cry of delight as the pup leaped at him. "It is truth," he began, "and sacrifice and honor. All these tied by love are stronger than a shield of ice and break the spell of the winter rose. When summer comes to Rose Castle, the Isle of Winter becomes the Isle of Flowers and the Sea of Ice becomes the Sea of Hope. And here, the good queen gives hand and heart to her valiant prince."

"It is a good ending," Kylar commented. "But perhaps you would wait until I ask the good queen for her hand and her heart."

She dashed tears from her cheeks. Her people, her love, would not see her weep at such a time. "You have my heart already."

"Then give me your hand. Be my wife."

She put her hand in his, but because she must be a queen, turned first to her people. "You are witness. I pledge myself in love and in marriage, for a lifetime, to Kylar, prince of Mrydon. He will be your king, and to him you will give your service, your respect, and your loyalty. From this day, his people will be your brothers and your sisters. In time, our lands will be one land."

She let them cheer, let his name ring out along with hers into the wondrous blue bowl of sky. And her hand was warm in Kylar's.

"Prepare a feast of celebration and thanks, and make ourselves ready to welcome the guests that come on the morrow. Leave us now, for I need a moment with my betrothed. Take the pup to the kitchen, Phelan, and see that he is well fed. Keep him for me."

"Yes, my lady."

"His name is Griffen." Her gaze met Orna's, and smiled as her people left her alone with her prince. "There is one last thing to be done."

She walked with him down the path to where the reddest roses bloomed on the tallest bush under thinning ice. Without a thought, she plunged her hand through it, and the shield shattered like glass. She picked the first rose of her life, offered it to him.

"I've accepted you as queen. That is duty. Now I give myself to you as a woman. This is for love. You brought light to my world. You freed my heart. Now and forever, that heart is yours."

She started to kneel, and he stopped her. "You won't kneel to me."

Her brows lifted, and command once again cloaked her. "I am queen of this place. I do as I wish." She knelt. "I am yours, queen and woman. From this hour, this day will be known and celebrated as Prince Kylar's Return."

With a gleam in his eye, he knelt as well, and made her lips twitch. "You will be a willful wife."

"This is truth."

"I would not have it otherwise. Kiss me, Deirdre the fair."

She put a hand on his chest. "First, I have a gift for you."

"It can wait. I lived on dreams of your kisses for days in the cold."

"This gift can't wait. Kylar, I have your child in me. A child made from love and warmth."

The hand that had touched her face slid bonelessly to her shoulder. "A child?"

"We've made life between us. A miracle, beyond magic."

"Our child." His palm spread over her belly, rested there as his lips took hers.

"It pleases you?"

For an answer he leaped up, hoisted her high until her laughter rang out. She threw her arms toward the sky, toward the sun, the sky, the rainbow.

And the roses grew and bloomed until branches and flowers reached over the garden wall, tumbled down, and filled the air with the promise of summer.

The Rose and
the Sword

Jill Gregory

*To my dear and extraordinary friend
Karen Katz, with love and friendship always*

1

"You sent for me, Your Highness?"

Smiling, Brittany curtseyed before Queen Elysia and waited quietly in the queen's drafty bedchamber for the snowy-haired woman wrapped in ermine robes to reply.

Outside the castle walls, in the small kingdom of Strathbury, fat snowflakes tumbled from a leaden winter sky, and the fields and hills were wrapped in gauzy layers of snow every bit as thick and white as the ermine of the queen's robes. Inside, the flickering candles illuminated the chamber's velvet bed hangings, the rich tapestries, the heavy, gilt-trimmed furnishings as Brittany shivered in her green wool gown and awaited the queen's bidding.

It was strange the way Elysia was staring at her, almost as if she had never seen her before — which was ridiculous, since Brittany had been her ward ever since she could remember. But Queen Elysia's kindly old eyes

143

were fixed on her unblinkingly, intensely, as if she was memorizing the face of the girl she had known for nearly twenty years.

"Your Highness, are you well?" Brittany asked uncertainly, as the woman suddenly lifted a hand to her brow and closed her eyes as if she were in pain. "How can I help you?" Without waiting for a formal invitation, Brittany hurried forward.

Queen Elysia took a deep, shuddering breath and clasped the hand of the girl who sank down upon the edge of her bed. "Ah, child, do not fear for me. I am in pain, yes, but it is not a physical ailment. My heart grieves because the time has come for me to tell you something, something that will change our lives forever. Something that will take you away from me."

"Take me away from you? Oh, Your Highness, no! Please, no. Whatever I have done, I will fix. If I have offended, please allow me to —"

"Child, child, you have done nothing — nothing but earn my love and respect, my admiration." The queen smiled at her through a glimmer of tears that made her faded blue eyes appear the color of the winter sky. "You have been an exceptional ward. A handful, perhaps, but a lovely handful. I care for you, child, as if you were my own daughter. If it

144

were up to me, I would have you with me always, safe and by my side. But that is impossible. I waited as long as I could to tell you the truth, but now your twentieth birthday will arrive in only a few days, and I fear I may have delayed too long. There isn't much time."

Brittany stared at her in complete confusion. It was unlike her to be lacking in either words or comprehension. The petite, dainty young woman with the smooth, honey-colored hair, delicate features, and wide-set green eyes that were flecked with gold had the spirit of an imp and the courage of a soldier. She had been raised at the queen's side as a lady, but from the time she was a girl she had been taught to ride, to shoot an arrow, and to wield a sword with the skill of a man. Brittany had never understood why the queen had allowed her man-at-arms to train her in these things, but she hadn't questioned it because she'd craved the challenge. She was a girl who loved to run, loved to race her horse through the wood and jump the streams that meandered behind the castle. There was no tree in the kingdom she hadn't climbed, no flower she hadn't gathered, and no person, high- or low-born, in the land whom she did not know by name and who did not bow or curtsey before her, out of respect for the beautiful girl whose laughter made even the sourest old man smile.

But now the young woman who was loved throughout the tiny kingdom felt her heart breaking into a thousand pieces. She was to be sent away! *Why?* a voice shrieked in her head.

"I don't understand." Brittany moistened her lips. The sad words and grave expression upon her guardian's face filled her with foreboding. "I don't wish to leave. Not you, not Strathbury. If I haven't displeased you, then why must I go? I wish . . . I wish to stay with you always!"

"If only you could, my child." Queen Elysia shook her head. "But this castle will hold no safety for you, not after your twentieth birthday has passed. The danger draws near. Every moment only brings it closer. To escape, you must go, you must find your betrothed and —"

"My betrothed!"

Shocked, Brittany stared at the queen, wondering if she had lost her senses. Then, suddenly, she understood, and she laughed aloud with relief.

"I don't have a betrothed, Your Highness." She couldn't contain a smile. "As you well know. Is that what this is all about? You wish to send me away so that I can find a husband?"

"Not just any husband, child. The one who is pledged to you. The one to whom *you* are pledged, have been pledged for all these past years. Oh, dear." Elysia's thin lips trembled. "I never should have delayed this long. But I . . . I wanted to keep you here with me for as long as possible. I didn't want this day, this moment, ever to come."

The ground seemed to shift beneath Brittany's feet. Nothing the queen was saying to her made any sense. But it filled her with dismay. If she was pledged to some man — had been pledged all her life — why was she only just learning of it? Why had she been allowed to dance at court festivities with handsome knights and dashing noblemen? Why had she been allowed to fall in and out of love half a dozen times, allowed to hope and to dream of one day finding her one true forever love?

Why hadn't anyone ever told her she'd been promised — and to *whom?* she wondered in mounting horror. A vision of a stout, ugly toad of a duke suddenly filled her mind, and she choked back panic.

It dawned on her that everything she knew about her life and her past now seemed to be unraveling. From the time she was a little girl, she'd been told that her parents had been well born, that her mother had died giving birth to a babe when Brittany was not yet two years old, that her father shortly after had died of a fever and she'd been sent to live with Queen Elysia because the queen was a cousin to Brittany's mother, and childless, and kind as could be.

No one had told her about any danger, about ever having to leave this castle — or about any "betrothed."

"I am trying to understand," she told the queen in a voice that trembled a little, though she strove for calm. "But your words are a riddle to me, Your Highness. I beg you, if you love me, explain what all this means. And tell me why I have never before heard a word about this man to whom I am supposedly betrothed."

"It was a secret, child. A secret I have kept for eighteen long years, in order to protect you. You could not know the truth. But now it is time. I must tell you all of it, so that you are prepared. The time is short, because I delayed, dreading this day of telling you what lies ahead." The queen's hands trembled upon the bedcoverings. "But you have a right to know, child. A right to the life that was stolen from you — and a right to be warned about the danger that will come. And once you know, you must leave. In the morning, at first light."

"So soon?" Brittany gasped. "I think . . . you had best tell me, Your Highness. Why must I go, and what is this danger?"

"You are more than what you know, my dear child. More even than the beautiful and brave young woman we have all come to love. You are royal, Brittany, every bit as royal as I, and more than that, you are powerful. Very powerful. Have you never felt it? Have you never felt the power deep inside your blood?"

Power? Brittany sat very still. Was that what it was? Power? Sometimes, at odd moments, there would come a chill. A chill that pervaded her skin and made her shiver, yet at the same time her blood would seem to heat and tingle. She would sense something, something in herself that was not quite of herself. She would feel that there was something she must do, something she would do, but then . . . the feeling would fade as quickly as it had come. Was that it — was that the power?

"I don't know," she said quietly, while her thoughts raced. She was royal and she had power. How could this be?

"Your Highness, perhaps it would be best if you tell me more, tell me all of it. For example, this power — what does it do?"

"Would that I could tell you, child." The

queen sighed. "I only know that it is in you, and that it must be very strong, very potent. Otherwise, Darius would not have tried to kill you along with the other members of your family."

"Darius!" Now confusion and the first inkling of fear settled over her. Darius was a wizard, the most powerful wizard of the times, and he ruled the land of Palladrin, a vast kingdom far greater and wealthier than Strathbury. Stories of Darius's cruelty and his seemingly limitless powers terrorized citizens of every land, and his name was mentioned to children as the source of ultimate evil.

"Darius . . . killed my family? Are you saying that my mother did not die in childbirth and my father of a fever?"

Brittany jumped up, no longer able to sit calmly upon the bed. She paced back and forth around the chamber, turmoil churning within her, and questions swirling through her brain, even though she tried to subdue the panic inside her. If she was going to have an enemy, why did it have to be Darius? Why not merely a dragon, or a troll, or some wild outlaw scoundrel? Why did it have to be Darius the Wizard, who was rumored to be able to turn an oak tree into an acorn with the flick of a finger?

"Your Highness, I beg you — tell me all of it. Tell me at once. I must know the entire truth or I shall go mad."

With sorrow and quiet understanding the queen studied the distraught girl pacing her chamber. "Come, my child. Seat yourself upon my gilded chair as befits a princess, and I will tell you. Listen carefully, though, Brittany, for there is not much time. Though what I am going to say will shock you, you must gather your wits and your resolve. My men will escort you upon your journey at first light — every moment of every day will be vital if you are to succeed. And," she added, her voice breaking, "if you are to survive."

The girl slipped into the golden chair facing the bed, her heart pounding. "I'm ready," she whispered, grateful that her voice sounded steadier than she felt.

The queen told her then, told her that even her name was not her own. Her real name was Britta, and she was the princess of Palladrin.

She was the youngest daughter of the royal family, all of whom had been murdered on Darius's orders when he came to power: her mother, Queen Alvina, her father, King Raulf, and her brother, Dugal, seven years old when he was slain.

"And you, child, were a babe of not yet two winters. But your mother somehow managed to save you and you were smuggled to safety. Another child, one from the village who had died of the fever, was substituted and shown to Darius with a blade through its heart."

Brittany gasped, all the color fading from her face. The tale seemed wild, impossible, but somehow, deep inside, she felt that it was all too true.

"That is why," the queen continued heavily, "all the world believes that the last of your royal line is dead. That there is no longer any threat to Darius. That, and the spell that your mother cast upon you, to shield you."

"What . . . kind of spell?" Brittany asked, her throat dry.

"One that hid you in a fairy mist, protected from Darius's sight. A spell that would not allow his evil eye to see or to sense your presence in the land of the living." A smile trembled across Elysia's lips. "And it has worked. If it had not, Darius and his soldiers would have found you. And killed you," she added with a shudder.

"How is it that my mother came by such power? It must be very great to deceive a wizard of Darius's skill."

The queen nodded. "Indeed, yes. You and your mother are descended from the great sorcerer Zared."

"Zared!" All the world knew of Zared the Powerful, the greatest sorcerer since Merlin himself. His powers were said to have surpassed even those of Darius.

"He is your grandsire, child — your mother's father. And he created the Rose Scepter for your mother and for you, and for all future generations of women in his line. There is a power in it that can be used only by the women descended from Zared. A power that you must claim now and use to unleash your own magic. Your mother used the Rose Scepter to save you — to conjure up a spell powerful enough to protect you from Darius's sight for all these many years. But the spell was conjured with only enough magic to last until your twentieth birthday — on that day, the fairy mist will fade as suddenly as morning dew, and Darius will be able to sense your presence. He will know that you live."

She hesitated, her face turning pale, but before she could say the final words, Brittany said them for her.

"And he will try to destroy me."

A silence fell, a silence so complete that Brittany was sure she could hear the snowflakes falling outside the window.

"Yes, dear child," the queen replied at last. "But he will not succeed — not if you can do two things. These two things will enable you to fight Darius — and win."

"I'm listening." The girl swallowed, trying to take in everything she'd been told, to comprehend that her true past and her true identity were far different from what she'd always believed, that she was someone whom the wizard Darius, with all his power and might, would want to seek out and destroy. "What must I do?"

"There is a legend, child, an ancient legend of Palladrin that foretold all of the events I have related to you. Even that of Darius coming to power, slaughtering your family, and taking the kingdom that was theirs — and that is now rightfully yours. According to the legend, the Rose and the Sword, raised together, can defeat Darius, or any evil that threatens the land of Palladrin."

"The Rose and the Sword? What does that mean?" Brittany cried, desperate for a solution, for something she could do to stop the series of events that she felt even now spinning into motion.

"The Rose Scepter — it is yours. You must find it. No one knows where it is, probably not even Darius — it was hidden at the same time you were smuggled out of your castle. But the scepter alone will not defeat him. For that you need your betrothed."

Her betrothed again. "Why do I need him? And who *is* he?"

She tried to banish the image of the old toad of a duke from her mind, and failed. "I think I would prefer to take my chances with Darius myself, rather than align myself with some stranger. I have no desire to marry a man I don't even know and who —"

"You are pledged to him, child, and he to you. Because of the legend of the Rose and the Sword."

"Well, it is up to me to find the Rose, but what is this Sword, Your Highness? Many men have swords, and I don't see why it makes any difference —"

"If you are going to defeat Darius and rule your people, child, you need to learn patience and you need to listen," the queen said, meeting the girl's gaze with a quelling glance. "I know this is all a shock to you, but you must let me finish and then you will see. Contain your impatience, and your ideals. They are well and good, and they become you, Brittany — I mean Britta," she corrected herself grimly — "but you would also do well to learn to subdue your temper, your

155

youthful impatience, and learn to think like the ruler you will become. If you find the Rose Scepter, great power will be yours. You must learn to wield it wisely and well — with a cool head, not a hot one."

Chastened, Brittany took a deep breath. What she wanted to do was to scream, to run out of the castle and race through the woods, losing herself in the darkness and the deep, drifting snow and the cold of the night. To leave behind this wretched tale, this frightening truth about who she was and what she must do.

But she couldn't. She had to face it, accept it. And deal with it. She forced herself to remain still, to keep a calm facade, and to heed the words of Elysia, remembering that there was little time.

"The Sword in the legend is that of the family of Marric. It is a jeweled sword from the time of Arthur, a sword blessed by Merlin himself, that is endowed with keen powers when it is raised against that which is evil. It was foretold that when the Rose and the Sword are raised together against evil, their magic will be powerful indeed — powerful enough to defeat the enemies of Palladrin. Such a joining of forces was foreseen long ago as the only way to defeat Darius, and that is why, long before the threat became real, you were pledged to the young prince of Marric and he to you. You were only a child in swaddling clothes at the time, and he was a boy of six. But the promise made then, that you would be joined in marriage, is binding as long as you both shall live. You are bound by honor to marry him — not only to fulfill the pledge between your families but to save yourself and your kingdom."

Kingdom. I have a kingdom. Brittany swallowed as the enormity of what lay ahead of her began to sink in.

"This prince of Marric, does he have a name?" she asked.

"His name is Lucius of Marric. I sent Sir Richmond in search of him more than a fortnight ago, and he has returned after searching near and far. Prince Lucius is in Gullvantium — two days' journey from here. You will leave at dawn, and you must find him, my child. Find him and call upon him to fulfill his pledge, to aid you and protect you as you try to find the Rose Scepter — and in the battle that will come between you and Darius."

Brittany closed her eyes. *The battle that will come between you and Darius.* Something shook her at these words — that feeling came over her again, sharper than ever before. A burning, icy feeling, and for a moment she heard wind whooshing through her ears. A faraway wind. For an instant she couldn't breathe; the wind seemed to be eating all of the air in her lungs.

The moment passed. Her head ached, but nothing else remained.

"What is it, child?" The queen's face was filled with concern. "You are whiter than my robes. Are you faint?"

"No, no, Your Highness, only . . . stunned by all you have told me." But Brittany knew, just as she knew that the queen's words were the truth, that what she had just felt was a taste of the magic and the power and the evil before her. She didn't know what it meant, or where it would lead. She knew only that never before had she experienced such a sensation.

Of course, never before had she been so near to her twentieth birthday.

This might be only the beginning of the changes that would come, of what she must face, learn, use. Brittany took a deep breath. A short time ago, she had been sewing in her own candlelit chamber, enjoying conversation with the queen's ladies-in-waiting, sipping spiced wine. Now her entire life had been turned upside down, and she was contemplating a journey, a quest, a marriage.

And a battle.

"How will I convince him — Prince Lucius

— that I am who I say I am? He thinks I'm dead, does he not?"

The queen beckoned her forward, and Brittany returned to kneel at the bedside of the old woman who had been her gentle guardian and the closest to a mother that she could remember. "The birthmark," the queen said. She touched a spindly finger to Brittany's shoulder. "Here, I believe?"

Mute with wonder, the girl nodded. Never before had it occurred to her — the birthmark in the shape of a rose upon her right shoulder. She'd never seen any significance in it before. But now . . .

"That is your proof. Your heritage. The mark of the Rose. Lucius will believe. And he will help you, child." She clasped the girl's slender fingers in her own and clung to them a moment, gazing into Brittany's face as if she was indeed memorizing every lovely, delicate feature.

"May the angels keep you safe," she whispered. "May you win all that is yours."

She was trembling all over, and Brittany saw with a surge of worry that Elysia looked wearier and older and more fragile than she had ever looked before.

"Sleep now, Your Highness. I will ready myself for the journey and come to you in the morning before I leave."

The woman nodded. "You are brave, Britta. Brave and beautiful and good. You will meet this challenge. With Prince Lucius's help, you will conquer Darius."

With Prince Lucius's help. Those words echoed in Brittany's ears as she hurried along the chilly stone corridor toward her own chamber.

Her heart was heavy. Her throat was dry. How she wished that this was only a dream, that she could remain here in Strathbury forever, wait for her one true love to find her, and live in peace among the good people she had always known.

But it was not to be. Her real family had been slaughtered. Slaughtered by a great wizard — who would be hunting for her soon. And she would need all her wits if she was going to survive.

Not only to survive, she told herself with determination and a sudden sharp flick of anger, but to take back what Darius had stolen. The kingdom for which her family had been murdered.

I'll need more than my wits, she thought, as she descended a narrow stair lit by torches and then rounded the corner to her own chamber. *And more than mere courage and determination. I'll need the help of that man. My betrothed.*

She drew a ragged breath. She had always thought she would marry for love. A forever love. The kind Queen Elysia had had with her husband, Coll, all the years they were wed, until he died, a year before Brittany had come to Strathbury.

Brittany had grown up on stories of how they'd met, courted, wed. Stories of the strength of their love and the gentle passion that flared between them always.

She had wanted the same kind of love for herself, a love that was true and deep and lasting. But now her dreams would have to be put aside.

Toad or no, it seemed she would need Prince Lucius's help. *Prince Lucius of Marric.* Her betrothed.

She shook her head as she entered her chamber and hastily began to gather what she would need for the journey.

If the Rose and the Sword together could save Palladrin from Darius's rule, then together they would be.

Tomorrow she would set out for Gullvantium and find her betrothed.

And marry him — even if he was a toad.

2

"Another jug of wine, Ula!" Lucius of Marric called to the lushly endowed serving wench bestowing kisses upon all the men at the Bones and Blood Inn as she made her way through the room.

"Make that two jugs," he added, laughing, and returned his attention to Drusy, sprawled in his lap, then forgot about his thirst as he drank in the redheaded serving girl's lusty kisses.

"Let's go upstairs, me lord," she suggested, her hands sliding all over him despite the crowded room. Of course, the air was so thick with woodsmoke, chances were no one could see, but Lucius only chuckled, yanked her closer, and kissed her some more. He would bed her before the night was through, but he wasn't drunk enough yet. Not nearly enough. He needed more wine, more merriment, maybe even a good fight — and then the girl. Then perhaps, when it was done with and his brain and body were sated, perhaps he would sleep . . .

And know a few hours of peace.

Ula brought the wine, and he shared the jug with Drusy while she brazenly jiggled her wares at him, teasing him into going up the stairs to the room with the rough hay mattress that smelled of a goat. Lucius never even noticed the inn door swing open, never saw the girl who slipped inside, bundled up to her neck in a blue woolen cloak, her cheeks flushed from the cold. He did glance up in time to see the gruff, bowlegged old soldier who stepped in after her, though, and his eyes narrowed in the firelight from the roaring hearth.

That the man was a soldier he had no doubt. Despite his plain dark cloak and filthy boots, Lucius would have wagered a chest of coins that there was chain mail beneath the deceptively simple garments. He hadn't been away from battle so long that he didn't recognize a trained soldier when he saw one. And seeing one here, in an inn as coarse and disreputable as the Bones and Blood, not exactly known for its high company, was almost as startling as seeing . . . well, as seeing a girl like the one who stood talking earnestly with the soldier in a place as low as this.

She was small and lovely. He could almost hear the soft murmur of her voice, but not her words. She didn't belong here, in this wild, smoky place amid the din of drunken men and the shrieking laughter of the serving women and the stench of sweat and ale and burnt meat.

What the devil were the two of them doing here? Lucius wondered sharply, then realized that he must not yet have consumed enough wine, if he was puzzling over such things. They didn't concern him. Nothing concerned him. Not anymore.

He wrapped a muscular arm around Drusy and laughed as he reached for the second jug of wine, while the girl squealed and giggled and squirmed on his lap.

In the corner of the inn near the door, Brittany spoke forcefully to Sir Richmond, Queen Elysia's man-at-arms.

"Go. Leave me now. Your duty is done."

"I will not leave you in a place like this, my lady. With men like this . . ." The old soldier glared at the noise and commotion all around, at the men arguing loudly, cursing, shoving against one another at the far end of the room, perilously close to the roaring hearthfire, while others tipped ale tankards or jugs of wine and sang at the top of their lungs, and brazen serving women bustled to and fro, waggling their hips. Richmond's glance included the tall, dark-haired man with a day's growth of beard upon his swarthy face, the man seated on the bench in the center of the room, practically undressing the red-haired wench in his lap.

"Your men confirmed that that is indeed Prince Lucius, did they not?" Brittany asked, trying to sound calm, though she was praying that there was some terrible mistake. That man, that giant handsome man who was practically swallowing the serving maid whole, he could not . . . could not be her betrothed. *Could he?*

Please, she prayed silently as she stared at that starkly handsome face, *I would so much rather have a toad.*

The man across the room was the opposite of a toad. He looked tough and dangerous and entirely unsuitable to be anybody's husband. He looked like an outlaw, she thought with a shock. And not a very pleasant one. And the way he was fondling that woman . . .

Her stomach felt queasy. It had been hours since she'd eaten even a morsel of food, and she and the small troop of soldiers Elysia had sent with her had been traveling for nearly two days. She was sore, stiff, and exhausted, and her stomach had been growling in a most unladylike manner.

Worst of all, the day after tomorrow was her birthday and after that — well, she didn't know what would happen after that, but it seemed likely that Darius might well get some inkling that she was alive. And then —

Then she would need a protector. Someone to help her find the Rose Scepter, someone to lift the Sword of Marric on her behalf.

But not him, she thought desperately. *Oh, please, don't let it be him.*

Yet even as she tore her gaze away from the black-haired man in the dark tunic and fixed it once more upon Sir Richmond's grim face, her heart sank. She saw the truth in the soldier's eyes even before he answered her.

"They did confirm it, my lady. That is Prince Lucius. May the heavens help you."

May they indeed, Brittany thought with a gulp as her stomach roiled again. Yet she spoke with firm resolve. "Then all will be well. He is pledged to me, and I have every confidence that he will keep that pledge. Please leave me so that I may . . . approach him," she finished.

"I prefer to stay and ensure your safety, my lady. I know that Queen Elysia would wish —"

"She would wish you to obey me." Brittany spoke quietly, but there was steel beneath the gentle tone. The knight stared down into those flashing green-gold eyes for a moment, saw the determination tightening the delicate features, then slowly nodded with respect.

"As you wish," he sighed.

"You and your men may break your camp and return to Strathbury at first light."

"Not before I have spoken with you again and assured myself that you're under the prince's protection," he countered swiftly.

Despite her determination, Brittany nodded. She was grateful for his concern. But she was concerned enough for both of them.

She wasn't at all convinced that the man on the bench kissing that woman and drinking wine as if his life depended upon it would actually agree to help her.

Or be *able* to help her. Why, he could be intoxicated for days. And they didn't have much time before Darius might be swooping down upon them like a great bloody-fanged dragon.

"I will see you on the morrow, Sir Richmond. Have you obtained lodging for me in this . . . place?"

"Yes, my lady. Such as it is."

"Then leave me now. The hour is growing late and I must speak with my betro—, I mean, with Prince Lucius. Now. Alone."

Gravely, the knight took her gloved hand, kissed it, then turned and marched out of the inn. A great gust of wintry wind swept in as the door banged shut behind him, and the firelight flickered eerily across the walls and the earthen floor.

It glowed on the dark face of the man on the bench and made him look as forbidding and dangerous as the devil himself.

But there was no time to waste, Brittany reminded herself, and taking a deep breath, she started toward him. Just as she did so, he swept the woman on his lap into his arms and arose from the bench with a great roar of laughter.

"Come along, then, wench, up the stairs with you. It is time for bed," he said with a wide, drunken grin.

"Prince Lucius," Brittany murmured quickly, stepping directly into his path. "Please wait . . . I must speak with you."

He halted, the serving girl clamped easily in his arms, her mouth dropping as she gaped at Brittany, who had planted herself between them and the stairway. The tall man with the close-cropped black hair and the sharply handsome features didn't gape, but he did frown at her as if her intrusion was most unwelcome, his dark gray eyes, the color of a stormy sea, piercing her.

"Do I know you?" he asked curtly.

"No . . . not exactly. That is, we have met before . . . but it was long ago. Very long ago . . . much too long for you to, er, remember," she finished lamely.

By the heavens, she was babbling. She never babbled. Not a good beginning, not at all.

Why couldn't he be a toad? Brittany thought. Then she straightened her spine, remembering her family whom she'd never known, how they'd been slaughtered by Darius. Remembering the quest for the Rose Scepter and the great danger ahead.

"My business with you is urgent," she told him, her chin lifting in a gesture of stubbornness and pride. "We must speak privately — at once."

"I'm busy."

The serving wench in his arms threw back her head and laughed.

"This is more important." Brittany drew herself up to her full height, which fell just short of his powerful shoulders. She ignored the woman and fastened her gaze on the man looming before her.

Lucius of Marric stared at her, a good,

long stare of the sort that had been known to shake the confidence of seasoned warriors. The woman blocking his path was a petite beauty wrapped up to her long, lovely neck in a blue woolen cloak. The hood was thrown back, however, revealing masses of hair the color of wild honey, hair that tumbled down in a cascade of curls around a delicate face of astonishing beauty. Fiery green-gold eyes regarded him from beneath winged brows. Her features were exquisitely chiseled, her mouth looked soft and full and eminently kissable. But it was not any of that which made his stomach tighten, made his senses suddenly come alert, despite the effects of the wine heating his blood. It was something in her bearing — a tension, a determination — and something even more in those brilliant eyes. Intelligence, spirit, and purpose glowed in them. Along with just a trace of fear.

Perhaps it was the glimmer of fear that he perceived in their depths that decided him. He set Drusy down, ignoring her loud protests, and gave the honey-haired girl his full attention.

"Urgent, you say? Somehow I doubt it. But come, be seated, and tell me your tale. If it's a champion you seek, however, you've come to the wrong place — and the wrong man. We who favor the Bones and Blood serve only ourselves."

Brittany peered swiftly around the dark, noisy room, taking in the drunken, brutish men who filled the place, then returned her gaze to the tall, midnight-haired man regarding her through those shrewd gray eyes, eyes that held no softness, only an icy calm. And something more — a deep, long-held sorrow that even the wine could not dull, she realized suddenly.

If he thought to convince her that he was just like the others here, aimless and coarse and indifferent, he had failed. He was not like them — she could see that much at once. She wondered suddenly if his words to the contrary were meant to convince her — or himself.

"Don't listen to her now. Come upstairs with me!" the serving wench shrieked, hanging on to his powerful arm.

He flicked her off with no more than a glance. "Leave us."

"But —"

"*Leave us.*" The ice in his tone stilled her shrill protests, and she dropped his arm, stepped back, and whirled on Brittany. For a moment Brittany thought the woman would strike her, but even as the serving girl clenched her hand into a fist and let out a

171

hissing oath, Lucius of Marric gave her a swat on the bottom that sent her staggering for several paces.

"Bring more wine, Drusy," he said lazily, his gaze still fixed on Brittany's drawn face. "And don't fret. I'll be finished with her soon enough, and then you and I will have our pleasure."

"Ah, fine, then." The woman tossed her head and planted her hands on her hips. "I'll hold you to that, don't think I won't." With one last glare in Brittany's direction, she flounced off.

Lucius gazed into Brittany's face for one more moment, then seized her arm and began steering her toward a low bench and table in the darkest corner of the inn, far from the fire, far from the center of the noise and the other patrons.

"This way."

3

No one paid any attention to them as they made their way through the thick smoke, the games of dice, and shouting matches. A man with a full black beard yelled something and shoved another man, who would have barreled right into Brittany, but Lucius thrust himself in front of her and grabbed hold of the man first, sending him reeling in the opposite direction.

"Thank you," she said quietly as she hurried past the fracas, but Lucius only clenched his jaw and made no reply.

By the time they reached the bench, Brittany was more than happy to sink down on it. Her stomach was rumbling in earnest now, and she was grateful that the din in the inn would prevent her companion from hearing it. But she was beginning to feel weak from lack of food, and as Drusy stalked over and banged a jug of wine onto the table, she quickly said, "Kindly bring bread and meat as well."

"All we have is boiled mutton," the girl retorted, but Brittany nodded.

"That will do."

There was no mistaking the soft elegance of her speech, nor the subtle air of command, which Drusy obviously resented, but felt compelled to obey.

As Drusy moved away, Lucius gave his companion a hard, curious look.

"You're going to have to sup alone, my lady," he told her shortly. "I won't be staying long enough to join you. I have business to attend to — upstairs." The drunken grin returned. It was clear he meant his business with Drusy. "Say what is so urgent and be done with it."

"I fear it won't be that easy to rid yourself of me, Prince Lucius."

His eyes narrowed. "Lucius will do." He took a swig of the wine, without inquiring if she wanted any. "How do you know who I am?" he asked with a scowl.

"Perhaps you ought to ask who I am," she countered.

His gaze swept over her once more, then returned to the jug of wine. "It doesn't matter," he said with a shrug. "Whatever you want, I'm not interested and I can't help you." He took another long, noisy gulp of the wine.

"I am your betrothed," Brittany said softly.

174

At that, Lucius of Marric choked on his mouthful of wine. Great coughs wracked him. He set the jug on the table with a thump as he bent over, gasping.

Brittany couldn't sit idly by and watch this. Without even thinking she jumped up and began pounding him on the back. "I probably should have broken it to you more gently. It's most awkward, I know. And highly unusual. I wish you would stop choking," she said sharply, in growing concern, as his coughs grew more violent. Her blows upon that broad, strong back became more rapid and fierce. "This usually helps. Samu the juggler did this for me once when I sneaked into the kitchen in the dead of night and choked on a sip of warm mead. I couldn't sleep, you see, because . . . oooooh!"

She gasped as his hand closed tightly around her arm and he yanked her around and onto the bench beside him so roughly that she cried out. Though she tried to pull free, she couldn't. His grip was like iron. Seated this close to him, so close she could see the dangerous-looking black flecks in his intense gray eyes, a strange dizziness washed over her.

At least he's stopped coughing, she thought as she tried to keep breathing herself. Being so close to him was unsettling, to say the least. A powerful jolt of heat ran through her, locking her breath in her chest. She couldn't tear her gaze from that darkly handsome and oh-so-furious face.

"What . . . did you say?" he managed to choke out, his voice low and raw, his grip on her wrist so tight she had to fight to keep from wincing.

"I said that I am your betrothed. And kindly let go of my wrist before you break it. Oooh, *thank you.*"

He released her abruptly, and she jerked her arm away and began to rub her bruised flesh. From the expression in his eyes, she could see that he hadn't realized how tightly he was holding her. He looked like a man in shock, a man who had just jumped into an icy river and could barely stay afloat in the shock of the cold.

He gave his head a shake and leaned toward her so that their noses were almost touching. "No," he said forcefully, his eyes like flint. "You're lying."

"I do not lie. I wish I were. I mean, I wish it was not true. I wish none of it was true." Brittany took a deep breath. She was babbling again. She never babbled. What cruel joke was this that this man whom she was bound to marry should have this effect on her, to make her chatter like a magpie.

"My name is Britta. Britta of Palladrin," she continued in a low whisper, glancing around uneasily. To her relief, no one appeared to be listening. No one except Lucius, who was frozen before her, an expression of utmost horror upon his face.

"When you were six years old and I was not yet two, our families pledged us to one anoth—"

"I know what my family did when I was six," he hissed, his hands shooting out and grasping her by the shoulders. "But you're dead. That is . . . *she's* dead. You're no more Princess Britta than I'm Arthur of Britain!"

"Everyone thinks I'm dead — but they'll know the truth soon enough if you don't keep your voice down," Brittany retorted, her heart thudding. This wasn't going well. Lucius of Marric wasn't exactly getting down on one knee and promising to serve her, protect her, and marry her. He looked like he wanted to strangle her.

"I am alive, but perhaps not for long unless you help me. Which you will do, I trust," she added hastily, her tone brisk as she tried to sound expectant and far more confident than she felt. "We must be married at once and you must help me to defeat Dar—"

"Hold on. Don't say another word. I know how to settle this."

He stood up, seized her arm, and dragged her away from the bench, even as Drusy appeared with a tray of food.

"Wait! Where are you — aaarrgggh!" The serving wench's shriek echoed as Lucius hauled Brittany up the stairs of the inn, ignoring her protests and futile attempts to pull free.

"What are you *doing?* I am not going upstairs with you. Let me go at once! I wish to eat my boiled mutton and . . . and this is most uncalled for. Not to mention improper. We . . . we are not married . . . not yet, and . . ."

Goodness, Brittany thought in panic as Lucius didn't even slow his pace. *He doesn't intend to claim his husbandly rights, does he? We have not yet been wed. Only pledged.* Apprehension rushed through her, and she tried again to get him to release her. But no matter how imperatively she flung orders at him, he paid no heed and continued to pull her helplessly up the stairs as if she hadn't spoken. Her strength was no match for his, and she could do nothing but be borne along, down a dingy corridor lit by a single candle. The hallway smelled repulsive, of spilled ale and rotting wood, but at last they reached a tiny chamber at the end of it.

Lucius dragged her inside and kicked the door shut.

Several candles illuminated a dank little room, with few furnishings aside from a lumpy bed covered by a moth-eaten woolen blanket and a plain wooden chest against the wall. The single window was shuttered against the cold.

There was no fire, no hearth, and the room was nearly as cold as a barn. Brittany shivered, not only from the cold but from the ruthless expression in Lucius's eyes as he surveyed her.

"Take off your cloak."

"I will not!"

"The hell you will not." He spoke between clenched teeth, and before Brittany could do more than gasp, he had his hands on her again and had ripped the cloak from her shoulders.

"You're a madman! How dare you!"

"Now your gown."

"I am *not* taking off my gown and if you try —"

"Slip it down off your shoulder," he ordered tersely. "Or I will do it for you."

Understanding came to her in a flash.

The rose birthmark.

"It's there. The birthmark. It's on my right shoulder. Everything I told you is the truth."

"Show me. *Now.*"

Her vivid green-gold eyes met his glittering gray ones. A silent battle ensued in that tiny, dim room while the clamor of the inn roared below.

Brittany, gazing defiantly at those hard, commanding features, knew that he meant what he said. He would remove her gown to see the birthmark — or lack of one — for himself if she didn't obey his request. What sort of man was he, what sort of past did he have, that his distrust ran so deep? That he was so cynical, so careful?

So hostile.

"Very well," she said at length, with all the dignity she could summon. "Once I prove it to you, may I trust that you will honor your pledge and help me?"

"I'll make no bargain with you. Not before you've shown me the birthmark. But if you're lying, I promise you this: I'll make you sorry you ever set foot in this inn. That's one pledge I *will* honor."

Brittany said nothing more. With her eyes locked on his, she began unfastening the bodice of her dark green gown, only enough to allow her to slide the fabric off her right shoulder. In the flickering candlelight, she watched Lucius's eyes. Her heart began to race as he took in the tiny birthmark in the shape of a rose. He stepped closer, stared harder, then swung his gaze back to her face.

"Satisfied?" she asked coolly, but an odd fluttering had sprung up deep inside her. She yanked her gown back up on her shoulder with hands that shook a little, all too aware of the intensity of his scrutiny. Quickly she began refastening it, but his hand shot out and stopped her, his fingers warm on hers.

"Just what the hell do you want from me?" he rasped.

"Only that you honor your pledge."

"Marry you, you mean?" He gave a jeering laugh, his mouth twisting unpleasantly, and the warm little flutter inside her went still.

"Are you that desperate for a husband, a comely wench like you?" He stepped closer, his fingers still clamped around hers, and Brittany felt the heat and energy of him searing her. She couldn't breathe for a moment, could only stare up into that angry, dangerous face. Then she reminded herself that it would not do to let Lucius of Marric intimidate or belittle her, that she was no longer merely the ward of a queen, she was royal herself.

"I'm not a wench, Lucius. I'm a princess, as royal as you, and you would do well to remember that."

Even as she eyed him haughtily, a tiny part of her again tingled with warmth. He thought she was comely.

Why should that matter? she asked herself. He probably thinks every hag within a hundred miles is comely. At least, comely enough for his purposes. She continued quickly. "I am desperate — yes. I won't deny it. I'm desperate for a protector. And since you were pledged to me by your family — by *our* families — then I expect you to fulfill that responsibility. I am about to find myself in very great danger and —"

"What sort of danger?" Suddenly, understanding lit his eyes.

"Darius." He spat out the word. "Of course. Ruler of all Palladrin. Don't tell me you want me to fight Darius for you?" He gave a great crack of laughter. "I wouldn't even fight Darius for *me*," he said, shaking his head.

"Are you afraid?"

"Let me tell you something, *Princess*," he told her with thinly veiled contempt. His hand tightened, but Brittany didn't even protest, so caught up was she in the bitterness reflected in his face. "I fought Lothbin the Giant and poked out both his eyes. I killed two dragons before my fifteenth winter, and I have fought in one war after another for almost half my life. I'm not afraid — not of anything — not of death, and by all the demons in hell, surely not of Darius."

"Then why —"

"I don't care. Understand? *I don't care.* I just want to enjoy some decent food, some good ale, and savor the company of whatever comely wenches cross my path. I'm nobody's champion, nobody's hero, nobody's fighting man — not anymore. And I'm certainly nobody's prince. So find yourself another champion. I'm out of the dragon- and wizard-slaying business."

"You don't care about your family's honor?"

He gritted his teeth, and she saw a shadow cross those deep-gray eyes. But when he spoke his voice was like a whiplash. "I don't care about anything — or anyone. So don't bother me again. I won't be so patient with you next time."

He turned on his heel and left her there. For a moment Brittany stood in shock. Then, trembling, she sank down upon the cot and covered her face with her hands.

Lucius wouldn't help her. Now what would she do?

Despair and the first twinges of terror began to creep through her. Soon Darius would be able to sense her presence in the world of the living — and she had no doubt that he would seek her out and try to destroy her. There had to be another way — besides the Sword of Marric — to gain her powers and claim her kingdom.

There had to be!

What that way might be, she had no idea, but she knew one thing. She couldn't waste time here at this inn. Not another moment.

Besides, after seeing the manner of men who frequented the place — including the prince of Marric — she felt it was clearly too dangerous for a woman to stay here alone, with no protector. She had to get her horse from the stable and find the camp of Sir Richmond and his men. Sir Richmond was a seasoned warrior, experienced in battle and strategy. Perhaps he could help her to devise another plan, a way to hide herself from Darius as she searched for the Rose Scepter. Or he might suggest another ally, someone who, unlike Lucius of Marric, *did* care about someone other than himself.

Blindly, she finished fastening up her gown, flung on her cloak, and made her way downstairs and through the crowded inn. She was too distraught to heed anyone around her, and she refused even to peer about for Lucius of Marric. She never saw him glance up from his efforts to soothe

Drusy's ruffled feathers in a warm, dark corner of the room, never saw him drop his hands from the serving girl's waist to stare piercingly after her, a scowl upon his face as she tore down the stairway and hurried toward the door of the inn. She'd been wrong about him, that's all she knew. He *was* a toad — for all his handsome face and powerful muscles and keen eyes, he was nothing but a selfish, lowly toad who cared only for himself.

She gasped as she threw open the door and a blast of wintry air struck her. Shivering, she plunged out into the night and with head bent, veered toward the stables as snow swirled around her and the wind bit into her flesh. But as she reached the stable doors, two men emerged from the murky depths of the structure and blocked her path.

"Whoa, what's this?" The first one grabbed her as the wind nearly knocked her over.

The second one paused, fingering his dark beard, which was encrusted with bits of snow and ice. His eyes were red-rimmed and bloodshot, and an evil scar stretched across his left cheek.

"What's a lovely thing like you doing out here in this ugly night?" he bellowed in a voice as thick as congealed gravy.

"Let me pass." Brittany spoke firmly and

tried to step around them, but the first man, whose sharp, narrow eyes were the color of horse dung, refused to release her. Instead he swung her up against his chest.

"Not so fast, my pretty. Come with us into the inn. We'll buy you some ale to warm you and —"

"Let go of me and be on your way!" Brittany kicked out at him and tried with all her might to pull free of his grasping hands. She suddenly wished she'd never sent Sir Richmond away from the Bones and Blood, that she'd had him wait here for the outcome of her meeting with Lucius. She'd been so certain that her betrothed would help her. So certain that she wouldn't need Sir Richmond's aid once she'd found Lucius of Marric.

"I'm warning you —" she began desperately, but the two men both threw back their heads and laughed. Panic bubbled inside her as she struggled in vain to break away.

Suddenly the man who held her yanked her closer and pressed his mouth against hers. Wet, cruel lips crushed hers, and Brittany nearly retched at the sour taste of him. Frantically, she kicked, clawed, struck out, but he only tightened his hold on her and bent her backward with the force of the kiss.

"Gangrin," the scar-faced man hissed, as

wind roared all around them and snow whirled in a fury, "take her into the stable! We'll both have her, then get to our ale. Quick, before someone sees!"

But even as he glanced over his shoulder toward the inn door to make sure no one was there to witness what they were about, a fist struck his jaw and sent him flying back into the snow. Brittany felt herself flung aside, and she stumbled to her knees as the man who had held her was thrown hard against the wall of the stables.

She heard the rasp of a sword being drawn, peered up dazedly as terror burst through her — and saw a towering man facing the two who had accosted her. He held a sword, a sword whose jeweled hilt glittered fiercely in the night, hurting her eyes with the brilliance of it. The man's feet were spread apart, planted on the ground, his face grim and deadly as the two who'd accosted her sprang upright and drew their swords as well.

"Defend yourselves as best you can. Then prepare to die," warned Lucius of Marric.

4

Gangrin gave a great bellowing yell and charged toward Lucius even as the scar-faced man raised his own sword over his head. Brittany screamed, but Lucius moved faster than either of the attackers and the scream died in her throat as he sliced his blade into Gangrin's heart, yanked it free in the blink of an eye, and spun about in time to slam it against the scar-faced man's head. Before the man could do more than grunt and stagger, Lucius killed him, plunging the sword into his throat.

It was over — over so quickly that Brittany's scream was still echoing in her chest. She gasped, fought the bile that rose in her at the gruesome sight of the dead men, and closed her eyes. "Are you hurt?" Lucius knelt beside her. His voice was rough, but his hands were gentle as he touched her. She forced her eyes open and stared at him, unable to speak.

"Are you hurt?" he repeated with a tinge of impatience.

She shook her head.

"Where's that damned soldier who entered the inn with you? Why were you out here alone?"

"Sir Richmond. I . . . sent him away."

"Brilliant."

"Those men —"

"Forget about them. They're dead." He scowled. "I'd best get you back inside before you freeze."

"Why . . . did you . . . help me?"

"I'll be damned if I know." He lifted her into his arms as if she weighed no more than one of the snowflakes melting on her lashes, and stomped toward the door of the inn.

Brittany had no strength to argue or to question him. A faintness had stolen over her, and she fought against slipping away into the warm blackness that loomed near. Only dimly was she aware of Lucius carrying her through the inn and up the stairs, then to the door of the very same room where he'd taken her before.

But this time the door was shut fast.

Lucius kicked it in, and there upon the cot Drusy was rolling about with a burly man who had wild straggly hair the color of straw. They both gasped in astonishment as Lucius stepped into the dim chamber with Brittany in his arms.

"Out," Lucius ordered between clenched teeth.

"Aucchh! *You* get out!" Drusy screeched, and the man surged to his feet.

"We got here first —" he growled, but Lucius cut him off.

"Out." The single word held so much menace that Brittany was stunned out of her half-fainting state. She saw the man look into Lucius's eyes, and whatever he saw there made him blanch.

He gulped, backed up a step, then grabbed Drusy's hand and tugged her behind him as he all but scurried from the room.

Lucius kicked the door shut behind them, still scowling, and lowered Brittany's feet to the floor.

Supporting her, he slid his cloak off and draped it over the rough mattress. Then he eased her down upon the bed.

"Sleep."

She shook her head. "Too c-c-cold."

He swore, a litany of words that she'd heard only when she had hidden once in the stable loft and heard the grooms talking roughly among themselves. With a grimace he pushed her back against the mattress and folded his cloak around her, as if swaddling a child.

He turned on his heel and would have strode to the door, but Brittany snatched his hand and held on to it for dear life.

"You're very kind. You don't want anyone to know it, do you? But you are — kind."

"You're as mad as Ejax the Gnome, Princess."

He would have yanked his hand away, but she gripped it still. Lucius stared down at the slender fingers entwining his larger, stronger ones, and his scowl deepened.

"What do you want from me?" he rasped.

"I want you to help me. Fight — not for me — but *with* me."

"Fight? Do you know what those cutthroats almost did to you back there? And they'd have killed you — slit your throat and left you to die in a horse stall — when they were finished with what they had in mind. So what do you think Darius, ruler of all Palladrin, will do to you?"

"If you help me, I can find my powers. I'm supposed to have powers," she said, as if trying to convince herself. "They'll help me once I find the Rose Scepter and you raise the Sword of Marric —"

"Fairy tales," he growled. "Stories of the past. Myths and legends that end well but reflect nothing of life in this world we know."

"And what kind of a world might that be?" she asked.

"A world of savagery. Of war and cold and hunger and death. A world where good men die and bad ones flourish —" He broke off and clamped his lips together.

"Go to sleep, Princess," he sighed.

But still Brittany clutched his hand. Her eyes held his, searching, but she knew not what she sought. "I need you," she whispered at last. In the feeble light, she saw the harshness of his gaze and wondered how she could breach the wall he'd built around himself. "Please. Whatever you've lost, whatever you've known or suffered that has brought you to this place, at this time, with such hardness in your heart, perhaps . . . we can heal it together. I need you. My . . . my kingdom needs you. The people are suffering under Darius's rule. Won't you help them? Help *me* to help them?"

Lucius stared down into her pale face, so lovely, so delicate. In the shadows of the dim room, her cheeks looked sunken, her eyes desperate. Afraid. She must have ridden far today, a grueling ride in biting cold and drifting snow. At the end of that ride, he'd rejected her, and she'd been accosted by cutthroats of the lowest order. And she would soon have Darius after her. Not a pretty prospect. Yet . . . in her eyes there was hope. Trust. A sweet, heartrending appeal that touched something deep within him, something he had thought was dead to all touch, to all life.

She was either incredibly foolish — or incredibly brave.

"By the devil's tail, why not?" he muttered. A harsh smile curled his lips. "Fighting Darius is as good a way to die as any." He shrugged those great shoulders. "So why the hell not?"

He stalked out of the room without another word and slammed the door behind him. Exhausted, and relieved beyond words, Brittany stared after her betrothed for a moment, then curled up in his cloak. Her pounding heart slowed, her limbs melted wearily into the mattress, and she allowed her heavy lids to drift shut.

To her own surprise, despite her worries and her troubles — chief among them the knowledge that in little more than a day an evil wizard would know of her existence and come after her — she felt strangely at peace.

She nestled within Lucius's heavy woolen cloak — and slept.

5

Lucius groaned and came awake with the first stirrings in the inn's kitchen below. The aroma of gruel and hot bread drifted up to him, and his stomach growled its hunger. Even his muscles grumbled a protest as he sat up in the inn's still darkened hall.

The pallet he had thrown down upon the hard floor directly before the doorway of the chamber where Princess Britta slept was not much softer than the floor itself, where a cold draft had flowed like a river all through the night. He still didn't understand why he hadn't availed himself of Drusy's bed — or Ula's — where he would have had warmth and comfort and pleasure. What odd notion of chivalry had compelled him to spend the night guarding the chamber where a honey-haired girl slept?

No doubt the same idiotic notion that had urged him to accept her plea for help.

Damn. He'd committed himself — to her,

to the fight ahead of her, to . . . marriage.

For a moment Lucius had to choke back the urge to howl with laughter. He, Lucius of Marric, whose poor judgment had lost him a kingdom, whose idiocy had gotten his most loyal friend killed, whose so-called skill with a sword had brought nothing but disaster, was about to take responsibility for an innocent and helpless princess on an impossible quest.

He scrambled to his feet, raked a hand through his hair, and scowled at the closed door behind which the princess slept.

For a moment he wondered if she indeed had already acquired her magic powers and cast a spell on him. There was no other explanation for it.

Even after he had donned armor and dressed himself in a black tunic of thick wool, had partaken of thin gruel and mutton and coarse bread, had seen Sir Richmond slip into the inn and settle himself in a chair in the corner near the door, no doubt awaiting a final word with the princess — even then there was no sound of stirring from the room where she slept.

Lucius pushed open the door and entered, his booted feet moving with remarkable quiet for so large and powerful a man. He stood over the bed, gazing down at the girl. She was curled on her side, her hair spread like lace across the pillow. One slender hand nestled beneath her cheek, and his cloak was still bundled around her. Her breathing was deep, even, and the long eyelashes that lay against her cheek did not so much as flutter.

Something tightened deep inside him as he gazed at her. She was utterly defenseless, utterly innocent of the evils of the world she was about to enter. If he had been an enemy, he could have killed her in an instant. If he were Darius . . .

"Awaken, Princess. We must ride far this day." He spoke harshly, shattering the calm of the little room, shattering whatever dreams held her. She jerked upright, a gasp in her throat, and her eyes widened upon him with terror.

"Oh, it's *you*." Relief filled her lovely face, and there was even the hint of a smile, which only made Lucius's muscles tense. By all that was holy, she thought he was a hero, her hero. Little did she know that he could well bring her to ruin, as he'd brought everything else.

"Dress and break your fast quickly. Your Sir Richmond awaits you belowstairs. If you wish to go with him, tell me now — if not, ready yourself for a hard journey. I won't hear any complaint."

"Are you always this grumpy in the morning?" Brittany asked, swinging her legs over the side of the bed. She scooped up his cloak and handed it to him.

"If we reach Dag Omer, you'll find out."

"Dag Omer? Where is that?"

"That is where the holy man lives who will marry us tonight. If you still want to marry me, that is. Then for certain you will know what I am like in the morning," he added.

She swallowed, staring into that dark, sardonic face so full of hardness and a bitterness she couldn't understand. Her heart trembled at the idea that she was surrendering herself, her life, her fate to this stranger. That by this evening, they would share not only danger but, if he chose, a bed.

"You are my pledged betrothed," she answered quietly. "An alliance between us is our only hope. Tomorrow . . ."

She took a deep breath. "Tomorrow is my twentieth birthday. After that, Darius will know that I am alive and that I am a threat to him." She shuddered suddenly as a thought occurred to her. "You should know that he could kill me before I ever find the Rose Scepter, before we have a chance to fight. He could kill you, too."

For the first time she realized the depth of the danger she was thrusting upon him.

"Are you sure you want to go ahead with all this?"

"A fine time you've chosen to ask me that." Eyes glinting, Lucius wheeled away from her toward the door. "As it happens, Princess, I don't have anything better to do. Life's been dull lately — ever since I lost my own kingdom," he added carelessly. "So why not take a stab at yours? It's my duty, as you reminded me. But don't keep me waiting. I've no patience for dawdlers."

And he was gone, the door slamming behind him.

Her thoughts in a whirl, Brittany soon found herself sitting down before a platter of mutton and thick bread in the inn's main room, after dismissing a reluctant Sir Richmond.

By the time she ventured out into the blowing snow beneath the dull gray sky, the hood of her cloak tumbling back in the wind that ripped through naked trees, she was wondering at her own audacity in challenging the great Darius.

Not even the sight of Lucius of Marric standing beside a black destrier of impressive height and muscularity reassured her. Beside the great steed, her own pretty brown mare with the snowy feet looked small and dainty as a toy. But she was sturdy and had a great heart, Brittany reminded herself, remembering how the mare had carried her through the woods of Strathbury on her daily explorations.

They rode throughout the day — long, cold, grueling hours with the snow biting into her cheeks, the wind whipping her cloak, the cold seeping into her bones. Stealing sideways glances at Lucius, she thought that none of it seemed to disturb him at all. He was all soldier, all warrior, riding tall and straight in the saddle, his keen eyes always fixed straight ahead.

What was it that he'd said? He'd lost his own kingdom. Questions fluttered through her. She guessed the answers would reveal something of the dark emptiness that tormented him. And though she knew she ought to keep her mind focused on the challenges besetting her, she couldn't help but wonder what those answers might be.

They rode through thick forests and through low brown hills, along the winding, frozen River of Moons, and finally they crossed into the rougher, wilder country of Llachdrum, a land Brittany had never seen before, which bordered the southern tip of Palladrin.

As the afternoon waned, so did the snow, but the wind rose, howling around them as the horses galloped through a forest knotted with huge trees and ancient twisted roots, where carrion birds wheeled overhead, screeching, and where there seemed to be no path to follow. Each time she began to panic that they were hopelessly lost, that they would wander in the dark depths of the forest forever, she would glance at Lucius and see him riding placidly along, intent on some unseen destination, stalwart as always.

And then at last the trees widened, not much, but enough, and she saw a series of dips and vales ahead. At the bottom of one of these, in a place where the sky now showed the blue shadows of night descending and the final glimmers of a rose-orange setting sun, there stood a hut made of bark and logs and mud.

Dark smoke puffed out of the chimney, and behind the dwelling, Brittany saw as they approached and the horses slowed, was a rough stable.

Her legs were so stiff from riding that they trembled and gave out when Lucius helped her down. He caught her around the waist and saved her from falling.

"Sore, are you? Not used to long rides? There will be more of the same on the morrow."

"I made no complaint," Brittany said quietly, mindful of his earlier warnings and all too aware of his strong arm around her waist and of his nearness. In the gloom his face was more handsome and more dangerously aloof than ever — yet his presence was warm, vigorous, giving off a vibrant heat that spoke of strength and vitality and raw male energy. He smelled faintly of leather and of pine, and of clean sea breezes — or was that the scent of the air wafting around them?

She knew only that while they stood like this, she no longer felt the bite of the cold.

Odd, when in the saddle only a moment ago, she had felt quite frozen.

"Inside," he told her, with a jerk of his head toward the hut. Clearly an order. "His servant will tend to the horses."

She allowed herself to be led toward the hut, suddenly wondering what kind of a holy man lived in a dwelling such as this.

The door opened as they approached and a diminutive figure in a pale-gray robe and a high crimson ruff peered up at the pair of them. He had no hair and no eyebrows, and his wrinkled layers of skin were pasty white above the ruff — whiter than the snow. His eyes were sunk deep within his lined face, yet they were not faded and dim with age. They were more like the eyes of a far younger man, bright and keen and the color of polished coal.

"Lucius!" The pasty face broke into a wide grin, showing small, rounded teeth every bit as white as his flesh. "I saw you coming in the light, but could not see your companion. Let me make you welcome, both of you —"

He broke off as he shifted his glance toward Brittany. For a moment he stared transfixed at the girl shivering before him in the blue cloak, her radiant face flushed with cold, a few strands of hair escaping her hood to tumble down around her cheeks.

"Come in," he said swiftly, opening the door wider. "Come in at once."

As they obeyed, he peered outside at the deepening shadows of the moonless night, looked furtively all around, and then closed the door with a thud.

"Casso will see to your horses. Come, sit. I have soup and venison and cheese. And wine. Yes, wine. It is good wine, the only thing in this humble dwelling truly fit for a princess."

Brittany froze where she stood and stared at him, fear surging through her. "You know who I am?" she gasped.

"Of course. How would I not know? I foresaw this day long ago — not clearly, you understand, but enough to know that it would come. I never saw your face, not until now, except for when you were a wee babe and —"

He broke off as suddenly as he had begun and shook his head.

"Forgive me, Your Highness, and you, too, my prince. There will be time for talk. Come and make yourselves comfortable."

"There's not much time," Lucius interrupted, frowning as the man led Brittany forward to a low couch set beneath flickering lanterns.

"I know that."

"And you know why we have come?"

"To be married. As agreed upon years ago. Who should know that better than I?"

"And who . . . are you?" Brittany managed to utter.

Lucius and their host exchanged glances.

The holy man stepped forward, his hands clasped before him. A ruby ring upon his right hand glinted in the lantern light. The brightness of its glow made Brittany blink and sent crimson shadows dancing through every corner of the hut.

"I am known now as Melistern, a simple holy man who serves the Visions of Right. Once, in another day, another time, I was known as Melvail, and I was a minor magician and counselor to Prince Lucius's father, King Raz. I was there, Princess, when the young prince was ushered into the castle of Palladrin, and when you, a wisp of a child cradled in your mother's arms, were pledged to him and he to you in a solemn ceremony that had been ordained years earlier by your grandfather, the great wizard Zared —"

"So it was my grandfather's wish that we be betrothed," Brittany murmured and threw a quick glance at Lucius. There was no reading his expression. He stood near the fire, his arms folded across his chest, apparently no more intrigued by Melistern's tale than by the howling of the wind.

"It was more than a wish. Zared ordered it," Melistern corrected her. "As he grew older and his own powers waned, he foresaw the rise of Darius's might. Darius had been his student, and at one time was both brilliant and good — but the dark side touched him and wormed its poison through him, pulling him away from the Visions of Right. As he came into his full powers, your grandfather's began to wane and he could not stop Darius. Your grandfather foresaw the fall of Palladrin, and the Rule of Darius tyrannizing your people, Princess. And he foresaw the deaths of your family. But he also saw that in you the power would be strong. That with the Rose Scepter in your hand, and the Sword of Marric by your side" — the holy man flicked a glance at Lucius, whose face tightened even more — "you could defeat Darius. You and you alone. Thus," he finished, "the alliance with the prince of Marric."

"You knew all along, then — that she was alive?" Lucius swung away from the fire, his eyes glinting with anger. "I have visited you over the years, but you never once told me —"

"You did not need to know. Not then."

"But how did you know?" Brittany broke in. "That I was alive, I mean. I've been told my mother cast a spell to hide me from Darius, so that he would not sense my presence among the living."

"Indeed she did. I taught her that spell. I helped her to perform it," Melistern said gently.

A silence fell as Brittany stared into that wise old face, at the shining black eyes. The ruby ring winked and burned like fire.

"You see, in my early days, I also was a student of your grandfather." The holy man's voice was soft. "My gift of power was never so great as his, or Darius's. I could do charms and spells, and my visions were true. But that was all. There was never greatness in me," he told her calmly. "Only goodness. That is what Zared often told me. When Darius stormed Palladrin and danger surrounded your family, I was on my way from Marric with a message from King Raz. Dragons and great beasts surrounded the castle, servants of Darius, but I found a way in — and your mother, who refused to leave your father and your brother, entrusted you to me in the precious seconds that were left before her death. With my aid, she performed the spell, and you were shrouded from Darius's sight. It was I who brought you to Queen Elysia. I, who have waited for this day. But," he said, directing a piercing look at her, "as Lucius has said, there is little time. You and the prince must be married at once. For on the morrow —"

He broke off.

"What? What will happen on the morrow?" Brittany asked, her hands at her throat.

"Have you foreseen something?" Lucius asked sharply.

"No. Not yet. What is to come has remained hidden from me. My powers, too, alas, now have weakened with the onslaught of years. But I know that the spell that was cast will be broken at midnight. From that moment on, you will be known to Darius. He will sense you, see you, know that you live. So you must marry the prince and make plans to retrieve the Rose Scepter at once — for when the morn arrives, there will be little time. And the greatest danger."

"Then let's get it over with," Lucius growled. He came forward and took Brittany's arm, raising her from the couch.

But as he looked into her face, he suddenly frowned.

"What's wrong?"

She looked alarmingly pale, her cheeks drawn, and there were shadows beneath her eyes.

"It's nothing. Let's get on with the ceremony."

"But you —"

"She needs food, my prince." Melistern regarded him with mild reproval. "Not everyone on earth is as strong as you, able to go days without food or rest. You have no doubt forced her to ride all day, haven't you? I think you have something to learn about the care of women."

"I know plenty about women," Lucius retorted, his eyes narrowing, and Melistern laughed.

"Some women," the holy man agreed smoothly. "But not this one."

Lucius looked down at Brittany, and she felt herself flushing under that dark scrutiny.

"I'm not *that* hungry," she muttered. "We can have the ceremony first and then —"

"We sup first and wed afterward." His tone was firm. "Then," the prince of Marric added, his gaze burning into hers, "if my bride is still weary, I shall gladly permit her to spend the rest of the night —" He smiled, an enigmatic smile that never reached his eyes. "Abed."

6

Brittany scarcely remembered anything of the meal that Melistern's servant, Casso, served them in the tiny hut. She remembered roasted venison and morsels of cheese, and light flickering from the lanterns. She remembered quiet talk and periods of silence.

She began to feel stronger after the food and the wine, which Melistern poured into thin silver goblets. Yet when Lucius led her away from the table, and they knelt before Melistern to be blessed in marriage, the room seemed to sway and blur.

She murmured the words Melistern instructed her to say, she gave her hand to Lucius. And she looked into the prince's narrowed eyes, as he held her slender fingers in his and promised to cherish and protect her always.

The aroma of incense filled her nostrils, the smoke from the fire stung her eyes, and a dreamlike aura overtook her.

Until the moment when Melistern raised them, when he placed his hands upon their heads and blessed them, and gave Lucius of Marric leave to kiss his bride.

Then her heart began to pound, and the sense of unreality faded like mist. The small room with the couch and the lanterns and the silk tasseled hangings upon the wall came flashing back, and so did the solid, handsome form of her new husband, still holding tight to her hand.

Lucius pulled her toward him, and his arm slid around her waist. His other hand came up to cradle her chin. She stared deep into his eyes and suddenly realized that she'd been married in naught but a plain midnight-blue gown of unadorned wool, without so much as a whisper of embroidery or satin, and her hair hung anyhow about her face. Surely this was no way for a princess to wed a prince?

Then Lucius's mouth touched her lips and she forgot about her gown, her hair. She forgot her weariness and the danger that would soon be upon her. She even forgot about Melistern, watching them through the golden candlelight. She forgot everything but the sweet roughness of a kiss that brought flames of heat alive inside her. A kiss that swept her into a churning sea that was strangely peaceful in its center. A kiss that made her toes tingle and her heart race and had her swaying in Lucius's arms. That only made him drag her closer, hold her tighter, and kiss her even more thoroughly, leaving her breathless and afire and dizzy when he let her go and stepped back.

He looked shaken. But not nearly as shaken as she felt, Brittany thought dazedly.

For a moment they stared at each other, their gazes locked, searching . . . searching.

"Melistern, where are we to slee—" But Lucius broke off as he glanced at the spot where the holy man had stood.

Melistern was gone.

Only the candlelight and the goblets of wine and the wind wailing at the door remained.

"Where did he go?" Brittany asked in wonder.

"No doubt to spend the night in the stable with the horses and his servant so that we may share our wedding night together. Alone."

Alone.

"How kind of him," Brittany managed, and Lucius shot her an amused look.

"Fear not, Princess. I don't bite. Not usually," he added, grinning as she froze.

He's teasing you. Trying to . . . to frighten

you. Or, she thought, suddenly realizing the truth, *trying to put you at your ease.*

Lucius found a straw pallet in a tiny rear chamber, tossed it down before the hearth-fire, and then threw down a sheepskin he had dug out of a carved chest, creating a thick nest.

Brittany came slowly forward and seated herself upon the soft bed he'd made for them.

They would sleep here together now — as husband and wife. There would perhaps be more kisses, she thought hopefully.

And what else?

A whisper of panic as well as a strange eagerness fluttered inside her.

She was breathless looking at him — frightened, and yet not frightened, and when he came to sit beside her, her heart leaped into her throat.

"You're afraid." He was studying her trembling lips.

"I am not."

His brows lifted, and he hunched closer to her. "You look afraid."

"I do not." Her chin angled up, and Lucius was struck by the magnificence of those green-gold eyes blazing into his.

"At a time like this, Princess Britta, every woman is afraid. It's nothing to be ashamed of."

"I am not ashamed. And not afraid. Not really." She hesitated only a moment. "You see, I could never be afraid of you."

"Oh?" Amusement, and more than a little skepticism, flickered in the gray depths of his eyes. "And why is that?"

"Because there is kindness in you." She couldn't hold back a smile even as the words spilled out. "I told you that last night," she reminded him. "There's a kindness that you try to hide. But I can see it."

For a long moment he stared at her, speechless. Then she did something impulsive, something she could never afterward explain. She reached out and covered his hand with hers.

A trembling heat passed between them. Lucius's skin burned. Her touch, the gentle gesture, and the simple trust he saw in her lovely face, as well as the saucy sweetness that emanated from her very soul suddenly made his blood roar. And sent a river of conflicting emotions coursing violently through him.

She thought he was a champion, *her* champion. She thought him someone she could count on, could trust. He, who didn't trust or count on anyone.

He wanted to laugh at the absurdity of it, but the laughter died in his throat. He wanted to hit someone, fight someone, but the only one there was this lovely, gallant girl who wanted to fight a wizard and liberate a kingdom.

Every muscle in his body tensed. Fury lashed him like a whip.

"You think you know everything," he snarled, and seized her by the shoulders so suddenly that she jumped. When she tried to pull away, he yanked her closer, right up against his chest.

"But you know nothing, Princess. Do you understand? *Nothing*. Nothing of what really awaits you on the morrow, nothing of true darkness, true evil — and nothing about me." It was a growl, wolflike, from deep in his throat. He saw the alarm in her face, saw the quick panic as she tried to struggle free, and felt a surge of bitter satisfaction.

She was scared at last. Good. She should be scared. Of him, of the world. But her fear, and his own role in it, only intensified his anger. But it was directed as much at himself as at her.

"You're so damned innocent!" he shouted and saw her eyes widen, then flash.

"So why don't you tell me — tell me about you?" Brittany gasped. She was finally afraid. Not much, but a little. He looked not the least bit kind now. Only dangerous and strong and unpredictable, like a wild wolf prowling beneath the moon.

"About me? You want to hear about me?" He gave a short, hard laugh. "What do you want to know?"

"You . . . you said you lost a kingdom. Your kingdom. H-how?"

He was hurting her. His fingers were strong, pressing into her flesh, but she refused to tell him. Yet he seemed to sense it in the breathless way she bit out her words, and his glance suddenly shifted to where his fingers gripped her.

They went slack at once and he released her suddenly. He scowled at her, then sprang up from the floor and began to pace with long, restless strides, sending the lantern light dancing.

"My father had two sons," he rasped at last. He had paused not far from the fire and was staring into the flames, his face a harsh mask. "I was the younger by a little over a year. For as long as I can remember, there was rivalry between Sedgewick and me. He hated me — because I happened to ride better than he, because my aim with an arrow was straighter, mostly perhaps because our father favored me. I tried when I was small to be a brother to him, to follow and admire him, but he would kick me and shout at me, and once he paid the village boys with gold to thrash me down near the bank of the river."

He ignored her gasp of horror and continued as if she hadn't made a sound.

"I never told our father, though he demanded to know the cause of my bruises, the reason I could scarcely walk for a week."

"Why didn't you tell?" Brittany burst out, gripping her hands together as she watched his face.

Lucius's big shoulders lifted in a shrug. "He was my brother," he said simply, "and I knew what my father would do to him if he learned the truth."

Silence fell but for the hiss of the logs in the fire, the scream of the wind. Brittany shivered and drew the sheepskin closer around her.

"What happened . . . to your brother?" she asked at length.

Lucius swung toward her. In the golden light, his eyes looked dark as thunderclouds. "He became king of Marric when our father died."

"But that was his right, wasn't it? He was the elder. How can you say you lost a kingdom when as the firstborn, he —"

"Listen," Lucius hissed, stepping toward her, seeming to loom like a dark giant in the tiny hut. "My father grew ill, feeble. But his mind was still strong. He knew that Sedgewick was weak and that he was a bully. By the time I was grown past the age of eight, I knew it, too." His voice lowered. "I came to fear for the kingdom because of it. I feared that the people would suffer —" He broke off and wheeled away from the wavering flames to stand before her.

"My father wanted me to succeed him — he told me so. But he couldn't order it outright, so he devised a way." His lip curled. "With the help of Melvail the Counselor, he came up with a challenge for the two of us. A test of sorts. I had already defeated my brother in a contest that won me the Sword of Marric. In every generation of my family it has always gone to the strongest son. But this contest would be for the kingdom. Sedgewick was furious. He argued that by all rights the kingdom should be his — and he was right. I didn't want the kingdom, didn't want the contest — not at first. I wanted only to lead our army, because it was clear that a great war was coming with Darius to the south. But Sedgewick told me that if he was king, he would never let me lead his army, that he didn't trust me, that I wasn't good enough —

"It was an ugly quarrel," he continued

softly. "And at the end of it we came to blows. Afterward, I went to my father and told him I agreed to the contest."

"You were right to do so." Brittany jumped up, still clutching the sheepskin around her. "Your brother wasn't fit to be king. Obviously, your father was very wise and knew that you were twice the man Sedgewick would ever be and —"

"Don't be so quick to spring to my defense, Princess. You don't know the rest."

"Tell me." She stood before him, small and lovely and shivering, and it was suddenly all Lucius could do not to take her in his arms, bury his face in her hair, let her softness and her beauty drown out the memories.

"We were supposed to hunt wild boar in the forest for a day. Whoever returned with either the most carcasses or the largest, if there should be only one apiece, would win the throne of Marric. Each of us was allowed to take one companion along on the hunt. I chose Connor, who had been my groom and my loyal friend since I was a boy."

"And how old were you at the time of this contest?" she whispered.

"Seventeen. Sedgewick was nearly nineteen. He chose Sir Geoffrey, one of the knights. I wish to heaven I'd chosen one of the knights as well."

Brittany's flesh prickled. There was a haunted look to his eyes, a grim bitterness that made dread knot inside her.

"What happened?" she asked in a soft tone, stepping closer to him without even realizing it.

"We rode through the forest all morning, following signs of the boar but unable to spot him. Finally, in the early hours of the afternoon, we found him — and I killed him. We staked out the spot for those who would come to retrieve the beast's carcass, and we continued deeper into the wood, for I was determined to kill at least two more. But then," he said, drawing a deep breath, "something happened that changed everything. We heard a scream, faintly, in the distance. A woman's scream."

Brittany went perfectly still. Lucius continued speaking, his eyes grim and hard as rock. "The scream came from the opposite direction of the tracks we were following. I hesitated, then heard it again. A woman's scream, again and again, filled with pain or with terror, I couldn't tell which." His mouth twisted.

"I couldn't ignore those screams," he said. "So I turned my horse toward the sound. Connor cautioned me, reminding me that an entire kingdom was at stake, a kingdom consisting of many people, and that all together, they were more important than a single inhabitant of Marric. We couldn't afford to turn aside from the hunt, the day was already waning . . ."

Lucius shook his head. "Such were his entreaties," he said in a bitter tone. "But I wouldn't listen. I told him I would find the woman and discover what had befallen her while he continued to follow the boar tracks. I told him that I'd catch up to him soon enough. But he begged me to let him accompany me instead. No doubt he felt compelled to act as a guard of sorts, though I was no longer a child and needed no escort. Still, I let him come. I suppose I felt I might need his help with the woman and that together we could dispose of whatever trouble afflicted her much more quickly. At any rate, Connor and I both veered from the path of the boar and followed the sounds of her screams."

"You found her?" It was a whisper.

"Oh, yes, we found her. Her screams had stopped by then, but we were close enough to complete the search. It was Eynneth, a girl from the village. She was in a clearing at the bottom of a gully — lying facedown upon the earth."

"Dead?" A quick chill of horror ran through her.

"Alive. Very much alive. The moment we reached her and I leaped off my horse, she sprang up. And at the same time we heard a great noise in the brush. In less time than *that*" — he suddenly snapped his fingers — "we were surrounded. Seven, eight, nine men," he said grimly. "I can't recall now exactly how many there were. All I know is that they were a filthy bunch of cutthroats, part troll, by the looks of them. Eynneth slipped away, right through their ranks, and they let her pass without shifting their gazes from us. By then, of course, I knew. It was a trap. Sedgewick had set a trap for me, and fool that I was, I'd ridden straight into it."

Brittany couldn't speak. She watched his face, reading the tortured shadows there, the darkness that haunted his gray eyes, and she shivered again beneath the sheepskin. In the silence a log popped and she jumped, gasped, but Lucius merely lifted his gaze from the fire to regard her bleakly.

"We fought them, Connor and I. But we were surrounded and outnumbered. And I, even with the Sword of Marric, even with the so-called skills with a sword for which I was so renowned," his voice grew thick with sarcasm, "could not slash quickly enough to kill them all. And Connor, he had only a short sword, and his bow and arrows. They had swords, knives, and cudgels. They killed him first, before I could stop it, and his blood ran slippery beneath my feet as I fought. He was the best man I'd ever known, the best friend to me of anyone, far more like a brother than my own brother ever had been — and then he was dead — murdered — in service to me."

"It wasn't your fault, Lucius —"

"Whose, then? *Whose?*" He spun on her, his face savage, and grasped her arms. "I chose to follow the screams, rather than the tracks of the boar. I allowed him to accompany me. And I watched them cut him down — watched three of them hack at him as if he was naught but a block of wood."

"You couldn't stop them, there were too many."

"Damn right there were too many. I allowed myself to be tricked and trapped. Now is that the judgment of a king, I ask you? I lost my kingdom and I lost my friend. This is the man you've wed, Princess, the man you think can help you defeat Darius."

He gave a rough bark of a laugh, full of pain and rancor, and released her arms, wheeling away. He stalked to the table where the wine and goblets were set, poured himself some, and tossed it back. As he began to refill the goblet, splashing some of the wine like blood across the fine silver-embroidered cloth Melistern had laid for them, Brittany went to him quickly and laid her hand on his arm

"Tell me the rest. What did they do to you?"

"It doesn't matter. As you see, they didn't kill me. They kept me busy, fighting, hacking, slashing — while Connor bled to death. I managed to kill three of them and wounded a fourth, but it didn't matter. They left as suddenly as they'd appeared. And there I was, nary a scratch on me, but the day of the hunt had waned and was gone, Connor lay dead, and my brother . . ." His lips twisted. "My brother returned to the castle having killed two boars. Besting me. Marric was his."

"And you had lost your friend," Brittany murmured, her heart heavy for him. "I suspect that was worse for you than losing your kingdom."

He said nothing, only stared at her, then slowly nodded.

She reached up, touched his face, then quickly let her hand drop to her side.

"My father knew, of course, as well as I did, that Sedgewick had hired those bastards, as well as Eynneth, to thwart me. But it couldn't be proved, for they were never found — alive, that is. And as for Eynneth, she was never seen again, so she could not be made to speak the truth. My father had already dared to offer the contest, he couldn't then refuse to grant the kingdom to the winner, his firstborn. So I left Marric, joined the army of Duke Valmoor, and from that time on spent my days fighting in one battle after another, in whichever army would pay the most for my services. I've traveled the six lands and across two seas, returning to Marric only once, to attend my father's funeral. I was glad he didn't live to see the day when Sedgewick joined forces with Darius in an unholy alliance that has bled Marric dry of all its former riches."

"So you have punished yourself by fighting all these years. Yet it brought you no peace."

Peace. Lucius's lips thinned. "What is peace?" he asked contemptuously. "It is something for fools and dreamers. The world is fraught with war."

"And you were between these wars when I found you in the inn," she murmured.

"You could say that. I chose at last to leave the battlefield for a time, to seek my pleasure in inns, with whores and dice and tankards of ale."

He shrugged, choosing not to tell her how hard he worked at fighting and at whoring to try to forget. "I'd thought to go back — but not as soon as this," he added with a hard smile.

"And not with a woman depending on you. On you — who doesn't trust your own judgment." Her voice was a whisper, but she was gazing at him steadily through the flickering lantern light. "Or is it your heart you don't trust, Lucius?" she asked softly. "The heart that led you to help someone you thought was in need?"

"My heart has nothing to do with this, or with anything," he said sharply, frowning at her. "And I do trust my judgment — now. Because I learned not to trust anyone else — no one. Not woman nor man. I learned to stay my own course and not be swayed by anyone else. I learned to do what's best for me. Only me. And to keep others at a distance."

"Yet you helped me at the inn." Though his frown deepened, she continued resolutely. "You killed those men who would have hurt me — and you brought me here, to shelter and safety. You wed me and took on this danger that we'll face any hour now."

"Another lapse in judgment," he said carelessly. "And here I thought I was cured."

He lifted the wine to his lips, but Brittany closed her hands over the goblet and gently tugged it away.

"You're a much better man — and a much better prince — than you ever thought, Lucius of Marric," she said impatiently. "You were seventeen when you made that mistake — if it *was* a mistake. I happen to think it was brave and good of you to choose to help a woman in need."

He groaned and would have argued with her, but she cut him off. "And now you've done it again. You're not nearly as callous and cold as you'd have the world believe."

"The devil save me from foolish women who see the world as they wish it to be!" He pulled the goblet from her grasp, slammed it down on the table, and seized her roughly in his arms.

"I told you once — I'm no hero. No noble knight ready to sacrifice himself for the sake of chivalry." His eyes were gray marble slits, and as his fingers tightened on her arms, he gave her a shake. "I'll help you — but do you know why? Because you're my last tie, my last obligation to who and what I once was, to the House of Marric. When this is over, I'm done. I thought you were dead, and that I had no more obligation to that stupid pledge made when I was a child, but now you've shown up, and heaven help me, I'm saddled with you. Well, so be it. I'll damn well live up to my duty so that I can be finished with the past once and for —"

He broke off at the flash of pain that crossed her face and cursed his own temper and his tongue. "Never mind," he muttered. His fingers slackened on her arms. "I didn't mean it that way. Now that we're in the thick of it, it isn't so bad. I have nothing better to do and —"

"Kindly let me *go*," Brittany ordered with all the dignity she could muster. She tried to twist free, but he still held her too firmly for that. His touch didn't hurt her, though. Only his words did. Words that repeated themselves in her mind, searing her in some intimately painful way.

I'm saddled with you.

Of course, that's how he sees it, she told herself angrily. *He didn't ask for this fight. Or for this marriage. I'm a burden to him, an obligation, nothing more.* Why had she thought, hoped, that there would be something more? She was furious with her own foolishness. And when had she started to think that way? Was it after their vows, when he kissed her? Because of the way she'd *felt* when he kissed her?

A tremor of dismay ran through her. He

was right. She was nothing but a dreamer, a fool.

"Let me go," she ordered again between clenched teeth.

His jaw tightened, and instead of releasing her, he hauled her closer. So close she could feel the iron hardness of his chest pressing against her breasts, so close that his breath feathered her eyelashes.

"Maybe now you see why you should be afraid. I can hurt you. I *did* hurt you."

"Don't be . . . silly. It isn't as if I didn't know that our marriage is . . . is only a matter of duty and need, that it has nothing to do with love —"

"Love?" He looked startled. Then he laughed. "Another word, Princess, like peace, that has no meaning."

"You've never loved anyone?"

A heavy silence fell. "My father," he said at last. "And my friend. But that's different from what you mean. I've never loved a woman. Bedded many, but loved — never."

Her gaze dropped from his. He reached out his hand and cupped her chin, forcing it up until she had no choice but to meet his eyes.

"I think, though," Lucius said softly, carefully, "that if ever I *would* love a woman, there's a good chance she would be . . . someone like you."

Now why in hell did I say that? Horror filled him. What devilish sprite had jumped inside his mouth and brought forth those words? He didn't know where they came from, but he saw the light fill her eyes. Light and wonder.

"She . . . would?"

The princess sounded dazed. Almost as dazed as he felt. Yet, as he stood there with her in his arms, gazing into that lovely face full of hope and beauty, he felt something quiver inside his heart. He'd told her more of his story than he'd ever told another soul. She now knew more than any human being except Melistern about Prince Lucius of Marric. And she hadn't turned away from him, or pitied him, or looked askance at him.

There was sympathy in her gaze, yes, but also something else — understanding, perhaps. Admiration, even.

"And if I were ever to love a man," she said softly, her eyes searching his, "I think he would be someone like you."

He wanted to laugh, but no sound emerged. He wanted to speak, but couldn't think what to say.

He was lost in her eyes, those soft, brilliant eyes that shone so intoxicatingly in the firelight.

He would be someone like you.

She lifted a hand, touched his face. The gentleness of it stunned him. The women he'd bedded, whores and serving maids like Drusy and Ula, touched his body with coarse lust, never with this exquisite tenderness, like the lightest flutter of a feather.

He'd never experienced anything like the storm of emotions that swept him then. Every muscle in his body clenched, his loins heated, his blood roared.

He tightened the circle of his arms around her and brought his lips down to hers. It was a light kiss, lighter than any he'd ever known. As tender as her touch.

When it was over, they stared at one another.

Then it was she who rose on tiptoe and once again swept her lips to his.

This time the fire exploded in him. All of the tenderness fled as he kissed her deeply, single-mindedly, plundering the soft, pliable mouth that she offered to him with such innocent joy.

Damn, she was delicious. Sweet, so sweet. Like a peach fresh from a sunlit garden. He wanted her, *needed* her — needed her then and there with a fierceness that annihilated everything else. She was kissing him still — kissing him with a passion hot as flame.

With a growl, Lucius swept her off her feet, crushing her to his chest. As she gasped and then moaned, his mouth laid savage claim to hers. A surging heat enveloped them as their tongues brushed and circled, battling softly as he bore her to the pallet near the fire, lowered her upon it, and covered her body with his own. She was his wife, after all. *His.* She was soft beneath him, soft and willing, and her hair was rich with the scent of wild roses, like those that grew in the north of Palladrin.

Lucius's blood surged. He captured her mouth again, tasted it, savoring her honeyed flavor and the rich musk of passion that clung to her. This girl, this Princess Britta, his *wife,* was kissing him as though she was starving, her hands raking through his hair, and her hunger and need intensified his a thousandfold until he was wild with it and fighting all his basest instincts to take care with her.

Go slow, go careful, he told himself desperately even as her arms wound around his neck and pulled him eagerly down to her.

He began to touch her — her skin, her breasts — and he was lost. He never stopped kissing her as somehow he got her free of her gown, and then his hands were exploring, stroking that lush, smooth body that shimmered golden in the firelight, the curves that seemed to fit so perfectly against his own hard frame. His mouth lingered at her shoulder, where the delicate rose birthmark was nearly lost in the satin smoothness of pale skin.

The birthmark, her heritage — the link between Palladrin and Marric, between princess and prince.

And between this man and this woman.

The hut was no more, and the wine was forgotten. Melistern might have been nothing but a memory, a ghost of another lifetime. There was only the lantern light and the firelight, the rush of the wind and the roughness of the pallet, the honey-haired woman and the dark, taut-muscled man. Heat and magic and want enveloped them.

They needed nothing more.

Brittany knew only that he was raining kisses upon her, stroking her, making love to her with such exquisite tenderness that her senses whirled. When Lucius touched her breasts, kneading them until she moaned aloud, he took her to a world like none she'd ever known. Sensations coursed through her and heat devoured her as Lucius licked her ear until she was awash in shivers. And then he whispered hoarsely that he would try not to hurt her.

"I trust you," she breathed, and her eyes shone into his as he kissed her until her body shook and glistened. He circled her nipples with his tongue, loving each in turn, igniting her with a torturous pleasure.

The night and the fire and the passion swirled around them as their touches grew more urgent, their kisses more frenzied. When at last he kissed her mouth, her throat, her hair, and plunged inside her, there was fleeting pain, sharp as starlight, and then wonder and joy, and a wild thrusting, deep and filling, as he surged deep inside her and she rocked with him in a sweet, primal dance. Her hands stroked his hard, corded muscles, and she breathed in the sweat and the power of him, even as her body welcomed him, clung to him. Their hearts and souls, their breath and their bodies joined, fused, linked by lightning and by passion and by sweet, sweet fire.

And after the dizzying fulfillment, the flood tide of passion, after the fire dwindled and the lanterns burned low, she lay in his arms beneath the sheepskin, weak with pleasure, half dreaming as their two hearts beat together, solid and strong, beating as one.

7

She awakened alone, to absolute silence.

Opening her eyes, Brittany saw that Lucius no longer lay beneath the sheepskin with her. She jerked upright, pushed her hair out of her eyes, and cast a glance about the hut. There was no sign of Lucius, no sign of Melistern. Or of the servant, Casso.

A strange stillness hung in the air.

She heard nothing from outside the hut, no birdsong, no trace of wind. She sprang up and hastily dressed, donning a clean gown from her pack, smoothing her hair with her fingers, and growing increasingly uneasy as the moments passed and Lucius and Melistern didn't return.

Had last night been only a dream? The sweet kisses, the fiery lovemaking, the warmth and strength of Lucius's body locked with her own?

No, no. Her skin still felt warm from his touch, her lips scorched from the heat of his kisses. The memories were too vivid — it was no dream. They were wed, husband and wife, and they had lain together in this bed, in each other's arms. All of it was real. Blessedly real.

But today was her twentieth birthday, Brittany recalled with a stab of apprehension. Perhaps even now, at this moment, Darius *knew* that she lived. What would he do? How much time did she have?

She fastened her cloak with trembling fingers and hurried to the door of the hut.

"Lucius! Melistern!" Her voice echoed in the eerie silence.

"Lucius!" she called again, stepping out into pale sunshine. The sky had never looked so blue, the bare winter trees etched sharply against it. She turned toward the tiny stable behind the cottage, and that was when she saw them.

Two men lying on the ground. The metallic glint of blood. One of the men on his belly . . . crawling . . .

"Lucius!" Her heart in her throat, she darted forward, only to see that it was Melistern crawling toward her, blood streaming from his face and arms, a hunting knife gripped in his fingers. Behind him lay the still, bloodied form of Casso, the servant.

"By the angels, what happened?" She

dropped down on her knees beside Melistern as he gazed up at her, his mouth working, but no words coming out. "What can I do?" she asked desperately. "Where's Lucius?"

"H-hunting. D-deer . . . and berries for your breakfast." His words were so low, so weak that she had to lean down, straining to hear. Terror filled her as she gazed into his black eyes, the life already draining from them.

"He left before . . . before . . . they came . . . you must get inside . . . they'll be back . . ."

"I'm not going anywhere without you." Brittany slipped her arm beneath him, trying to lift him, but he grew more agitated and the knife slid from his fingers to thud against the ground.

"Run, Princess . . . it's you they're after. They'll carry . . . you off . . . you must . . ."

She saw his eyes widen then, staring past her, and she swiftly whipped her head in the same direction. Her breath caught in her throat, and icy fear rose within her.

Half a dozen giant carrion birds, black crows as big as young stags, perched upon the branches of the trees, where before there had been nothing but scrawny limbs. Now those limbs sagged beneath the weight of the huge birds, all of whom were watching Brittany through dark, wickedly gleaming eyes.

"Leave me," Melistern begged. "Get . . . inside, while you still may . . ."

Brittany swallowed. "Not without you," she whispered back, and with desperate strength, tried to help him to his feet.

All the while she watched the great crows, whose gleaming eyes were fixed unblinkingly upon her.

The holy man leaned heavily upon her as they inched forward, toward the hut. One step. Two.

The largest of the birds, on the lowest branch, jutted his great beak forward, and a rough squawk came from his throat. Some kind of command, Brittany realized with a gasp as all six of the birds swooped as one to the ground, blocking the doorway of the hut.

"Princess . . . I beg you . . . run . . . into the wood —"

To Brittany's horror, Melistern slumped to the ground despite her efforts to hold him up. She bent over him, tears filling her eyes, then she straightened and stared at the leader of the crows. "Begone with you," she commanded. "Return to your master."

With a great rush the birds all flapped their wings and soared upward, then zoomed straight toward her and Melistern, their claws outstretched.

Brittany screamed and whirled, lunging for the knife Melistern had dropped. The leader of the crows swooped in upon her, and she stabbed upward with the blade, but missed as the creature veered out of reach. Two more plunged at her, screeching, and she slashed out in terror.

"Britta, get down! *Down!*" Suddenly there was a rush of hooves, a violent blur of motion, and she saw Lucius charging toward her on his destrier, the Sword of Marric swinging at the great birds as they dove and screeched and tried to soar above the danger.

Quick as a bolt of lightning, the glittering blade cut a deadly swath through the air. Two birds tumbled, the others screeched even louder, and the leader screamed to the heavens and dove at Lucius in a blinding rush of wings and claws.

The destrier reared, the sword arced, and Lucius sliced off the head of the great carrion bird. The creature crashed to earth, and the other crows cried out, circling, dipping, and then with a great rush of wings they flapped off over the treetops toward the distant hills of Palladrin.

"Are you hurt?" Lucius was already swinging down from the destrier, running toward her, but Brittany shook her head.

"No, but Melistern is greatly injured! And Casso is dead." She spun back toward the holy man, who lay slumped and bleeding, his eyes glazed now with pain. "Oh, Lucius, I fear he's dying. We must get him into the hut!"

His face grave, Lucius lifted Melistern in his arms. By the time they had the holy man settled upon his bed, he could barely summon the strength to speak. Yet somehow, as they began to clean and stanch and bandage his wounds, he whispered to them to fetch certain herbs from a golden pouch within a carved chest, and told them how to prepare a broth using the herbs.

"It will kill the poison," the holy man whispered, his voice as dry as dead leaves, and Brittany realized then that the poison in the punctures he had sustained from the crows' beaks was far more serious than the wounds themselves.

Within moments of consuming the brew, Melistern's eyes were clearer, and his speech held more strength.

From his bed, he lifted a hand to beckon Brittany closer, and the ruby ring winked on his finger.

"Princess — now you must go. You and Lucius. Tarry no more."

"We won't leave you until you're better."

"You must!" His glance shifted to Lucius, standing in grim silence behind Brittany. "Even now the potion is working. The effects of the poison are fading. By sunset, my strength will return."

"But until then you're weak, Melistern. And vulnerable." Lucius studied him intently. "And they may come back."

"They will indeed come back. Perhaps with other servants of Darius, servants even more deadly, more difficult to defeat. But they won't come here, not unless the princess is still here. Do you wish to bring them down upon my simple hut again?" he asked Brittany.

She turned pale. "You know I don't!"

He nodded, and offered a feeble smile. "Go, then. Now. They will follow you, for Darius will direct them. Your only hope is to find the Rose Scepter. The powers it will grant will be your best protection. Lucius and the Sword of Marric alone cannot withstand the full force of Darius's magic. Those creatures were only a hint of the evil he can send against you."

"But where do I look for the Rose Scepter? I don't even know where to begin."

"I know."

The whispered words stunned her. She stared at Melistern's face, remarkably tranquil for a man who had just been nearly killed, a man still fighting for his life.

"I have always known. For I am the one who hid it."

"*Where?*" Brittany and Lucius spoke the question at the same time, and the holy man permitted himself another wan smile.

"It is in Palladrin — in the Valley of Ice. I have frozen it deep within the heart of the Devil's Cave."

"Frozen it?" Lucius asked sharply.

"Within the walls of the cave. It is encased in ice, hidden by rock. Here."

He suddenly tugged the ruby ring off his finger and pressed it into Brittany's hand. The stone seemed to burn into her palm.

"The rose carved into the scepter has a ruby dewdrop atop it," Melistern said. "That ruby is the sister of this one. They will speak to one another when you draw near."

"Speak to one another?" she asked, baffled.

"You will see. Take the ring, Princess. And leave me. *Now.*"

Lucius came forward and grasped Brittany's arm. "You heard him."

"But he's ill. Shouldn't we wait until —"

"Until you bring some other beasts or perhaps a demon or two down on him? Is that what you want, Princess?"

She stared into his eyes, shocked by the sharpness of his tone, the impatience underlying it. She was still trembling from the encounter with the crows, from the horror of the attack upon Casso and Melistern. And now Lucius was regarding her with coldness, as if she were a silly, wayward child — not his bride, not the woman whom he'd kissed and stroked and made love to last night.

That gentle lover was nowhere to be found in the hardened soldier who gazed back at her.

She felt a staggering sense of loss, and her heart seemed to sink to the pit of her stomach. But even so, she suddenly saw that he was right. The danger would follow her. She must lead it away from here, away from Melistern.

And above all, she had to retrieve the only weapon that would be of use against Darius. The Rose Scepter.

Suddenly another thought occurred to her. Lucius was every bit as much at risk as she — until she had the scepter, and thereby her powers. For his sake, as well as her own, she had to find it.

And quickly.

"How far from here to the Valley of Ice?"

"A day's ride. We could reach it by tonight."

She nodded and turned away from the coolness in his eyes. "Then let us get started."

They rode without speaking, the only sound the clattering of their horses' hooves upon the rock path. Lucius sat the destrier with apparent ease, but she noticed the way he looked from side to side, up at the surrounding hills, back down the trail from which they'd come, even scanning the sky. She knew he was watching for the next attack. His outward calm was reassuring — but she sensed his keen alertness, a wariness in the set of those powerful shoulders. Yet she couldn't read his face at all. Did he even remember all that had passed between them in the night, the fire and the storm of their lovemaking, the blinding pleasure of kisses that she'd wanted never to end?

She knew that he was riding with her to help her and protect her in the most dangerous battle of his life, but only because of his obligation to his family honor — his *last* obligation, he'd said. She felt lost and adrift. And more alone than she'd ever felt before.

"Do you want to stop for a while? To rest?"

"No." Though he'd slowed his mount, Brittany kept hers at the same hard pace. She shook her head as she rode past him. "I want to get to the Valley of Ice — the sooner the better."

She spurred her horse forward, leaving him in a cloud of flying snow, determined not only to get to the scepter as quickly as possible but to hide from him the hurt festering inside her.

Hurt over a man she'd only just met? How could he have this effect on her so quickly, so powerfully?

Grimly, Lucius followed, staying close. She was angry with him. Which was just as well, he reflected. Better if she kept her distance and he kept his. Last night . . .

Last night had brought them too close. Not only physically, but in some other way he couldn't explain. When he'd returned to the hut this morning and seen the crows attacking her, he'd gone cold with fear. Fear for her — for the honey-haired princess with a spine of iron and skin as soft as the petals of a rose.

For the woman who had lit a fire in his blood last night. Who'd planted herself in front of Melistern and faced the crows with knife in hand, like some ancient warrior goddess. The woman who was now riding straight into danger.

He'd been casting about in his mind for some way to spare her, some way that he could go alone into the Valley of Ice and find the scepter for her — instead of escorting her right into Palladrin virtually under Darius's nose.

But it was futile, he realized. The danger would follow her. He dared not leave her alone, unprotected, for it was as certain as the imminent rising of the moon that Darius would attack her once more.

His mouth tightened with resolve. His horse quickened its pace. He had to protect her — somehow.

Throughout the ride, he maintained strict vigilance, constantly expecting the attack to come. When they reached Palladrin and began to cross the plain that would lead them to the cliffs and the Valley of Ice, he saw that her shoulders were beginning to slump with weariness and her face looked flushed from the cold.

"We stop here and sup," he ordered, riding up alongside her. "You'll be of no use to me or your people if you collapse from hunger."

Brittany was only too glad to rein in and join him in a meal of berries, bread, and cheese. The light was beginning to fade, and night would fall fast.

"How long before we reach the Valley of Ice?" she asked as they broke their camp and he came to help her into the saddle.

"No more than a few hours. The moon is full and will light the path — that'll make it easier."

She nodded, but as he took her hand to help her, she suddenly clasped her fingers around his. "Lucius, I'm sorry."

"For what?"

"For entangling you in this. It isn't that I didn't know the danger when I began. Queen Elysia made it clear and I . . . I was afraid. But . . . it was something I had to do. Darius killed my family. My parents, my b-brother. A brother I never even knew I had. He has enslaved my people. I'm their only hope."

"Then what are you sorry for, Princess?"

"For dragging you into it. If I didn't need your help, if I didn't know that I can't succeed without the Sword of Marric, I would release you from your pledge right now. This isn't your fight, and I . . . I don't want anything to happen to you."

He stared at her. Her words rang in his head. *I don't want anything to happen to you.* It had been a long while since anyone — other than Melistern — had cared at all about what happened to him.

"I've fought in plenty of tough battles before, Princess. Don't worry about me."

"I can't help it." Her eyes were troubled as they searched his. "You didn't ask for this fight."

He boosted her into the saddle before he could give in to the temptation to pull her into his arms. To taste just one more kiss.

"Neither did you," he said roughly, fighting the urges she stirred in him, trying to focus his mind only on keeping her alive.

Britta of Palladrin stared at him for a moment, then clamped those lush lips together. She urged the horse forward without another word, and Lucius vaulted upon his destrier and followed. He had the feeling that he'd lost something, something precious, more precious even than the kingdom that had been taken from him when he was a youth. But he didn't know for certain what it was.

Lavender shadows deepened to a heavy purple darkness as they rode across open fields and through a forest gilded by moonlight, at last nearing the cliffs and the sea and the Valley of Ice.

8

The Valley of Ice was the coldest place in Palladrin — cold even at the height of summer. Now, in the winter, ice layered the dead brush and trees and slicked the pathways, and they could hear the frosty roar of the sea in the distance. By the time Brittany and Lucius entered the valley and picked their way, shivering, to the base of the towering cliffs, Brittany felt as though she herself was about to freeze into a block of ice. She huddled in her cloak and gazed up toward the top of the cliffs, and there at last she saw it.

The castle of Palladrin. Her onetime home.

It rose against the sky, beautiful and strong, shining silver in the moonlight. But to her eyes, a shadow, like a low-hanging cloud, seemed to hover over the parapets.

Something evil, she thought, and a chill went through her.

Was Darius at one of the windows or parapets, even now? Was he watching her?

Her throat tightened with fear.

"Quick," she said with a certainty she didn't understand. "I think there isn't much time. The Devil's Cave — where is it?"

"Here. This way."

She followed him, suddenly feeling that her powers were starting to awaken, that her senses were sharper and clearer. The Rose Scepter — it must be near. Reaching out to her.

Warning her. Darius was coming.

They rode beneath the overhanging ledge of a yawning cave entrance that opened into thick darkness.

"Wait here," Lucius told her in a low tone. She heard him dismount, his boots scraping softly against the rocky floor of the cave.

Then he lit the end of a stick at the cave entrance, and the makeshift torch glowed, revealing the long, tunnel-like depths of the cave.

They left the horses near the entrance and, side by side, made their way along the glimmering rock wall, moving carefully over the uneven floor of the cave.

Brittany stuffed her gloves into her cloak pocket and held up her hand in the torchlight. The burning of the ruby ring nearly hurt her eyes.

"It's glowing stronger. We must be near the scepter." She moved closer to the wall and saw the brightness of the ring flicker. When she moved to the opposite side, it began to burn brightly once more.

"It's on this side. We're close to it — I'm certain!"

Even as the words left her lips, a huge chunk of rock ripped away from the roof of the cave and crashed down straight at her. Lucius pushed her aside just in time, but an instant later more rocks dislodged and began raining down upon them.

"This is Darius's doing!" Lucius shouted over the crash of the rocks splintering all around them. He extinguished the torch and shoved Brittany flat up against the wall, then closed in behind her, shielding her body with his. They were now in utter darkness, and she trembled against him as the rocks continued to slam down. But suddenly she saw a glimmer of red light.

The ruby ring. It was sending off a stream of light, glowing red light, which burned like fire right into the wall of the cave. Snatching it off, she pressed it against the wall and saw the light begin to burn even hotter. Suddenly, as she stared at the wall, her heart pounding, even the sounds of the falling and crashing rocks faded. She saw the Rose

Scepter, clearly outlined within a block of ice, set at arm's length within the wall of the cave. It was wrought of silver bright as stars, and gracefully made. Its tip was shaped like an exquisite rose and upon the delicately sculpted petals a ruby dewdrop sparkled with a fiery radiance.

"Lucius — the scepter! It's here! We have to get it out!"

He looked at the wall. "Where?" he demanded as a rock smashed behind him.

"Here. Right here," she gasped. "Don't you see?"

But he could see nothing, though she pointed, still clenching the ring, directly at the rock wall.

Even as a rock struck his shoulder with a glancing blow, Lucius dragged out his sword. He began to hack at the wall, though the rocks flew faster.

As he gouged out an opening, Brittany saw the ruby dewdrop begin to glow brighter, and the scepter shimmered with silver fire.

"Wait! I think I can reach it . . ."

She shoved her hand into the opening as far as she could, but she still couldn't touch the block of ice that encased the scepter. But as she stretched her fingertips toward it, straining to touch the gleaming silver, the ice began to crumble. The scepter shone

251

brighter, the ice broke apart, and suddenly the scepter shot toward her outstretched hand.

A tingling jolt shuddered up her arm, then a burst of heat, followed by a burst of cold. Her head swam wildly. But only for a moment. It cleared abruptly and she knew a cool serenity as her fingers closed tightly around the scepter's hilt.

"Lucius, I have it!" She slid the scepter out of the wall just as a rock slammed into his back. She felt him tense, heard his grunt, but he never shifted from his protective stance.

Suddenly a calm voice reached their ears.

"Give that to me."

Brittany and Lucius both became aware that the rocks had ceased to fall — that a deathly stillness had come over the cave. Lucius turned, and Brittany, clutching the scepter and the ring, moved away from the wall of the cavern and confronted the figure who stood blocking the passageway that would lead out of the cave.

The man who stood there was tall and gaunt, and his face was kind. The face of a benevolent grandsire. Snowy white hair glistened atop his head, and he wore robes of black edged with gold. A wavery gray light surrounded him, dim as mist yet strong enough to light the cavern so that Brittany could see every crevice in the walls, every rat scurrying in the corners. His voice was soft and cool as a running river.

"The scepter. Give it to me."

She felt the scepter slipping out of her grasp and sought frantically to hold on to it, even as it strained to escape her. She stared at it, and at the ring she held, Melistern's ring.

"Stay," she whispered and felt a jolt through her veins.

Then with a whoosh, the ring flew from her grasp and sailed across the dim cavern, as Darius held up his hand. The ring flew onto his finger.

And the scepter began to follow.

"No!" She squeezed her hand more tightly around it and managed to keep it within her grasp.

"It's . . . mine." Her eyes blazed at the wizard standing calmly before her. "The royal blood of Palladrin flows through my veins. You have no right to this scepter. You are an interloper."

"Foolish girl." Darius chided her as if she were a petulant child. "You have no knowledge of what you speak. You cannot wield the power of the scepter — it will destroy you. Just as those rocks might have destroyed you if I had allowed them to do so. I wanted only to show you a taste of true power, so that you may realize how unfit you are even to attempt to wield it."

Suddenly the scepter burned her fingers like a lighted torch. With a cry of pain, Brittany dropped it and sank to her knees. Lucius knelt beside her, his face taut.

"What did you do to her?" he demanded, throwing Darius a look of fury.

The wizard shrugged, but the smile curling his lips now held a hint of malice. Yet his voice remained gentle, almost regretful.

"I merely showed her how trying to wield great power can harm someone who is not trained to do so, who is not fit to use it for the right purposes. The scepter burned her hand. If she tries to touch it again, it could prove deadly."

"Let me show you something else that's deadly." Lucius straightened and strode forward, straight and tall, his sword drawn. It glittered even in the dimness, but the wizard didn't shrink from the dark, broad-shouldered warrior advancing upon him.

He lifted a hand in a circular motion, and immediately three specters appeared. As Brittany watched, their indistinct forms became solid and turned into large, rough men wielding swords and cudgels.

Lucius froze, and she saw the blood drain from his face.

"How can this be?" he croaked in a hoarse tone.

"Lucius!" She scrambled up and ran to his side.

"It's . . . them. The same men. The ones who killed Connor the day of the hunt. But . . . they're dead. I killed them . . . I know I killed them . . ."

"What magic is this?" she cried, spinning toward Darius.

"The kind of magic you cannot even fathom," the wizard replied slyly.

"They are visions, Lucius." She gripped his arm as he stood motionless. "Men, perhaps they might be, but he has given them the appearance of the men who attacked you that day. To make you remember, to hurt you —"

"They will indeed hurt him. They will kill him."

Suddenly Darius laughed, and the facade of kindness fell away, like a mask removed. His eyes were thin, gleaming, cruel, his skin drawn tight, his lips curling with malevolence.

The men advanced. Still Lucius didn't move, only stared at them, frozen in shock. It's some kind of spell, Brittany realized in despair.

How could she break it?

"Lucius . . . please, please, my love." She jumped before him as the men closed in. "No, I won't let you touch him."

Behind her, Lucius felt his head clearing. It had been filled with sickly greenish light and with memories — memories of that day when Connor's blood had run beneath his feet.

He hadn't even been able to see the wizard — only the men, with the faces of his old enemies.

But now . . . now something had penetrated the greenish haze.

Please, please, my love. My love.

It all became clear, crystal clear.

Brittany stood before him, her slender form braced as if she could somehow ward off the men circling, closing in. She had no weapon, no magic — only courage.

And love?

My love.

Did she love him? Had it been love in her voice? Was that what had yanked him from the mire of the spell?

He grabbed her, thrust her behind him, and sprang forward, his sword slashing out.

Brittany's heart leaped into her throat as the three men attacked and Lucius fought them, all three at once. His strength was powerful, his skill superior. There was naught but single-minded determination in his face, and the same deadly ruthlessness that she'd glimpsed the night outside the inn when she'd been accosted. He fought with a dazzling ferocity that soon cut down one of his enemies and left the other two sweating and pressing forward much more cautiously.

Before she could think how she might help him, there was a burst of light and Darius appeared directly before her in a puff of smoke.

He extended his hand, on which Melistern's ruby ring now glimmered, and reached down toward the Rose Scepter on the floor of the cave. It flew up, fairly leaping into his grasp, and as his fingers closed around it a smile of triumph lit his face.

"No!" Brittany cried, trembling.

"Yes, you foolish child. It is mine, clearly. See how it came to me. When you tried to hold it, it scorched your flesh. That should tell you that you're not meant to have it."

All around her clanged the sounds of the battle between Lucius and the specter men. Grunts and hisses, the clatter of swords, the thump of feet on stone. She smelled sweat, fear, death in the cavern, and she saw the smug, cruel smile on the wizard's face.

In his hand the Rose Scepter gleamed, the ruby dewdrop afire.

And her hand stung and burned. The scepter had scorched her, turned against her. Perhaps Darius was right . . .

Then came the voice of Queen Elysia. *You are more than what you know, my dear child. . . . You are royal, Brittany, every bit as royal as I, and more than that, you are powerful. Very powerful. Have you never felt it? Have you never felt the power deep inside your blood?*

"In the name of the people of Palladrin and of my slain family, the rightful, royal rulers of this land, I order you to hand over the scepter, to leave this place, this land — and never again to darken its borders with your evil."

Her voice rang out pure and clear, echoing in the cavern even as she heard a scream of pain from the men fighting. She spun around and saw that Lucius had killed a second man — she could smell the acrid odor of spilled blood — and she glimpsed the harsh weariness of her husband's face.

Fear clawed at her as Darius began to laugh. How she yearned for power, the power to help Lucius, to vanquish Darius. She felt no different than before. What powers was she supposed to have?

There was only one way to know. She had

to have the scepter — hold it, wield it. She had to get it back.

"For the last time, give it to me!" she said, aware that her voice shook with desperation and that Darius could see how close she was to despair.

"Come and take it." Taunting her, he held the scepter aloft. "But if you touch it again, it will burn you alive."

Her hand stung. His eyes mocked. Fear filled her, even as the Sword of Marric rang and clashed in the murky gray light.

She fixed her gaze on the scepter.

My grandsire fashioned you for the women of my family. Not for this evil interloper. Come to me.

It seemed to her that the scepter glowed brighter, the silver nearly blinding.

"Come to me," Brittany whispered.

Darius frowned, lifted a hand, and a gust of wind hurtled through the cavern, and blew Brittany straight back against the wall.

"Come to me!" she called over the raging gusts that blasted her. "You are mine — you were fashioned for good, not evil. Hear me, for I am Britta of Palladrin!"

She thrust her hand forward, and watched as the Rose Scepter jerked free of Darius's grasp and flew across the cavern straight into her palm.

She braced herself for the fiery pain as the silver touched her skin, but there was none. Now the scepter felt cool and smooth, the rose atop it glistened, and the dewdrop alone burst with ruby fire.

The wind blew and whistled, pressing her back. She lifted the scepter, waved it from side to side, and the wind died as swiftly as it had begun.

Power.

She saw Darius's lips move, knew he was trying to cast another spell upon the scepter, to turn it against her. She quickly pointed it at him.

"Let this evil one speak no more."

The wizard's mouth froze, and his face contorted as he tried to break the spell. Yet no words would emerge from his throat.

Brittany whirled toward Lucius in time to see him run the third man through. He yanked the Sword of Marric free as the man crumpled to the ground beside his fallen companions. Immediately, their bodies vanished, leaving no trace, not even a speck of blood.

But as Lucius turned toward Brittany, fear coursed through him, stronger than any he'd ever known. Darius had grown to thrice his size — he was now a veritable giant — and he loomed over the unsuspecting girl whose gaze was fastened upon Lucius.

In his hand he held a spear of fire, brilliant flames bursting from it as he arced it over his head and slammed it down toward the princess.

"Britta!" Lucius's roar sent her spinning around just in time to see the spear coming at her, the wizard towering over her, his face suffused with hate. At the same moment, Lucius sprang forward with a desperate slash of his sword and Brittany instinctively brought the scepter up to intercept the wizard's blow.

The Rose Scepter and the Sword of Marric crossed and rang together just as the spear came down. The blow struck them, and so did the fire — yet they were untouched, strong and whole and solid. Instead the flames of the spear jumped back onto themselves, leaping up the base of the spear and in an instant bounding onto the sleeve of Darius's black-and-gold robes.

He couldn't scream — the magic of the Rose Scepter still held his lips frozen — but his eyes shrieked his rage and his agony as the fire consumed him. Snapping blue flames spread in a blink and a roar, and in a moment the wizard was swallowed up in them. Black smoke exploded, then dissolved into a hissing shower of sooty dust.

When the dust settled, there was nothing left of Darius, nothing but a faint odor of rotting leaves and the ruby ring of Melistern glinting upon the ground.

Darkness filled the cave once more. Brittany lowered the scepter, her arm shaking. Lucius let fall his sword and pulled her to him.

"Are you hurt?"

"N-no." She clutched at him, trying to peer through the darkness into his face, but all she could see was the faint gleam of his eyes. "Are *you?*" she asked tremblingly.

"Nary a scratch." She heard him grin in the darkness. "Come on, Princess, let's get out of here."

He scooped up his sword and the ruby ring, and together they made their way to the horses at the mouth of the cave and led them out of the darkness.

The night was clear, cold, bathed in ice and moonlight. Brittany carefully tucked the Rose Scepter deep into the pocket of her cloak and lifted her gaze to the castle of Palladrin. The shadow that had hovered over the castle's parapets was gone.

"Lucius," she breathed, turning to him, lifting wondering eyes to his face. "We did it. And we're *alive.*"

"Barely."

She laughed, and his arms went around her, pulling her close. His eyes bored into her lovely upturned face, glowing softly in the light of the moon.

"When I saw that spear coming at you, I couldn't breathe," he said, his voice thick.

"When I saw those three men coming at you, while you stood frozen, my heart stopped," she whispered.

She lifted a hand, touched his face. "Lucius."

"Princess?"

"Nothing," she murmured, her eyes shining at him. "Just *Lucius*."

Gazing at her, he felt as if someone had just whacked him in the stomach with a battering ram. Did she really have to look so beautiful? So . . . wonderful? So full of life and hope and happiness? All the things he'd decided years ago to abandon — all the things he'd banished from his warrior's existence.

And she was looking at him as if he were some perfect knight, some hero from the legends.

He scowled at her as ferociously as he could. "If you keep looking at me that way —"

"Yes?"

"I'll —" He stopped, sucked in his breath. "You'll what?"

"You don't want to know, Princess."

Her lips curved upward in an enchanting smile that made his chest ache. Suddenly she flung her arms around his neck. "Yes. I do."

The tension of the night must have been affecting him, he told himself, because instead of pushing her away, he drew her even closer. She was trembling from the cold, and instinctively he wrapped his arms tight around her to protect her from the biting night air.

The Valley of Ice. Strange, here in this frozen place, everything he'd been holding frozen inside of himself seemed to be melting.

Especially with her arms around his neck, her vivid eyes gazing searchingly into his.

"What are you going to do, my prince?" Her voice was softer than the velvet collar of her cloak. Teasing, daring. Enticing. "I assure you I'm not afraid."

"That much I know. After tonight I doubt you're afraid of anything."

Her eyes danced. "Certainly not of you."

"Maybe you should be," he muttered, and his eyes glinted a warning at her.

"Why? Because you slew those crows for me, you married me, you faced an evil wizard for me and fought the demons of your past? You raised the Sword of Marric and helped me to defeat Darius? For all these things I should fear you?" It was she who pulled him closer, she who tightened her arms around his neck and nestled her body even more snugly against his as the white stars beamed down and the moon sailed through a jet sky, and the Valley of Ice glittered like diamonds.

"If you want to know what I think, Prince Lucius, I think you're the one who's afraid. You're afraid of what you feel, afraid to trust your instincts, afraid to imagine that you could be on the brink of getting everything you want."

"And just what do you imagine I want?"

"Your kingdom back. A chance to rule it as wisely and well as your father knew you could. A chance to cease fighting and begin leading. And . . ." She hesitated only briefly. "A chance to put the past behind you, to come to peace with it — and with yourself."

Her words shook him. His jaw clenched. "You talk too much, Princess," he told her, but his voice held a trace of amusement and of awe. *Were all women so wise?* he wondered. *Or just this one?*

She stretched up on tiptoe so that her lips were only a breath away from his. "I know I do. But you haven't seemed inclined to silence me."

His hand caught her chin, tilting it up even as his head lowered, dipping toward hers. "Let's remedy that," he said as he captured her mouth with his and kissed her long and deep and hard.

Brittany clung to him throughout that dazzling, heart-stopping kiss. She had no choice but to cling to him because her bones seemed to melt and she lost all trace of reason and sanity and will.

There was only Lucius and the frozen night, joy and heat and splendor.

When he finally pulled back, her eyes were radiant, her cheeks flushed. He scooped her up into his arms and spun her around and around until her laughter grew breathless. Then still holding her, he kissed her again, gently this time, as if she were a precious, fragile treasure.

"I love you, Britta of Palladrin. Whether you knew it or not, you had magic even before you found the Rose Scepter. You enchanted my heart almost from the first moment I set eyes on you. The spell has only deepened since then, and now I'm hopelessly in your power."

Her eyes softened on his, and he lost himself in their gold-flecked depths. "Then I command you, my prince — kiss me again. Because I love you, too." Her lips brushed his mouth, slid across his jaw, gently nibbled his ear. "And if you even think about kissing anyone else ever again, I'll simply have to turn you into a toad."

His laughter joined hers, as their lips met tenderly. By moonlight and starlight, in the shadow of the castle, they celebrated victory, hope, and the wonder of love.

Epilogue

Of course there was a feast.

Torchlight shimmered and the long tables in the great hall of Palladrin groaned beneath the overflowing platters of roasted venison and capons and pheasants, and dishes of sweetmeats, jellied eggs, and tarts. There were golden goblets filled with spiced wine, sweet music of harp and flute, jugglers and minstrels, much dancing and laughing and cheering. The castle was alive and vibrant with merrymaking as noble and villager alike celebrated the return of Britta of Palladrin — and the demise of Darius.

A week had passed since the night the Rose Scepter and the Sword of Marric had been raised together, ending the wizard's cruel reign. During the intervening days, Lucius had spent his time organizing and deploying an army of men loyal to the princess, unearthing those who had served Darius, and making the borders of the kingdom secure. Brittany had met with counselors and nobles and villagers, learning much about the land and the people from whom she'd been exiled since her childhood.

From far and wide people had come for the feast, to catch a glimpse of the beautiful princess with the honey-colored hair and gold-flecked eyes, the princess whom all had believed dead for so long, and who had in the end recovered the legendary Rose Scepter and rescued all of Palladrin from tyranny.

Queen Elysia had traveled from Strathbury, accompanied by her ladies-in-waiting and a company of nobles and knights led by Sir Richmond. Melistern, fully recovered from his injuries, sat beside Lucius on the dais and, preceding the first of the many toasts and songs, had made an announcement to the hushed crowd: upon learning of Darius's defeat, the neighboring people of Marric had risen up against King Sedgewick. Sedgewick had fled and was being hunted by his subjects — and Prince Lucius was to be crowned king in his stead. A formal treaty had been drawn up that very day, joining the kingdoms of Palladrin and Marric, uniting them in peace and freedom from this time forward under the joint reign of the soon-to-be-crowned Britta and her husband, King Lucius.

But the best part of the feast, in Britta's royal opinion, came when Lucius absconded with her as the midnight hour neared and swept her away from a most boring conversation with the minister of Palladrian taxes, bundling her out of the hall and down a corridor, up a flight of winding, torchlit stairs, and finally into her bedchamber. He shoved the massive door shut behind them, surveyed her in her low-necked gown of ruby velvet, her braided hair bound with jeweled ribbons, and grinned the wolfishly appealing grin that made her heart turn over.

"You look most beautiful in that gown, my love, but I think I'm ready to see you out of it."

"Lucius!" Laughter bubbled in her throat. "You *did* see me out of it — you saw me out of *everything* every evening and every morning all this week. And have you forgotten this afternoon, in *your* bedchamber — just as poor Cook was searching for me high and low to ask if thirty pheasants would be enough —"

"Of course I remember this afternoon," he chuckled. His eyes gleamed at her in the candlelight, and Brittany thought she had never seen him look so handsome. In his dark tunic trimmed in gold, he was sleek and tall and powerful, and her heart skittered happily merely at the sight of him. "I enjoyed it so much I've scarce been able to think of anything else," he continued, coming toward her, his lips curving. "Except a continuation of all our frolic."

"Frolic?" Brittany laughed softly and her cheeks flushed a delicate pink as he took her in his arms. "Is *that* what you call it, my husband?"

"What would you call it, my wife?" His hands cupped her face, then slid down her arms and came to rest at her slender waist.

"I would call it wonderful. Intoxicating. And most gratifying," she whispered, reaching up to brush her lips against his.

"Then let us delay no longer." He was chuckling deep in his throat as he began to kiss her, long, deep, delicious kisses that nearly distracted her from realizing that he already had her halfway out of her gown.

"But, Lucius, our guests —"

Her words were lost as he rained kisses upon her eyelids, her cheeks, her mouth — gentle, exquisite kisses that made her forget everything but this man and the love she felt for him. A lasting, forever love, just as she'd once dreamed about. Breathless and dizzy, she clutched him, her fingers raking through his hair, her mouth sipping eagerly from his. When his hands found her breasts, she gave a desperate moan of pleasure.

"What was that about guests?" he whispered, nuzzling her throat.

"They . . . won't . . . miss us," she murmured, opening her lips and, as always, her heart to him, as he chuckled again and backed her toward the bed.

As he gently lowered her to the silken coverings, the Rose Scepter suddenly twitched upon its crystal shelf and a shower of rose petals drifted over them, rich with sweet fragrance.

They were only dimly aware of it, for they were lost in each other, lost in joy and in passion.

As the guests drank and danced and laughed far below in the great hall, Brittany and Lucius lay in each other's arms upon the rose-strewn bed and practiced a brand of magic that was all their own.

The Roses
of Glenross

Ruth Ryan Langan

For Nora, Jill, and Marianne,
who share my belief in the healing power
of love and friendship

And for Tom, my partner in magic

1

"Not yet, lads. We'll wait until they're closer."
Jamie Morgan stood with his comrades,
hoping to calm their fears as wave after wave
of invaders marched out of the mist, swords
poised for battle.

" 'Tis said they violated the women, and
even children, before burning Penrodshire to
the ground, Jamie. They left not a soul alive.
And what livestock they couldn't take with
them, they slaughtered." Duncan MacKay
was Jamie's oldest and closest friend. The two
had trained as warriors together from the time
they were lads. And though Jamie was descended from the royal house of Moray, and
Duncan's father had been stablemaster to the
laird, the two were closer than brothers.

"This isn't Penrodshire, Duncan. I swear
on my father's grave that these barbarians
will not take Ballycrue. This day we will
drive them back to the sea from whence they
came."

275

"What if we can't, Jamie?" Duncan shivered in the cold, driving rain.

Jamie pressed a hand to his friend's shoulder. "Then we'll die like warriors." He turned to the men who huddled under the thin protection of their plaids. "They've not seen us yet. That gives us our only advantage, since we're badly outnumbered. Keep yourselves concealed as long as possible. Once they spot us, we fight to the death, lads. Is that understood?"

The warriors nodded, united not only by love of their country but also by their devotion to their leader.

As the invaders drew near, the men clutched their swords and dirks and tensed, awaiting Jamie's command. When it came, they ran forward, screaming like banshees, catching the barbarians by surprise. Soon the air was filled with the clash of steel and the cries of the wounded. And though the ground beneath them ran red with blood, one man continued calling encouragement to his men as he leapt from skirmish to skirmish, determined to drive back the invaders.

The battle had been raging for hours. And though Jamie Morgan and his warriors fought valiantly, the barbarians had relentlessly inched their way through the tiny village, and beyond, to the forest, where the old men had taken refuge along with the women and children.

Alexa MacCallum huddled in the shadows with her family. Besides her frail mother she had two sisters, one with a babe at her breast, and her father, who had to stop every few steps as a fit of coughing overtook him.

Hearing the crunch of booted feet behind them, Angus MacCallum motioned his family to take cover. Then he stood, sword lifted, ready to protect his loved ones from these barbarians.

There were half a dozen of them, their nakedness covered only by pelts of fur, their eyes hot with blood lust. Though Angus fought with a courage born of desperation, he was no match for these giants, who laughed as they easily dispatched him.

Seeing her father fall, Alexa raced out of her place of concealment and took up his sword, determined to protect the rest of her family. For a moment the invaders were caught by such surprise that they merely stared and laughed at the lass holding a sword as big as she.

Finally one of them stepped forward to engage her. He wasn't prepared for her courage or her skill with a weapon. As he advanced, she refused to retreat, choosing instead to stand and fight. The first swipe of her sword caught his arm, and he choked back a cry of rage before calling to his comrades to join him. Within minutes they had driven the lass back against a tree, where they easily disarmed her. Though she could no longer defend herself, she lifted her head high in a final act of defiance as she awaited death.

Instead, one of them held her while the others plunged into the thicket, easily driving the rest of her family out from their places of concealment.

With tears streaming down her face, Alexa was forced to watch as they brutalized her mother and her sisters, as well as the infant, before finally killing them.

Then the barbarians turned back to Alexa. And though she couldn't understand their words, she was well aware of their intentions. Her blood turned to ice. She crossed herself and whispered a prayer for courage, then closed her eyes, helpless against what was to come. She was resigned to whatever sort of horror would be hers at the hands of these barbarians before they snuffed out her life.

Suddenly she heard a strangled cry and opened her eyes to see her enemy falling to the ground and a magnificent Scots warrior standing over him, brandishing a sword.

Blood streamed from the brave warrior's wounds, completely soaking his plaid, but he took no notice.

Jamie Morgan took one look at the lass and felt his heart swell with admiration for her courage. She was as brave and proud as any of his warriors. And so beautiful that she had his breath catching in his throat.

He swept her behind him for protection, while he turned to face the others. And though he was badly outnumbered by his enemy, he drove them back with each lunge of his sword, easily disposing of one after another, until all lay dead.

Weeping uncontrollably, Alexa dropped to her knees, too weak to stand. Jamie longed to take her in his arms and comfort her. But before he could utter a word he heard the cries of his comrades. With a last lingering glance at the lass with the fiery curls and green eyes swimming with tears, he was gone — leaving Alexa alone in the forest, surrounded by unspeakable carnage.

She stared around as though in a daze. All she saw was death and destruction. All those she'd once loved were gone, their lifeblood slowly seeping into the soil that had once nurtured them.

Numb beyond belief, she remained with the dead as darkness overtook the land.

★ ★ ★

"How does our patient fare, Sister Fiona?" Mother Superior stepped into the room and paused at the bedside.

"His wounds would have killed a lesser man." A brown-robed nun pressed a cool cloth to the forehead of a still, silent figure swathed in coarse linens. "He must fight for every breath, Reverend Mother." She shook her head sadly and began to weep. "I fear he will never awaken."

"Here now." The older nun touched a hand to her shoulder. "We must have faith, Sister Fiona. After all, this is no ordinary man. Were it not for the laird, we would already be enslaved by our enemies."

"Aye, I know, Reverend Mother." The younger sister wiped at her tears. "That's why it grieves me that there's so little we can do for him."

"You're wrong, Sister Fiona. There is much we can do. Besides the herbs and balms, there is our faith. I believe that we are all part of a great, eternal plan. Laird Jamie Morgan was brought here to us for a reason. Now we must do what we can and put the rest in the hands of the Almighty." She turned away. At the door she added, "I shall gather the rest of the sisters in chapel now. If we must, we will storm heaven on our laird's behalf."

280

"Have you seen him?" The young novice, in her stiff white gown and apron, stood in the midst of a huddle of brown-robed nuns. Though she kept her voice to a whisper, it was obvious that she was nearly bursting with news of their patient. "He's so noble, his face so bonnie, it fair breaks my heart."

"Aye." A hunched old sister limped forward to join in. "I heard Mother Superior telling Father Lazarus that the young laird must indeed be blessed with very special gifts from heaven, for, despite his wounds, he is with us still."

The novice, eyes as big as the covered dishes on her tray, leaned closer. "All of Scotland is rejoicing, and singing the praises of our laird. They are calling Laird Jamie Morgan the laird of lairds, the hero of Ballycrue. While all around him men fell, he stood alone, displaying uncommon valor as he took punishing blows and continued beating back the barbarians until they were forced to flee for their lives. This day our land is free once more, because of him. They are even saying —" She looked up and caught sight of Mother Superior swooping down on them, her face as dark as a thundercloud.

"Gossiping, young Mordrund? When there

is work to be done? If your chores are finished for the day, Sisters, I expect you to be on your knees in chapel, praying for those in need."

Properly chastised, the cluster of women scattered. But all along the hallways they whispered among themselves about the heroic warrior who had been brought to their abbey, and who even now lay on his pallet, fighting for his life.

Mother Mary of the Cross stood at the window, watching the slight figure at work in the garden.

She marveled as the lass patiently tended the fragile flowers. When she'd first arrived here, the lovely walled garden had been nearly destroyed by the invaders. One wall had been smashed, the graceful old stone benches overturned. There had been deep grooves in the earth from the booted feet of the barbarians. But as soon as she was physically able, like someone driven by an inner frenzy, the lass had begun single-handedly restoring the garden to its former beauty. Though she never spoke and rarely acknowledged those around her, the work in the fresh air had brought color to her pale cheeks and had begun restoring her strength.

The transformation in her had been amazing to watch. For weeks after she'd been brought to them, she'd done nothing more than lie on her pallet, staring silently at the good nuns who had patiently bathed her, fed her, and forced her to live when she'd wanted nothing more than to die. Yet she had lived. Against all the odds, she had lived.

It would be the same for the laird, Reverend Mother thought. In time his health would be fully restored. She believed fervently that he had been brought to their care because he was meant to live. There was, she believed, a purpose for everything, even the simplest of events.

She turned away from the window and hurried out to the corridor to relieve Sister Fiona, who had sent a request that she be allowed to go to the chapel.

"How does our patient fare this day?"

"It is the same, Reverend Mother." Poor Sister Fiona seemed always on the verge of tears these days. "I can think of nothing more now except prayer."

"Then go, and I'll stay here with the laird. Send the little novice, Mordrund, with more of the healing balm."

The old nun knelt beside the pallet and bowed her head in prayer. Suddenly she heard a whisper, low and raspy, as though spoken with great effort.

"So. I'm dead, then?"

"My laird." Her head came up sharply. "Nay. You're very much alive, my laird." She touched a hand to his forehead and was relieved to see that the fever that had burned for days was now gone. "Praise heaven."

"You praise heaven? A robed angel?" His words were slurred as he struggled to focus. "What is this place, then? Heaven or hell?" He thought, by the fire that raged through him, that it couldn't possibly be heaven.

"Neither heaven nor hell, my laird. I am Mother Mary of the Cross. You're at the Abbey of Glenross."

"The abbey?" He could vaguely recall the great stone structure with its tall spires and the bells summoning the villagers to take refuge inside its walls when the battle had begun. "It wasn't destroyed, then?"

"Nay, my laird. Though it was badly damaged, it survived, thanks to you."

"The invaders?" He started to sit up.

"Gone, my laird. Again, because of you." She pressed him gently back against the fur throw. "You were gravely wounded. Now you must rest so that your health can be restored to you."

"My comrades-at-arms?"

She shook her head, wishing to avoid the question. "We'll not speak of that now, my laird."

Despite the gravity of his wounds, his fingers gripped her wrist like claws. "You will tell me of my fellow clansmen. What has been their fate?"

"It is said that . . . they did not survive."

She saw the light go out of his eyes, to be replaced with something dark and dangerous. A whisper of fear clutched her heart. "You must rest now, my laird, and regain your strength."

His handsome face was dark with fury. "Why must I?"

She sighed. "Because the work of rebuilding the land will fall on the shoulders of the young and strong. And because your people will look to you for guidance."

He could feel the room beginning to spin. He closed his eyes, cursing this weakness. Though the physical pain had lessened considerably, there was an even more intolerable pain around his heart that was almost crippling in its intensity as the knowledge began to seep into his consciousness. Duncan. His comrades. The men who had been family to him. All gone.

He gave himself up to the darkness, embracing it as it took him down and down until he was at the bottom of a great, bottomless pit of misery. A pit from which there seemed no way out.

It was just as well, he thought. He deserved no hope, no light of day. He'd led his friends into the viper's den. Now they were all gone. And he alone had survived.

That knowledge shamed him to the core.

2

"I hate this weakness. I'm as useless as a bairn." Jamie fell back against the bed pillows, exhausted from the effort of walking across the room.

"Aye, my laird. It's to be expected at first." Sister Fiona caught his hand and easily hauled him to his feet before draping his arm around her sturdy shoulders.

"Where are we going?" He moved weakly by her side, allowing her to steer him only because he had no choice. Her strength was matched only by her determination.

"Outside. 'Tis a lovely day, and a bit of sun will be good for you." She helped him through an arched doorway and into a walled courtyard, where a chaise had been set in a patch of sunlight.

"You should have seen this just scant weeks ago, my laird." She pointed to the wall, where new stones now replaced the ones that had been battered and smashed by the invaders. "When the barbarians came, they destroyed everything in their path. The flowers, the trees, the beautiful old stone benches."

After easing him into a comfortable position, she wrapped him in fur.

He gave a hiss of annoyance. "You needn't treat me like a frail old man, Sister."

"Not frail, my laird. Merely weak. But it'll pass soon enough, you'll see. Now enjoy the sunshine, and I'll be back in a bit with some broth."

"Broth." He sighed as she bustled away. If he were home in his own castle, he would order a servant to fetch him ale strong enough to curl a man's beard.

He stroked his chin and felt the smooth skin where the beard had recently been removed. The ever-efficient Sister Fiona had even shaved him.

He frowned at the thought of being shaved by a nun. But, as she'd explained to him, before joining the convent Fiona MacGillivray had raised seven younger brothers, giants all. And, according to her, full of the devil all. There was nothing she didn't know about caring for the male of the species. Her brothers had tormented her unmercifully, so the rigors of convent life had seemed like play. She was, she boasted, perfectly suited to the life of a healer here at the abbey.

Still, as competent as his nurse was, and as peaceful this setting, there was no peace within him. Only torment. The knowledge that he had survived when those he loved had died ate at his heart and lay festering within his soul.

He longed for his home and his people. And yet the thought of sending a messenger to the Highlands informing his clan that he had survived, when all others had not, was repugnant to him.

As Jamie sat hunched in his furs, he caught a blur of movement in a sheltered corner of the yard. A hooded figure was kneeling in the dirt, painstakingly turning the earth with a small hand tool. Each time the tip of the tool encountered a rock or stone buried in the earth, it would be dug up and piled atop a broken section of the wall, where stone steps led to the top.

There was a time, he thought, when such work would have seemed like child's play to him. Now it tired him just to watch. He leaned his head back and closed his eyes. But instead of enjoying the warmth of sunlight on his face, he was plunged once more into the horrors of the battle, seeing the faces of his comrades as they sustained mortal wounds. In his mind he could hear their cries and the low moaning of those who lay dying all around him.

He had hoped by now to be back in the Highlands, celebrating their deliverance from the barbarians. Instead, he found himself alone with strangers who wanted to hail him a hero.

A hero. He experienced a flash of pain. It was an empty victory to learn that, though the barbarians had fled, the cost had been the lives of all those he'd held dear. And yet he couldn't regret his life as a warrior. It was all he knew. All he'd been trained to do. As his beloved father had explained to him so many years ago, it was not a life a man would choose. But because of that choice, other men would be free to make their own choices.

Jamie had always thought that a noble truth. Now it was hard to see nobility in the death and destruction left by war.

He closed his eyes. The peace and silence of this place mocked him as he heard again in his mind the echoing cries of the dead and wounded.

Alexa set another stone in place along the top of the wall, then stood back to admire her handiwork. It felt good to be out in the sunlight doing hard physical work. She'd lost track of how long she'd been toiling in this place. At first she had taken on this task as her punishment for living when those she'd loved had been less fortunate. Then, as the work progressed, she had embraced this as her payment to the good sisters, who had nursed so many tormented souls through the suffering caused by this terrible war. Now she had taken a vow, which she'd written on parchment. It had been witnessed by old Father Lazarus. She would remain here, tilling, planting, trimming, until the garden had been completely restored to its former beauty.

The first plot she'd restored was an herb garden, since the sisters had need of herbs for the treatment of so many ills. She tugged at the weeds and loosened the soil around the shallow rows of agrimony, aloe, wood anemone, and angelica. A second flower bed held lady's mantle, lavender, and myrtle.

She worked slowly, methodically, weeding and working the soil as the sun climbed high overhead.

There was something magical about this place. When she worked here, the fears that plagued her throughout the night were dispelled. The sounds of her loved ones' voices, calling to her to come to their aid, were silenced. The pain of her loss seemed to melt away. If she could, she would work here day and night, just to avoid the demons that stalked her in sleep.

She paused a moment to catch her breath. As she did she realized she wasn't alone. She turned to see a hunched figure wrapped all in fur, seated on a chaise.

A warrior. She'd heard the whispers. It was impossible not to hear all the things being said about the one they called the laird of all lairds. But Alexa had no curiosity about this Highlander. To her he was just another warrior, trained to kill.

She felt the trembling begin in her legs, and knew that just thinking about war had brought back the fears. She slumped down in the dirt and waited until the weakness subsided. Then she returned her attention to the task at hand, blotting out every other distraction.

"Here's your broth, my laird." Sister Fiona was trailed by the little novice, Mordrund, who was carrying a small wooden table.

After the table was placed beside the chaise, Sister Fiona uncovered a bowl, releasing fragrant steam.

"This will not only warm you, but also give you strength." She could see the sudden frown line between Jamie's dark brows. "Are you feeling ill, my laird?"

He shook his head. "Nay. Just . . . weary."

"Well, then." Sister Fiona looked up as the noon Angelus bells were rung. "I'm needed in the refectory now. If there's anything you want, you're to ask Mordrund. I've directed her to stay with you until I return, my laird." She sent the little novice a warning look before hurrying away.

Mordrund, honored at the prospect of caring for the laird, dipped a spoon into the broth and held it to his lips.

Annoyed, Jamie waved her away. "I can feed myself."

"Aye, my laird." Flustered, the little novice ran damp hands down her stiff skirts before handing him the bowl. She stood back, watching as he ate listlessly. "Are you enjoying the broth?"

"Not particularly." After only a few sips he placed the bowl on the table and leaned back, feeling utterly exhausted.

Deflated, Mordrund looked around for something that might interest the laird. "Isn't the lass doing a fine job restoring our garden?"

"Lass?" He looked over and saw the figure kneeling in the dirt. "I thought it was a lad from the village."

"Oh, nay, my laird." Mordrund gave a laugh, delighted to have found something she could discuss with this important man. "The lass was found in the forest, more dead than alive. From her garments it was determined that she was of the same clan as the dead lying around her. She appeared to have been there without food or water or shelter for days."

"Has she not spoken of it?"

"She hasn't spoken at all, my laird. She seems incapable of speech, though it is unclear whether she was born mute or has been rendered that way by her injuries. The sisters here at the abbey have begun calling her Eve, not only because she was the first woman found alive after the battle but because of her love for our garden."

"Why does she hide away out here? Has she been maimed?"

"Not that we can tell. But Reverend Mother says that not all injuries are visible to the eye. Many who survive war must endure grave pain to the heart, and sometimes to the very soul. As healers we must treat these with the same compassion that we treat the body's wounds." She barely paused for breath. "I hope one day to be a healer, as fine as the sisters here at the abbey. It was my reason for joining their number. But Reverend Mother has told me that I must

first learn to curb my tongue. She says —"
The little novice stopped and clapped a hand to her mouth. "Here now, I've done it again, saying far more than I ought. I . . . hope you won't mention to Sister Fiona that I discussed the lass. For it wasn't my place to do so. In fact, Reverend Mother has said that our first duty is to our patients. We must always respect their privacy."

He shook his head, his gaze narrowed on the figure near the wall. "You need have no fear. I've no intention of repeating what was said here. It will be our secret, Mordrund."

"Thank you, my laird." Delighted, she turned away suddenly, taking the wooden table under one arm and the bowl of broth in the other hand when she caught sight of the nun returning to her patient. "I'll go now and visit the chapel. Perhaps, if I pray hard enough, I'll remember to think before I speak again."

Sister Fiona studied the flushed face of the novice as she dashed past her. "Did our Mordrund pester you with her silly gossip, my laird?"

When he merely lifted a hand in dismissal, the nun gave a sigh of relief. There was no telling what the foolish child would say. "Do you wish to return to your room now, my laird?"

He surprised her by saying, "I believe I'll sit here in the sun a while longer, Sister."

"Do you need anything, my laird?"

"Nay."

"Then I shall return in an hour or so to fetch you back to your pallet."

He made no response. But she noted that this time, instead of closing his eyes, he seemed to focus on the lovely flowers in the garden.

Perhaps, she thought as she walked away, Reverend Mother had been right to suggest this place. There was magic in a garden. Magic that could begin to heal the wounds that were outside the realm of their experience.

Jamie sat for almost an hour, but the diligent gardener never once looked his way. She painstakingly hoed, shoveled, and removed stones and rocks from the soil. She pressed seeds into tiny rows and tended delicate seedlings that had just broken ground.

He found himself mystified by her. Despite the heat of the afternoon, she was completely covered by a hooded cloak. Why did she hide herself so? Mordrund had assured him that the woman wasn't maimed. Yet her actions said otherwise. How could anyone keep up this pace for hours on end without stopping for food or drink? She worked like one driven by demons. She was so intent on it, in fact, that she seemed to have slipped away to another world.

When Sister Fiona came for him, he was actually reluctant to leave. Yet he felt foolish admitting such a thing to the nun, and so he allowed her to help him to his feet. At once he was surprised by his weakness. For the brief time he'd spent here in the garden, he'd been able to forget about his wounds and their lingering effects.

"I'm afraid I'll have to lean on you, Sister."

She smiled. "That's why I'm here, my laird." She gathered the fur throw around him, then put a strong arm around his waist, helping him across the short span to the arched doorway.

As they stepped inside, she saw him glance over his shoulder and felt a rush of pleasure. "You enjoyed the flowers, my laird?"

"Aye. They were . . . most pleasant."

"You see?" She helped him along the silent corridor until they came to his room. Like all the other rooms in the abbey, it was nothing more than a cell, with a pallet, a washbasin, a fireplace, and in his case a wooden chaise draped with furs pulled up before the fire.

"Reverend Mother thinks you're still too

weak to take your meals in the refectory, my laird. So I've asked young Mordrund to bring you some food."

"Thank you, Sister." He was grateful when she eased him onto the chaise and left with a rustle of skirts.

He leaned his head back and closed his eyes. Soon now he would have to send word to his clan to come and fetch him home.

Home. That word should have brought such pleasure. Instead, the very thought of returning without his friends left him utterly bereft.

He leaned forward, pressing his hands to his face in a gesture of weariness.

By the time the young novice arrived with his meal, the black mood had descended upon him once more. He refused the food, choosing instead to crawl onto his pallet, where he closed his eyes and sank into deep despair.

3

Misty mornings gave way to gentle summer afternoons. As the flowers began bursting into bloom, more and more of the sisters of the Abbey of Glenross found excuses to spend time in the walled garden. There, walking the narrow paths or sitting on the carefully restored stone benches, they would recite their formal prayers or occasionally lift their voices in songs of praise.

They had learned to avoid the laird, who had also taken to sitting in the sunlight. Though he often remained there for hours, he spoke to no one unless it was necessary, and then only replied to questions in a monotone.

Sister Fiona walked to the window in Mother Superior's office and glanced out the window with a sigh. "It isn't the laird's physical wounds that worry me, Reverend Mother. Those are healing nicely. In no time he'll be able to wield a sword with the best of men. 'Tis the wounds to his heart that have me concerned. Look at him. How can anyone sit in that garden and not be moved by its beauty?"

"He cannot yet see the beauty, Sister. His eyes are clouded by the horrors he saw on the field of battle. He witnessed too much death. It is with him still, keeping him from the light."

"But we call ourselves healers, Reverend Mother. How can we consider our patient healed if the life he has been restored to only brings him pain?"

The older woman smiled gently. "We do what we can, but some things are completely beyond our control. For now, you must give the laird time. Time often proves to be a great healer. As does faith."

The younger nun gave a weary nod of her head. "If only I knew how to reach out to the laird."

"Perhaps it is now up to the laird to reach out to others."

Sister Fiona walked away, shaking her head. She hoped Mother Superior was right. But she'd come to know Laird Jamie Morgan during these long days and nights of his recovery. He was a proud man, perhaps too proud to ever reach out to anyone for help.

The voices of the sisters singing evening vespers drifted from the chapel window. Alexa sat back on her heels to listen. She'd been so absorbed in her work she'd been unaware of the passing of so many hours. Could it possibly be evening already?

Pressing a hand to the small of her back she got slowly to her feet. As she did, she realized she wasn't alone. She whirled to find the warrior standing directly behind her. There was no chance to see his face. Just the sight of that tall, muscled body sent terror rippling through her. She seemed to shrink back into her hooded robe, as if to escape.

Jamie had long ago discarded the fur in favor of his plaid. He wore it in the manner of a warrior, tossed over one shoulder, leaving the other bare to the sunlight. His legs, too, were bare and bronzed from the sun.

"You can hear." He saw her back up a step and turn away from him so quickly that she nearly fell over the hoe at her feet.

At once he closed a hand over her upper arm to keep her from falling. Though it was no more than a touch of her through the heavy woolen cloak, he felt the sizzle of heat through his veins. It shocked him to the core. As soon as she was steady on her feet, he drew his hand away as though burned.

She kept her back to him, refusing to look at him.

He struggled to keep his voice soft so as not to frighten her more. "Forgive me for startling you. It wasn't my intention. I do admit that I've been watching you. The little novice told me that you don't speak. But I saw you listening to the singing."

She bent and picked up the hoe, then started walking away from him.

His voice, so close behind her, warned her that he was following. "I'm told you're called Eve. My name is Jamie. Jamie Morgan."

She opened a small door in the wall of the garden and set the hoe inside, then reached into the pocket of her cloak and removed a hand tool, which she set on a shelf. Closing the door, she latched it, then started toward the arched doorway.

"Wait." Again Jamie touched a hand to her arm. Just a touch, but the heat was there again, burning a trail of fire through his veins. He knew now that he hadn't imagined that first time. "I grow weary of doing nothing more strenuous than lifting a spoon to my mouth. I thought I might help you. Now that my wounds have begun to heal, I could till the soil while you plant. And I could prune the branches of those trees too tall for you to reach."

302

She shivered and drew the cloak around her, before walking through the doorway without a backward glance.

He stood watching as she hurried along the dim corridor until she'd disappeared around a corner. Then he turned in the opposite direction, along a moonlit path, deep in thought.

She had heard him. Of that he was certain. But she'd chosen to ignore him. Was she frightened of him? Repulsed by him? That thought brought him up short, and he crossed his arms over his chest to consider. As a son of privilege, he had seen many maidens glance his way. And later, as a warrior, there had been too many to count. He'd taken his looks, as he'd taken his life of privilege, for granted. But here was a lass who refused even to look at him.

What a strange creature was this Eve. She both puzzled and intrigued him. Though he didn't wish to cause her alarm, he knew there was no way he could turn away from her now that he had taken this first step.

But how to win her over?

He stood very still, thinking.

When he'd been a lad of no more than six or seven, his father had taken him hunting. In the middle of the forest his father had taken aim at a great stag. Just as he'd drawn back his bow, a doe had stepped in front of him, taking the arrow meant for the stag. While his father regretted the mistake, he had no choice but to skin the doe and carry it home with the rest of their game. While he bent to his chore, young Jamie saw a fawn step out of the forest, in search of its mother.

Seeing his young son trying to coax the animal to him, his father had said, "Nay, Jamie. That's the wrong way to deal with a frightened creature. Be very still, and let it come to you."

"But it's afraid."

"Aye, lad. But there's something stronger than fear. And that's need. The fawn needs its mother, and now she's gone, it must turn to another for help. You see? Even now it starts toward you, eager to see if you are friend or foe."

Jamie found himself remembering that summer when he and the young deer had become inseparable. And by summer's end, when the deer, now grown, had disappeared into the forest, Jamie had been bereft, until his father comforted him with the thought that his animal friend was now with creatures like itself.

The mere thought of those idyllic days had him smiling.

The smile froze on his lips when he caught sight of a shimmering image taking shape before him. While he stood, unable to look away, a beautiful woman came toward him. She didn't so much walk as float. Her hair was as golden as the moonlight that seemed to glimmer around her in a halo of light. Her gown was a lovely column of gold and silver cloth that skimmed over her body as though it had been spun by angels.

She hurried past him without even a glance. As she climbed the stone steps to stare out over the wall, she wore the eager look of a maiden awaiting her lover.

Transfixed, Jamie stood watching for more than an hour while the woman waited patiently, hands clasped at her waist, a smile on her lips. When a bank of clouds blotted out the moon, she suddenly shivered and descended the steps, weeping softly. On her face was a look of such sadness and despair, Jamie instinctively reached out a hand to comfort her.

"What is it, my lady? Is there something I can do to . . . ?" Shock rippled through him when he realized that his hand had passed completely through her. Though she continued on, his hand was as cold as if it had been dipped into a frigid Highland stream.

He stood perfectly still, eyes narrowed in

concentration, as he watched the woman pause by the far wall before dissolving into a shimmer of light. In the blink of an eye there were only shadows where the light had been.

Though he was a practical man, Jamie knew what he'd just seen. And what he'd touched. Or almost touched.

Still wearing a frown, he went in search of Mother Superior.

"So. You've seen her." Mother Mary of the Cross listened to Jamie's description of the woman before nodding. "She is Lady Anne, our benefactor. It was she who gave us this fine castle to be used as an abbey more than one hundred years ago."

"You've seen her?"

The old nun shook her head. "I've not been so fortunate. There are, in fact, few who've actually seen Lady Anne. But over the years there have been enough to know that she is still here, waiting."

"Waiting for what?" Jamie walked to the window, unable to keep from scanning the garden in search of another glimpse of the famous ghost.

The Mother Superior folded her hands atop the desk. "Lady Anne was the daughter of a Scots mother and an English nobleman.

She was raised gently here in this magnificent palace, where she was tutored in music and art by French and Italian teachers. It is said that she spent many happy hours in the lovely walled garden, painting the flowers on canvas. There were many visitors to her father's home, and one of them was a bold, handsome warrior, who was so taken by the beautiful young maiden, it's said he lost his heart in an instant. The same was true for her. They became lovers in that very garden. He enjoyed watching her paint, and could have happily spent the rest of his life with her here. But when the country was plunged into war, he had no choice but to go off to do battle. Before he left, he begged her to marry him and come with him. According to legend, though she loved him more than life itself, she couldn't bear the thought of leaving the comfort of her home and garden to follow him into battle. And so she refused, saying on the day he returned, they would wed."

Jamie nodded, already anticipating the end of the tale. "And so she waits to this very day for a warrior who will never return."

Mother Mary of the Cross turned to him. "Aye. But there's more. She never married. And when her melancholy became more than she could bear, she invited our sisters to her castle to care for her until her death. In payment, she offered the castle and grounds to us for all time. We've been here ever since, using our simple skills to care for others."

Jamie turned away from the window and studied the profile of the old nun. "You say she died. Why can she not simply" — he nodded toward the heavens — "go the way of the dead?"

Mother Superior shrugged. "It's said there is something she must do before she can join those who have gone before her."

"Do?" Jamie crossed to her desk. "What can a ghost possibly do?"

The old woman steepled her hands. "I know not, my laird. But it's said that it was her selfish desire for ease and comfort that kept her from going with her lover. Perhaps she must find a way to make amends before she can finally take her leave of this place. Until then . . ." She smiled. "You must consider yourself most fortunate, my laird. There are few whom the lady deems worthy to visit."

"Aye. Thank you, Reverend Mother. Though I doubt you could call our brief moments in the garden a visit." Deep in thought, Jamie let himself out of the office and made his way to his room.

As he lay on his pallet, he found himself thinking about the sad tale of Lady Anne. She had chosen comfort over love and was now paying the price for all eternity.

Lady Anne. So beautiful. So heartbreakingly sad.

He'd actually had a better look at a ghost than he had at the mysterious Eve. The hooded cloak made it impossible to see her. In that one moment when she'd turned to him, he'd had a quick impression of eyes wide with fear and a mouth rounded in silent protest. But there had been no time to see more before she'd turned away.

"Why are you hiding from the world, little Eve?" he wondered aloud. "What secrets do you carry in your heart?"

It occurred to him that this was the first night since he'd arrived at the abbey that he hadn't once been plunged into the depths of despair with thoughts of the battles and the comrades who'd fallen. Instead his thoughts were of two very intriguing women, one dead, one hiding.

As a lad, Jamie had always loved a mystery. How could he possibly resist this one?

4

"Look, Reverend Mother." Sister Fiona, slightly out of breath, bustled into the office and pointed out the window. "At first I couldn't believe what I was seeing. But young Mordrund tells me the laird has been in the garden since early this morning."

Mother Superior pushed away from her desk to stand beside the younger nun. What she saw had her smiling. "It would seem that Laird Jamie Morgan has begun to heal."

"Aye. See how easily he wields a shovel? His leg, which once caused him to limp painfully, now presses the blade into the soil without hesitation. And his arm, which recently couldn't even lift a sword, now lifts the damp earth as though it weighs nothing at all."

The older sister smiled indulgently. "I wasn't speaking of his physical healing, Sister Fiona. It would seem that the laird is finally able to look beyond himself."

"Oh. Aye." The younger sister shot her

superior a brilliant smile. "I hadn't thought of that. It's just so grand to see him standing tall and becoming involved. Even though it is merely with the mundane work here at the abbey."

"It is indeed grand." Mother Superior continued watching. "What of our Eve? How does she accept his help?"

Sister Fiona sighed. "Grudgingly, I fear. When he first began to dig beside her, we all expected to see her run and hide. But though she shuns the laird, at least she remains in the garden."

"A very big step for our Eve as well, wouldn't you say, Sister Fiona?"

The younger nun looked startled. It hadn't occurred to her until this very moment that the healing of one patient might affect the other. She gave a weak smile. "Aye. I would indeed, Reverend Mother. Is there anything you would like me to do?"

"Do?" The old sister shook her head. "I think we should leave the laird and the lass alone, to work things out as they will."

"Very well, Reverend Mother."

As the younger nun hurried away, the older one remained at the window watching for long minutes. Finally, looking pleased, she turned away and returned her attention to the work at hand.

The healing had taken a turn none of them had anticipated. But a turn for the better all the same.

Jamie stopped to mop his face with the edge of his plaid. "The sun's hot this day."

The lass said nothing as she tugged at a weed.

He stared down at the hooded figure kneeling in the dirt. She had to be maimed. Aye, that was it. It was the only reason he could think of for staying hidden in that infernal cloak during the warmest part of the day.

"Sister Fiona has brought us a jug of water." He thrust the shovel into the earth and started toward a stone bench. "Shall I bring you some?"

The lass moved away to another patch of soil, where she began methodically pulling weeds.

Annoyed, Jamie took a long drink, then splashed some of the water over his head. He stood for a moment watching her, then picked up his shovel and stepped up beside her, turning the earth in smooth, easy strokes.

"Ah." He gave an exclamation of delight as he stooped beside her to touch a hand to the plant at his feet. "Yarrow. Now this is a plant I know well. In our home in the Highlands, my mother used to make an ointment of this and apply it to our wounds. And as we were a family of warriors, there were many wounds that needed healing." Seeing no reaction, he added, "Did you know that this is also used to find one's true love?"

He was pleased to see that she actually looked at the plant for a moment before returning her attention to the weeds.

Warming to his subject, he said, "It's well known that a lass should sew an ounce of yarrow into a small pouch and place it under her pillow before going to bed. Then she must repeat this verse twice. 'Thou pretty herb of Venus's tree, thy true name it is yarrow. Now who my bosom love must be, pray reveal it on the morrow.' "

Her hands had gone very still. Because of the hood, he couldn't tell where she was looking. But at least he knew that he had her attention.

His voice lowered. " 'The wise lass will wait for a knock on her door on the morrow. When it comes, the enchantment of true love will begin.' "

He thought he heard a hiss of annoyance. The sound brought a smile to his lips.

The lass could hear. He was now more certain of it than ever.

So why did she not speak? Was it because she couldn't? Or wouldn't?

The intriguing question fueled his energy and kept him going until dusk. And though he might have continued working longer, he made no protest when the lass suddenly walked to the small door in the wall and began to store her tools. He followed her, carefully putting away the hoe and shovel. When he turned, she was already walking through the archway. All that could be seen of her was the hem of her cloak swirling around her ankles. It wasn't the sight of those shapely ankles that had him sweating, he told himself. It was merely that he had become unaccustomed to the rigors of hard work.

It had been good to work. He'd missed it. Missed the pleasant ache of straining muscles and the good feeling that came after a day of honest sweat.

He took himself off to his room to bathe away the grime of the day and to eat the food he knew would be waiting on his table. He had no doubt his muscles would protest the hard work he'd undertaken this day. He hoped it would help him sleep through the night without waking in a cold sweat, something he hadn't accomplished since first arriving at the abbey.

★ ★ ★

Mother Mary of the Cross looked up as the shadow of the man fell over the doorway. "My laird. You are up late tonight. I would have thought all that work in the garden would persuade you to sleep."

"So did I, Reverend Mother." He crossed to her desk, a frown upon his handsome face. "I'm here with a request."

"Anything, my laird." She sat back, folding her hands on the desktop.

"What can you tell me about the lass you call Eve?"

The old woman arched a brow. "It is not our way to speak of one patient to another, my laird. If the lass were to ask about you, I would tell her the same."

He gave a sigh of impatience. "I understand. I have no wish to violate her privacy, but I wonder about her devotion to the garden. What fuels it?"

"I know not, my laird. She seems driven in her determination to restore it. In fact, she has taken a vow to remain here until the garden is exactly as it once was."

At that his frown deepened. "How would she know the way it once was? I was given to understand that, like me, she is only recently arrived at the abbey since the battle."

"That's true, my laird." Mother Superior

paused, as though considering how much to tell him. Getting to her feet, she beckoned him to follow. "Come. I wish to show you something."

She led him up the stairs to a gallery that ran the length of the upper abbey. It was lined with ancient portraits. "This is Lady Anne's mother, and this is her father."

Though he wondered what this had to do with the lass called Eve, Jamie studied the lovely flaxen-haired woman and could see that her beauty had been passed on to the ghostly maiden he'd seen in the garden. As for the handsome man, he seemed both aristocratic and haughty, characteristics that had also been passed on to his daughter.

"I don't have to tell you who this is." Mother Mary of the Cross paused beneath a portrait of the woman Jamie had seen in that single encounter.

He nodded. "She looks exactly the same. Even down to the gown she wore when I saw her." He glanced around. "But what has this to do with Eve?"

The old nun led him further along the gallery until they came to several framed watercolors of colorful flowers and graceful trees.

"These are some of Lady Anne's paintings of the garden as it looked when she was a young lass."

Studying them, Jamie nodded. "Her talent is most impressive. It's easy to see that she had a special gift." Suddenly he muttered a word of surprise. "But how can this be? They look the same now as they did in these pictures."

"Aye." Reverend Mother gave him a measured look.

"Then Eve has been up here to see these? She used these as her guide?"

The nun shook her head. "Not that I know of. In fact, I don't believe our Eve has ever been anywhere in the abbey except in her room and in the garden. Almost from the day she was strong enough to leave her pallet she began working the soil, and it was as if she knew exactly where everything should be. Where to plant the herbs, and the flowers and climbing vines. No one has coached her. At least no one here in the abbey."

"Are you saying that Lady Anne may have befriended her?"

The old nun gave an expressive shrug of her shoulders. "I cannot say, my laird. Since the lass has never spoken, we have no way of knowing what she has experienced. But since Lady Anne showed herself to you, it isn't so difficult to imagine that she may have visited the lass as well. Though for what purpose, I cannot imagine."

He saw at once that the old nun had given him the route he would take to break through that wall of silence Eve had built around herself. He felt a sense of growing excitement. "You believe the lass has seen Lady Anne?"

"It seems a reasonable assumption."

"Thank you, Reverend Mother."

As he walked away, the old nun's sharp eyes suddenly danced with undisguised merriment. It would seem the laird was taking an inordinate interest in someone other than himself. It was another step away from the illness that plagued his soul. Now if only he might persuade the lass to do the same.

It was only a step, she reminded herself. But then, each journey had to begin in just such a manner.

Jamie knew that after the day he had put in he ought to be asleep. But he couldn't stay away from the garden this night. Not after what Mother Mary of the Cross had hinted in the upper gallery. He was eager to see Lady Anne again. Now, knowing her story, he wouldn't find himself awed in her presence, as he'd been that first time.

He drew the plaid around his shoulders

and walked the length of the wall, then back again. For more than two hours he remained there, occasionally sitting on a stone bench before resuming his pacing.

Just as he was about to give up and return to his room, the clouds that had been rolling across the heavens suddenly drifted off, leaving the land awash in moonlight. It was at that moment he saw her.

At first there was just a shimmer of light. Then it grew brighter and seemed to take shape as the woman drifted toward him. He waited until she climbed the stone steps to stare out over the wall. Then he walked up beside her.

"I know you wait for your warrior."

She turned her gaze fully on him, and he could actually feel her sadness. "It is my punishment. I must spend eternity waiting for my Malcolm."

"Why are you being punished, my lady?"

"Because I was given the gift of true love and squandered it."

"You were a gentle lady, reared in this lovely setting. Many would understand why you would be reluctant to leave it for the discomfort and danger of a field of battle."

She gave him a sad smile. "It is obvious that you have never truly loved."

"Why do you say that?"

"When you love, with all your heart and soul, you cannot bear to be separated from your lover for even a moment. That's how it was for my Malcolm. And so I sent him not only into battle alone but with a heavy heart. As a warrior, you must know the advantage that gave to his enemies."

"Are you saying that you feel responsible for his death?"

She gave no answer before turning to stare out over the land.

Jamie took a deep breath, hoping he wouldn't drive her away with his questions, for they needed to be asked.

"Do you know of the lass Eve, who toils here each day in your garden?"

"Why do you call her Eve?"

"It is the name the sisters have given her. Do you know her?"

"I do. She has taken a vow to restore the gardens to their former beauty." She continued staring into the distance.

"Do you tell her where you want the soil tilled and the seeds planted?"

"I do."

"Then she can hear you." He paused a beat before asking, "Does she answer you?"

"Sometimes."

The sigh of relief rose up from deep inside his chest. "I'd hoped it was so. Can you tell me why she chooses not to speak?"

"Perhaps she shall, when she has something to say." She turned and descended the steps, then began drifting slowly away.

As before, there was a bright glimmer of light, and then she was gone, leaving only shadows where the light had been.

Jamie stayed where he was, thinking over what Lady Anne had said. Of all the things she'd told him, the only thing that mattered was the fact that the lass could speak.

Now he must find a way to get her to speak to him.

He would begin his assault on her defenses first thing in the morning.

5

Jamie stood just inside the arched doorway, staring sullenly at the rain that had been falling all morning. He'd been awake since dawn, planning the many cunning ways he would trick Eve into talking while they worked together in the garden. Now the rain had spoiled everything. Eve had remained closed in her room. Not a single soul dared to venture outside.

By the time the bells tolled the noon Angelus, the rain had slowed to a trickle. Though he feared the soil was too wet to work, Jamie dutifully opened the door in the wall and removed a hoe and shovel. He worked alone for more than an hour, and had begun to realize that the day was slipping away, when suddenly he saw the cloaked figure step through the arch. He felt a sizzle of anticipation and tried not to stare as she retrieved her tools and began working alongside him in silence. Suddenly the sun burst through an opening in the clouds, bathing the land in brilliant light.

All his well-made plans were gone in the blink of an eye. Without thinking, he stopped work and leaned on the hoe, staring down at the hooded figure as she knelt in the dirt.

"Lady Anne appeared to me in just such a manner. One minute I was alone in the darkness. The next she was there, in a blaze of light, walking toward me."

"Truly? The lady showed herself to you?" Then instantly, realizing what she had done, she clapped a hand to her mouth.

He bent down and caught her by the upper arms, lifting her to her feet. On his face was a look of absolute delight.

"I knew you could talk. And now you have."

The hand trowel slipped from her nerveless fingers as she looked at him for the first time and caught sight of his eyes. Though she'd seen them for only a moment one other time, they were eyes that had been indelibly imprinted in her mind when a brave warrior had leapt to her defense, sweeping her behind him for protection while he fought off her attackers.

These were his eyes. The warrior's eyes.

Blue they were. Not the blue of the sky in summer, but a deep midnight blue, the pupils ringed with gold. There had been such kindness in them. And such fierce determination. Minutes later, with a slight bow of his head, he'd been gone, rushing headlong into yet another battle, leaving her the lone survivor of her clan.

"It's you." Her voice was little more than a hushed whisper. "The bold warrior who saved me."

"I saved you? Where? When?"

"In the forest of Ballycrue. You came to me in my hour of need and slew my enemies."

The story of her family's flight, and their fate at the hands of the barbarians, tumbled from her lips. Like a stream that had long been dammed up and had finally been set free, the words spilled one after the other until finally she was forced to pause for breath.

As she did she lifted a hand to the hood, slipping it aside to reveal a mass of fiery hair that tumbled down her back in a riot of curls. "I've never forgotten you, my brave warrior."

His breath caught in his throat when he recognized the lass who had so tugged at his heart that day in the forest. "Nor I you. Had I but seen those eyes as green as a Highland loch, or this hair like autumn leaves, I'd have known you long before this, lass." He touched a hand to her cheek. Only a touch, but the heat spread through his veins like liquid fire. "Tell me your name. For on that fateful day, there was no time."

"Alexa. Alexa of the clan MacCallum, my laird."

"Alexa." He couldn't tear himself away from the fathomless depths of her eyes, which seemed to glow with some inner light. "My name is Jamie, of the clan Morgan. You've never been far from my mind, Alexa MacCallum. So often I wondered what had happened to you. In my despair, I feared that your fate had been the same as that of so many others who had come to mean something to me."

"Are you saying you lost loved ones as well?"

"All my friends and clansmen who fought beside me are gone, I'm told. And there was no time to bid them farewell. When I awoke, I found myself here at the abbey."

She lay a hand gently over his. "I know how you have suffered, for it was the same for me. The worst was wondering why my life should have been spared when there were so many more worthy."

"Aye. That's it exactly." He looked down at her small hand touching his and felt such a rush of tenderness it almost overwhelmed him.

He kept his eyes steady on hers as he framed her face with his big hands. "But now, suddenly, seeing you, hearing your voice, I feel as though I've just awakened from a long, deep sleep and have been given back my reason for living."

Though she could feel the heat flooding her cheeks, she couldn't look away. "It's the same for me."

"Is that why you stopped speaking? Because it was too painful?"

"Aye, my laird. The pain was so great that at times I felt as though my heart must surely break from it. Each morning when I awoke and realized I was still here, I was sad, knowing that I would have to suffer through another day alone."

He shook his head and touched a finger to her lips. "You're not alone, Alexa Mac-Callum. Nor will you be ever again."

Her eyes widened. "What are you saying?"

"Shhh." He lowered his face and brushed her lips with his. It was the merest touch of mouth to mouth, but both of them took a step back as though jolted.

Then, because he couldn't seem to help himself, he drew her close and pressed his lips to her temple. "Oh, Alexa. My beautiful, wonderful Alexa. We're alive. We're here in this lovely place. And we've just been given a reason to be grateful for the strange twist of fate that brought us both here."

At a burst of voices in the doorway they looked up and stepped apart as a group of novices walked out to enjoy the late-afternoon sunshine.

As they smiled and nodded and walked on, Jamie leaned close to whisper, "I suppose we must find some task in the garden or invite their gossip."

Alexa nodded and bent down to retrieve her hand tool. As she did, Jamie knelt beside her and gave her a smile that had her heart doing strange things in her chest.

"I wish it were nighttime."

"Why, my laird?"

He couldn't help laughing at her innocence. "If you don't know, my sweet Alexa, perhaps you'd consent to meet me here tonight. I'd be happy to show you all the things I'd like to do when no one is around to watch."

"My laird!" She turned her face away to hide the blush that bloomed on her cheeks.

He cupped a hand under her chin and lifted it for his inspection. "Oh, Alexa. Your sweetness is such that I do believe I have to kiss you right this minute."

"You mustn't." She got to her feet and shook down her skirts. When she looked up, he was laughing. Her heart took another quick tumble in her chest before returning to its natural rhythm.

For the rest of the time she spent in the garden, tilling the soil, pruning, weeding, she was achingly aware of the handsome young man who worked alongside her. Whenever she glanced his way, he would pause in his work to smile or wink, causing the most delicious flutter deep inside her.

Though she blushed often, and quickly turned away to hide it, there was no denying the fact that this day something strange and wonderful had occurred. Her heart felt lighter than she'd ever known before. All the darkness that had so often clouded her vision seemed to have lifted.

She felt as if she'd been reborn.

It was all because of the bold and handsome warrior Jamie Morgan.

Jamie mopped the sweat from his brow and looked up in surprise to see that the sun was already setting in a glorious display of color. Where had the day gone? He hadn't wanted it to end. Not when he had just discovered sweet, beautiful Alexa MacCallum.

He liked working beside her while they

talked and talked. She told him about her childhood with her parents and sisters. Told him about growing up in the Lowlands, always fearful of attack by the barbarians who came from across the sea. He told her about growing up in the Highlands, and his training as a warrior with his friend Duncan. After so many days and weeks of silence, they couldn't seem to get enough of the sound of one another's voice. She loved the deep timbre of his, and the rumble of easy laughter. He loved the way her words seemed to whisper over his senses, causing a prickly feeling inside. He even loved the fact that they could go for long stretches of time without saying a thing, yet feel completely comfortable in each other's company.

Not exactly comfortable, he thought, glancing over to catch sight of her shapely backside. Now that she'd shed the heavy cloak, he could see the lithe, slender body that she'd kept hidden from view. Even the coarse gown the sisters had provided her couldn't hide the softly rounded breasts, the waist so tiny that his hands could surely span it with room to spare, the gentle slope of her hips. At the sight of her his throat went dry and the heat rushed to his loins. He found himself spending a great deal of time thinking about the way her lips parted when she smiled.

He wanted to taste them again.

At once he felt that quick rush of heat, the sudden jolt to his heart. What was he going to do about these wild, reckless feelings that stirred inside him?

Without taking the time to think his intentions through, he ambled across the garden to where she stood putting away her tools.

As he set the hoe and shovel inside, he leaned close to whisper, "Meet me out here tonight when the others have retired to their pallets."

She gave him no answer as she turned away and started through the arched doorway.

He watched the sway of her hips and felt a hunger building inside him.

He glanced at the gathering shadows and found himself eager for the darkness.

Alexa stripped off her coarse robe and gown and stood beside the basin of water in her room. The tray of food on her night table lay forgotten. She was too nervous to think about eating. Instead she began to wash away the grime of the garden. As she did, she studied her body.

What did Jamie Morgan see when he

looked at her? Surely a Highland laird would have had many women eager to please him. He could choose from the most beautiful maidens in the land.

Though she'd had scant opportunities in her young life to be kissed, there had been a time or two. But they'd been mere lads. Jamie Morgan was a man who'd kissed her the way a man kissed a woman. When he'd brushed his lips over hers, she'd felt the flash of heat all the way to her toes. And with the heat, something more. A strange, hungry yearning, unlike anything she'd ever known before.

Oh, what was she to do about these feelings?

She tossed aside the square of linen and began to wring her hands. What sort of woman would even consider meeting a man in the garden, under cover of darkness? Worse, what would he think of her if she did?

She slipped into the coarse gown and began to pace the length of her room. Then she resolutely climbed between the covers of her sleeping pallet, determined to put such foolishness out of her mind for good.

Jamie had been in the garden for hours, walking the paths, counting off the number of paces from one side of the wall to the other. He'd watched the candles in the abbey windows slowly being extinguished, until finally the one in Mother Superior's office went out and the structure was in total darkness.

Still the arched door remained closed.

Where was Alexa? Why hadn't she come to him as he'd asked? Was it fear that kept her from him? Or was it simply that she had no wish to be with him?

That thought had him sighing as he once again turned and made his way along the wall. Suddenly he caught sight of the shimmering light that told him of the arrival of Lady Anne. He stood perfectly still, fascinated as always at the way the light took on the shape of a young woman standing before him, the hem of her silvery gown billowing around her ankles.

"Like me" — her voice was a mere whisper on the wind — "you await the arrival of your love."

"Aye." He couldn't keep the sadness from his tone. "I fear that like you, I may be waiting in vain."

"Then we shall wait together." She began to climb the stone steps, and Jamie found himself following her to the top of the wall.

She looked out over the countryside, bathed in pale moonlight. "He comes for me soon now. I can feel it."

"What will you do if he doesn't appear?"

She shook her head, sending golden waves tumbling around her hauntingly beautiful face. "What I've done for all these years. I shall wait. For I know that one day I'll be given a chance to make amends for having squandered his love. And when that day comes, I'll be free to leave the bonds that hold me here and join my beloved in that other life for all eternity."

Jamie thought of the green-eyed maiden who stirred his soul as no other had. What if she never came to him? What if he had to spend a lifetime thinking about what might have been? Would he return to his Highlands and mourn his loss? Or would he give his heart to another?

A scant day ago he'd have scoffed at the idea of mourning the loss of the love of a lass he hardly knew. And yet there was something about Alexa MacCallum that was like no other.

Lady Anne turned soulful eyes to him, eyes brimming with unshed tears. "Beware, my laird. True love is a rare and precious gift. Once you have tasted it, nothing else can satisfy the cravings of your heart."

"Are you warning me to walk away now before it's too late?"

She gave him a sad smile before descending the steps. Over her shoulder she called, "For some, love is a slow-growing flower that takes many seasons to bring to bloom. But for some, all it takes is one look, one touch of the pretty petals, to seal a fate for a lifetime."

As she stepped into the shadows, her light began to shimmer and fade. When she was gone, Jamie stood perfectly still, allowing her words to play through his mind.

It was true, he realized. It had taken but one look from Alexa MacCallum to touch his heart and to unlock all its secrets.

If she didn't come to him, he was doomed to wait, as did the lovely ghost of the abbey.

6

Jamie draped his plaid about his shoulders to ward off the midnight chill. Though he knew he was behaving like a foolish, lovestruck lad, he couldn't bring himself to give up and return to his room. It wasn't sleep he craved. It was Alexa.

The thought of holding her, kissing her, had him alternately pacing, then dropping onto a bench, his head in his hands. What was he going to do about this wanting? Sweet heaven, he wanted her with his heart, his soul, his entire being.

"You look so sad." At the sound of that whispered voice, his head came up sharply. There was a flood of warmth where a hand was touching his shoulder. "Do I dare hope that at least some of that sadness is because of me?"

"Alexa." He was on his feet, his hands at her shoulders. "You came to me."

"I tried not to. I couldn't stay away. I

couldn't sleep. And I fear I've worn a path in the floor of my room from all my pacing."

"Oh, my love." He couldn't stop staring at her. He wondered if she had any idea how truly beautiful she was. "I'd given up hoping that . . ."

She stopped his words with a finger to his lips. "You, my laird? Now I know you jest. 'Tis said of you that you never give up."

"I don't?"

"Nay, my laird. No matter how many of the enemy you faced on the field of battle, you continued fighting even when all around you had fallen. It was you, and you alone, who drove the barbarians from our land."

He closed a hand over hers and absorbed the familiar rush of heat through his system. "Now where did you hear all that?"

"The sisters and the novices." She gave a soft laugh that wrapped itself around his heart and gently tugged. "They talked easily around me, since they thought I could not hear."

"You little vixen. What else did you hear?"

"That you are called the laird of lairds. The one most loved in your Highlands." She looked up at him. "Is this true?"

He shrugged. "I don't wish to speak of me. I'd rather speak of you, Alexa. Tell me why you came to me."

"How could I not?" She slid her hands along his arms and lifted her face to his. In the moonlight her eyes gleamed like emeralds.

"Oh, my beautiful Alexa." The touch of her, the look of her, had his heartbeat thundering. He drew her close and covered her mouth with his, drinking in her sweetness like a man starved for the taste of her. He couldn't seem to get enough of her. Even when she tried to pull back, he took the kiss deeper, until they were both breathless.

He felt her tremble and thrilled to it, gathering her even closer, until he could feel the pounding of her heartbeat inside his own chest. Still he continued kissing her, taking them both higher, then higher still.

In her entire life, Alexa had never felt like this. Icy needles seemed to be racing up and down her spine. Yet she was hot. So hot she could hardly breathe. The strong, workworn hands moving along her back were causing the most amazing sensations to curl through her veins. Somewhere deep inside a fist seemed to tighten. She had to clutch at his waist for fear of falling, for surely her legs would soon fail her.

She could feel herself quivering, her breath coming harder and faster as he continued assaulting her senses. His mouth was so warm. So firm. When his hands moved slowly up her sides and his thumbs encountered her breasts, she gasped and pulled a little away. Moments later, her fear was forgotten as he kissed her eyes, her cheeks, the tip of her nose.

She seemed to hold her breath, waiting for his mouth to find hers once more. When it did she sank into the kiss with a sigh that sounded very much like the purring of a cat.

This time when his hands found her breasts, she had no will to resist. Instead she sighed again and lifted her arms to his neck, needing to anchor herself to keep from falling.

"You know I want you, Alexa." He spoke the words inside her mouth.

"Aye, my laird."

"Not 'my laird.'" He lifted his head, his eyes hot and fierce. "The one who would love you is not the laird of lairds. It is the man, Jamie Morgan. Do you understand?"

He could see that she didn't comprehend. He felt a quick twist of frustration. "Why did you come to me, Alexa? I need to know."

"Because you asked." She offered her lips for another kiss. "And because I owe you my life."

"You owe me . . ." He went very still before drawing away.

All that he'd felt, all that he'd wanted, all

that he'd hoped, was shattered by those simple words.

As he withdrew from her, she felt the cold seep into her, where only seconds earlier she'd been so hot.

With his arms crossed over his chest, he said simply, "Go to bed now, Alexa."

"To . . . bed?" She studied the taut, rigid line of his jaw. The haughty lift of his head. The angry flare of nostrils. "I thought you wanted me."

"I thought so, too. I was wrong. Now leave me."

She touched a hand to his arm and felt him stiffen and pull back. "Tell me what I've done wrong, my laird."

His voice seemed more sad than angry as he turned away from her. "You've done nothing wrong, Alexa. I was the one who was wrong. So very wrong." His tone was the harsh command he'd used with his comrades when he needed to be obeyed. "Go now. Quickly."

For long minutes Alexa continued watching him, seeing the rigid, unyielding line of his back. He didn't move, standing as still as a statue, his gaze on a distant star. It was as though he had already cut her out of his life. Out of his heart.

Oh, if only she knew how to make things right between them. Something she had said or done had changed everything in the blink of an eye. One minute he'd been kissing her as though he would never stop. The next he'd behaved like a stranger, ordering her to go.

Was it her inexperience? Was that what had changed everything between them? She felt like such a fool. It was all she could do to keep from weeping.

Gathering her cloak around her, she turned away and started across the garden. Though tears welled up in her eyes, she blinked them away. She was not going to shed tears over Jamie Morgan. The laird of lairds indeed.

His words began playing through her mind, taunting her.

The one who would love you is not the laird of lairds. It is the man, Jamie Morgan. Do you understand?

How could she understand when he made no sense? How was it possible to separate the man from the title? Was not the king the king? Why would one so far above all others also desire to be a mere man?

She stopped in her tracks as the answer came to her in a flash of understanding.

When he was in love.

He was, in fact, a mere man. It wasn't her gratitude he wanted; it was her love. Not the love of a grateful subject, but the pure, simple love of a woman for a man.

She clapped her hands to her mouth to keep from crying out.

How could she have been so blind?

Now, if only she could find a way to make him listen.

She had to find the way. For unless she made him understand now, this very moment, all would be lost.

Alexa hurried back along the path she'd just traveled, then came to a sudden halt. For a moment she almost lost her nerve. Jamie looked so distant and untouchable. Then she thought about the man who had held her and kissed her until her bones had melted. This was the man to whom she would pour out the secrets of her heart.

"I've hurt you, my lair—" She caught herself in time and moistened her lips with her tongue. "I've hurt you, Jamie, though it was not my intention to do so."

Even though he was caught unawares, he didn't bother to turn around. "I told you to leave me."

"Aye. In truth, you commanded it, as the laird might order one of his underlings." She took a deep breath and forced herself to lay a hand on his arm, feeling him flinch as she did. Though his reaction momentarily stopped her, she was determined to see this through, no matter what the outcome. "But you are not my laird, and I am not your subject. I come to you as a woman would come to a man." Her voice faltered. "A man she loves."

He turned, his flesh still burning where she'd touched him. It took all his willpower to keep from dragging her into his arms. Instead he merely looked at her with such intensity that she almost lost her nerve.

Though she was trembling, she lifted her chin. "Do you doubt that I love you, Jamie?"

"You confuse love with gratitude, my lady."

"Nay." She lay a hand on his cheek and saw his eyes narrow fractionally.

So. He was not as unmoved by her touch as he pretended. That knowledge gave her the courage to continue. "On that point I have never been confused. I confess that I spoke myself badly. I was . . . overwhelmed. I've had little experience speaking of love. You are my first."

His fingers curled around her wrist as he held it a little away from him. "You want me to believe that in these last few minutes you've come to the conclusion that you love me, Alexa?"

"Is that what you think? I have loved you from the first moment I saw you, Jamie Morgan. That day, on that bloody field of battle, you were the most magnificent man I had ever beheld. But so much happened on that day that I was forced to lock those feelings in a tiny room in my mind, where they stayed until today. Today, when I looked at you, I remembered, and the door to that room opened, even though I tried desperately to keep it closed. Now, having seen you again, there is no going back. I know, as surely as I know my name, that I love you, Jamie. Only you. And I believe that you love me, too." She stared deeply into his eyes. "Can you deny it?"

He continued holding her away, his eyes as hot and fierce as they'd been in battle. She feared for a moment that he would turn away from her once more and order her to leave.

If he did, her heart would surely shatter beyond repair.

She held her breath, afraid to breathe. Even her heart forgot to beat as she waited.

He shook his head slowly. His voice was little more than a whisper. "I can't deny it, Alexa. I love you. Only you."

"Then kiss me, Jamie. Before I die from the wanting." She started to reach for him, but he stopped her.

"I cannot."

"And why not?"

"Because if I kissed you again, I would never be able to stop."

"And why should you stop?"

"You're a maiden, Alexa. You said yourself that I'm the first."

"Aye." This time she did reach for him and felt him flinch. "My first. My last. My only."

Still he held back, as if unable to believe what he was hearing. "I'll not settle for mere kisses this time. I'm a man, Alexa. With a man's hunger. I want you. All of you. The way a man desires a woman. Do you understand?"

She gave a slight nod of her head. "I understand, Jamie."

"This is what you want? Truly?"

"Truly." Though she felt a moment of pure terror, she managed a quick smile. "Please, Jamie. Kiss me now."

At her words he knew there would be no holding back.

"Oh, my darling." He dragged her roughly into his arms, and his mouth covered hers with a savageness that had them both gasping. "I'm not certain I can be gentle. The wanting is so fierce."

She felt her heart nearly overflow with relief. With love. With wild, exuberant joy. "Aye. I know, Jamie, for it's the same for me."

7

Alexa wrapped her arms around Jamie's neck and returned his kisses with head-spinning fervor. She loved the rough texture of his cheeks and chin, which just this morning had been clean-shaven. She delighted in the quick, fluttery thrills each time his tongue mated with hers.

She could feel herself melting into him. Becoming aware of so many things she'd never felt before. The way the backs of her hands tingled where his hair brushed them. The way her skin warmed and heated at his touch. The way his warm breath tickled the hair at her temple as he pressed soft, moist kisses to her face.

Just as quickly the kiss softened, gentled, as he lingered over her mouth, drawing out all the sweet, fresh flavor that was uniquely hers. There was a sweetness, a freshness about her that put him in mind of a Highland meadow when the heather was in bloom.

He lowered his mouth to the sensitive skin of her throat, running nibbling kisses lower, to her collarbone, then lower still to her breast, until she gasped and clutched at him.

He lifted his head. His voice was gruff. "Would you like me to stop, Alexa?"

"Nay." The word came out in a long drawn-out sigh.

"Ah. Praise heaven." He nibbled the spot between her neck and shoulder until she shivered and clutched at his waist. "For I'm not sure I can."

He slipped the cloak from her shoulders and let it drop to the ground, then reached for the buttons of her gown. When the bodice parted, he untied the ribbons of her chemise until it, too, was parted. At the sight of all that soft, lovely flesh he gave a sigh of pleasure. "You're even more beautiful than I'd dreamed, Alexa."

When he bent to her and took her breast into his mouth she thought she would surely die. Waves of unbelievable pleasure seemed to wash over her at her very core. Her skin was damp, her breathing labored as she reached for his plaid and tugged it free.

Now at last they were standing flesh to flesh in the moonlight. She wrapped her arms around him, greedy for another kiss. He dragged her close, his mouth feasting on hers while his clever hands drove her higher and higher until she thought she would go mad with the need.

"Jamie." Her voice was a desperate plea. Heeding it, he took her hands, and together they dropped to their knees on the cloak.

He couldn't get enough of that soft, soft skin and those luscious lips as he lingered over them, savoring each taste, each touch.

Needing more, he lay with her on the cloak in the cool grass of the garden. He moved over her, his hands and mouth taking her higher, then higher still. She writhed beneath him, her hands and mouth as eager, as avid as his.

With each kiss, each touch, they drew ever closer to the edge of a high, steep cliff. One step, and they would surely soar. Still he held back, wanting, needing, to take them both higher.

He loved the way she looked, steeped in pleasure. Lips moist and swollen from his kisses. Eyes heavy-lidded with passion. Her body taut as a bowstring, desperate for release.

"Alexa. My beautiful Alexa." He kissed her long and slow and deep, drawing out the moment until she gave a low moan, wrapping her arms around his neck, her body rising up to meet his.

Despite the coolness of the air and the dampness of the grass beneath them, heat rose up, clogging their throats, threatening to choke them.

He'd never known a need this powerful. A desire so overwhelming, it seemed to take over his will. He knew he had to have her. Now. This moment. Or go mad. For there was a demon inside, struggling to be free.

As he entered her he heard her little gasp of shock.

"Dear heaven, I've hurt you." At once he started to pull back.

"Nay, my love." She pulled him close and wrapped herself around him, drawing him even deeper. Then she began to move with him, climb with him, and whatever protest he was about to make was lost.

Now, he knew, there was no turning back. Though in truth he'd known it as soon as she'd returned to him in the garden. From that very first moment he'd been lost.

"I love you, Alexa. Only you," he whispered as they began moving faster, climbing higher.

"And I love you, my brave, handsome warrior. Only you, Jamie."

The words were torn from her lips as she felt herself hurtling out of control.

Wrapped around each other, they took that final leap and found themselves soaring through space. It was the most amazing, breathless journey of their lives.

Moments later they shattered into millions of glittering stars before drifting slowly to earth.

"I didn't mean to be so rough." His face was buried in her throat.

They lay, still joined, their breathing ragged, their bodies slick with sheen.

"You weren't." She gave a weak laugh. "Well, not much."

"Am I too heavy?"

"Nay." She thought she could lie just so for the rest of her life. The feel of his heartbeat, as unsteady as her own, was oddly comforting. The press of his lips against her throat more wonderful than anything she'd ever known. She felt deliciously sated and happily content.

"Alexa. My Alexa." He shifted, rolling to one side and drawing her gently into the circle of his arms. "Isn't that better?"

"Aye."

"Are you cold?"

"Not a bit." It occurred to her that she ought to be, for they were naked, with nothing but a cloak to shield them from the chill night air. But the warmth of his body was enough to warm her the way nothing else ever could. "Are you cold, Jamie?"

"How could I be cold when I'm holding you, my love?"

My love. She thought she'd never heard two more beautiful words. She traced a finger over the dark hair that matted his chest until she encountered a long, raised scar.

"What is this?"

"Nothing." He closed a hand over hers to still her movements. "Just an old wound."

"I hate knowing you've been so hurt."

"It doesn't matter now, love. Now that I have you here in my arms, all my wounds are forgotten. They no longer have the power to cause me pain."

It was true, he realized. He felt healed. Reborn. He framed her face with his hands. "We've all been scarred by wars, Alexa. But we've survived, you and I. Until now I hated that I had survived when others had died. Now, because of you, I realize that we've been given much more than the gift of life."

"And what is that?"

"The gift of love," he whispered against her lips.

He held her a little away, then drew her close and kissed her again, this time lingering over her lips before taking the kiss deeper.

"My lovely Alexa. You're so incredible. And I love you so very much."

Love. She hugged the word to her heart, knowing there was nothing he could have said that would mean as much.

"You're cold." He began to draw the cloak around her. "I felt you shiver."

"It wasn't from the cold, Jamie." She wrapped her arms around his neck and pressed her body to his, thrilling to the fact that he was once again fully aroused. "It was from this. Only this."

Growing bolder, she pressed moist little kisses along his throat, then lower, to his chest. When he gave a groan of pleasure she grew bolder still, until he caught her by the upper arms to still her movements. "Woman, do you have any idea what you're doing to me?"

"I do indeed, my laird." She chuckled and brushed the damp hair from his eyes, loving the look of love she could see there. "Do you object?"

"I'll object only if you stop, my lady."

As he lost himself in her, he realized that he felt as if he'd been waiting for this woman, this moment, and this unexpected gift of love all his life.

"Jamie. What have you done?" Alexa awoke to find Jamie sitting cross-legged beside her in the grass. On his face was a look of smug confidence as he began removing items hidden beneath his plaid.

"I've brought us food. And some fine wine as well."

She looked up to see that it was barely dawn. The two lovers had spent the night in the garden, huddled together in her warm cloak. And though they'd managed a little sleep, most of their time had been spent loving.

At times they'd felt as if the very earth shook with the enormity of their love. At other times their loving had been as easy, as gentle, as if they'd always been together.

It was how she felt, Alexa realized. As though this man had been her lover from the very beginning of time.

She sat up, shoving fiery curls from her eyes. "Are the sisters awake already?"

"Nay. There was no one in the refectory, so I helped myself to whatever I wanted. And as I was rummaging around I discovered a jug of church wine." He filled a goblet and offered it to her. "I'm sure old Father Lazarus won't mind if we enjoy a bit."

"Church wine?" With the goblet halfway to her lips she paused and shot him an incredulous look. "You stole church wine?"

"I didn't steal it, love. In fact, I'll be more than happy to replace whatever we drink."

With a roguish smile he broke off a hunk of cheese. "You have to admit that we're in need of sustenance, Alexa, love."

"Aye." She returned his smile and sipped the wine, feeling the warmth flow through her veins.

When he offered her a bite of bread and cheese, she accepted it gratefully.

"Of course —" His smile grew as he sipped from the goblet before passing it back to her. "I had a selfish reason for fetching all this food and drink."

"And what would that be?"

He leaned close to brush his mouth over hers. At once they both absorbed the quick rush of heat.

"I want you refreshed and renewed, my love, so that we can take advantage of these last precious moments before the sisters awaken for the day."

"I should have known your motives weren't entirely noble, my laird."

He took the goblet from her hands and set it aside before framing her face with his hands and covering her mouth with his.

Against her lips he murmured, "You must admit that my idea was a fine one."

"A fine idea indeed." With a purr of delight she wrapped her arms around his waist and gave herself up to the pleasure.

"Reverend Mother, something is amiss."

The older nun looked up from her desk. "What is it, Sister Fiona?"

"When young Mordrund took a tray to the lass's chamber, she found it empty. She said that the bed linens don't appear to have been slept in, for they were cold to the touch."

"Perhaps she went to chapel with the novices."

"She didn't. I already looked there. But there is more, Reverend Mother." The nun worried the skirt of her coarse gown. "When I checked the laird's chamber, it was also empty."

Mother Superior pushed away from the desk and began to pace. As she did, she glanced out the window and stopped in her tracks. Then she stepped closer to the window and gave a long, deep sigh.

"What is it, Reverend Mother?" The younger nun hurried to her side, then let out an exclamation of surprise at the sight of Alexa and Jamie seated side by side on a stone bench, their shoulders brushing as they carried on an animated conversation.

"The lass is without her cloak, Reverend Mother."

"Aye. I noticed."

"I've never seen her with her head uncovered. Look how her hair blazes in the sunlight."

"I see it."

"And she appears to be . . . laughing."

"She does indeed."

"It's nothing short of a miracle." The younger nun turned to her superior with a look of amazement. "Wouldn't you agree, Reverend Mother?"

"Aye, Sister Fiona. It would appear that both the lass and the laird have finally come out of the darkness."

"I must go and share this good news with the others. Perhaps Father Lazarus will offer up a prayer of thanksgiving."

"A fine idea." Mother Mary of the Cross waited until the door to her office closed behind the eager young nun. Then she returned her attention to the couple in the garden.

She had been praying for a miracle, and at first glance it would seem that one had been granted. Still, though she had taken a vow to turn away from the things of the world, she considered herself a practical woman. Practical enough to know that love alone was sometimes not enough to cure the ills of body, heart, and soul.

She hoped and prayed that she was wrong. She desperately wanted a happy ending for these two wounded people.

She saw the laird touch a hand to the lass's shoulder before leaning close to say something that made her smile.

Mother Superior turned away, feeling very much like an intruder.

8

"Look at them, Reverend Mother." Sister Fiona paused in the arched doorway to stare at the young couple working side by side in the garden. "It does my heart good to see them so happy." She sighed. "And so in love."

"Aye." The older nun nodded.

There was no denying it. The transformation in Alexa and Jamie was amazing to all who saw them. The sound of their laughter couldn't help but lift every heart at the abbey. The sight of them, shyly holding hands as they walked the garden path after their evening meal, had the nuns and novices openly smiling. Especially when they recalled how wounded these two had been such a short time ago. Now that they had heard the tale of the lass's painful loss of family, they were even more amazed that she had emerged into the light.

Mother Mary of the Cross glanced

around approvingly. The gardens had never looked better. There were dahlias as large as serving platters, in every color imaginable, and behind them, in stately rows, snapdragons as tall as a man. Some beds were overflowing with bright yellow and orange nasturtiums, while others boasted pale pink verbena and deep purple foxglove.

Even the walls were abloom with color. Pink and white sweet peas and vibrant purple wisteria snaked along the stones and spilled over the top, filling every available space with fragrant blossoms.

It was as though the flowers, like the people who resided in the abbey, were basking in the luminous glow that emanated from these two lovers.

While he worked beside her, Jamie paused and tried to keep the excitement from his voice. "Do you know what I love best about this garden?"

"What?" Alexa looked up.

"The knowledge that it brought us together. First as a refuge from the world, and later as proof that there can still be peace and beauty in a world torn apart by battle."

She smiled. "It's true. This is our world now, Jamie."

Something about the way she said it had him shaking his head. " 'Tis only a brief respite, my love. Our world still awaits us, out there." He pointed toward the distant forest. "There in the Highlands is my home. My people. Now that I'm well and strong again, I long to be with them. I want you to go with me and accept them as your people, too, Alexa."

She went very still. Seeing it, Jamie dropped to his knees beside her. "Forgive me, love. I'd meant to set a more solemn tone when I asked you. But you must admit that we've been here long enough to heal our bodies and souls. Now it's time to return to the real world. I've already sent a message to my people, letting them know that I'm alive and well and strong enough to return to lead them. I want you to return with me, Alexa, as my bride. I hope I'm not too bold to ask that you marry me, my love, and return with me to the Highlands where we'll make our home together."

"Make a home in the Highlands?" The hand tool dropped from Alexa's fingers. She seemed unaware as she got to her feet. "I thought this was our home now, Jamie."

He stood beside her, too happy to note her little frown. "This is an abbey, love. It was a fine refuge while we recovered from our wounds. Now we must get on with our lives. Since you no longer have a clan of your own, I offer you mine. My people will love you as I do."

As he gathered her close he heard her sudden sigh of distress and held her a little away from him. "What is it, Alexa?"

"I thought you understood. I can't possibly leave here."

"Why not?"

"Because I took a vow. Because" — she looked around wildly, her mind awhirl with sudden fear — "my task here is not yet complete." At his puzzled look she knelt and retrieved something from the ground. "You see? How can I leave when this has happened again?"

"What has happened?"

"This." She opened her hand to reveal several shriveled rosebuds. "There's a blight. No matter what I do, they refuse to open. Instead the buds fall off and die."

He laughed. "Then we'll pull out the roses and replace them with something else. Something that will fill the garden with glorious blooms."

"Nay." She shook her head vigorously. "The roses must be here, in the center of the garden."

He tried to rein in his impatience. "Why must they?"

"Because." She lowered her head, avoiding his eyes. "What is a garden, after all, without roses?"

He lifted her chin. "Such a simple problem as this shouldn't upset you so. What is it you're not telling me, love?"

She pulled away, again avoiding his eyes. "There must be roses here. Without them the garden isn't complete."

He spread his hands. "Look around you, Alexa. See what you've accomplished. Without you, this would still be barren earth and tumbled stones. Thanks to you, the abbey's garden is once more a place of beauty and serenity. Why can't you simply enjoy what you've done and replace the roses with something that will thrive?"

"You don't understand." She looked up, and her eyes glittered with unshed tears. "I see the garden as it once was."

"You see it?"

She nodded, afraid he would think her mad, yet needing to admit the truth. "Each time I close my eyes, I see the garden as it was a hundred years ago. It . . . haunts my dreams. As do Lady Anne and her sadness."

"I see." Jamie drew her close and felt her shiver. "No wonder you were so withdrawn from the world, love. By day you were back on the field of battle, and by night you were thrust into the distant past. But what about the present, Alexa? And the future? Our future, together?"

She took a deep breath. "I know not, Jamie. I know only that I have given my word to Lady Anne that I will restore the gardens to their former beauty. That way, she will have a measure of comfort while she is confined to this earthly prison. Furthermore, I took a vow before Father Lazarus." She gave a deep sigh. "So you see, I cannot leave here until the roses are brought to bloom, or I would be breaking my vow."

"And if my men come for me and the roses have not yet bloomed? What then, Alexa? Will you send me away alone?"

She swallowed. "If I must."

Jamie's eyes narrowed. "Are you saying that you love this garden more than you love me?"

"Nay." She clenched her hands at her sides, to keep from reaching out to him. "I will never love anyone or anything as much as I love you, Jamie Morgan. But I made a vow."

"Vows can be broken."

She shook her head. "Nay. I gave my word to Lady Anne."

"Your word to a ghost is more important than your love for me?"

"You don't understand."

"I understand this: You feel safe here, Alexa. This place offers you peace, and beauty, and a refuge from the reality of life beyond these walls. The life I offer you is one of hard work and strife, and yes, possibly war. But I also offer you undying love. Can there be anything more important in life than that?"

When she remained silent, he said, "Heed my word, Alexa. The women here, both those alive and the one whose spirit walks the garden, can never love you as I do. Nor can these flowers."

"You sound as though" — she blinked furiously to hold back the tears that burned her lids — "you intend to leave with or without me."

"My people look to me to lead, Alexa. When my men come for me, I must leave with them. Though my heart will be heavy, I will abide by your decision."

She lifted her chin, as determined as he not to back down. "I love you, Jamie. Only you. I would be proud to make your people my people, but only if my task here is complete. I gave my word to Lady Anne, to restore her gardens exactly as they were when she first walked them."

His tone rang with challenge. "If the roses bloom, will you take that as a sign that your task here is complete? Or will you find another excuse to hide from the world?"

"Is that what you think? That I'm using my vow to keep me here?"

His voice lowered. "I ask again, Alexa. If the roses bloom, will you go with me?"

She nodded.

"And if they should not?"

She shook her head and turned away, unwilling to let him see the tears she could no longer hold back.

For long minutes he stood watching. Then he turned away and strode through the arched doorway, his booted feet echoing in the silence of the abbey.

Word of the lovers' disagreement swept through the halls of the abbey, casting a pall over everyone's joy. Throughout the days that followed, the nuns and novices watched as the roses continued to shrivel and die.

Each day Jamie walked to the garden with eager expectancy. Each day, as Alexa knelt in the soil to retrieve the latest fallen rosebuds, he turned away with a look of such sadness, it tore at the hearts of all who saw him.

Too soon, word of a procession of Highland warriors approaching their village swept through the abbey. As always, it was the novice, Mordrund, who first heard the news and carried it to the others.

"Giants they are," she reported to her superior. "And so fair of face that all the maidens are weeping with joy."

Mother Mary of the Cross shoved away from her desk and started toward the door, saying dryly, "I'm sure we'll be able to maintain our composure at the sight of them, Mordrund. Go and inform the laird that his clansmen approach."

"Aye, Reverend Mother."

By the time the line of warriors arrived at the gates, the nuns and novices had assembled in the courtyard, along with Alexa. Jamie rushed forward to welcome his kinsmen. When he caught sight of their leader he gave a shout of delight.

"Duncan. By all that is holy, is it truly you?"

The two men fell together in a fierce embrace before laughing and stepping apart.

"I'd feared that you were lost to me, Duncan."

"Aye, Jamie lad. I'd feared the same, for my wounds were grave, but a kind family took me in and nursed me back to health. I made my way back to the Highlands only a fortnight ago. When we got your missive that you were alive, there was great rejoicing, for we'd feared the worst."

Jamie turned to Alexa. "This is my oldest and dearest friend, Duncan MacKay." His tone softened. "Duncan, this lovely creature is Alexa MacCallum."

Duncan bowed before her and saw the way she shrank back from him. "I realize I look a bit wild, my lady. We all do." He swept a hand to include the other warriors, who still sat astride their mounts. "We've come a long way to fetch our laird home."

To smooth over the awkward moment, the head of the abbey stepped forward. "I am Mother Mary of the Cross, the superior here. You and your men are most welcome to refresh yourselves for as long as you please before you return to the Highlands. We have a meal ready in the refectory, and Father Lazarus has added pallets on the floor of the chapel for your nightly comfort."

"My men and I thank you for your kindness, Reverend Mother." Duncan threw an arm around his old friend. "Will you join us in the refectory?"

"Aye."

As Jamie was surrounded by his clansmen, he tried to draw Alexa into their circle. She backed away from him and fled to the garden.

He kept his smile in place as he greeted

his old friends and walked with them into the abbey, but his thoughts were on the lass who, like a motherless fawn, was trying to find her way in a frightening new world.

Supper was a grand affair, with much shouting and laughter as the men washed away the grime of the journey with ale provided by Father Lazarus.

Jamie sat at a table with his men, while Alexa sat with the women in a small alcove to one side, since it wasn't considered proper for the nuns to be seated in the company of raucous warriors.

"Will we leave on the morrow?" Duncan asked.

Jamie glanced toward the table where Alexa was seated. "I . . . would think you would desire some rest before you undertake the return to the Highlands."

"There's no time to be wasted, Jamie. There is much disarray among our people." Duncan emptied his goblet, more than a little surprised at the quality of ale at the abbey. He was even more surprised when the elderly priest produced a second jug as soon as the first one was emptied.

Duncan refilled his goblet and drank deeply. "There are some who claim that you aren't really alive. They claim that your friends are trying to hide your death from them in order to keep the clans together. There are even a few who whisper among themselves that it is time to appoint a new laird from among the remaining warriors. I would advise you to leave at first light, Jamie, in order to stop the rumors and assure peace in our Highlands."

Jamie digested this news before giving a grudging nod of his head. "I hadn't realized the seriousness of the situation. You're right, of course, my friend. We'll leave at first light."

He saw Alexa excuse herself and knew that she was going to the garden. Though he still felt a small measure of hope, there was a heaviness in his heart, for he'd seen that same look on her face before, and he knew that she intended to keep her promise to Lady Anne. No matter what the cost.

All the lights of the abbey had been extinguished. From the chapel came the rumble of snoring as the Highland warriors slept.

Jamie stepped through the arched doorway. The garden was bathed in moonlight, giving the flowers, the trees, even the stone benches, a luminous quality. The air was sweet with the perfume of hundreds of flowers.

He took no notice of the beauty of the place, however. Instead he crossed directly to where Alexa stood studying the roses in the middle of the garden. Seeing the look on her face, he felt a hard, quick tug at his heart.

"They continue to die?"

She nodded and held out her hand. "The latest buds have already begun to shrivel." She couldn't keep the pain from her voice. "By morning they'll be littering the ground like all the others."

He absorbed the blow at the knowledge that he would be returning to the Highlands alone. His heart lay like a stone in his chest as he gathered her into the circle of his arms.

Against his throat she whispered, "I can't bear the thought of your leaving, Jamie."

Heat pulsed through his veins at the warmth of her breath against his skin. "Then come with me, Alexa. It's the only thing I'll ever ask of you."

"Don't do this, my love. You know I can't do as you ask. A solemn vow once made cannot be broken on a whim."

"You call our love a whim?" His voice was made deep with pain. "You were a gift to me, Alexa. A very special gift. Because of you I'm healed in body and mind. Now, because of a vow made to a lost, tormented soul, you would condemn us both to a life of loneliness." He couldn't hide the bitterness in his tone. "Could this be why she remains here? To see that other lovers are denied the happiness she denied herself?"

"Is that what you think? That she somehow extracted a promise from me in order to bind me to her?"

"Can you think of another reason?"

Alexa lifted brimming eyes to his. "I'm so weary of thinking, Jamie. So weary." She touched a fingertip to his mouth and saw the blaze of desire flare in his eyes. "If we can't have a lifetime, at least we can have tonight."

"It will only make the parting that much more painful on the morrow."

She shook her head. "I care not about tomorrow. I need you now. This night."

He framed her face with his hands and covered her mouth with his. Against her lips he muttered, "How could I refuse you, my love?"

He kissed her long and slow and deep, until they nearly wept with need. Then lifting her into his arms he strode across the garden and carried her to his room.

As the couple disappeared through the arched doorway, a shimmering figure appeared in the garden.

As always, she climbed the stone steps to the top of the wall, where, as she had for a hundred years, she stared off into the distance, her expression a mixture of hope and despair.

9

Thin ribbons of dawn light streaked the sky as the Highland warriors trooped out of the chapel and began the preparations for the journey home. The courtyard of the abbey rang with shouts as horses were saddled and provisions were loaded in wagons.

Alexa choked back tears as Jamie wound the plaid about his shoulders and reached for his sword and dirk.

All night there had been such urgency, such passion to their lovemaking. A passion born of desperation. The knowledge that this was to be their last time had them clinging to one another as though to life itself.

His face was devoid of emotion as he turned to her. "Will you walk with me to the courtyard?"

"Aye." Though she dreaded the thought of the entire assembly witnessing their good-bye, she knew it would be cowardly to hide here in his room. He deserved the same courage from her that he'd shown on the field of battle. And so she reached for his outstretched hand and moved woodenly along beside him.

"Will we stop first in the garden?"

She glanced at the still-darkened sky before reluctantly shaking her head. "It will only add to the pain of our farewell."

"I suppose." He walked with her into the courtyard.

The Highlanders stood beside their horses, awaiting their laird. When they caught sight of him, their voices grew hushed, for they had heard of his painful dilemma. The love between him and the lass, and the vow that would now separate them, was all that was being discussed in the abbey. Even the old priest had spoken of it.

The sisters, too, fell silent at the sight of Jamie and Alexa, heads high, staring straight ahead as they made their way among the waiting men.

Duncan was holding the reins of two horses. As Jamie approached, his friend handed him the reins to a magnificent black stallion. It occurred to Alexa that the animal suited the man. Both looked a bit untamed, and more than prepared for whatever task lay before them.

She touched a hand to Jamie's arm, determined to get through this with as much dignity as she could. "Good-bye, Jamie Morgan. Godspeed."

He didn't touch her. Couldn't. For he knew if he did, he would surely take her in his arms and force her to accompany him, and to hell with her solemn vow. But now, as he had with the fawn of his childhood, he must let go and take comfort in the knowledge that she would be with her own kind.

"Farewell, Alexa MacCallum. I'll never forget you."

He pulled himself into the saddle and stared straight ahead as Mother Superior stepped to the head of the column of Highlanders and lifted her hand in a blessing.

Before she could speak the words, there was a shout. Everyone turned as the young novice, Mordrund, came rushing into the courtyard, her skirts hiked up in a most unladylike fashion, her chest heaving from the exertion of her run.

Reverend Mother's eyes flashed in a rare display of anger. "You will take yourself to the chapel, Mordrund, and pray for the humility befitting a servant of the Lord."

"Aye, Reverend Mother. I shall. As soon as I tell you . . ."

"Now." Mother Mary of the Cross could

feel her patience snap. "Can you not see how difficult this moment is for all of us? I'll not have it made worse by your impertinence. Now leave us."

"I will, Reverend Mother. But first . . ." The poor novice looked from her superior to the laird seated upon his steed, and then to the lass, who was close to tears. "I must tell you that a miracle has occurred in the garden."

"A miracle?" Reverend Mother's head came up sharply. "What are you saying, Mordrund?"

"The roses are abloom! Not just a few, but dozens of them."

For the space of a heartbeat there was complete silence at her announcement. Then, as her words sank in, there seemed to be complete chaos. While the sisters ran ahead, Jamie scooped Alexa into his arms and turned his mount toward an opening in the wall, with the Highlanders following on their steeds.

"Oh, my sweet heaven." Alexa clapped a hand to her mouth as she stared at the rosebushes, bathed in streams of morning sunlight in the middle of the garden.

Where only last night there had been shriveled buds, there were now dozens, perhaps hundreds of perfect blooms.

"Do you know what this means, my love?" Jamie brought his lips to her temple.

"Aye. It is as young Mordrund said. A miracle. A sign that my work here is finished."

"You're prepared to come with me to my Highland fortress, my love? Now? This very hour?"

"I will. Oh, Jamie. I know now that what you said was true. I've been hiding out here, lost and afraid. Now, though I'm still afraid of the world beyond these walls, I'm even more afraid of life without you. I need you, Jamie. Only you. And I love you so." She wound her arms around his neck and hugged him fiercely. "I feel so useless. I have nothing to bring with me, for I came here with nothing."

"You'll bring everything that matters, Alexa. Your sweetness, your goodness, your love." He lifted his voice. "Reverend Mother, give us your blessing, for we must leave you now and return to our home."

"Home." At the sound of that word Alexa began to weep. Softly at first, and then more openly, as she realized the enormity of what had just occurred. "I had no home to return to, Jamie. No clan to call my own. And now I will have both."

"Aye. And I'll have the woman I love beside me always."

As silence settled over the crowd, Reverend Mother's voice rose above the sigh of the wind. "Go with God, Laird Jamie Morgan and Alexa MacCallum. We hope you will think of us from time to time. And when you do, we hope you will whisper a prayer. For the two of you will be in our hearts and our prayers forever. Each time we walk our beautiful garden, we will think of you and remember the time you spent here."

Mordrund came bounding forward. "Shall I pick you a bouquet of roses for your journey, Alexa?"

Before she could reply Duncan shouted, "There's no time, my laird. We must leave now."

Alexa smiled at the little novice. "I thank you, Mordrund. But the memory of all those lovely roses will be enough for me. I leave the blooms for all of you to enjoy in my stead."

Jamie wheeled his mount, and a great shout went up from his men as they followed their laird through the courtyard and up the grassy meadow beyond.

Atop a hill Jamie reined in his mount for a final look at the place that had brought them both healing and love. Then, with matching smiles, they turned toward home.

As the Highlanders disappeared into the mist, the sisters hurried to chapel to pray for a safe journey.

Reverend Mother was just turning away to follow when Mordrund called to her. "Reverend Mother, you must come at once."

The old sister gave a sigh. "What is it now, Mordrund?"

"Look, Reverend Mother." The young novice pointed to the rosebushes, where a breeze was causing the blossoms to blow about. She lifted her hand and caught hold of one.

"It's perfect," Mother Mary of the Cross said.

"Aye, Reverend Mother. But feel it."

As the novice pressed the blossom into her hand, the old nun gave a gasp of surprise. "What is this?"

"Parchment, Reverend Mother."

"What are you saying?" She held it up to the sunlight and could see that it was indeed made of parchment. She reached for another, and yet another. Some were made of parchment, others of cloth. Each had been perfectly painted to resemble a rose. "But how can this be? Who . . . ?"

Mordrund pointed, and Reverend Mother looked up to see Lady Anne on the top step of

379

the wall, holding out her arms. As they watched in wonder, they saw a warrior coming for her on a golden cloud. With a shout of triumph he gathered her close, and as they embraced, they shimmered with a blinding light before disappearing from sight.

The old nun and the young novice stood transfixed, watching until the vision dissolved.

Mother Superior's voice was hushed. "What we have witnessed this day is truly a miracle. Lady Anne has finally learned the truth. When her gifts were used for purely unselfish reasons, she was set free of the bonds of this world. Free at last to be with her warrior for eternity."

"What of Alexa and the laird?" The little novice seemed genuinely concerned. "Should we not send word of the truth?"

"What is the truth, Mordrund? Did not the roses bloom, thus freeing our Alexa from her vow?"

"Aye, Reverend Mother."

The old woman's eyes burned with inner fire. "The love we saw between a wounded laird and lass was quite extraordinary. Such a love is rarely found. When it is, nothing should be allowed to stand in the way of love's special healing. We are, after all, healers, are we not?"

"Aye, Reverend Mother."

"Come, then, Mordrund. Let us join the others at chapel and praise heaven for the miracle of healing granted this day."

The little novice dutifully followed her superior to chapel. Though she prayed that she would one day learn to curb her tongue, it wasn't to be. Only two women witnessed Lady Anne flying into the heavens with her warrior, and from the lips of one, the story was passed from village to town until it became a legend.

In the Highlands, the laird of lairds wed his beloved before his entire clan. It is said they raised up many fair sons and daughters. Though all were trained as warriors, their true task on earth was to preserve the peace among all clans in the Highlands.

All who knew them said that their love blazed so brightly even death could not extinguish it. To this day, each time the roses bloom in the garden of the Abbey of Glenross, it is seen as proof that the love of Jamie and Alexa, like the love of Lady Anne and her warrior, Malcolm, endures for all time.

The
Fairest Rose

Marianne Willman

To Nora, Ruth and Jan,
the fairest roses of them all

Prologue

"Today my true love returns home to my arms!"

Deirdre smiled before the small looking glass on her cottage wall. She'd dressed her dark hair with wild pink roses that she'd plucked from the riverbank, still fresh with morning dew, and a length of silver ribbon the same shade as her clear gray eyes. Her lover had bought it for her at the Beltane fair.

A ring of hammered gold circled her finger, gleaming in the warm morning light. He'd placed it there at midnight, to symbolize their vows to one another: In the midst of war, there had been no time for priests and marriage bans. They had pledged their love in the ways of old, by clasping hands and leaping together over the sacred Beltane fire. Afterward, they had lain together in the sweet scented grass and whispered their undying love while the stars danced overhead.

She smoothed the blue fabric she'd woven herself over her swollen belly. Nine long months had passed since that magical night. Soon she would bear the fruit of their love. The precious babe within her womb would be born before the moon came full.

Ah, Gilmore! What a happy surprise you'll have when you learn of it.

He had answered the call to arms and ridden into battle with his loyal followers, not knowing that he had fathered a child. Those had been lonely and terrible times for her. Months of fear, endless rumors of defeat and banishment. Or worse.

She shivered, remembering. Indeed, for the last month she'd fought dark despair. The news from the war had been bad, and she'd feared for Gilmore's life. Then, as she stood by the beckoning river seven nights ago, she'd seen something blaze across the night: a shimmering golden bird that left glittering trails of jeweled light against the midnight sky.

She had recognized it at once: the mystical phoenix, symbol of eternal life and beauty. Legend said the magical bird lived in the high reaches of the Misted Mountains, an enchanted no-man's-land between Airan and the borders of the Eastern Lands. Some debated whether the creature existed at all.

The occasional sightings, they claimed, were of falling stars, such as could be seen on any summer night.

But she had seen it, soaring and shining brighter than the stars. She'd taken it as an omen, for the phoenix was Gilmore's emblem. She'd known then that he would return to her in triumph.

Her instincts had proved right. The very next day the countryside had rung with the news of his victory. He'd rallied the troops and won the day with his fierce courage, and had been rewarded for it with the highest honor. Where before he had been a landless knight, Gilmore was now king of Airan.

Her lover had always been ambitious, and she had championed his dreams of uniting the country — but she had never imagined it would come to this! Some even whispered that he would be named High King of All the Western Lands when the clans met again. He'd been crowned upon the battlefield, with all the nobles and their allies pledging support. Only the stubborn men of Far Islandia had refused to bend their knees and take the oath of allegiance.

As Deirdre was tucking the last of the fragrant roses into the silver ribbon, she heard it: the song of golden-throated bugles announcing the arrival of the new king.

Her heart gave a leap of joy. She raced out of the cottage, her lovely face radiant. Nothing could be seen of Gilmore and his soldiers yet, except the cloud of dust churned up by the approaching cavalcade.

Movement closer by caught her eye. It was Elva, the wisewoman who made simples and remedies for the village. She came out of the deep woods, thin as a birch stick in her light gray gown. There was a basket of fresh-gathered herbs and medicinal plants over her arm, smelling of green forest and damp summer earth.

She turned to greet Deirdre, a slight frown between large eyes as dark as peat. For a moment a shadow seemed to sweep across Deirdre, as if a great black bird had flown between her and the sun.

"You should not run so near your term, mistress. You must save your strength for what is to come."

"Indeed, my feet have wings today. Gilmore has returned to Airan," Deirdre said. "He has come for me. For *us*."

She looked dreamily across the river, to Castle Airan. It rose above the rushing water, all white towers and turrets and crumbled stone walls. Soon Gilmore's phoenix pennant would fly there. And they would live out their lives together in happiness, with this child she carried, and all their children to come.

It seemed like a fairy tale, too astonishing, too good to be true.

She turned and smiled down the road. Already she could see Gilmore's banner topping the rise: a golden phoenix on a ground of royal blue. Deirdre's heart was so full the joy spilled over in tears of happiness.

A moment later the colorful cavalcade poured through the dark gap in the rolling hills and down into the river valley. The breeze carried faint sounds to them: the jingle of harness, the rumble of hooves, and the creaking moan of treasure-burdened wagons. Down the dusty road the villagers were hurrying out of their cottages to greet the victors, but Deirdre waited patiently at her gate for her lover.

First came the outriders, with their festive banners, then Gilmore's private guard in their dark blue tabards, his phoenix insignia embroidered with gold thread upon them. Then he was there, Gilmore himself, on a prancing white steed with a golden bridle. He was so splendid she hardly recognized him. A cloak of crimson velvet hung from his wide shoulders, and his tunic was woven of cloth of gold. The glinting coronet upon his thick red hair was centered with a sapphire that was no bluer than his eyes. Deirdre's heart stood still with love for him.

"Your father," she whispered to the child within her womb.

He reined in as he reached the curve before the cottage and slowed his horse to a walk, frowning slightly. *He is looking for me among the throng,* she thought. What a surprise he will get!

"Gilmore!" Her face shone, and she lifted her arms in greeting as he pulled abreast of her.

But the young king kept his handsome head high and his gaze straight ahead as he rode past in his newfound glory. Not so much as a single glance did he cast her way.

Deirdre was stunned. Why hadn't he stopped? Why hadn't he acknowledged her? She was hand-fasted to him, as much his wife as if they'd exchanged vows before the high altar.

Then Deirdre saw what she hadn't noticed before: A woman rode beside him. She was gowned in cloth of gold, with a cloak of emerald satin, and a thin gold circlet rested low on her brow. Her skin was white as milk, her hair and eyes as gold as coins; but her beautiful face was hard with arrogance, and her red mouth a disdainful slash.

As she passed Deirdre her golden eyes

narrowed as if in recognition. Her gaze was cold and dagger-sharp. Deirdre staggered back in pain, as if she had been impaled on a poisoned blade. Although the sun was hot, she felt a darkness filling her chest, congealing her blood. It thickened and slowed in her veins.

While she stood frozen to the spot, the line of soldiers and wagons rumbled by. Elva stepped out to accost one of the men-at-arms who was her kinsman. He pulled over at the roadside.

"God save you, cousin. Who is the woman riding at Gilmore's side?" she asked.

"Why, that is Bryn, daughter of wily Monfort."

"But Monfort is our sworn enemy," Elva said.

"No longer," her kinsman said. "They have signed an accord and sealed it in blood." He made a grimace of distaste. "The Lady Bryn is now queen of this land. She and Gilmore were wed in high ceremony, before all."

Deirdre heard, and the words slammed into her, almost knocking her off her feet. The man rode on to join the rest, but it seemed to her that it happened in total silence. Her ears went deaf to the glad shouts, her eyes blind to the bright summer sky and the green hills spilling down to the winding river. She stumbled back toward the cottage.

Elva saw. She caught Deirdre's arm and guided her inside. "Lie down upon your bed beneath the warm blankets. Your skin is like ice!"

Deirdre stared at her blankly. "He did not stop. He did not so much as acknowledge me!"

Elva's black eyes filled with anger. And fear. "Gilmore has not abandoned you — he has forgotten you."

"How could he do so? We grew up together in this valley, playing beneath the castle walls. He has had my heart since I was a mere child, and I, his."

"Do not judge him too harshly. His new queen has cast a spell upon him. I know a wicked sorceress when I see one!"

"There must be some way to break the spell." Deirdre's eyes welled up with tears. "You know the ancient arts. Can you not find a way to free Gilmore from the enchantment of this sorceress?"

The wisewoman shook her head. "I know the healing ways, and the charms to draw love, or make crops bloom with abundance. But I have never studied evil. She has, and her power is too great for such as me."

Suddenly Deirdre doubled over. The birth pang caught her by surprise, and her silver-blue eyes glazed with pain. With fear. "Ah, no! Not yet."

But the babe within her was eager to be born. It would not be denied.

Elva helped her to the bed and prepared for the confinement. It was not long at all before the child came, a girl, small and vulnerable, born into a world that was hostile to her. Exhausted, Deirdre lay back against her pillow. She sipped the wild cherry cordial that Elva held to her lips, but it gave her no strength or warmth. Her thoughts were only for her newborn daughter, nestled in her arms. She smoothed the soft, dark auburn curls, caressed the velvet cheek, and marveled at the tiny fingers wrapped around her own.

But even as she felt the heat of that small body nestled against hers, her own grew increasingly colder. She saw the sorrow in Elva's eyes. Knowledge of what was to come burdened her gentle soul.

"Elva, I know I am beyond your help — I knew my fate the moment that woman looked at me with such hatred. She has cast a curse upon me, and my hours on earth are numbered. But what of my daughter? Can you save her, at least?"

Elva hesitated, remembering. "Once upon

a time, when I was very young, I was told the Spell of Forgetting. Perhaps I can use it against Bryn's curse, turn it inside out upon itself to suit our purpose. If only I can recall it now."

She struggled to dredge it up from the depths of memory. But true to its name, the spell kept sliding away from her, as if it were mist. A bit here, another there. Shifting, shifting. She began to fear it was beyond her reach.

Elva threw herself back in time, past her memory and her mother's memory, into the realm of long ago. Her dark eyes went flat and opaque. Then her breath came out in a sigh of relief, and the corners of her wide mouth turned up in triumph.

"I have it now! I know what I must do."

If only she could bring it all together. The old woman who had been her mentor had passed on before she could share all her accumulated wisdom.

She smoothed the damp hair back from Deirdre's cold cheeks. "Rest for a while," Elva told her. "I must fashion an amulet."

"Keep her safe for me," Deirdre whispered. She felt the cold and dark closing in with every beat of her heart.

"I shall," Elva said fiercely. "I swear it."

She hurried from the cottage. Time was

running out. The distant hills shimmered with misty rain, but the river still lay in dappled sunlight. The water shone gold and brown and silver, singing softly as it rushed down to the sea. She plucked green moss from the rocks along the verge.

The wisewoman's fingers moved in a blur of speed while she murmured ancient words in a low, sweet voice. She wove the strands of dark moss into a slender chain. It changed to gleaming silver in her hands.

Next, she reached into the rippling stream and brought a quartz pebble from among the water weeds. It was oval and clear as glass. "Ah! Perfect!"

Elva held the pebble high, toward the rainbow that now arced across the far hills, and murmured another phrase in the language that few mortals remembered. The rainbow vanished from the sky and reappeared as shifting planes of dancing color within the stone's transparent heart.

The crystal grew warm in her hand. Her spirits soared. Yet she must not grow overconfident. There was more she must do to bind the spell.

Back in the cottage, she saw that both mother and child were asleep. It was better so. Her skills might fail them yet. Elva pushed the thought away.

Taking one of the wild roses discarded from Deirdre's hair, she pulled the petals loose and wrapped them around the shining stone with trembling fingers. She smoothed each one carefully in place. Then she caught the single tear that trembled on Deirdre's dark lashes and the tiny tear that lingered at the side of the infant's closed eye.

As the tears mingled and fell upon the petal-wrapped stone, it was instantly transformed. The crumpled petals turned smooth and glossy. Their color deepened until they were red as heart's blood.

Elva closed her eyes and lifted her head, then threw off the protective barriers of self, became open and defenseless, naked to the universe. "I command the Power of Good and summon it to this place. Hear me!"

For a moment she seemed to be tumbling head over heels through the air. Then she felt it stirring around her, like a summer breeze through the trees. The power grew and shook her as if she were a leaf in a storm.

Sweat broke out on her forehead and her breathing grew labored. Taking the silver chain with its amulet, she wrapped it around the wrists of mother and child so it bound them together.

"By the Power of Heaven and the Power

of Good, by the magic of earth and water, wind and fire, I weave the Spell of Forgetting. May this amulet protect against all who would do you harm. May only those who wish you well remember you. May you be kept safe until one day a hero comes, a man with a noble heart that beats to the rhythm of yours, and a soul as true and passionate as your own. Then, and only then shall this spell I have woven, unravel."

Something jolted through her, like a lightning blast. A torrent of sunbeams poured through the small cottage windows, bathing the room in a powerful crystalline light. It haloed the sleeping mother and child in the bed. Then the air blazed a rich, vibrant gold. Elva had to blink her eyes and turn away from what was an almost painful radiance. Her heart hammered with excitement.

The brightness vanished as suddenly as it had come, but she was so dazzled it took a moment before her vision cleared. When it did, the sun had sunk behind the hills, plunging the room into twilight.

Nothing else seemed to have changed at all.

Elva leaned back in the chair, completely drained.

Had the phenomenon been a true response to her summons, or merely a trick of the eye, caused by the angle of the setting sun? Only time would tell.

While the baby slept and Elva watched, Deirdre dreamed. Of Beltane, and a red-haired man who smiled down at her with love in his eyes. Of a glittering golden bird that streaked like a comet across the dark night sky, aflame with light.

She took wing and followed it, soaring up among the stars.

1

Tor reined in his mount beneath an ancient oak and waited for his companion to catch up with him. The twisted silver torque around his throat gleamed in the half-light of the grove, and his eyes — as jet-black as his long, thick hair — shone with bold resolve.

The light breeze sighed through the oak leaves and brushed like tasseled silk against his sun-bronzed cheek. The cool green dimness was welcome after his hard ride, but rest was not his goal. That lay on the far side of the river.

Castle Airan.

There it rose, beyond the river's green verge, like a sorcerer's illusion. Soaring white towers and crenellated battlements burned bright against the deep-blue summer sky. For a moment Tor was dazzled by it.

He'd journeyed long and far to reach this place. He only hoped it would prove worth his while. His gloved hands gripped the reins tightly.

He would make it so.

Dismounting lightly, he tied his horse by the little stream that flowed down to the river, and rubbed it down. Once his mount was settled, Tor removed a cloak from his saddlepack. It was of wool, finely woven and as dark as the heart of a forest. He fastened it in place with a simple bronze ornament, set with polished agate.

Another rider entered the oak grove and reined in beside him. He was a grizzled warrior, with hard blue eyes and leathered skin. A third horse was tied behind his, a noble creature with a restive manner.

"Why do you stop?" the man said. "The castle is across the river."

"We'll leave our horses here, Broch, and go afoot."

"And likely come back to find them gone," his companion said darkly. "I don't like this place. There might be thieves lurking about. Or trolls. They steal travelers' horses. Airan is said to be thick with them."

Tor laughed. "I don't believe in trolls. No one I know — including you — has ever seen one."

"Well, I've seen enough thieves in my time." Broch eyed the grove as if one thief might be lurking behind each massive trunk.

"Enough of your grumbling," Tor told him. "The beasts will be safe enough here in the grove. Look how their dark coats blend into the shadows."

He rubbed the nose of the third horse, and it whickered softly. "As for the thieves and cutpurses who prey on crowds, they will be too busy fleecing the fine lords and ladies to bother with us."

Broch shot him a mistrustful look. "You're a deep one. I wish I knew what deviltry you are up to."

Tor turned away hiding his smile. "If I told you, you'd throw me into the river!"

"I may do it anyway."

"Don't worry, old friend. You'll know soon enough."

Tor's laughter died away and his face grew sober. He stood with arms akimbo, eyes on the bright banners flying from the castle ramparts. Each blue pennant was emblazoned with the insignia of a golden bird.

It was a familiar symbol in the Western Lands: the rising phoenix was the emblem of Gilmore of Glendon, a man who had risked all in a desperate battle — and had won himself a kingdom by his wits and skill. Although there were some who felt another warrior had had more right to Airan's crown.

"Airan is a place where dreams can come true," Tor said, "if a man only dares to risk enough!"

Broch swung down beside him. He patted his mount and went to the other horse they'd brought with them, grumbling the whole time.

"I'm a highlander. I've no use for Airan. The mountains are too low, and the sky is too far above to suit my tastes."

Tor shook his head. "By the gods! I swear you'd find fault with heaven." Taking down the worn leather case that held his harp, he slung it over his shoulder.

The other man eyed it suspiciously. "Can you even play that harp?"

"Aye, you sorry doubter! And sing like an angel, too." Tor's wide grin was back. "Come, Broch. Destiny awaits us!"

"Or the dungeon."

"Not if I succeed, my friend. Try and have a little faith in me."

"You have enough for both of us. I pray it's not misplaced."

"You, pray?" Tor slapped the old warrior on the shoulder. "I'd give half my purse of coins to see it."

With the horses hidden deep inside the ancient grove, they crossed the meadows and the stone bridge that spanned the river, joining the others thronging in through the castle gates.

The great outer courtyard had been cleared of its usual hucksters and clutter, but it was crowded with people. There were minor dignitaries, wealthy merchants, and their wives at the back.

Nearer the wide stone steps to the inner court, Tor saw, were ranks of princes and lords in bright silks and velvets, their household retainers in gold-threaded tabards, and burly men-at-arms with the glint of chain mail beneath their tunics. He found a space near the back wall and claimed it. The few who started to protest took one look at his wide shoulders and determined face and held their peace.

Broch glanced around. "Fah! I've never seen so many strutting peacocks," he said in disdain. "We have no place among them."

"Not yet."

Broch stared. "I mislike it when you speak in riddles."

"You'd like it even less if you knew what I have in mind."

"By the Great Dragon, you try my patience. I've half a mind to knock you on the head and carry you out over my shoulder."

"I wouldn't try it," Tor said with a hint of steel in his voice.

"Well, I wouldn't waste my breath. You've a head as hard as granite."

A small smile curved Tor's firm mouth, but his dark eyes were unreadable. He folded his arms across his chest and leaned against the sun-warmed stone.

Up on one of the parapets, a young woman of eighteen summers peeked down at the scene below. She was called Mouse, although her hair was not dull brown but a rich, dark auburn, and her dark-lashed eyes were the same sparkling silver-blue as the sea that pounded Airan's western shores.

Mouse was the youngest of the castle's weavers, and as quiet as her namesake. No one had called her by her given name in many years. Indeed, she doubted that any even remembered it.

Someone jostled her, and she looked up.

"Oh, it's you, Mouse. I didn't notice you there." It was Luce, a bold and pretty girl who worked in the spinning room, making yarn for the looms. Mouse moved to make room for her.

Luce leaned against the rail, her long yellow braids dangling over it. "Well, well. A fine lot of likely lads," she announced, and busied herself happily in ogling the men below.

A few ogled her back. Luce was a pretty,

slender girl. With her full bosom and the enticing swing to her walk, she attracted men's attention wherever she went — but Mouse was used to going about unnoticed. At times, she thought, it was almost as if she were invisible.

Mostly she was glad of it. If no handsome youth brought her flowers and fairings, or asked her to walk out among the summer meadows, neither did she have to fear being accosted by some amorous knave. Not even the off-duty soldiers, who flirted with the serving wenches and bawdy laundresses, called out to Mouse to dally a while.

At least it gives me the freedom to wander about at my will when my work is done, she consoled herself. Mouse knew the maze of corridors and the hidden courtyards within the castle's great curtain wall as well as she knew the workings of her loom.

But still there were times when she felt lonely and odd, different from the other girls in a way that seemed obvious to everyone but herself.

Perhaps my luck will change. There might be some handsome lad among the servants of the noble visitors who will catch my eye and who will find me pleasing in return. Perhaps a lad who would sweep her away to the life of stirring adventure that filled her daydreams.

On May Day she'd joined the other maidens to go gathering hawthorn blossoms along the hedgerows. Legend said that a young woman who put a sprig of hawthorn beneath her pillow would dream of her own true love.

Mouse *had* dreamed.

In those airy fantasies, she had left the castle's gleaming towers far behind. She'd ridden through clinging silver mists and dark forests. Along high, treacherous mountain passes in the heat of day, and across wide meadows in starshine. In one, she'd stood in utter silence and watched a streak of multicolored light arc across the heavens, as the flight of a jeweled phoenix lit up the night.

Of course, the phoenix was only a legend. She knew there was no proof that it existed or ever had. There was no reason to believe that the bird in her dreams was real — any more than the black-haired man who'd accompanied Mouse on each of her dream odysseys.

Common sense said he was not real, but in her heart Mouse believed that he did exist.

Somewhere.

Why else would she have that feeling of recognition each time she slipped into her dreams to find him waiting there?

The breeze snapped red and blue banners atop the tower. It tugged loose stray wisps of Mouse's auburn hair and filled her with restlessness.

She looked out over the thatched cottages and slat-roofed buildings that nestled in the bowl of wooded hills. Once upon a time this had been a small village, but it had grown with Airan's power over the years. In the distance carved ships rode at anchor in the bay, with the bright face of the limestone cliffs beyond.

In her free time she went there, sometimes afoot, other times on the cob that Elva, the village wisewoman, kept stabled in her shed. There were plants she picked to dye her wool, or for Elva's herbal remedies. In time Mouse had come to know the overgrown trackways, the forgotten ruins and secret coves that lined the shore very well indeed.

But of the world beyond Airan, she knew little.

Was it true that there were humped animals that lived in the desert of Persiod, who drank no water and needed only air to survive? Or creatures larger than the largest ox, that swam in the cold seas beneath the shining ice-mountains of Far Islandia?

Mouse longed for adventure, for the sight

of distant and exotic lands; but certainly there was no way a simple weaver could experience such things on her own. Unless the man in her dreams arrived to claim her one day, she would likely live out her life like old Elva — busy and alone.

Her quick blue gaze skimmed over the would-be suitors below, in their gold and gems, their splendid cloaks and richly embroidered tunics. They were a colorful sight against the pale stones of the courtyard. Then her eye, trained to distinguish among a great variety of hues, was caught by something unexpected: a lack of color at the very back of the cobbled court.

A tall man leaned against the stone inner wall. Here was no elegant courtier, she saw, but someone who, by the look of him, had traveled long and hard to reach Airan. His body was hard-muscled, his skin deeply bronzed by wind and weather.

Like his companion's the man's garments were simple and foreign: He was dressed all in black, except for a cloak of deep, dull green. For all that, she noticed the subtle drape of it across his wide shoulders. It had been fashioned by an expert weaver. Light glinted off the twisted silver torque he wore about his muscular throat, but his thick, dark hair was clubbed back at the nape of his neck, restrained only by a simple knotted cord.

She wondered from where he had come, and what he was doing here among this gilded company. *Perhaps he is guard to one of the princes or lords who have answered the king's summons.*

Mouse wished that she could see his face. There was something familiar about him. . . .

She examined him more closely. There was a small harp in a battered leather case slung over one shoulder. *A bard,* she realized, *come to sing for his supper.*

But his hands were strong and looked more suited to wielding a sword than plucking harp strings. He stirred, and beneath that deceptively simple cloak, she saw the glint of a broadsword buckled to his side.

He was not only the musician and storyteller that the harp in its worn covering proclaimed, she was sure of it.

A wolf among lapdogs.

The thought caught Mouse by surprise, and she shivered.

A fanfare of trumpets shattered the air. The tramp of boots echoed from the stairs leading down into the castle's courtyard. "Make way! Make way!"

Mouse turned her attention away from the dangerous-looking stranger. The king and queen were coming to formally greet their illustrious guests. There had never been such a glorious gathering in the castle's long history.

Gilmore, High King of all the Western Lands, had invited every eligible prince and nobleman from the surrounding kingdoms to a great tournament. They had come eagerly from far and wide, spurred by rumors that the king was seeking a husband for his daughter, the beautiful Princess Camaris.

Someone jostled Mouse again from the side. Another trod on her toes. Luce elbowed them away. She grinned at Mouse.

"The princess will be hard to please if she doesn't find a husband among them. I'll wager she'll take one of those dainty princelings. She'll settle for no less."

"Hah," snorted the old woman beside them, pursing her wrinkled lips. "The queen will accept no less than the wealthiest one. And it is her that has the say in such matters."

Mouse said nothing at all, only listened.

Once again her eyes were drawn to the dark-haired man in the leather jerkin and green wool cloak. His quarter-profile was to her now, displaying a well-shaped nose and a decidedly firm chin. She caught her breath. Could it be? The resemblance to the man in her dreams was uncanny.

Turn this way! Look at me!

But he did not obey her silent call, turning away instead.

Mouse fingered the amulet she wore, taking comfort from the smooth coolness of it. It was a habit she'd had since childhood, whenever she felt uneasy. Her earliest memories were all bound up in the pretty talisman. The dark red stone on the fine silver chain had swung above her cradle from the day she was born until she was old enough to wear it around her neck. It was her dearest treasure.

Suddenly her fingers froze and she gave a small cry of dismay. The surface of the stone had turned rough and crumbly in one spot. Lifting the amulet by the chain, she cupped it in her palm. What she saw startled her.

She'd always believed the stone to be a solid piece of jasper, but she'd been wrong. A long section of the polished red surface had peeled away, like a petal separating from a tightly curled rose. Inside was something odd.

Mouse stared down at it. Prodded it with her finger. The core of the amulet felt smooth and cool, and gleamed with inner light.

It looked, she thought, like a clear quartz pebble.

Or perhaps a tear.

2

Cheers rang through the courtyard as the king and queen appeared at the head of the stairs. Tor watched in silence, assessing the royal couple as they ascended the dais.

Gilmore was still a handsome man, but time had placed its mark on him. The weight of responsibility had furrowed his brow and streaked his ruddy hair with silver. He'd won the crown of Airan in battle, and gone on to unite the Western Lands, and his peers had elected him High King. For eighteen years he had ruled with wisdom and dignity.

His only weakness had been his choice of queen.

Broch muttered something, and Tor leaned down to hear. "How," the older man said, "a man so good and fair in judgment could have taken a woman so spiteful to wife is beyond my ken."

While he didn't know much about the details, Tor knew that his companion had fought beside the men of Airan in the wars. Broch always spoke well of the king. But where as Gilmore was loved and respected, Queen Bryn was feared and disliked.

No one, it seemed to Tor, had anything good to say of the queen. Nor did they voice their disapproval aloud. "Perhaps," he replied quietly, "it is true what rumors say: that Queen Bryn holds him under an enchantment."

He'd heard that the king might quell the boldest knight with a word, a single glance, but bowed to his queen's slightest wishes like a lovestruck moonling.

No one would guess it by the king's manner as he rose from his throne. He looked regal and very much in command.

"In this courtyard today," he proclaimed, "I see the greatest gathering of nobles and knights that has ever assembled in all the Western Lands. You have come as my guests, hoping to win honors and prizes upon the field of tournament."

His eyes glinted in the sunshine, and the great ring upon his finger glowed darkly blue. "There is a greater prize at stake," he said softly. "One far greater than I have ever given before."

The king watched the effect of his words upon his assembled guests. He smiled, secrets shifting like mists behind his hooded eyes. He held out his battle-scarred hand, and the sapphire bearing his royal seal blazed again with light.

"Behold," he called out, "the Flower of Airan: my daughter, the Princess Camaris."

Silence fell as a vision in azure silk and cloth of gold came through the archway to join him upon the dais. A sigh went up from the assembly, like the whisper of wavelets on smooth sand. The Princess Camaris was far more lovely than any of them had dared to believe.

Her hair was as finespun as the gold threads that lined her cloak, and her eyes as amber as the topazes in her delicate diadem. She moved with exquisite grace across the dais and took her place on the smaller throne beside her father. Gems winked on her fingers and at her white throat. Her smile was small and aloof, a mere curving of her full, red mouth. If there was haughtiness and perhaps bored amusement in her expression, it only added to the sense that she was a rare treasure.

Up on the parapet, Mouse was pleased to see that the princess was wearing the cloth she'd woven for her. It suited her delicate coloring. "How beautiful Princess Camaris is! There is not a man among them who will not strive to win her hand in marriage."

Luce folded her arms. "Pretty is as pretty does! Camaris would be the better for it if the good fairies had granted her the sweetness and wisdom to go with her beauty."

Someone shushed her. King Gilmore was speaking again. "My daughter is ripe for marriage, and I would have an heir to succeed me. The man who wins the princess shall have half my kingdom as well!"

His announcement rang from the walls of the great court, stirring echoes in the hearts of the assembled men. Airan was a kingdom with fertile green fields, deep blue harbors, and misty purple mountains thickly threaded with veins of gold and silver, copper and iron. A very great prize indeed.

At the back of the courtyard, Tor leaned against the thick stone walls and smiled. His eyes shone with appreciation.

"All that, and half a kingdom, Broch," he said, eyeing the princess. "A man would risk his life for far less!"

The older man stroked his scarred chin. "There's a trick in it somewhere, mark my words. Gilmore is a canny ruler and still in his prime. He has fought hard to keep his throne. He has no intention of handing over the reins of even half his kingdom to another man!"

Tor shifted, resting his weight on the cross-handle of his unadorned sword. "Not even the High King would dare to make so public a challenge and then go back upon his word."

His black gaze scrutinized the Princess Camaris, stripping away her silks and brocades with the ease of experience. Her fair face, graceful figure, and full, sulky mouth were the stuff of fevered dreams.

The smile that Broch mistrusted spread across Tor's face. "By the Great Dragon, I've a mind to try for the prize he offers."

"Hah!" Broch shook his head. "I'd give all I own to see you decked out in jeweled chains and satin boots, like these pink-cheeked lordlings. And believe me, the Princess Camaris would demand no less of any man aspiring to her hand." His blue eyes were shrewd. "You can tell that she's one as knows her own worth."

Tor laughed. "You're a sour old man these days." He slanted a glance at his comrade. "I've never met the woman I couldn't bed and pleasure. Aye, and make her smile for days afterward, just for the remembering of it."

" 'Small dogs bark loud,' " Broch grunted.

"And large dogs bark loudest," Tor replied with a twinkle in his eye. "That old

416

proverb does not apply to me."

"Let's see how you boast when all is said and done!" Broch narrowed his eyes. "I'll wager the Princess Camaris has as much iron in her will as you have in your sword."

"Then," Tor said, grinning broadly, "she has met her match."

Gilmore's challenge stirred his interest. The Princess Camaris stirred his loins. His face sobered. "By the gods, she's a beauty. I'll have her, kingdom or no!"

Broch sent him a sharp look. "You are too cocky by half. Gilmore did not send *you* an invitation to take part in his tournament. And if he had, what makes you think that you could meet the challenge?"

A hard light gleamed in the depths of Tor's dark eyes. He had his own reasons, and Gilmore's offer was only half of it. The gleam was gone as quickly as it had come. His bronzed hand clasped the old man's shoulder.

"How can I fail in any feat of arms? Did I not have the finest teacher in all the world?"

Broch's mouth twisted in what passed for his smile. "Aye, you did." His fingers tightened on the stout blackthorn staff he used for support. "And if the Beast of Cullen hadn't snared my thigh with his great claw, I'd best you still, you proud young pup."

Tor's voice softened. "Aye. Aye, you would."

Broch's seamed face reddened. Seeing that he had embarrassed his companion, Tor turned his attention back to the Princess Camaris. Like every other man in the chamber who didn't have one foot in the grave, Tor was smitten. And determined.

The beautiful Camaris would be his.

While he watched her, he was unaware that he was himself the object of much speculation. Luce pointed down at him.

"Look at that rude fellow smiling at the princess, as if she were a dainty sweetcake. He is not even fit to touch the hem of the princess's skirt!"

Mouse felt a tingle dance along her skin. *I wish he would look up and smile at me,* she thought, and was surprised when the other girl jumped. She hadn't realized that she'd spoken aloud.

Luce stared. "Do you? Well, I wouldn't say no, myself. Such a fine set-up man can touch my skirts anytime he pleases. Aye, and lift them as well!"

Mouse didn't say anything at all. She couldn't.

The dark-haired stranger had glanced up at the parapet, casually. For a few seconds before he turned back to his companion his gaze locked with hers. From that moment she'd been robbed of speech. Of breath.

She grasped the worn stones for support. She didn't believe in love at first sight. Mouse knew that was merely attraction, the mating lure between the sexes. Old Elva had told her so, many a time, and that she must respect the soul of the man she loved more than she did his face.

But Mouse believed that if she ever met her soul mate, she would recognize him instantly. And she recognized this man.

Perhaps he was not her true soul mate, but at any rate he was the man who had haunted her dreams in recent weeks. He had the same dark eyes alight with inner fire, the same strong nose and square, stubborn jaw. And that mouth! Oh, yes. She knew that mouth. She'd awakened from its hot kisses, tangled in her sheet and aching with need.

Closing her eyes, she tried to blend their images. It was the same man. In her dreams, though, his gleaming dark hair had been unbound, flying out behind him as he raced his night-black steed along the causeway to the castle. And in his gauntleted hand, he'd held aloft something that sparkled and shone with jeweled fire.

There was fire of a different sort in his eyes now as they gazed upon the princess.

Mouse saw it, and her heart plummeted. Every man who set eyes upon Camaris was taken with the princess's beauty. No, more than that. Blinded and enchanted.

Pain gathered and swelled like a molten bubble in her chest. The man of her dreams was real. But she'd dreamed that he came to her. To *her!* Not to the Princess Camaris, who had beauty and grace and learning, and all the riches that the world could offer.

Look at me, Mouse willed him. *Over here!* Every fiber of her soul resonated with the yearning. *Look this way. Look at me!* See *me.*

He turned his head, frowning up at the parapet. It was as if, she thought, he'd heard her unspoken command. But his gaze passed lightly over her and returned to the princess. A flush rose up his windburned cheeks.

Mouse bit her lip. He had eyes only for Camaris.

It was too cruel.

She gathered her will and found her voice. "Who . . . who is he?"

"I don't know, but I'll find out!" Luce told her. She had made it her business to know everything about the men who entered the castle precincts.

"A handsome devil, is he not? But after all, only a border ruffian come to see the tournament, and no more fit to mingle with the lords and princes in the courtyard below than we. I've a mind to set my cap for him, but nothing would come of it. I know a man with wanderlust in his heart. After the festivities he'll be on his way, and we'll never set eyes on him again."

You are wrong! Mouse wanted to cry out.

But she realized, with a sinking heart, that her dream was not wrong. She had only misinterpreted it, out of sheer romantic folly. He was not for her.

The black-haired stranger would go away, it was true. But he would return as she had seen, racing across the drawbridge with the wind whipping his black hair wild and free.

Her fingers pressed tightly against her amulet. The small fracture inside the quartz pebble grew. Mouse heard something crack — a small crystalline sound — and thought it was her heart. When he returned — and she had no doubt that he would — it would be to claim the Princess Camaris for his bride.

She slipped away and vanished into the shadows of the tower.

No one noticed that she was gone.

No one remembered that she had been there at all.

3

"Fetch the princess her cloak of gold wool, and the feathered cap," Queen Bryn commanded. "And do not snag it with your harsh hands!"

Mouse hurried across the tapestry-hung hall to one of the carved chests that stood between the windows, hoping she would open the right one first. The princess was suffering from a fit of the sullens, and the queen was in a rare temper.

Mouse's duties as a weaver seldom brought her into contact with the royal family, and she had rarely set foot inside the princess's private quarters. But today she had been walking by when Camaris's waiting woman had slipped and broken her arm. She'd responded to the cries for aid — and had been pressed into temporary service in the woman's place.

Kneeling before the chest, she caught her reflection and that of the princess, in the polished brass lock. What a contrast they made: the princess in burgundy cut velvet draped over yellow satin, Mouse in her simple round dress of periwinkle blue.

And not merely in our garments, she thought.

She knew she looked well enough. Her figure was neat, her features pleasing, her auburn tresses thick and shining. *But even if I were gowned in splendor, I would still be a pale moon to Camaris's sun.*

Mouse was conscious that she lacked something the princess had in abundance: the power to turn men's heads. To weave herself into their dreams, waking and sleeping.

The only weaving she could do was with flax and wool dyed with plants she gathered from the woods or along the rocky cliffs, and the reels of vibrant silk thread imported from exotic lands. From warm cloaks to keep away the cold to transparent veils shot with gold and silver, there was nothing she couldn't create.

I am more fortunate than many, she reminded herself. At least she could earn her own keep, by the intricate work of her clever fingers. She would never starve or lack a warm fire and roof over her head.

But, oh! How she would have liked to turn the head of that handsome stranger her way!

The queen paced the chamber. "Hurry,

girl! The duke of Ragnor is awaiting the princess in the rose garden."

"I don't wish to walk with him in the garden." The princess shuddered. "He has yellow teeth and the face of a halibut!"

"You are a fool, Camaris! He is the most powerful ruler outside of Airan, and his coffers overflow with gold."

The princess bit her lip. "He might rule the entire world, for all I care. He would still look like a fish!"

Queen Bryn strode up and down the chamber, her eyes snapping with anger. The argument had been going on all afternoon. All because a handsome young lordling in blue velvet had caught her daughter's eye. "I will not let you throw yourself away on a mere nobody!"

Bryn glanced at the looking glass. She was in her prime, the most powerful woman in all the civilized world. But no longer the most lovely. That title belonged to Camaris now. Ungrateful girl that she was!

Along with the spells and potions to ensure the girl's beauty, the queen had raised her daughter with one aim — to make herself alluring to men. If a woman did not inherit her own wealth and estates, it was the only way that she could hope to wield power. The queen was determined that her lovely daughter would contract a brilliant marriage.

Bryn had used her own beauty and cunning to raise herself up from her beginnings as the eldest daughter of a very minor king to her current position as the highest lady in the Western Lands. From the moment she'd first set eyes on Gilmore, she had known he was her destiny.

To that end, Bryn had schemed and plotted to ensnare him. She had even delved deeper into the Dark Arts.

A mistake, that!

A shudder ran through her frame at the memory of it. She had been unable to control the forces she'd conjured, and her body bore the scars of that terrible miscalculation. Her profile was still lovely; but beneath the scarf that shielded her throat from view was a mass of ropy purple scar, like a coiled serpent.

Her mouth curved bitterly. It was a hard thing for any woman to bear. Especially one used to wielding her great beauty as a lure — and a weapon.

But, Bryn assured herself, there were still glory and power to come, and that would be worth every sacrifice. She would not let Camaris ruin everything!

Adjusting the veil more securely, she forced herself to smile.

"Consider yourself fortunate that the duke

wishes to ally himself with the kingdom of Airan. You will walk with the duke, and you will be at your most charming."

The princess leaned back upon the silken cushions. "I do not wish to wed the Duke of Ragnor. And I will not!"

"This is what comes of spoiling you." Queen Bryn fought the urge to slap her daughter's lovely face.

Under the best of circumstances, the princess had the casual arrogance that too often accompanies beauty and wealth. But her mother wasn't blind: Camaris was as demanding as a child, and she had neither wit nor charm to recommend her. In time the attraction of her fair face would pale. And where would they be then?

Bryn was aware that her own power over the king had faded with time. Although Gilmore was still under her spell, the hold it had upon him was not as strong as it had been. She could feel him struggling to free himself from its web.

But if Camaris wed the duke, it would consolidate Bryn's power considerably. If she played her hand well, in time she would rule two kingdoms: Airan and the Western Lands through Gilmore and another, vaster one through her daughter's chosen husband.

Chosen by *her*.

It *must* happen. She must make it so! Then, even if Gilmore cast off the spell, he could never set her aside.

Her temper frayed like a raveled hem. She would allow nothing to come between her and her ambitions. Not even the king.

"I will brook no defiance in this matter! Youth and beauty fade. You must secure your position in the world before that happens." Bryn clenched her hands. "If you do not come down of your own free will, I will have the sergeant-at-arms drag you to the garden by your hair!"

Camaris went white with shock. The queen had never used such words to *her*.

Mouse hunched over the cedarwood chest, pretending she'd heard nothing of the altercation. The brass catch was hard to lift. She winced as she banged her finger against it, but succeeded on the second try.

Inside were a multitude of beautiful cloaks, each more lovely than the other. She found the one the princess wanted at the very bottom. The fabric was the same tawny shade as the princess's eyes.

Mouse shook it out and carried it to the princess. Camaris rose and stood rigidly while the cape was settled over her shoulders.

Suddenly the queen stiffened.

"Stupid girl!" She clouted Mouse across

the shoulders. "See what you've done!"

Mouse was aghast. Although her hands were smooth from the oils in the wool she wove, her fingernail had snagged thread of the fine wool like a bur. She must have torn the nail on the faulty catch. As she drew her hand away, the thread pulled away with her fingers, puckering the cloth.

Bryn turned on her in a fury. "You fool!" Snatching the garment away, she flung it across the room toward the hearth, where a fire was always kept burning against the chill of the thick stone walls.

"I won't have such a clumsy cow waiting upon the princess," she said viciously. "Go back to the kitchens, or the scullery, or wherever you belong — and stay there!"

Without warning, her hand lashed out at Mouse again. She was caught off guard, and the force of the blow sent her sprawling on the floor.

For a moment Mouse couldn't hear anything at all. Then her head rang like a great brass bell, and her ear burned like a white-hot coal. The rest of her face felt numb.

No one had ever struck her before. She struggled to her feet, while anger rose like a white-hot flame within her. She tried to repress it, but felt it burning like a torch. Could almost smell the singe of it in the air.

Then she realized that the odor came from Camaris's discarded cloak. The hem of the garment was on fire. An ember had fallen out of the hearth, and little licks of flame danced along the cloth.

"Oh!" Snatching up a pitcher of water from the table, Mouse dashed it over the burning cloak. Smoke, black and pungent, filled the air. She grabbed the damp garment and held it up. The ember had burned through several folds of fabric, leaving a series of blackened holes.

"Now it is ruined beyond repair," the queen said through gritted teeth. "I could have you whipped for this!"

Mouse bit back a hot retort. It would only fetch her another blow. "The rest is still good, Your Majesty. I am handy with my needle. I could fashion it into a cape."

"You've done quite enough for one day! Get out, and take this sorry mess with you. I never want to see it again." Her eyes narrowed. "As for you, keep out of my sight. Show your face to me again, and I will have you flogged within an inch of your life!"

Mouse scooped up the scorched cloak and hurried out of the room. Her ear throbbed and buzzed like a hornets' nest, but at least she had a quantity of warm wool for her troubles. She would take it to the woman who had raised her and use it to line her cloak. Elva's cottage was across the river, beyond the village.

This will keep the old dear snug when the winds come down from the north.

In her haste, Mouse rounded the corner and collided with a tall figure coming the other way. Only his strong arm kept her from falling. She looked up into a pair of eyes as deep and black as midnight. And as impersonal as air.

The dark-haired stranger she'd seen in the courtyard! Mouse was too embarrassed to speak. He was impressive at a distance, overwhelming so near at hand. His muscles felt like steel beneath the sleeve of his black leather jerkin.

"Watch your step!" Tor exclaimed. "You might have tumbled down the stairs."

The bundled cloak was caught between them, but Mouse realized she was pressed tight against his broad chest. Was that his heart pounding, or hers?

His touch was firm, and sent heat penetrating beneath her delicate skin, racing through her to coil in her belly. She felt dizzy and closed her eyes. A great mistake. Her every sense was heightened by his nearness.

A gasp of breath, and she inhaled the heady, masculine scent of him. Sun-warmed earth and the rich, cool green of wild grass. She colored and pulled away.

Tor released her at once. "Your pardon," he said.

She was obviously an upper servant or craftswoman, by her clothing and demeanor. A fetching little thing, small and willow-slender, with shining auburn hair plaited loosely at her nape. She smelled like wild raspberries, and her eyes were like no color he had ever seen. Hues shifted in them like the sea in sunlight, in multiple shades of silvery blue.

He flushed when she continued to stare at him. "I meant no harm, mistress," he said. "My only thought was to save you from a fall."

"I thank you, sir, for your quick action." Mouse averted her face from his level gaze. "And now I'd best be on my way."

Tor saw the scarlet mark along her cheek and the swelling purple bruise. All his gallant instincts were aroused. Was this why she'd flinched?

"By the Great Dragon! Has some scoundrel accosted you? Only say his name and I'll have his hide!"

Mouse bit her lip. "Nay, sir. I . . . I was merely clumsy and was punished for my lack of grace."

"You have a harsh mistress," Tor declared. "Her temper should be checked. Where I come from, no lady of quality would treat a servant so!"

"Alas, sir, there is none to stop her," Mouse said.

"Then you should petition the queen. Surely she must take an interest in the welfare of her household."

Mouse gave him a tight little smile. "You are mistaken. The queen's only interest is the welfare of the queen."

She clamped a hand to her mouth. She couldn't believe that she'd blurted out such a dangerous truth. *If anyone heard me . . .*

She dipped a slight curtsey and whisked herself away, down the winding staircase. Tor stared after her, frowning. The episode left him frustrated, angry, and determined to look into it further.

But by the time Mouse reached the bottom step, he had forgotten the incident entirely.

4

Mouse approached the half-timbered cottage and ducked beneath the low door. Elva sat at the pine table by the window, sorting through her dried herbs. Stone jars were lined up neatly along the whitewashed wall, waiting to be filled.

She looked up when Mouse's shadow fell over her.

"Ah, Rosaleen, my love!"

Mouse smiled. It always startled her to hear Elva call her by her given name. No one else did. And it always comforted her, as well. At least here in this little cottage she was known and loved.

Her heart swelled with deep affection for the old woman. "Blessings on you," she said in greeting. "I see you've set two mugs out for tea."

"I knew you would come today." Elva noticed the bundle beneath Mouse's arm. "What have you there, child?"

"I've brought you something. A goodly quantity of fine wool — woven, I might add, on my own loom."

Elva's thin fingers touched the soft fabric with its intricate weave. "It's beautiful work you've done. But why have you brought it away from the castle to show me? It's a terrible risk. You'd be punished if anyone knew."

"That I won't. The queen gave it to me herself!"

"I've never heard her to be generous before." The old woman looked worried.

A dimple peeked at the corner of Mouse's mouth. "It wasn't hers. It belonged to Camaris." Shaking out the cloak with its burned hem, she told Elva the story of how she'd obtained it.

"You are so small, there is enough to line your cloak and boots, and make a shawl as well."

"My old bones will be grateful when the snows come. I've the kettle on the boil. Sit down and I'll make some tea, while you tell me all the castle gossip. Rumor says that King Gilmore means to marry off the princess."

"And a great quarrel it's provoked." Mouse folded the wool and smoothed it carefully. "The queen has her eye on the Duke of Ragnor, but Camaris wants a young and handsome prince. Not that it matters who is wanted by either, for whichever knight wins the tournament will win the hand of the princess in marriage."

Elva poured boiling water into two earthen cups. The scent of elderflower and lemon balm filled the air. "Do not be fooled. Gilmore rules the kingdom, but the queen rules him. Bryn will do whatever she must to make the duke win the tournament."

"Do you mean she will cast a spell upon the others?" Mouse was shocked.

"Nay, girl. No need of the Dark Arts to make sure the man she had chosen will be tournament champion, when simple means will do the trick. A few loyal servants willing to maudle the wine. Or stablehands willing to slip certain herbs into the feed of the other's men's horses, in return for a handful of coins."

A shiver ran up Mouse's spine. She shook it off. "I am glad my role at the castle is a minor one. It makes life much simpler all around."

She looked up suddenly, ears pricked. A shadow had passed by the window. Rising, Mouse went to the open casement. Twice on her way to the cottage she'd had the sensation that someone was keeping pace with her along the track through the woods, but had dismissed it as her imagination. Now she leaned out the window, but there was no one in sight.

It must have been the shadow of a hawk flying by, she told herself. *Or perhaps another bird.*

Elva was lost in her own thoughts and hadn't noticed anything beyond them. For three nights her sleep had been troubled with portents of danger. Neighing horses, the clash of armor, the thunder of discord.

But last night she'd dreamed of a jeweled phoenix, flashing across the night sky like a falling star. And of Mouse's poor mother, God rest her soul.

Try as she might, she could not shake her forebodings. "You are as dear to me as if you were my own, Rosaleen. If the queen is in a foul mood, you must take care to stay out of her path. Promise me."

"Today was a rare occasion. My path rarely crosses hers." Mouse put her hand over Elva's. "Do not fear. Except for the tournament, I will keep myself busy all day in the weaver's room. I give you my word."

The old woman glanced anxiously at Mouse. She curled her hands around the mug for warmth.

I failed her mother, but I have not failed her. At least she is in no danger. My Spell of Forgetting has kept her safe.

Unseen beneath Mouse's plain bodice, another layer of petals crumbled and turned to dust.

5

The sun was slanting over the far hills when Mouse left Elva and hurried across the bridge and up the dusty road to the castle.

Perhaps it is all this talk of spells and sorcery that has me on edge, she thought.

Whatever its cause, the peace she'd felt in Elva's thatched cottage fell away as she crossed the moat and entered the castle's outer courtyard. With the commotion of housing all the nobles' guests, the morrow's tournament, and the tension between the princess and the queen, the place was buzzing like a hornets' nest. Servants were scurrying to and fro, intent on their errands.

She slipped up the stairs and into the minuscule room near the weaving chamber that she shared with Luce. Mouse opened the small chest that held her possessions and took out a folded dress. She had made it with wool that Elva had gathered from her own sheep and dyed with the dark red juice of winterberries. She'd never worn it before.

As she dressed her hair and tied it back with a matching band, Mouse knew she was doing it all in hopes that the dark-haired stranger would notice her.

Except that his name was Tor, no one knew anything about him. She imagined that as a traveling bard he would earn his supper and a place to sleep by entertaining the court with his music and then go on his way again.

Her heart beat a little faster thinking of him. She hoped very much that he would be inclined to linger. She was drawn to him like iron to lodestone. There was something about him that was more than the sum of his handsome face and wide shoulders and strong physique. More than the humor and intelligence she'd seen in his keen dark eyes.

If she closed her eyes Mouse could still imagine the wild, summery scent of him, the dizzying thrill of his nearness. He was the reason she'd made the decision to brave the queen's wrath tonight and take her usual place at the servants' table. *Chances are that she has already forgotten me,* she told herself.

Certainly Tor had. He'd passed her in the great hall twice without so much as noticing her. But she was determined that she would make him do so.

The bells rang out, announcing the hour. It was time for the company to assemble. Mouse didn't want to draw attention to herself by arriving late. She ran down a little-used stairway to a quiet courtyard. She stopped in dismay when King Gilmore stepped from the shadows. She dipped into a low curtsey, expecting him to continue on his way.

"You are in a dire hurry, lass. Do you rush to meet your handsome young lover?"

She shook her head. "Nay, Majesty. It is but love of my supper that calls me to the banqueting hall with all good speed."

He laughed. "Then be on your way. It would not do for you to arrive after the king."

She curtsied again and hurried away beneath a stone arch.

Gilmore stared after her. A pretty thing! She reminded him of someone. . . .

He spied something lying on the stones at his feet, winking like a jewel. He bent to pick it up. Only a broken bit of glass-clear quartz, and the dried petal of a rose. He wondered if the girl had dropped them. As his fingers closed over them he felt suddenly dizzy.

Flickers of memory teased him. A dark-haired woman — surely the very image of the girl, with eyes of the same silvery blue.

Visions came tumbling into his mind, sensations assaulted him. The smell of woodsmoke and the leaping flames of the Beltane fire. Words of love whispered, acts of love consummated, with no other witness than the whirling stars. He saw her clearly now: the beautiful lover to whom he'd pledge his heart and troth. Her name . . . her name was . . .

Suddenly Gilmore felt caught in an invisible net. It tightened around him inexorably. He struggled, but in a matter of seconds the woman's face vanished. Everything was gone: name, images, every vestige of memory, leaving him with an aching head and pervading sense of loss.

He stood alone for some time in the silence of the courtyard, while twilight drifted down around him.

6

As Mouse entered the great hall, her heart thudded with mingled hope and fear that this time Tor might notice her. She wished that she had gowns of gold-shot sendal, exotically scented perfumes to lure his attention. Jeweled earrings to dangle from her lobes that would wink in the candlelight to catch his eye.

But as always, once she slipped into the great hall, no one seemed to remark her presence. She took a seat along one of two tables set at angles to the dais. The amulet that hung around her neck brushed against her bodice. Unnoticed, another piece of dried rose petal flaked away.

Like others with valued skills, Mouse was fed and housed by the king. The weavers' appointed place was above that of the ordinary household servants and the carvers of fine wood but below that of the jewelers, whose baubles of gold and glowing gems adorned the royal family.

The highest nobles and princes were seated at the head table, quaffing mead and wine from glass cups encased in intricate silver. Light from the torches glimmered from their embroidered robes and silk and velvet tunics and glinted from jeweled collars and hammered gold torques.

She scanned the sides of the hall, searching for Tor, but he was nowhere to be seen among the other musicians. Her disappointment was keen.

When the royal family took their places, she sighed. Camaris the golden. The princess was gowned in azure satin, decked with pearls. Her bright hair was confined in a matching snood. She was so beautiful that everyone else suffered in comparison. *What a fool I am. If Tor were here, he would not notice me at all.*

It was only when the candles beside the head table had burned low in their iron branches that Tor made his entrance. His dark hair gleamed as he bowed before the king and queen. King Gilmore leaned back on his throne, his favorite wine goblet of rock crystal and gold in his hand.

"I am told you have great skill upon the harp. You are welcome to my court, sir bard. I bid you play for us."

Tor took a place at the foot of the dais in

profile to the king and placed his hands upon the harp. Notes rippled from it, dancing through the air like motes of light. He was a master harper, and he caught his listeners in a net spun of sunshine and moonbeams. He conjured up the ice-clad mountains of his homeland, shining against a sky so blue it hurt the eyes, and they felt his yearning. When he sang of Airan's heroes who had fallen in freedom's name, their blood roused to the echo of ancient war drums.

Mouse listened raptly. The music of the harp was sweet, but it was his voice that captured her heart. Deep and true, it resonated through her, stirring emotions she had never known before. Wild longings and unspoken desires that swirled like storm winds off the sea.

All her life she had lived in the shadows, moving cautiously, attracting no notice. It was something as integral to her as the color of her eyes. Yet as she listened to Tor play and sing, watched the sure movements of his hands upon the harpstrings, she wished that he would look up at her.

Only at her.

When the last lovely note died, the great hall was completely silent. A moment later it erupted in cheers. The king held up his hand, and gradually the clamor ceased.

Gilmore inclined his head toward the bard. "We thank you for the gift of your music. What is your name, and from whence do you come?"

"I am called Tor," the man replied, green eyes glinting. "Like my fathers before me, I have been raised in exile, among the wild peaks of Far Islandia."

A ripple of tension ran around the room. Mouse noticed that the guards suddenly laid their hands upon their sword hilts. When Gilmore had united the Western Lands, only the hardy people of Far Islandia had refused to acknowledge him as their ruler. There was bad blood, legacy of an ancient feud, between them. Gilmore's ascent to the throne had driven the two countries further apart.

The king rubbed his beard and eyed Tor steadily. "Far Islandia has been a thorn in Airan's side for a hundred years. It breeds rebels like no other place on earth."

"Aye," Tor said softly. "It does."

Then the king smiled. Perhaps his goal of uniting their countries in friendship could begin here. "And brave men and women. I welcome you to my court, Tor of Far Islandia. Will you play another song before the hour grows late?"

"Aye, Your Majesty."

Tor surveyed the room, and his gaze fell upon Mouse, sitting with her hands folded beneath her chin. He frowned. There was something familiar about that lass. Something of importance. He struggled to recall it, then shook his head.

Try as he might, he couldn't place her.

Touching the strings again, he played a tune that wound around and around upon itself, then launched into a tender ballad. The tale of a fair maid who loved unwisely and too well. Who waited faithfully for her lover to return from war, only to find that he had wed another. And who died giving birth to his child, without his ever knowing it.

It wasn't what Tor had intended to play. In fact, it was a new song, pouring out of him — or through him — as if it came from another realm. He felt the wrenching of his heart with every word, the sorrow of the brokenhearted maid with every poignant note. It left him shaken.

The last notes echoed among the high, carved rafters like the maiden's soul ascending to heaven. No one who heard the song was untouched by it.

Except the queen, who wore a fearsome frown upon her white brow.

Gilmore gripped his empty cup in his fisted hand. He stared down into it for what seemed like a long time, then slowly lifted his head. His eyes looked dazed. "A sad song, sir bard, terrible in its power and beauty. But well worth the hearing."

He rose suddenly, every inch the king, and pulled the massive emerald off his finger. "Take this ring in payment for the pleasure you have given."

Tor rose and bowed. "I am a simple man and have no use for fine jewels."

"Then name your prize!" Gilmore commanded. "Whatever you wish shall be yours. I give you my word as High King."

A look of triumph flashed in Tor's eyes. He slanted a glance to where Broch stood along the wall. *Did I not tell you?* that gaze demanded. His mobile mouth quirked up slightly at the corners. He lifted his head and faced the king squarely.

"I ask the right to fight in the tournament tomorrow, for the hand of the your daughter in marriage."

A murmur at his audacity ran through the assemblage. It was the last thing anyone expected. Mouse put her hand to her mouth in dismay.

A muscle ticked at Gilmore's jaw. He regretted his hasty vow. "Have you lost your wits? You are a weaver of song, not a knight trained to battle!"

The queen glared icily down. "And insolent beyond forgiveness. He is not even fit to speak the name of the Princess Camaris aloud!"

Tor's voice rang out through the hall. "A bard I am, but the blood of kings runs through my veins. I am trained in the art of combat, and as skilled with sword and lance as any here."

The king scowled. "Ask me for another boon instead," he commanded.

"No, sire. I will not take back my words. Nor," Tor challenged, "can you take back yours."

The tension in the room heightened. It was true. Gilmore had given his royal oath.

Reaching out, the queen grasped her husband's wrist. Her fingers dug into his wrist. "You must deny this absurd request!"

Gilmore turned on her, his eyes glittering with anger. "You heard the man — and you heard me as well. I have pledged my word. Now we must all live with the consequences."

No one had ever heard the king speak so roughly to the queen before. Even Bryn was taken aback. She went very still. Panic fluttered inside her breast, and her knuckles blanched whiter than the sleeve of her pale silk gown. She examined Tor from head to toe. This man, whoever he was, had power. That was undeniable. She feared him.

It was a new emotion for the queen, and it rattled her. She rallied quickly and addressed her husband, gathering her robes around her as if they were protective armor.

"You will do what you must do," she said. "And let me warn you, my lord, that I shall do the same!"

Queen Bryn signaled her daughter and their waiting women, then swept off the dais and vanished behind the tapestry that hung in front of the stairs to the royal chambers. The Princess Camaris followed her, her lovely head held high.

For a moment King Gilmore looked old and ill. His kingdom had been at peace for eighteen years, but he hadn't known a moment of it in his own heart. He rubbed the bridge of his nose wearily.

Then he drew himself up, as regal as ever. "You are a fool, Tor of Far Islandia, and you shall surely die a fool's death. May God have mercy upon you."

Tor bowed. "I do not ask for mercy, Your Majesty, only your word, which you have freely given."

King Gilmore rose. "Let it be on your head, then. Your boon is granted. Tomorrow you shall fight in the tournament."

He left the dais, followed by his retainers. The princes and lords murmured among themselves, then left their places. As the hall emptied, people flowed away on either side of Tor, like a river streaming around a rock.

Broch joined him beneath one of the tall windows. "They flee from you as if you were diseased."

"Like the king, they think I am indeed a fool," Tor said with a harsh laugh. "Or a dead man."

Broch eyed his protégé. "They may be right on both counts. Tomorrow will tell the tale."

Mouse clenched her hands in frustration. In the past hour she had learned many things about dark-eyed Tor, who haunted her dreams. His singing was so beautiful it could make the angels weep. He had pride, courage, and great daring.

And it seemed that he was hell-bent on self-destruction.

She fled to her chamber and wept herself to sleep. Her dreams were comforting. She was back at Elva's cottage, snug in her bed. A woman with roses in her hair sat at a loom weaving by candlelight. In and out the shuttle darted, trailing gleaming threads of gold and silver that shaped the image of a glorious bird whose eyes glowed redder than any ruby.

Mouse smiled in her dreams.

7

Pennants waved from the grandstand where King Gilmore sat in state with his family and noble guests. The sun shone down on the already defeated, resting beneath the trees, and the two remaining combatants preparing to take up arms.

Gilmore wished the day already over. He had slept ill, assaulted by dreams. He'd been young again and filled with idealism. There had been a phoenix, his chosen symbol, blazing a rainbow of fire so bright that it dimmed the glory of the starry night. Once the bird had flown free over Airan, and sightings were common. There had been none in many years now. Perhaps it was an ill omen.

But there had also been a woman, her dark hair twined with roses and gleaming silver ribbon. She had smiled at him so sweetly, her eyes filled with love. He knew her name now: Deirdre.

Gilmore rubbed his temples. He'd wakened before dawn, filled with emptiness and an ache so profound that he felt as if a sword had pierced his heart. Deirdre the fair. How could he have ever forgotten her?

He glanced at his queen beside him. The answer lay in her. Not in her beauty, which was still potent, nor in the charm she could still summon when she wished. It was something deeper, darker. He fought it with all his might.

Trumpets sounded, announcing that the next challenge would be starting soon. Liveried pages swarmed about the Duke of Ragnor, helping him into his full battle gear: gilded armour, a red-crested helm, and a rectangular body shield as tall as a man.

The king brooded. Old enemies were working in the background to bring Airan down. If he could no longer keep the peace by persuasion and diplomacy, he could still do so through the marriage of his daughter. An alliance with a powerful duke like Ragnor would make them back away like cringing dogs.

Now Tor, the dark stranger from Far Islandia, had loosed a cat among the pigeons.

Gilmore was distracted by the arrival of his most trusted aide. The man spoke low so that only the king could hear. "I have made the inquiries you wished, Majesty and have information you may not welcome."

The king rose. "I will walk with you, while the contestants prepare."

The queen watched them leave the grandstand. Something was wrong. Gilmore struggled against her power. She could feel it, more and more. She reached beneath the veil wound around her throat, and touched the thick scars there. A shiver ran through her. It had been several years since she'd dared to call up the Dark Forces. Much as she feared another spell might go awry, she would have to attempt to work her magic upon the king again.

Her golden gaze settled on Tor, as he mounted his steed. As far as the barbarian from Far Islandia, she had no concerns. Ragnor was a powerful warrior, despite his unfortunate appearance. He would make short work of the upstart. If only Camaris had not set her heart against him! The girl was a fool. *I shall have to work a spell on her, as well. A love spell so that when my daughter gazes at the duke he will appear to be the most handsome of men.*

Tor steadied his mount and shielded his eyes against the glare, unaware that he drew the queen's attention. Despite Broch's dire predictions, no thieves had stolen their horses and gear from the hidden grove. Beneath his black silk tunic was the finely woven chain mail, and his boots rose high on his muscled thighs. He had less protection than the duke, but the advantage of greater speed and agility.

Tor wiped away a trickle of sweat from his brow. The day was hot and the exertion of the tournament great. In the last pass, he had shattered his lance, and his opponent's horse had fallen.

The thrill of battle was upon him. Of all the eager men who had fought this day for glory, and the hand of the princess, only he and the Duke of Ragnor had vanquished all previous challengers. Now they faced each other at either side of the greensward again, each one determined to win the challenge and the hand of the Princess Camaris in marriage.

"Strike well," Broch said, handing Tor another lance. "One blow and it will all be over. Whether it's you or the other," he added grimly.

"Fear not for me! I will prevail."

The king had returned to the grandstand. Tor saluted to show his readiness and King Gilmore acknowledged the gesture. Between the royal couple, the pampered princess sat rigid with dismay, awaiting the outcome.

Neither champion was to her liking.

"If looks were arrows," Broch muttered, "the princess would have slain you both ere now."

"I'll bring her 'round," Tor said with grim humor. "I shall make it my life's work."

Broch scowled. "A poor choice of careers," he said sourly.

Tor ignored the remark. Camaris looked more lovely than ever, in a cloth-of-gold gown. Emeralds and purple spinels wreathed her smooth white throat and glinted in the gold net that held her shining hair. The disdain in her face didn't daunt him. He liked a woman with spirit and fire. Taming her would be a delight.

She is proud, that one, but she will learn to love me. I will make her love me!

Determination steeled him. *By the gods, I will have her!*

Broch shook his head. "You look like a moon-calf," he said curtly.

"I feel like one in her presence. She is like the sun. She blinds me with her beauty."

"I've never yet known a lusty young fellow who didn't turn imbecile at the sight of a pretty face." Broch gave him a disgusted look. "Left to your own devices, you would choose a smoothly gilded rock over a nugget of pure gold — and all for the glitter of it."

Tor's brows knit. "You forget yourself. I'm a grown man and a warrior, not the stripling boy who came to you so long ago seeking wisdom and advice."

The older man folded his arms. "You'll get it anyway. Remember this, boy-o: The spawn of a serpent is still a snake, no matter how pretty her scales!"

He stepped away, and Tor took his place at the starting line.

King Gilmore waited for the action to begin again with concealed impatience. Where as once such a grand spectacle would have filled him with energy, now he found it displeasing. The desire for glory made heroes of men. The desire for power only made men desperate. And the desire for a beautiful woman could make the wisest man a fool.

He knew that all too well.

He glanced at his queen. He'd been battle-weary when he'd taken refuge at her father's tumbledown keep and had fallen under the spell of her beauty almost immediately. She had been trained from birth to marry well. Bryn was accomplished, and as clever and devious as any of his counselors.

There were times when he wondered what on earth had possessed him to marry her.

He turned to their daughter. Camaris

pouted beside him, unhappy with the way things were going. She had set her spoiled heart on a minor prince, a handsome, delicate fellow in sky-blue silk, with hair like spun gold. He knew she didn't really believe that she would be forced to wed the victor.

She has twice her mother's beauty, but half her charm. And less than that of Bryn's intelligence.

Thank the gods!

Two of them, strong-willed, able to cloud men's minds and bent on having their way, would have been more than he could handle.

He watched Tor rein in his mount. A brave fellow, and lucky, too. Now was the moment to see how far he could take this opportunity he had grasped so eagerly.

Yes, a clever young rogue, Gilmore thought with a smile. *But he'll find that he has met his match in me, whichever way this journey ends, I will turn it to my advantage.*

Mouse watched, too, with fear. A man in a brown jerkin pushed past, treading on her toes. A moment later the cry went up: *"Stop, thief!"*

Looking back, she saw a rotund merchant sprawled on the ground at the back of the crowd. His manservant was in pursuit of the thief, but the young cutpurse had fled, melting into the crowd.

Fortunately, the soldiers on peace patrol caught him near the hot-food booths. Without a word they clapped him on the shoulder. The next moment they'd lifted him off his feet so that his toes barely touched the ground and carried him away, to the cheers of the gawking onlookers.

"That will teach you, young ruffian!"

"There's another," someone shouted. "The girl is his partner." No one else was apprehended, though. The altercation ended, and the bugles announced the start of the tournament. All eyes were drawn to the jousting field.

The crowd fell silent, and tension built. Mouse could hardly stand it. Off to the side she saw two men standing by with a litter, waiting to remove the loser's body from the field. This would likely be a battle to the death. It was whispered that the duke would settle for no less.

Everyone seemed certain of the outcome. Everyone but Mouse. She prayed that Tor would somehow emerge from the battle unscathed. The odds were against him. One of the soldiers had wanted to get up a wager as to who would win. There were no takers.

She wished that Elva were here with her, but the old woman had been called to the bedside of a farmwife in hard labor. Gripping her hands together tightly, she waited.

The signal was given. Tor spurred his horse and charged his opponent. Hooves thundered and churned clouds of dust in the still, bright air.

Mouse held her breath. She wanted to be anywhere in the kingdom but here, yet she could not look away. In the back of her mind was the secret thought that by sheer will-power, she could keep him safe. She would rather see him wed to Camaris, than dead on the field of valor.

Horses and riders came at one another full tilt. It was hard to see it for all the dust that rose up as they met in a clash that shook the ground. When it was over, one horse lay still upon the ground. Ragnor had fallen hard.

Tor stood back, waiting until the older man struggled to his feet in his heavy armor. They reached for their swords.

Steel rang on steel as they thrust and parried. The duke was strong, but the weight of his armor impeded him. Tor danced around behind him and delivered a whacking blow with the flat of his sword. The duke went sprawling in the dirt.

A great cry went up from the crowd. Tor cut the strap that held the other man's helmet and placed the point of his sword at the duke's throat. "Surrender!"

Mouse squeezed her eyes shut as the duke signaled to acknowledge his defeat.

Then Tor's voice rang out. "You have fought with honor and courage, Ragnor. Rise to fight another day."

She looked in time to see Tor hold out his hand to the vanquished man and help him to his feet. A great roar of approval went up from the crowd.

The duke's men hurried out and helped him stagger back to his pavilion, where the red flag of Ragnor fluttered. Only a few of all those gathered remained voiceless among the shouts and ovations. King Gilmore eyed the scene from beneath lowered brows, while the queen sat grim and impassive.

The princess had apparently fainted.

A great stillness settled over the company as Tor moved toward the grandstand. He crossed the dusty field of combat in silence. Even the breeze held its breath.

The slanting rays of the lowering sun turned the air golden. His dark hair gleamed like polished onyx as he removed his helm and knelt before the king.

"I have come to claim my prize, Your Majesty: the hand of your daughter in marriage."

Mouse turned away. So this was the end of it. So much for her foolish daydreams.

She tried to leave, but king's men in their chain mail stood just behind her. The path to the village was blocked by the throng. She bit her lip. There was no way to escape. The servants and villagers and guildsmen would leave when the pageant was over, and not a moment before. There was nothing she could do but stand and watch it all unfold.

A soldier crowded her. Mouse gave a squeak of dismay. "Kindly give me room to breathe," she protested.

They ignored her, and she did her best to ignore them. The light was failing fast and a pale mist was rising. Although torches were lit beside the grandstand, it was becoming difficult to see. Mouse strained her eyes for a better look at the commotion on the grandstand.

The king held up his hand and the assembly fell silent again. "You have been victorious, Tor of Far Islandia."

The Princess Camaris had come around from her swoon. She sat up and her shrill voice carried across the field. "No!" she wept hysterically. "I will not marry him! I am a *princess!* He is a commoner, an ill-bred rustic! Father, you cannot mean to force me!"

Gilmore held up his hand. "Silence!"

He looked down at Tor, long and hard. "A

man who marries ill will surely live to regret it. Would you be content to wed a woman whose heart is set against you?"

"I will do aught I can to win her heart," Tor said. "I have no crown of gold or fine estates, but noble blood runs through my veins." He lifted his head proudly. "I am the grandson of Orgus, who ruled Far Islandia in olden times."

The queen gave a scornful laugh. "As are a score of others — bastards and barbarians all! You are not fit to stand in the shadow of the Princess Camaris."

Tor's black eyes glittered with anger in the circle of torchlight. "I do not intend to stand in her shadow, madam. I will stand at her side."

"Enough," King Gilmore said. "You are champion of the tournament and have earned the right to claim your prize. Is it indeed your wish to wed my daughter?"

"My most heartfelt one, sire."

"Do you swear on your soul that you will take her to wife, protect her and guard her and honor her all your days?"

"I do indeed swear, sire."

"Then your wish is granted. You shall have her hand." Gilmore gave a signal, and trumpets were raised in a bright fanfare.

Mouse gasped in alarm as she was caught

beneath the arms and picked up off her feet. Two burly men-at-arms held her in their grasp.

"Let me go! Put me down!" she cried. "I have done nothing wrong."

"You'll come with us," one said curtly. Without further ado, they carried her off as if she weighed no more than a windblown leaf.

"Well, well," someone nearby said. "They've caught the thief's accomplice. Look, they're taking her away."

Mouse couldn't believe what was happening. The toes of her shoes skimmed over the warm summer grass and the dusty tournament field. The soldiers delivered her straight to the foot of the grandstand, where they released her so abruptly that she fell all in a heap in the circle of torchlight.

"Ah, here she is, Tor of Far Islandia." King Gilmore smiled coolly in the flickering light. "Your prize!"

Tor looked from the frightened girl struggling to rise to the monarch. "What trickery is this? Who is this girl?"

"No trickery at all, sir bard." Gilmore's voice was stern. "This indeed is my daughter that you see before you. Her name is Rosaleen."

Mouse was filled with confusion. "R-rrosaleen is my name," she stammered. "But I am an orphan, the child of simple weavers. My father was killed in the wars. My mother died shortly after my birth."

The king touched the pouch at his belt, where a dried rose petal, and the small crystal stone he had found in the courtyard were hidden fast away. Memories were becoming more clear with every passing moment.

The king's face was lined with sorrow. "Your mother was Deirdre the weaver. We were hand-fasted at Beltane, before I went to battle. You have her silvery eyes and delicate features. But you got the fire in your hair from me, daughter!"

Mouse heard the ring of truth in his words. She lifted her chin. "If what you say is so, Majesty, why have you waited until now to claim me as your own?"

"The truth of your parentage has only just been revealed to me. I claim you now, before all the court and my noble visitors. You are mine."

He turned to Tor. "Come! Claim your prize, sir bard."

Tor saw the resemblance then, between the girl in the plain blue gown and the king. Rage filled him like roaring flame. "Daughter or no, this woman has nothing to do with me. It was the Princess Camaris I fought for!"

"Think back over my words. Never once was Camaris's name said by me to you."

Tor felt as if he'd been struck by a nailed fist. It was true. And it was wrong! "I will have Camaris," he said through clenched teeth.

Gilmore's eyes were cold as the northern ocean. "As I have kept my word, so must you keep yours. Tor of Far Islandia, grandson of the great Orgus, I grant you the hand of my daughter Rosaleen as reward for your valor today. You will be wed in the castle chapel tomorrow at noon."

8

Mouse stared at the king in horror.

The same emotion was reflected in Tor's black eyes. "I do not wish to marry her."

Unseen in the torchlight, a flush rose up Mouse's throat and covered her cheeks. She had endowed the stranger with all sorts of wonderful qualities. For her efforts, he had repudiated her before the entire court.

"Nor do I wish to wed this man," she said hotly. "I would not have him were he the last alive on the face of the entire earth."

The king rubbed his hand across his face. "Well, then. If neither of you is willing, let no more be said."

Mouse was giddy with relief. Tor held his ground. "There is still a prize to be claimed," he stormed. "I accepted the challenge — and I have won!"

Gilmore smiled, but his eyes were hooded. "Once again you misheard me. I mentioned a challenge to win the hand of the Princess

Camaris. You all jumped to the conclusion that it was the tournament to which I referred. But there is another quest I had in mind for the man who would claim half my kingdom."

He snapped his fingers, and a page handed him a sealed scroll. "The challenge is here, dated a week past. I will read it to you now."

Breaking the seal with his thumbnail, he unrolled it. "The challenge I set is this: The man who will share the throne as co-regent must first complete a quest. He must find and bring to me the egg of the fiery phoenix!"

The crowd murmured like sea waves against Airan's towering cliffs. A few snickered. The king had set an impossible task, and everyone knew it.

Tor eyed him warily. "Does this creature even exist in Airan?"

"It is your task to find that out. In legend," the king said, "the home of the phoenix is in the Mystic Mountains, which divide Airan from the Eastern Lands. A rugged place, not one for the weak of heart. Both my daughters will remain safe in my care while you are on your quest. Bring me the egg of the phoenix. Then, Tor of Far Islandia, I shall grant any wish you desire. You have my word of honor."

"I am not inclined to take your words at

face value," Tor snapped, "so facile are you at twisting them."

Gilmore shrugged. "Ah. I see. If the task is too difficult — if your courage fails you — then you may leave this country in peace, and none will call you coward!"

Tor was so angry that a red mist filled his vision and a muscle twitched in Tor's jaw. "If the phoenix exists, I shall find it!"

The king smiled grimly. "I shall order everything made ready for your journey. You will remain at the castle as my guest, of course, until such a time as you can set out."

"I will not stay a moment longer than is necessary," Tor said, in a voice that rang like steel. "I shall fulfill the quest you've set me and find this phoenix egg." His entire body was taut with anger. "And you will rue the day that I return!"

Mouse gasped. *He must be mad to utter such a threat!*

It was evident that others thought the same. In the stunned silence, Tor turned his back upon the king and strode away. The captain of the guards stepped out, his sword drawn and ready. Other weapons slithered from their scabbards.

In a movement so quick it seemed like a stroke of magic, Tor's own broadsword was in his hand. Battle light gleamed in his eyes,

468

like cold stars in a January sky. He had fought against high odds before, and won.

"If my quest starts here, so be it!"

"It will end here as well," the captain said.

"No!" Gilmore thundered. "Let him pass freely, and in peace. He is still my guest and still under my oath of safety."

Tor sheathed his sword and strode away into the darkness.

In the commotion that followed, Mouse slipped through the crowd and vanished as well.

9

The hour was late, the noble guests gone to bed, when the queen sought her husband. She found him alone in the tower, sipping from a goblet of wine.

Bryn smiled sweetly at her husband. "How clever of you, my lord! I admit I was terrified to think of my sweet Camaris wed to that oaf who came to claim her!"

Gilmore drained the wine from the silver-and-amethyst goblet. "He is not such a barbarian as you think, my dear. We might do worse for a son-in-law."

Bryn blinked, and her smile froze for several seconds. Then she rallied quickly. "He is bold, I grant you that. But on the wrong side of the blanket!" Orgus had no legitimate heirs.

The king took another gulp of mead. "There are some who would dispute that. Orgus wed Maire — but he was hand-fasted to another long before."

"I am no fool," the queen hissed. "You are reminding me that there was another woman before me. But," she said pointedly, "you did not wed her. You wed me!"

He gazed down into his cup, seeing years past in the reflected light. "This you should know: Had I not wed you, I would have married Deirdre upon my return from the war that won me my crown."

"What, wed a *peasant?*"

"Her mother was a freeholder," Gilmore said, bristling. "I knew her from the time we were children. We fell in love. . . ."

The queen was alarmed. He should remember none of this! "And yet you said nothing to me? And yet you let the girl, Rosaleen, grow up like one of your servants inside these walls? What kind of love is that?"

"*I* cannot explain it," he replied softly. "But perhaps you can."

Bryn's eyes shone hard as diamonds, but her heart was filled with fear. The spell she had cast over Gilmore was losing its power more rapidly with every passing hour. She must find another, stronger one to hold him in thrall.

"I am but a woman. How can I hope to judge what was in your mind or heart all these years? It has been a long day, my love," she said in honeyed tones, "and we are both weary. Seek your bed, my lord. We will speak of this another time."

Gilmore tossed back the last of his wine. "Yes. The hour is late. But it is my daughter Rosaleen I must seek out, first. I've given her a suite of rooms in the west tower. You must find servants and garments worthy of her status."

Bryn clenched her hands. "Do what you like. *I* shall never acknowledge her. Never!"

She whirled around and left Gilmore's chamber in a rustle of silk brocade. In her own quarters, she dismissed her servants and sent her ladies to their beds. When the castle was asleep, Bryn locked the door and then lit a candle and set it in the window of her bedchamber. Taking a seat in her gilded chair, she waited. It was not long before her signal was answered.

She heard the tap on the hidden door, and moved the tapestry aside to open it.

A steely-eyed knight entered, his burly shoulders brushing the sides of the narrow door. He knelt before her and kissed the hem of her gown. "Majesty!"

"Yes, yes," she said impatiently. "Rise. I have a commission for you."

"Anything you will, my lady, even though it cost me my life!"

She smiled. "Such loyalty! But be reassured. It is not your life I seek, but another's." She drummed her long nails on the seat of her gilded chair. "Rid me of the girl Rosaleen! I do not care how it is done."

10

A sickle moon rode low in the black velvet sky as Tor thundered across the moor. A prudent man would have waited for morning to set out, but he had been too angry to be prudent.

Consequently, he had spent the last hour cursing and trying to maintain his bearings.

Night and weather were closing in more quickly now. One by one the stars were obliterated, as a luminous fog rose up from the valley. It was proving increasingly difficult to see the road. If he meant to seek shelter for the night, it would have to be soon.

Tor urged his black horse across the turf, sending up clods of earth, trying to outrace the humiliation of Gilmore's trickery. The king had made him a laughingstock in front of the entire court. Tor gritted his teeth.

Even Broch had scoffed at him. That had rankled. Tor had been sent to Broch for training when he was just a lad, and the older man had been like a surrogate father. He'd taught Tor the arts of swordplay and horsemanship, and had given him good counsel along the way.

"I warned you not to come to Airan in the first place," the older man had told him after the tournament. "Let us leave this accursed country before you come to grief."

Broch had been outraged when he'd realized that Tor had no intention of letting Gilmore hold the upper hand. "The king has made a fool of you once, and now you are letting him do it again. I won't accompany you on a fool's errand. There is no phoenix, and never was," he'd snorted. "It's as imaginary as your love for that haughty princess!"

And in the end, driven by anger and ambition, Tor had agreed that it was better if their paths diverged. The quest was liable to be both long and dangerous. He did not wish to put the old man in jeopardy. Broch could be more useful in other ways.

Once he reached the heights, Tor wheeled his mount and looked back the way he'd come. The great black horse whickered and pawed the air. Tiny lights glimmered where Castle Airan thrust up through the fog, looking as distant as the stars. Tor's jaw squared. He was a warrior who lived by his wits and his sword, but he was the equal of any man. The blood of kings ran through his veins. He would not forget it.

Nor would he let anyone else do so.

"I will be back to claim my true bride," he vowed to the night wind, raising his gloved fist. "And when I return, woe to the house of Gilmore! For I shall claim not merely half the kingdom, but the whole of it!"

His pride was no protection against the fog. It swept in around him, relentless as the tide. The damp gray air thickened and congealed. It was impossible to see more than a horse's length ahead. Much as he wanted to push on, Tor knew he would have to seek shelter for the night.

Fortunately, he had studied the old maps before arriving in Airan and knew the general lay of the land. If memory served, the old coast road branched down from here. It was rarely used these days, but dotted with ruined watchtowers that had guarded the coast from invaders centuries before. If he judged correctly, one of them was at the end of this downward slope. Even if it were nothing more than a pile of stones, it would provide some protection for the night.

Of course, if he was wrong, he might be heading out over the cliffs. Tor dismounted and led his horse through the undergrowth.

The ground dipped sharply on the far side of the woods just ahead.

At first there was only earth beneath his boots, but after a few minutes he felt that give way to paving stones. They were crooked as a crone's teeth, but eventually they led him to his goal. The fog shifted and the tower loomed up without warning.

There was no door, only a high, open arch and the remains of rusted hinges. When Tor tried to lead his gelding into the shelter at the tower's base, the creature balked and rolled its eyes.

"Easy, old friend." He ran a hand over the beast's warm muzzle. "There's a hard storm brewing out at sea. We'll stay warm and dry enough here while we wait it out."

The horse refused to budge. "Is there some ghost or magic here that frightens you? Very well. You'll be fine in the lean-to."

Visibility was worsening, but the animal went docilely enough into the place where other horses had been stabled years before, comforted by their faded scent. After removing the saddle and pack, Tor rubbed his steed down. Suddenly the beast whinnied softly.

Tor went still. He heard it, too. The sound of another horse picking its way along the old coast road.

He drew steel and waited. Was it merely some other poor wayfarer, lost in the smothering grayness? Or had Gilmore sent someone to follow him? Someone, perhaps, who would rid the king of the man who aspired to the hand of the princess?

Sure and relentless as the lapping of waves against the shore, the sounds came nearer. Soft jingle of harness, and muffled hooves. Tor smiled grimly. No one would be heading here without some dark purpose.

The hoofbeats slowed, then ceased. Now there was only the occasional skitter of stones along the path leading to the tower. The rider had dismounted. Fog distorted sound and made it difficult to pinpoint his exact position. Tor strained his ears to listen.

A rattle of stones startled him. Whirling toward it, he saw a shape come hurtling out of the night. As his sword flashed through the mist, he glimpsed a pale heart-shaped face filled with alarm. Tor cursed and leapt back, checking his powerful swing. Not a soldier, but a woman.

She slid down the rest of the way in a hail of tiny stones and fetched up against the base of the tower.

"I mean you no harm," she gasped.

He stifled a laugh and leaned on the hilt of

his broadsword. "A good thing, then," he said, "for you would have failed utterly. What is your business abroad at such an hour, on such a foul night?"

The woman sat up warily. "I was making my way to the old coast road. When it became too difficult to see the way, I sought sanctuary here."

"Not refuge, but sanctuary?" Tor frowned. "An odd choice of words."

"I am fleeing for my life, sir."

The mist thinned suddenly around them. She stared up at him and the naked blade gripped in his hand. He froze. Who else but Rosaleen, the king's daughter?

"Is this another trick?" he asked harshly, dragging her to her feet.

"Let me go!"

Mouse swallowed around the dryness in her throat. What a cruel jest of Fate, to send her on a path straight to the man who had rejected her!

Humiliation filled her mouth like bitter tea. Tears of helpless anger stung her eyes and spilled over her thick lashes. She turned her head so that he wouldn't see them.

Tor stabbed his sword into the ground and gripped her shoulders. "Why has he sent you after me? And where are the king's soldiers?"

She shivered and pulled back at the strength in him. He could snap her like a twig. "The king has not sent me. No one has."

"Oh, you merely decided to risk your pretty neck by riding out in a fog as thick as lambswool? Tell me another lie. Spinning them seems to be the favorite pastime here in Airan."

Mouse wrenched away. "I speak truth. My life is worth nothing now. The queen is my mortal enemy. She will not let me live to see many more days."

She lifted her chin. "As for soldiers, my lord, there are none. Only myself, armed with nothing but my wits and this dagger."

Her cloak fell open, and the crystal pendant at her throat seemed to burn with a pale, elfin light. In its glow he saw her eyes, dark as sapphires. And the small dagger with a twisted silver hilt, in the grasp of her fingers. The blade shone wickedly. She could have shoved it between his ribs at any time while he questioned her, and they both knew it.

Tor stepped back warily. "Perhaps this is another trick, to earn my trust. If you are truly the king's daughter, tell me why you are treated as a servant within his castle — and why the queen wishes to see you dead."

Leaning on the hilt of his broadsword, he eyed her shrewdly and waited for an explanation. Mouse was too weary for anything but the truth. Lies would do her no good in any case.

She bit her lip. "I am indeed Gilmore's daughter, although I never knew the full story of my birth until today."

Elva had told her everything after Mouse had fled the scene of the tournament. "The king is wise in all things — except where it concerns his wife," Mouse said. "But the blame is not his. The queen has ensorcelled him."

Tor's eyebrows rose. "A poor sorceress, if she could not keep the king from dallying with your mother!"

"It is not as you think," she said hotly. "My mother and the king hand-fasted before he won the crown." Her mouth trembled with emotion. "Bryn is a wicked woman. After casting her spell upon the king, she was not content until she destroyed my mother. I was orphaned mere hours after my birth."

Tor was startled. "In Far Islandia magic is used only for good — for healing and growing crops and calling up fair weather. What of the princess? Is she an acolyte of the Dark Arts?"

"No." Mouse shook her head. "Camaris is a spoiled and rather foolish girl, but there is no true wickedness in her. She is merely a pawn to further the queen's great ambitions."

Spoiled and foolish? Tor bridled. Surely such words could not apply to the lovely Camaris. He thought he'd found a flaw in her story. "You are clever with your tongue, but the tale does not ring true. Why did the queen not dispose of you, as she did your mother?"

The fog swirled in around them while Mouse told him about Elva and the Spell of Forgetting. "Only Elva remembered the truth of my birth, and she kept her own counsel. I was raised as a weaver, learning on my mother's loom. When the princess admired my work, I was brought to the castle. It was pleasant enough and I was well paid for my work." Her voice hardened. "And so I would have lived out my days quite happily, had *you* not arrived in Airan!"

"A spell of forgetfulness." He smiled cynically. "How convenient for everyone concerned — especially for the king!"

"I assure you it is the least convenient for me!" Mouse sent him a resentful look from beneath her winged brows. "I would much prefer to spend the night beneath a warm roof than out here in the fog and cold!"

Tor heard the conviction in her voice. He sheathed his sword. "I accept your tale. But it does not explain why you followed me here."

"I, follow *you?*" Mouse was furious. "It is the other way around. I came through the ravine."

He remembered it now, a wide slash of crumpled lines upon the map. "A dangerous journey."

"Not so dangerous as remaining beneath the same roof as Queen Bryn," she snapped. "Go on your way and leave me in peace, sir."

"Neither of us can go any further in this thick mist. Let us seek shelter in the tower while I decide what to do about you."

Anger flared in her eyes. "You need do nothing about me. I am off to seek my own fate. You have no part in it."

Tor's jaw squared. "Yet you just said in your own words that the blame for your troubles rests on me. You cannot have it both ways. And if I take the blame, lady, then I accept the responsibility as well."

"It's too late to argue. Come inside the tower. I've a fire started."

"Not very wise of you. The smoke will send us out coughing into the night, and the scent of burning wood will lead the soldiers here." He could smell it now that the wind had died away.

"The roof is mostly gone," she answered, "and there are no windows at all at the tower's base. The smoke will rise up high, and its scent will seem to be coming from the valley. We'll be safe enough."

She stopped suddenly and looked behind her, alert and wary. "There was another man with you. Where is he?"

"On his way south."

Mouse frowned. "Running away from danger? He didn't look to be a coward."

"He is not!" Tor said shortly. "I've sent him on an errand."

He ducked beneath the low doorway and followed her inside. She sat down in front of the fire. It was small and did little to keep back the blackness.

Two fat turnips were roasting over it. "I have sausage and cheese as well, and a pouchful of raisins," Mouse told him. "If the hungry little ermald didn't eat them all."

He looked down and saw a tiny creature poised upon its furry white haunches. He'd seen one only in paintings. Its body resembled an ermine, but its large green eyes were very like a cat's. It gobbled up the raisin it held in its paws and vanished into the darkness.

"Oh, you've frightened it away."

Tor sat on the far side of the fire and eyed her warily. Some believed that ermalds were the spirits of those who'd lived before.

"Are you a sorceress? I'd heard that ermalds never come into the presence of humans. No one I know has ever seen one alive."

"They are very shy," Mouse said. "I used to have one as a pet when I was younger. Elva taught me how to win the confidence of shy creatures."

She handed him a portion of cheese. "I've plenty to spare. I took everything I could get my hands on when I fled the village."

"Taming ermalds and cooking turnips. You're a practical woman," he said. "But a woman traveling alone will be easy enough to track."

"I've brought boy's garb with me. My trail ends here."

She twisted her hair up atop her head, tucked it beneath the boy's cap, and tried to look tough. The effect was spoiled by the streak of ash her knuckle left across her face. She looked, Tor decided, less like a farm lad than like a mischievous urchin. He wasn't sure if he liked it or not.

"You still look like a girl. There's no disguising your delicate features." *Or those high, firm breasts.*

She saw it in his eyes before he looked away, as clearly as if he'd spoken aloud. Hot color flooded her cheeks. "I'm not a fool. I'll bind them."

"A pity."

Tor flushed. He'd said it without thinking — but it was still true. And the rest of her was lovely as well. How odd he hadn't noticed that earlier.

Mouse cupped her chin in her hand. She'd been mulling something over in her mind for some time. "You risked everything in the tournament, including your life. I am wondering why."

That took him aback. "The Princess Camaris is very beautiful."

She made a dismissive gesture. "That is no answer. It's clear to me that your strategy was all planned out long before you so much as set eyes on her."

"Ah, but the moment I saw her, my heart was lost."

Mouse was sorry she'd asked.

His gaze was coolly appraising. "Why do you think I came to Airan?"

"The others — the dukes and lords and princes — came in hopes of increasing their status and wealth." She tipped her head and surveyed him. "You have neither, so I suppose that is the reason."

"You are an annoying girl," he said shortly. "And you know nothing at all about me. Perhaps I have five thousand acres and five hundred head of cattle. As to what drew me to Airan — I decided that I should like to have a few more adventures before I settled down."

That intrigued her. "What kind of adventures have you had?"

"None of your business, my girl. You ask more questions of a stranger than is considered polite!"

"Ah." She regarded him from beneath her lashes. "You have no land or cattle. I thought not."

He fought the urge to throttle her. She was a most maddening girl!

Tor took a deep breath. If he had to put up with her for the night, he could at least get information from her, for his knowledge of Airan's more remote geography left much to be desired.

"If I will find this fabulous phoenix, I must know more about its habits. Tell me, what lies in the mountainous regions that the phoenix calls home?"

"Ho! Now who is asking the questions?" But she laughed softly when she said it. She considered how much to give away: Part of the truth, she decided, would be sufficient to prove her use to him.

"The Misted Mountains are a place of enchantment. The source of Airan's legends." Mouse laced her hands behind her neck. "They also are home to thunder giants who use lightning bolts to spear their prey, and to trolls with eyes as red as fire and teeth like rusted knives. Many an unwary traveler has been frightened to death by them."

Tor was not amused. "Do you think me a rustic, with hay between my teeth?" He stuck his knife tip into one of the turnips. It was still hard as wood. "I wouldn't nibble at your troll tales, any more than I would bite into this half-cooked root. Such stories are spun to frighten country bumpkins."

She eyed him steadily. "Then why do you believe in the phoenix?"

He hesitated again. "Because I have proof."

Reaching inside his jerkin, Tor withdrew a flat piece of leather. When he opened it, the looming shadows jumped back. The chamber at the base of the ruins was lit with sparkling, iridescent light.

"Oh!" Mouse blinked and shielded her eyes. "What is it?"

"The feather of a phoenix. It is my talisman." Tor held it reverently. "I had the story from my grandfather, Orgus, and this feather from his own hand before he died. He came to Airan on a quest in the long-ago and found one of the creatures captured in a trap he set. When he removed it from the snare, it spread its plumage, dazzling him so greatly that he let go of it. The phoenix flew away, leaving only this feather behind."

Mouse was awed. "May I touch it?"

He nodded, and she came around the fire to sit beside him. "It is the most beautiful thing I've ever seen."

She reached out to the relic of the legendary bird. Little rainbows flickered over her slender hand. Her fingertips caressed the feather. It wasn't like anything she'd ever touched before. It felt warm and cool at the same time, and it tickled, as if hundreds of little golden bubbles danced against her skin.

"Thank you." She was enchanted. "Never in my life did I expect to see such a marvel. How did he capture it?"

"That," Tor said, "is a secret."

She pulled her hand back. "And how to find the phoenix is mine."

He placed the feather carefully inside the flat leather and tucked it away in his jerkin. Except for the glow of the small wood fire, the chamber was dark once more.

Mouse moved back to the other side of the fire. "I could aid you in your quest," she said quietly. "I know all the old legends and songs, even those that have been forgotten by all the rest." Elva had taught her, hoping to keep them alive. "You are an outlander. I doubt you have the smallest inkling of where the phoenix can be found."

"Tell me, then."

"For a price."

"Abominable girl!"

"It isn't gold I seek. I will aid you in your quest to find the phoenix if you will pledge to help me in mine."

"I might agree," Tor said, "but first you must prove to me that you have the knowledge I lack."

Mouse folded her hands and rested her chin upon them. Her eyes were like dark sapphires in the fire's glow, her hair like burnished copper.

"To find the phoenix, you must first locate Phoenix Pass. There's a rock that marks it, shaped like a woman. Legend says she was turned to stone by a basilisk, the sly reptiles that hatch from roosters' eggs. You can only look at them in a mirror," she added.

"Roosters do not lay eggs. Hens do," Tor exclaimed in exasperation. "No more of these faradiddles. Tell me about the phoenix, and tell me true!"

"You needn't shout!"

"Tell me, sweet Rosaleen, I beg you."

His voice was gentle — but the words

490

came through gritted teeth. She almost laughed aloud. She had him now.

"The phoenix is very shy. It makes its nest in the topmost branches of the silver rowan tree. They grow only near the summit of the tallest mountain and . . ."

"But of course," he broke in sarcastically. "It couldn't be just around the bend, lying by the side of the road."

". . . and are very difficult to find," she continued as if he hadn't spoken. "But the leaves of the tree are hammered silver, and the trunk is of purest gold. If the light is right, it can be seen from Phoenix Pass at sundown."

"And how do I find Phoenix Pass?"

Mouse couldn't restrain her smile. "You won't find it on your own. It can only be found by a virgin."

That let him out. He'd lost his virginity as a lusty lad of seventeen. Tor sent her a hard look across the low flames. "Very clever."

"Of course," Mouse offered, "I would be glad to be of assistance on your quest, in return for your vow to aid me."

He considered her thoughtfully. She had courage — and a wit as keen as a honed steel blade. A strange creature, this girl who was sired by a king and then forgotten. A fetching one, too.

"What is it, that you want?"

"You must promise to see me safely over the mountains to the Eastern Lands," she told him. Her face was aglow in the firelight. "There is a city there. A small but wonderful city called Penambra, with houses of gold-colored stone."

Elva had told her all about it. The wise-woman had visited relatives there long ago, when she was a young child, and remembered its honey-tiled roofs and gleaming domes. Mouse intended to send for Elva as soon as she was settled. "The moment my foot touches the ground in Penambra," she told Tor, "you are free of your vow."

He raised his brows. "And that is it?"

"Yes. I'll be safe there," she said confidently. "I have only to find the weavers guild, and they will take me in. I'll earn my way with my skills."

Tor's gaze was unreadable. "If you help me realize my quest, I vow that I will do everything in my power to see that you are safe and comfortably established. Word of a Far Islandian! And I will give you a dowry of gold."

Her eyes widened. "I didn't ask for gold!"

"It's the least I can do, after bringing the queen's wrath down upon you. Do we have a bargain?"

"I'd like something more than your word," she said. "Words can be twisted. Give me the phoenix feather as token of your faith. I swear that I will give it back once you've redeemed your vow."

Tor crossed his arms over his chest. "Unlike your father," he said, "my word is my bond. But I cannot give you the feather. It is a sacred trust."

He'd promised Orgus that he would give it someday to his own firstborn son.

Mouse didn't know if she could trust this black-eyed stranger. Her fingers caressed the fractured stone that was all that remained of her amulet while she decided. *I cannot leave Elva, aging and alone. I must get her away before the queen suspects that she had any part in my birth.* But first, she would have to reach the city beyond the mountains. *I will have to risk it.*

She took the silver chain from around her throat. The clear pebble shone like a ruby as it gathered the firelight. "This is all I have of value in the world," she said simply. "It is worth more to me than gold."

Mouse held it out to Tor. "Let us exchange necklaces as a token of faith. Your talisman for mine."

Tor saw the tear trapped in her eyelashes. He could not even begin to guess what it cost her to make the offer. She was risking far more than he by exchanging tokens — and by putting her honor and trust in him.

"My pledge is not worthy of yours, Rosaleen of Airan. But my solemn oath goes with it. I will keep my vow to you."

He accepted her amulet, then pulled the twisted silver torque from around his neck.

She smiled tremulously, accepting his token. She slipped the torque on. It was warm from his body, and far too large. Tor reached over and bent the ends closer to one another, forcing the twisted silver into a smaller circle to fit her slender throat.

As his fingers brushed her skin, something passed between them. The air hummed with it, like a plucked harp string. Mouse quickly pulled away. She still felt it, a vibration in her bones. A resonance in her soul.

Tor looked down at her talisman in his hand. The chain was far too small to go around his throat. Taking the thong that bound his hair, he threaded the amulet onto it, knotting the silver links to each end. "We have a pact, Rosaleen of Airan. I give you my solemn oath that I will help you, as you help me."

Mouse closed her eyes and sighed with relief. The silver torque seemed to throw a ring of protection around her. It was an illusion, she knew, but it comforted her never-theless.

Although initially she'd been distressed to find that her unwelcome visitor was Tor, she was glad now that he had chanced upon her hideaway. Practical she might be, but there was no way she could cross the mountains to safety alone. He had a sword, a strong arm, and the courage to wield both. Her odds had just improved greatly.

"I pledge the same to you, Tor of Far Islandia. You have my oath as well."

She saw that the turnips were done, and she removed them from the fire. They ate in silence while the flames leapt up inside the black maw of the tower. Mouse finished half of hers and put the rest aside. "It will do for breakfast."

"Hold still, Rosaleen. You've a smut on your cheek."

He tried to rub it away with his thumb, but she pulled away. "You wouldn't be cleaning a lad's dirt off," she told him sharply. "And I am called Mouse, sir."

"Not," Tor said, "by me."

"Why?"

"It is not a dignified name for the daughter of a king."

She plopped down on her knapsack. "I am not a very dignified person."

Tor wrapped himself in his cloak and lay down on the other side of the banked fire. "Nor I."

Her sudden smile flashed. "Then we shall be disreputable together for the night."

A swift intake of breath and an awkward silence followed her gaffe. "That wasn't an invitation," she said in a gruff voice.

Tor hid his laughter. "I didn't take it as one. Go to sleep, Rosaleen of Airan. And sleep well."

She turned her back to him and lay unmoving in the dim glow. It was only a few minutes, however, before her breathing slowed and she was fast asleep.

Tor pondered the situation. He doubted whether the girl had thought further than the first day or two. The food she had with her would run out by then, and as far as he could tell she had no warm garments or leather boots to protect her from the cold of the high mountains.

Tor doubted she had the heart to wring a chicken's neck, much less the skill to trap even the weakest game. If he hadn't stumbled upon her, only the gods knew how long she might have survived on her own.

Not very long, he decided. *She is no more fit to survive in the wilds alone than an infant is. And she would prove a hindrance to his own* survival, no doubt about that either.

It wasn't just her knowledge of where the phoenix lived that had swayed his judgment — although he believed her. It was something else she'd said that rang terribly true: If not for him, she would have lived out her life safely between the thick stone walls of Castle Aidan, her royal identity unknown.

By winning the tournament he had jeopardized everything that mattered to her. It was a burden he must bear for both of them.

Wrapped in her blanket, Mouse murmured something in her sleep. *She is having a nightmare,* Tor thought. He rose and went around the fire to kneel beside her.

In the glow, her hair was like dark flame spilling around her shoulders. Her lashes lay against her cheek, casting a shadow. She was really quite beautiful. And he recognized where he'd first seen her now.

The knowledge came all at once. She was the girl he'd encountered in the castle, fleeing as if her life depended upon it. If he hadn't caught her she might have hurtled down the stairs.

He reached his hand out. There was the mark of the bruise upon her smooth skin, fading to yellow. Gently, so as not to awaken her, he placed the back of his hand against her cheek.

So lovely, and so brave. Life has used her hard. She should have been born to silks and satins, not to a life of servitude to a cruel mistress.

Tor made another vow then and there. *Fair Rosaleen of Airan, I will do all in my power to see that you get everything your heart desires, and more.*

Although at the moment he didn't have a clue as to how he would bring it all about. Instead of going back to the other side of the fire, Tor wrapped himself up in his cloak and lay down beside her.

He was still awake at dawn.

11

At half-light Tor saddled up their mounts. Mouse watched him place his bow and quiver of arrows within easy reach. "I hope you are as handy with them as you are with a broadsword."

"They are not for show!" he said stiffly.

Just then they both stopped and listened. The fitful wind had carried an ominous sound to their ears: men and horses in the distance. "We'd best be on our way."

She used a rock for a mounting block before he could help her. Tor swung up into the saddle, and they took off over the sand. Row upon row, the waves flashed dull silver as they crumpled and spilled onto the beach. The retreating surf washed away their hoofprints, and the roar of the sea covered the sound of their passage.

They went on for some time. The sun was rising over the hills when Mouse led him back toward the cliffs. A shadow behind a fall of giant rocks proved to be the narrow entrance to a cave.

"A shortcut," she said. "The coast curves in and out, like lace on a lady's gown, but this cavern tunnels deep. We'll save many miles this way, and no one the wiser."

Tor followed her, frowning. He wasn't fond of enclosed spaces, but he wasn't going to let this mere slip of a girl know that.

Mouse glanced at him from beneath her lashes. "It's all right," she said. "You won't feel smothered."

He muttered an oath and rode in.

It wasn't dark once he got inside. Weak sunshine filtered down through small crevices hidden from above by the wild grasses. The walls were a soft lavender-rose color and glittered as if they were covered with hoarfrost.

Once the seas had been higher, he guessed, for the first hundred yards of the cavern floor were covered by wave-packed sand. He saw small footsteps winding over it and realized they must be hers.

"You know this place well."

"Yes. Elva showed it to me. We used to ride out on the back of her cob to gather the wild mosses." She lifted her head, glancing up at the domed ceiling. Stalactites gleamed like tinted icicles.

"Beautiful, isn't? I've been coming here since I was a child."

"You're still . . ." He stopped and looked away.

Then he glanced back at Mouse, assessing her in the filtered green light. She wasn't a child. Not by any means.

She was truly quite lovely. During the long night hours he'd grown increasingly aware of it. Her breasts were high and firm, her hips and thighs softly rounded. And, he remembered keenly, her hair had smelled exactly like wild raspberries.

The ground underfoot rang as their horses left the sand and entered a long gallery hollowed from rock. Mouse led them through the forest of stone formations, some bridging the span from floor to high ceiling like fancifully carved pillars. Gradually the light dimmed as the way grew cramped.

"We must go single file from here," she said. "Stay well back. The cavern floor is slippery." *And,* Mouse thought, *you won't be able to question me further.*

Or see her face and realize that she'd never before gone so far into the winding maze of passageways.

Her heart beat a little faster. All she had guiding her now was Elva's instructions. The wisewoman had taught her a set of rhymes to get from the seashore caverns to the secluded valley far beyond the cliffs. Mouse prayed that she had memorized them well.

Tor didn't guess her secret. He fell in behind her, trusting her to lead the way. They rode in echoing silence for a long time, picking their way over the stone floor. At one point his horse almost lost its footing. It skittered sideways, but he held it in check. When he looked up Mouse had vanished.

There were several routes she could have taken. He called out to her. His voice came echoing back, ever fainter.

Cursing beneath his breath, Tor stopped and listened. The only sound was a soft sighing. He urged his horse toward it. There was an opening somewhere ahead. The closer he got to it, the more he felt the gentle breath of air moving past his face. He rounded a turn and came out into daylight.

They were in a narrow valley surrounded by sheer rock walls. The sky was a thin blue ribbon high above. Mouse was just a little way ahead, looking back over her shoulder.

"You should have made sure I was behind you," he said, with a hint of temper.

Her eyebrows rose. "Were you afraid that you were lost? I would have turned back and found you."

"No, by the gods! My concern wasn't for

myself." Tor reined in beside her. "The queen's men are after you, and you are unarmed!"

"They would never find their way through the caverns." She pointed up toward the mouth of the valley. "The trail leads up to the rim. It's long and steep. Best to rest and water the horses before we set out along it."

Since he was about to suggest the same thing, her advice annoyed him. He didn't know why. They took the horses to the stream that trickled down from the heights and let them quench their thirst.

Mouse had seen the frown flicker across his brow. "You are accustomed to giving the orders. You don't like taking them from a woman."

"In Far Islandia, women and men walk on equal footing. But I am not used to meekly bringing up the rear, as if I were a beardless stripling."

Mouse saw she'd stung his pride, and hid her smile. "We've a long way to go, and many adventures ahead of us. We'll take the lead in turn."

"I'll take it here," he said, with a mocking smile. "In case we run into any giants or basilisks or trolls along the way."

"If it makes you happy, lead the way. Give me a boost into the saddle."

Tor swept her a formal bow. "I am at your service, lady."

She expected him to lace his hands together to form a step for her to mount. Instead he stepped in close. The moment his strong hands spanned her waist, a curious shock of pleasure zinged through her.

Before she had time to think, he tossed her into the saddle as if she weighed no more than mist. Mouse clutched the reins and steadied her horse. *What power there is in him!*

She felt his tongue against her throat, and remembered how it had lain against his skin. Her heart skipped and fluttered like a startled bird, and her head was light with agreeable confusion. She looked quickly away.

Tor waited until he was sure she had command of her mount, then leapt up on his own. The moment his hands had closed upon her waist, he'd had the urge to pull her hard against him, and kiss her senseless. It left him startled and wary.

She's learned the legends from the village wisewoman. What else had she learned? Spells of enchantment? Certainly that would account for the suddenness, the potency of the urge that had almost overwhelmed him.

He feared, however, that it was something more difficult to keep at bay: the age-old lure of man to woman. And beneath that boy's garb, she was all woman.

Heat pooled in his loins. He remembered the feel of her narrow waist and delicate ribs. The feminine flare of her hips and the soft swell of her breasts. Her wild berry scent that teased his senses. And the king had offered her to him.

Tor gave himself a mental shake. He would not follow that line of thought: that way lay disaster.

He started up the narrow trail and left her to fall in behind him. The way sloped gently upward, then became considerably steeper. Ancient hardwoods gave way to dark fir forest. The heady scent of the trees filled the air.

Tor rode with an easy, masculine grace, sword at his side and his quiver and bow behind his saddle. Mouse was quite content to watch him. Dappled light brushed his wide shoulders and outlined his formidable physique. Although she was becoming tired, he looked fresh and alert as ever.

If trolls and giants do exist, she decided, *he could dispatch them with the same ease he vanquished Ragnor.*

She imagined Tor, then, his chest naked and sweat-slicked, sunlight gilding his body. It was so clear in her mind, she could almost feel the heat rising off him. Then she realized that the heat was inside her, burning deep in the pit of her belly. Her breath hitched in her throat.

Need and want poured through her, filled her to overflowing. It was not the sweet, innocent yearning of her dreams: It was a woman's throb of hot desire.

She fought against it. Only a fool would get caught in that trap. *I will not want a man who doesn't want me,* she vowed. *I value myself more highly than that!*

A shudder of mingled fear and anticipation shook her. Although she was a virgin, she knew the ways of the world. Fate had bound them together. Isolation in each other's company would serve to draw that bond tighter. The attraction she felt to him would tempt her sorely, and somewhere in the days ahead — it was inevitable — there would come an opportunity to quench her longing in his arms. She knew that she must guard against succumbing to it, fight it with all her might.

Mouse realized they'd reached the rim of the valley as they came out from the narrow defile onto a ledge. The sun was blinding and she shielded her eyes against the glare. They were in the foothills now, with the Misted Mountains rising above, their weathered summits wreathed in smoky veils.

Tor tipped his dark head back and gazed up at them. Excitement thrilled through his veins. *Somewhere in their mysterious heart, Destiny awaits.*

Mouse had ridden up beside him. She gestured to him. "Look. Over the cliff's edge."

Tor moved closer to the dizzying drop. Far below, a band of soldiers galloped along the coast road. They were heavily armed and wore the scarlet tunics of the queen's men.

And they were riding in the wrong direction.

"We've eluded them!" Mouse sighed in relief, and pushed damp tendrils of auburn hair away from her brow. She'd done it! Triumph surged through her.

Until this very moment she hadn't been quite sure that she could pull it off.

"You're worth your weight in rubies, fair Rosaleen!" Tor smiled at her, a flash of white in his tanned face.

Mouse flushed rosily. She felt that smile all the way down to her toes. It melted her bones and made her head spin — just as it had in her dreams.

Tor's eyes kindled. "For now we dance to the king's piping. But when I ride back to Castle Airan to claim my prize, he'll whistle another tune!"

Mouse felt as if she'd been slapped. She'd been so dazzled by his smile that, for a few seconds, she'd forgotten the true purpose of their journey.

Her hands jerked on the reins. The horse sidled and reared in alarm. For a wild moment it seemed that she would be thrown from the saddle.

"Have a care!" Tor leaned across his saddle bow. He pictured her spinning out over the void, falling down and down through the cool blue air, to shatter like glass on the valley floor below.

Reaching out at an awkward angle, he grabbed her horse's bridle, and wrestled the bit down with strength and sheer willpower. The jolt of it was severe. It almost wrenched his arm out of the socket.

Again, Mouse was startled by his great strength and power. And by the pleasure it gave her.

She mistook his grimace of pain for one of anger. "I could have brought the horse under control without your interference," she said hotly.

His brows knit in a scowl. He'd risked death to save her pretty little neck, and this was the thanks he got for it!

"You little fool! Do you know how near you came to disaster?" he said.

"Much you'd care!" Mouse's voice was sharp. "You didn't value my companionship so highly yesterday."

Tor's temper flared. "Ah," he snapped, "but that was before I learned that *you* can lead me to the phoenix."

Mouse recoiled from the anger in his voice. "You are right. I am a fool! If I had any wisdom at all, I would have lost you in the caverns. Or better yet, I would never have agreed to this bargain we made!"

"With all respect, lady, it was you who suggested the bargain."

She had indeed. "At the time it was the lesser of two evils."

Nudging her horse, Mouse sent the beast galloping across the meadow. Clods of earth and mangled wildflowers flew out behind them, as she tried to outrace her wild emotions. She was so furious with herself that she was shaking with it.

Earlier, for a bright, fleeting moment, she'd forgotten something she must never forget again: it wasn't the thrill of the quest that drove Tor on, nor the desire to obtain the phoenix egg.

It was his desire for the Princess Camaris.

12

Tor threw another brand upon the leaping fire and held his hands out to its warmth. The ebony sky was studded with myriad diamonds, and a chill wind blew down from the mountain's crest. The stars were cold and distant, but they could not have been more remote than his companion.

Mouse sat a hundred feet away, silhouetted against the night, with her back to him. She'd been sitting there for hours.

Seven days and seven long nights they'd been traveling together now, higher and higher, into the heart of the Misted Mountains. She intrigued him greatly. With every mile, his interest in her grew. At the same time, hers seemed to wane. He didn't know what to make of her.

Rosaleen. Her name suited her. She was lovely as a rose in bloom. And just as prickly. Every time he tried to get too close, he ended up bloodied.

It wasn't that he expected to charm every woman whose path he crossed, but she had barely spoken to him for days. Her silence unnerved him. She made no comments on the weather or the beauty of the scenery, and she uttered no complaints about the tiring journey, or the cold nights. On the rare occasion when she did speak, she was civil, but that was all.

It isn't natural, he reflected. *Women are supposed to chatter.* He'd never known one who didn't. But then, he'd never known any woman quite like her.

Tor frowned into the fire. He had enough experience with women to know that he'd offended her somehow — just not enough to figure out exactly what his offense was.

There was another thing niggling at him. For the first two days the course she'd led had been sure. Today, it had seemed at times that she was wandering along without a clue to guide her. At other times, he wondered if she might be purposely leading him astray. But why?

To complicate matters there was an attraction between them. He felt it keenly. At first she was so reserved that he had believed it to be one-sided. Then he noticed how she watched from the corner of her eye when he stripped off his shirt to bathe at the edge of the stream on a hot afternoon. The way her skin flushed and her pupils widened when he smiled down at her. Ah, yes. She felt it, too. And the longer they were thrown together, the more likely it became that one of them would act upon it. Just thinking of it aroused him.

That made the situation increasingly awkward. He tried not to think about it. About *her.* Nothing must distract him from his true goal.

Once Airan and Far Islandia had been united under one crown. During the chaotic war years, a despot had wrested the kingdom of Airan away by treachery. Tor's father had gathered his army and marched to battle, pledging to bring back Airan's crown and unite the countries once again.

Instead he had perished on the battlefield in tarnished glory. Tor had come to Airan not to seek a wife, however beautiful, but to make good his father's vow.

Tor rubbed his aching shoulder. He wouldn't let his focus be diverted by anything. Not by Gilmore's trickery. *Not even,* he vowed, *by the nearness of a beautiful young woman on a starry summer night.*

Try as he might, it was an impossible task not to think of her. His thoughts circled like a hawk riding the air, and each time they came back to his companion.

And she calls the queen a sorceress! he thought. Certainly the fair Rosaleen had put some sort of spell on him.

He looked at her and felt that hot tug of desire. She was lucky that her lot had fallen in with him. After all, he wasn't the type of foul villain who would tumble a pretty maid without a by-your-leave. But then, as she'd reminded him, her predicament was one of his making.

What would have happened to her if I hadn't come along to poke a stick in the hornets' nest of the past?

She was a fetching lass, as clever as she was lovely. Likely some fortunate fellow would have taken her to wed and bed. Fathered some red-haired sons and daughters on her. She might, as she'd said, have lived out her life in a little cottage contentedly enough.

Tor's reflections gave him no satisfaction. Guilt and regret filled his heart. *She deserves far more than that.*

Indeed, if matters had stood differently between Gilmore and the girl's mother, she would have been raised as befitted a daughter of royalty. He scowled. *Poor brave girl! She's been robbed of her birthright. If the king had honored his hand-fasting with her mother, Rosaleen should have worn a golden diadem upon her brow, and robes of embroidered sendal.*

She should have worn jewels at her throat and wrists and fingers. Flowing garments of rose-colored silk, trimmed with ribbons of the same hue as her silver-blue eyes. He imagined her in them.

He imagined her out of them.

A vision of her rose before Tor, sweet and enticing. That glorious dark red hair tumbling over her bare shoulders. Her ivory limbs as smooth as satin, her breasts rosy-tipped and inviting. They would pleasure a man with their texture and taste — like the wild raspberry scent that rose so tantalizingly from her skin.

Heat smoldered in his belly, curled out along his veins at the thought of it. She was more than lovely, she was beautiful. And she was incredibly desirable. If he hadn't been blinded by rage after the tournament, he would have seen it then.

He realized that now every day spent in her company would be more difficult than the one before. The long nights would be torture.

Even at a hundred yards, Mouse felt him looking at her. She was intensely aware of him on every level. He was a magnificent man. His sculpted muscle and sinew pleased her eye, and his face pleased her even more. Those eyes, as dark and light-filled as the starry sky above her. That firm, determined mouth roused feelings in her she didn't wish to examine any closer.

Mouse imagined him in the midst of war, the muscles of his back and shoulders rippling beneath his leather armor, the flash of steel in his strong right hand.

She imagined lying naked beside him, amid a crumpled toss of linen, his sun-bronzed hand dark against the whiteness of her breast. Her body tingled as if he'd touched her bare skin.

I will not think of you anymore than I must, Tor of Far Islandia. I wish I'd never agreed to set out with you in search of the phoenix.

She rose, meaning to walk further away from the camp. A moment or two ago she'd glimpsed a falling star. There would be a better — and safer — view from there.

Suddenly her body tensed like a bow. *Yes! There it was again.*

"Tor! Come here!" Mouse called out softly. "Quickly!"

Tor jumped up in alarm and raced toward her, his sword drawn and ready. "What is it?"

"Wait! Watch."

He did. There was nothing to see but the

immense stretch of velvet sky. Time slipped away like silk. Tor became aware of the utter stillness around them. Not an animal scurrying, not a single insect rustling in the darkness. Only the beating of his heart as he became attuned to her nearness.

Her beauty addled his head like mulled wine on a winter's night, and her scent rose around him in the darkness. He wondered what it was she wore that made her smell so enticing. He wondered what she would do if he gave in to the sudden and overwhelming urge to take her into his arms and kiss her breathless.

The air tingled. It seemed to Tor that invisible stars danced between them. Did she feel it, too? He held his breath as she stepped closer. Her fingers curled lightly over his wrist.

"There! Look!" Mouse whispered, shattering the spell. "Do you see it?"

A streak of scintillating light shot across the face of the dark. It vanished as quickly as it had come. "The phoenix," she said softly.

Excitement poured through Tor. Could it be? Certainly he had never witnessed anything like it before in all his travels.

"There's another!"

A shimmering golden ribbon unspooled against the blackness. It died to embers and winked out. Scant seconds later the night bloomed with light and color, closer still.

Mouse held her breath. Her whole body was trembling with the wonder of it. Tor's arm steadied her and they stood at the edge of the cliff. Watching. Waiting.

They waited for a long while, but the streak of gold didn't reappear. She became aware of Tor's breathing, the warm strength of his arm around her. The urge to lean into his embrace and see where the dangerous moment led them. Mouse knew he felt it, too.

They heard a rush of wings. Suddenly the air was on fire over their heads. Sparks of silver and gold rained down around them. Pulsing jewels of multicolored light were everywhere.

They stood transfixed. They could barely make out the creature's shape amid the darting beams. Up and down and around, in great looping spirals the resplendent phoenix flew. Its glory dimmed the stars and dazzled their eyes.

Tor stood with his head thrown back, his dark eyes gleaming with reflected fire. His arm tightened and Mouse leaned against his shoulder, not even aware of doing so.

A fountain of sparks fell around them, bright gold and silver plumes, glowing clouds of scarlet and blue and green. Mouse blinked and held up her hand. It was too much, this brightness, like staring into the noonday sun.

The light blazed, soared up and up, then disappeared for good.

They were left standing in the darkness, while images burned like flame against the insides of their eyes.

Neither spoke for some time. They had experienced something wonderful together, and the magic of the moment held them both in thrall.

He turned to smile at her. "We've almost reached the end of our quest. Tomorrow we'll be there, at the nesting grounds of the phoenix."

"Oh," she said softly, "I wish that we would not!"

He wasn't sure if he'd heard correctly. Was that a sneeze or a sob she'd stifled? Were those tears in her eyes? Tor lifted her chin in his hand, and saw that it was. He felt a little shaky himself.

"Don't cry, Rosaleen. Hush, my sweeting."

His fingers brushed away the tear that spilled down her cheek. She swayed against him, more blinded by his nearness than she had been by the light. He inhaled the now familiar scent of her. Berries and woman and dark summer night.

He felt the rapid beating of her heart, the small shiver that rippled through her body as his embrace tightened. All the feelings he'd suppressed so long would not be denied. Nor could hers. Warm and willing, she curved into the shelter of his arms. He pulled her close and lowered his head to hers. The moment his mouth touched hers, the high mountains and dark valley, the joyful dance of the phoenix, were all forgotten. The world fell away.

He angled his kiss and pulled her hard against him. As she curved into him, heat layered his body, rising in ever demanding waves. She trembled as he took the kiss deeper, but her arms rose up to wind around his neck. Her body felt so light — as if only his embrace kept her from lifting off the ground and floating away to the stars.

She'd dreamed this moment. Dreamed it a hundred times. The hardness of his lean body against hers, the steady thud of his heart. The warmth that poured through her, melding her to him. She kissed him. Not a tentative, fleeting kiss, but a full-mouthed, heated one. *Love me,* she whispered silently. *Love me.*

His mouth skimmed her cheek, her

temple, her closed eyelids, soft as a whisper of eiderdown against them. This was what she'd longed for, the protective circle of his strong arms. The power and demand of him. She ached with the need to answer it. To plunge recklessly into the moment without regret.

Her breasts strained against him, her fingers wound in his hair. Her ardent response surprised and delighted him. And by the gods, he ached for her! He kissed her again and savored it, long and deep. His blood sang.

Cupping her face in his hands, he kissed her until they were both breathless. He was like a beggar at a feast. He wanted to consume her. This past week had been hell . . . watching the sunlight dance on her flaming hair and caress the sleek lines of her body.

His hands, so large and calloused, opened her tunic with infinite care. Every touch, every move, was filled with heat and tenderness. Her body was like silk and velvet beneath his questing hands, her passion like a flame. He warmed himself with it. He cupped her breast gently, trying to soothe the wild beating of her heart. Starlight turned her skin to alabaster, tipped her breasts with silver. She was so beautiful, so very desirable.

A wildness came over him. His breath came faster, in time to the pounding of his heart. The same fierce need coursed through her blood. As if he sensed it, his hands became less gentle, more urgent in their explorations. She arched with pleasure and moaned against his mouth. It was a sound of victory and surrender. Of her delight in her feminine allure and power, and her yielding to his passion. *Yes,* she thought, *yes!* and didn't know she spoke aloud.

He swept her off her feet and lifted her, his mouth hot on hers as he swirled her around and around beneath the stars. Her cap flew off and her hair tumbled over her shoulders, spilled across her body in a scented cloud. She laughed with delight and anticipation.

When he placed her softly on the ground, she was reeling with desire. He pulled his shirt over his head, and her hands reached out and touched his naked chest. Her fingers trailed over the chiseled muscle, down his ribs. Her mind was filled with the touch and scent and sight of him. She moved against him, wanting . . . wanting.

He lay down beside her on the mossy ground. His hands danced lightly over the curve of her breasts, and down. His mouth followed where his hands had been, and everywhere he touched, she burned with fire. Light kisses, soft nibbles. The delectable shock of his tongue against her flesh.

He stroked and caressed and explored, all the while murmuring soft words of love. He led her gently but inexorably on. Along the way she lost her garments and her inhibitions. She was clothed in moonlight and sudden sensual awareness.

The light skimming of his hands tantalized her, and she arched against his questing hands, opened herself to more. Sensations shot through her, a mingling of desires so strong, so deeply pleasurable that she could scarcely bear the joy of it. She was shocked at his boldness, and at her reckless response. Tension coiled inside her, building fast.

There was no shyness in her when he touched her intimately. She pressed against him, eager to follow where he led. She was lost in a world that he knew full well, and she trusted him to guide her. To take her to places she had never even glimpsed in her fevered night dreams. His body was fully alive to the changes in hers, his mind numb to the consequences. The need to pleasure her, to claim her for his own, grew with every moment. With every soft gasp of her breath, every beat of his heart.

Again his fingertips touched, retreated, touched again. Her scent was on him now, ripe summer and woman, and he knew he couldn't hold back much longer. He wanted to lose himself in her. The urgency to claim her almost drove all else from his mind. He struggled against the madness. Against the need. The intensity of it shook him.

Lovemaking had always been a game of giving and taking erotic pleasure. This time it was something different. He wanted her with a primal ferocity he hadn't known was in him. To give in to it would be insanity. He'd never meant this to happen. He fought for control. One wrong step and he could jeopardize everything he wanted most.

Muttering an oath, he kissed her hard, then pulled away. Whether they took this to the next step or not, the choice must be hers. If she chose to stop, he would return to the fire and lie awake the whole night through, yearning for — what might have been. But if she chose to continue — ah, then he would lead her surely through the dark woods of desire, and he would lead her deep.

She cried out in protest as he drew away. She looked up at him in confusion as the cool night air caressed her skin. She ached to be immersed in the heat and passion of him. To feel the strength of him against her and around her and in her.

He felt her need as strongly as he felt his own. She was passionate and eager, but as innocent as he was experienced — and he had already turned her life upside down.

"Tell me what you want," he said hoarsely, "but tell me now. One word and we'll end this, before it goes too far." Too far was only a heartbeat away. "Tell me now, love."

Her emotions were like a tangled skein of silk. She couldn't tell one from another, they were so entwined. She wasn't sure of anything except that she wanted him to hold her and make love to her, banish all the loneliness as his passion met hers in equal measure.

She lifted her head and her hair fell across his chest like a satin veil. He groaned as the sensation rippled through him. She was exquisite and exciting, and he couldn't breathe for wanting her. In the night silence, he imagined he could still hear the blood pumping through her veins and the wild fluttering of her heart. She parted her lips and he waited for her answer.

She was caught in the grip of desire, and almost beyond words. Intuition guided her, and she arched up against his hand with a soft little cry of need.

The instant she brushed against his fingers she lost all control. Her head arched back and her eyes closed. She didn't know if the light was real or was bursting outward from the very core of her. It pulsed in waves of heat and pleasure. She bucked and cried out in delight.

In that same split second, an incredible light exploded through the clearing, showering their bodies with tingling sparks of gold and silver. In their blinding midst was its cause: a graceful bird with fiery plumage and jeweled wings.

"The phoenix!" Tor shielded his eyes against the white hot pain of it.

As he cried out, he felt her hips buck and writhe beneath him. Felt the honeyed heat of her against his flesh. Felt her twist and pull away.

She huddled on her side, spent and still. Alone. Shame blazed through her, as the phoenix burned a lonely path across the stars. *How could I forget?* she thought wretchedly. *How could I?*

He shook his head to clear his vision and glanced down, expecting to see her face still filled with desire. Instead she was curled up on her side, eyes closed. The change in her startled him. One moment she'd been as eager as he, the next she was rolled up like a hedgehog. He bent down and lifted the heavy spill of hair away from her face.

He touched her check. "Rosaleen?"

She wouldn't look at him.

"What is it, love? Did I hurt you?"

"No," she whispered. *I fear I have hurt myself. I let desire lead me, not my head, and this is the result.*

He leaned down to kiss her, but she pushed him away. Her eyes opened, glittering like cold blue diamonds. "Answer me this: Do you mean to continue your quest for the phoenix egg?"

He rocked back on his heels, astounded. Here they were, on the verge of plunging into the act of love, and she stopped to ask such a thing?

"Well?" she asked in a dangerous tone.

"Of course I intend to fulfill my quest. What else are we doing here in this isolated place?"

"What else, indeed?"

I am a fool. Why did I expect anything more? It is Camaris and a kingdom he covets, not me. Never me!

The cool breeze danced over her naked flesh, with no more effect upon her now than if she had been a statue. All the heat of her passion was turned to fury.

Once again Tor reached out to her. "Rosaleen . . . !"

She jerked back as if his hand were a firebrand. "Do not call me that!"

It was her own secret name. A part of herself that she'd kept hidden from the world.

She fought against the angry tears that stung her eyes. Her body had played her false, giving in to passion. He had breached her solitude and come close to doing the same to her virginity. She would not give up anything more to him.

Mouse grabbed her crumpled garments and rose. "I gave you my solemn vow, and I must keep it. And *you* must keep your distance. Dare to touch me again and you'll feel my dagger in your ribs!"

"You're being unfair," he said hotly. "I never took anything but kisses. You gave them freely enough." *And would have eagerly granted far more.*

The unspoken words hung between them like a sword.

She turned and walked away into the darkness, all bare and slender limbs. She was stunned by what had happened. Her breasts ached with fullness for the touch of his mouth. Her loins ached to know the feel of him inside her, the shock and glory of victory and surrender. And she would die before she let him know it.

Mouse went back to the campfire, dressed hurriedly, and lay down, wrapped in misery and her blanket. She heard Tor follow her there and mill around before rolling up in his own.

He'd taught her things she'd never even guessed at. He'd brought her body arching to fulfillment, and then . . . Her hands fisted at her sides, and fresh tears stung her eyelids. He was right in his silent assumption. She would have given her innocence to him — not just willingly, but eagerly. Hungrily.

He had said the choice was hers, but he had been the one to stop. She knew why. It wasn't the distraction of the phoenix; it was the knowledge that only a virgin could actually lead him to its nest in the silver rowan tree.

She would never forgive him for it.

Tor cradled his hands behind his head and glared up at the sky. The fire crackled in its ring of stones, and his body ached with all the heat and passion that had just been thwarted by the untimely arrival of the phoenix.

He remembered what he thought she'd said earlier. Now there was no doubt in his mind. She'd wished that they hadn't found the phoenix, yet she had given him her oath to do so. Only a virgin could lead him there, according to legend. Had she for those few moments of passion, wanted him? Or had she hoped to prevent him from finding the phoenix. And if so — why?

Rolling on his side, he watched the flames

burn low. He knew how to tease a maiden and make her smile, how to pleasure a woman's body until she came alive with fire and passion. But despite all the women he'd known, he hadn't a clue to the inner working of this one's mind. *Or,* he thought savagely, *her heart.*

His hands curled into fists. If he'd had them around that bloody bird a few minutes ago, he'd have wrung its bloody neck!

Well, perhaps he still would, after she led him to its nest.

If she led him to it.

13

Mouse was heavy-eyed and silent, Tor moody as they rode off in the morning light. He turned in the saddle to glance back at her, and his breath caught in his chest. Last night they had stood side by side and shared the magical flight of the phoenix. Afterward, they'd soared in each others arms, explored each other with a hot, greedy passion.

Now she couldn't even bear to look at him.

Her hair was bound up and tucked beneath her boy's cap, but the morning sun struck fire from it nevertheless. The plain tunic she wore belted loosely around her hid her feminine contours, but he remembered every lush curve of her body. Their silken textures. Their heady tastes.

He felt a dull flush rise up his face. The desire for her was still there, but hedged with caution. He pushed the tantalizing memories away. Last night they'd come so close . . .

Mouse felt him watching her but kept her gaze averted. She was trying not to think of it. Of him.

Once he had the phoenix egg, he would take her over the last line of mountains and down to the city Elva had described to her. Their ways would part forever.

Her horse stumbled suddenly, but she righted it. The beast was old and growing tired now, as if it had spent its last burst of energy in reaching this place. She guided it between the heaps of fallen granite that littered the mountainside, but as the hours passed they lagged further and further behind. She was a hundred yards away when Tor disappeared from sight.

Urging her mount on, she hurried to the place where she'd seen him last. She came around a pile of tumbled granite blocks, scanning the path for signs of him. There he was, at the foot of a weird formation — a spear of rock, cleaved from the face of the mountain. Wind and time had sculpted it into the semblance of a female form.

Mouse stared at it. *A woman turned to stone.*

That meant that Phoenix Pass, and the bird's nesting grounds, lay just beyond.

Tor had waited for her to catch up. He'd spied the stone formation and the narrow pass beyond it. "If your information is accurate, that pass should lead us straight down to the plateau — and to the phoenix."

"It might not yet have laid its egg," she warned him. "Unlike other birds, the phoenix broods in high summer. It might be anytime in the next two weeks."

Tor shrugged. "That doesn't matter. I'll capture the bird and take it back to Airan. Then it will be merely a matter of time."

Mouse bit her lower lip. The closer they came to their goal, the more she regretted her part in it. "That would be both cruel and unwise. The egg will only hatch within the nest of silver rowan leaves."

He shot her an annoyed look. "You seem determined to find obstacles. I'm not a fool. I'll take the nest as well."

"You still have to catch it," she said. "It won't be easy. You saw how it dipped and plunged and streaked across the sky. Like lightning!"

He laughed. "That was at night. But during the day the phoenix sleeps. I'll have my net around it before it even opens its eyes."

She went still and pale at the thought of it.

"What's wrong? Is it the height?"

"No. I . . . I think we should turn back. It's a trap. I just remembered another part of the legend," she lied. "It says the pass is guarded by trolls."

"My friend Broch says Airan is overrun with them — but have you ever seen a single one?"

"N . . . no. But that doesn't prove anything! I'd never seen a phoenix before last night." She twisted the reins around her hands.

Tor's black eyes surveyed her keenly. "Why are you trying to turn me aside from my quest, now that we're so near its end?"

Can he read my mind? Mouse shifted the attack. "It isn't an idle question! Suppose there *are* trolls? What will we do if one attacks us?"

Tor was impatient. "If our luck holds, we won't have to find out."

He led the way, and they came through the pass without incident. The first thing they saw was three squat lumps of weathered stone. "There are your monsters," he laughed. If she squinted her eyes, they did look a bit like gnarled trolls.

Tor couldn't resist sending her a wry look. "So much for the legends."

He rode on, to the edge of a high ledge overlooking the plateau. The view was astonishing. And infuriating. The Misted Mountains were not jagged ridges set row on row. They wound around in concentric circles, like a bizarre maze.

He scanned the area to get his bearings. To one side lay the Eastern Lands; to the other, Airan. He could clearly see Airan Castle and the river that flowed past it like molten silver. "By the gods! We could have gone out the northern gate and followed the river to its source — and reached this place by easy stages in a single day."

She shaded her eyes and saw nothing but high ridges and veiled peaks. "Impossible! There is no northern gate to the castle. And the river doesn't even flow toward the mountains!"

Tor realized that she was right. He'd stood on the castle's ramparts and looked to the Misted Mountains. There had been no river. No road.

He blinked. The terrain had shifted. The castle was gone. Nothing was there but a dead salt sea. Tor rubbed his eyes and the sea was gone. A fairy city rose against the sky, taller than the highest mountain peak, with towers of spun glass.

He knew that if he waited, the scene was likely to change yet again. "There is an enchantment upon this place. It is no wonder that strange legends abound!"

"Let's turn back!"

"The mirage can't fool me. That plateau beneath us is where the glowing streaks of light vanished last night."

She peered to where he pointed. Still nothing but swirling mist. Then something flashed with bright metallic luster. The mists parted and vanished, to reveal a grove of pines and the silver rowan tree in their midst. Its leaves shone gold in the bright sunlight.

Tor was baffled. Ahead lay nothing but a haze of mist and fog. But *she* saw something.

"The silver rowan," she breathed. The words were no sooner out than she wished she'd bitten her tongue.

"So it is true!" he said. *Only a virgin can lead the way.*

Mouse felt her heart drop. Vow or no, she couldn't go through with it. She tried to turn around, to go back the way they'd come. The pass had vanished. There was nothing but solid rock as far as the eye could see. The same magic that had led them there had closed any hope of retreat.

"Can you find the path?" he asked.

She stared at him. "Of course. It's as wide as a road."

It led down, straight and smooth, to the plateau. There was no way to go but forward. Mouse started down the track, leaving

Tor to follow. He plunged down into the fog, ignoring the flickers of light and shadow seen from the corner of his eyes. There was no sense of descending, no feeling of up or down or sideways. She was his beacon, his safe guide through the enchantment, and he kept his fixed gaze upon her back.

Mouse wondered at his cautious progress. In a matter of minutes they were at the start of the pine grove. The lowest branches grazed her head as she dismounted. *There must be a way out of this predicament,* she thought with rising panic. *I must think of something!*

Tor swung down, breathing in the scent of invisible evergreens, and went to her. The moment his hand touched her shoulder, his vision cleared.

They were in a wild place. The rocks were black marble heavily veined with rose, the trees like none he'd ever seen before. Huge flowers like cups of gold, like cups of blood, turned to watch their passage. Their leaves whispered softly.

A dainty creature leapt up beside the path and bounded away in a flash. Mouse had only a glimpse of it. Just enough to see the twisted gold horn that rose from its forehead.

"Did you see that?" Mouse exclaimed. "A unicorn!"

Tor kept his hand on his sword. This was an ancient place, and fraught with magic. They came to a place where steam vents opened from the rock and the air stank of sulphur. He eyed a striped lizard sunning on a slab, its scales a shimmer of lavender and violet and stunning deep purple. Another strange reptile slithered away into the shadows, all rippling gold and silver. The wide neck frill that covered its shoulders gave the illusion of wings.

He tipped his dark head back and gazed up through the green branches. Something flashed, like a sunbeam dazzling through the shining leaves.

But the sun was shining from the opposite direction.

Was it another trick of magic? It all seemed real enough. The ground was soft beneath him and covered with a blanket of pine needles. Branches stirred in the wind, and a brightness caught his eyes. *The silver rowan.*

Its leaves danced in the heart of the pines, reflecting light. But near the very top of the tree, there was something brighter still. He shaded his eyes.

It was a nest woven of the rowan's silver

leaves, and inside it was the most beautiful bird he'd ever seen. *The phoenix.* It was elegant, exquisite, with gleaming golden plumage that flickered with light. Its delicate tail feathers were so extravagantly long that they curved down over the edge of the nest, and its lovely head seemed crowned with sparkling jewels. Rainbow prisms shot from the bird like darts of colored flame.

Triumph burst through Tor. *Everything I want is within my reach.*

He looked again, in chagrin. So near and yet so far!

The trunk of the tree was smooth and gleaming as polished silver. There was no way he could climb up and snare the creature with his net while it slept.

There was only one way to do it. He unslung his bow from the saddlehorn. Plucking an arrow from his quiver, he nocked it carefully in place. Every move was slow and precise. Only a fool would rush at such a moment. Tor drew back his bow and took aim.

A second later a screaming fury struck him from behind.

"No!" Mouse shouted, pummeling him with her fists. "You mustn't kill it!"

Tor went sprawling facefirst onto the pine needles as her weight knocked him flat. The arrow went wide of its mark, whistling harmlessly through the long tail feathers of the phoenix. The creature cried out in a crystal voice and flew up toward the sun in a flurry of beating wings.

He rolled over, but Mouse straddled him. Her small hands pushed against his shoulders and her face was bright with wrath. She was magnificent.

The bird, the quest, were forgotten. He wanted her with a fierceness he'd never imagined possible. He grabbed her and rolled over so that she was beneath him. He grasped her wrists and held them fast. Held on to his own wild needs with all the willpower at his command.

"You little fool," he said harshly. "You've spoiled my best chance!"

"I only told you I would lead you to it," she said hotly. "I never said I'd let you take it! You tried to kill the phoenix."

"I didn't intend to harm it! I only meant to lodge an arrow in the tree so I could fix a rope to it from the pines and pull myself across."

Mouse bit her lip. She hadn't realized his intentions. Still, given the same chance, her reaction would have been unchanged.

"The creature is flown. But," she said firmly, "it doesn't matter. My part in this is over. I brought you here as I promised. Now you must keep your share of our bargain."

Tor released her wrists and rose to tower over her. "Do you really expect it of me?" His eyes were harder than his voice. "If you'll think back, fair Rosaleen, I never said I'd take you over the border."

Mouse recalled his words with a shock. He was right. He'd never said it. It had all been her words, her doing. She struggled to her feet, trying to think of a way to hold him to them. There was none.

"I don't need your aid," she said with scorn. "I'll find my way myself!"

Tor's mouth twisted. "No. You cannot. The city you seek does not exist. It was sacked and abandoned before you were born. There is nothing left of it but a pile of ruins."

His words hit her like stones. There was the ring of truth in every one of them. She went white and blank with shock. "What will I do? Oh gods, what will I do?" He was sorry. He hadn't meant to be so brutal about it. "You need not fear. I will see that you are safe once this quest is ended."

"The bird has flown," she reminded him in a flat voice. "You have lost your chance because of me."

Tor lifted his head. "No. I vowed to return

to Airan with the egg of the phoenix. I will find it and redeem my vow."

His arrow had gone wide, but it had still hit its intended target. The silver nest had tumbled from its lofty perch, coming to rest on the lowest branch. "The bird must return to the silver rowan to lay its egg. You told me so, yourself. I'll place the nest lower down and bide my time."

"It might be days before that happens."

"No. It will be soon." He pointed upward. A blur of gold shot across the blue sky, and a thin cry split the air above them. It was not the ringing crystal note they'd heard earlier. It was the sound of breaking glass.

Tor took out his harp and played a chord. Then his voice rang out, rich and full. The silver rowan's leaves danced.

A moment later the phoenix plummeted down. Just when it seemed it would smash into the ground, it flapped its wings and settled gently into the fallen nest.

The golden feathers were streaked in places, and looked like tarnished brass. The creature turned its jeweled head and looked at them, its grave eye glinting like a dulled ruby.

"You see?" Tor murmured. "Its time has come."

"It remembers," Mouse said sadly. "It

knows what will happen to it."

He wasn't listening. "The egg will soon be laid — and thereby make my fortune. This time the king will not dare refuse me what I ask!"

Her hand tightened on his arm. "It is not the king who wants the egg," she told him. "It is the queen. He would never have asked for such a thing of his own will. While she lives, he will never be completely free of her evil spell."

"King or queen, it matters not to me. All that matters is that I claim my prize."

Mouse's throat felt dry. "Queen Bryn knows the legend in its entirety. She will mix the egg with wine and drink it down, hoping that it will restore her youth and beauty."

"What is that to you or me?" Tor shrugged. "An egg, whether chicken or firebird, is just an egg."

"Oh, no," Mouse cried. "You don't understand. There is only *one*, you see. One phoenix. One egg."

"*What?*"

"Don't you know the rest of the legend?" Mouse brushed at the loose auburn tendrils clinging to her cheek. Her fingers came away wet with tears.

"The phoenix lays her egg and dies, consumed in glory. The warmth of the ash incubates the egg. When the egg hatches, the phoenix is reborn."

Tor struggled with the concept. "As long as the egg hatches successfully, it is immortal? No." He shook his head. "Impossible. How can it be reborn? It is just a legend. . . ."

A tear stole down her cheek. "How can you say that? You've seen the phoenix with your own eyes. It is unique in all the world. It is as real as you or I. And when it is gone, there will be no more!"

His finger grazed her cheek. "Sweet Rosaleen, only think! There is no such thing in nature as one of anything."

She lifted tear-drenched eyes to him. "There is only one of *me!*"

14

"You are not the man I once thought you to be," Mouse said angrily.

Her tears had long since dried, and her arguments had been to no avail. Tor meant to take the bird back to Airan with them. Bryn would make her magic potion with the egg it laid — and the phoenix would become extinct.

He opened his saddlepack and withdrew something, avoiding her eyes. "And what kind of man was that?"

One to whom I gave my trust. My heart. One I thought I loved!

She felt a sharp pang of loss. "A man I could respect."

He flinched as if she'd struck him. A dark flush rose in his face. He hadn't yet done anything to deserve that.

"And what qualities do you respect, Rosaleen?"

Her chin lifted defiantly. "Honor and integrity above all else."

"I am sorry to have disappointed you so gravely." His jaw set. "But I must do what I must do."

Tor unfolded the bird snare he'd taken from his saddlepack. He draped it over the bird and its nest and staked it down tightly. The phoenix made small sounds, like the tinkle of discordant chimes, and gazed sadly at him with an eye like frosted pink glass.

"You didn't have to do that," Mouse said angrily. "It is in no shape to fly away. See how dull its plumage is?" She touched a feather. It was limp and lusterless. The color had darkened to bronze.

"The creature might brood quietly in the nest until it lays its egg," he said, "but I'm taking no chances. I have some exploring to do. You stay here and keep watch over the phoenix. I'll find us a plump fish for dinner."

"I don't want dinner." Mouse turned her back.

"Well, I do."

Mouse leaned back against the tree and murmured comforting words to the bird. The aging phoenix rubbed its golden beak over Mouse's finger, acknowledging her presence. Then it held its graceful head aloft, waiting for the magical moment when its proud heart would burst into flames of joy, leaving nothing of its tired body but sparkling ash and a glowing rainbow egg. The moment was almost at hand.

Tor stalked off into the pine grove with a small wicker creel. There was a stream that cut through it, and he was bound to find a fine fish. But first he wanted to see more of this enchanted place.

He set off in the direction of the rocks where the lizards sunned. There were none to be found. He foraged for a while, wandering closer to a strange hummock that rose in the midst of the plateau. As he approached, he heard an odd metallic sound, like the gnashing of rusted steel. Wide, three-toed footprints covered the ground nearby, and the mound was studded with holes large enough for a man to enter. Tor gave the place a wide berth. He was curious as to what lived inside the burrows, but he had no intention of going in to find out.

I have other fish to fry.

Tor walked and walked, and always the stream seemed just ahead. A furry creature ran out across his path. It looked like an ermald — except for the tiny silver crown upon its head. Entering a clearing, he spied another lizard basking in the sun. This one was a fiery red, spangled with rose. A wide shadow passed over the ground, but when he looked up the sky was deep and clear.

Butterflies larger than his hand flitted through the dappled light, and the pinecones underfoot seemed carved from copper. When he touched them with the toe of his boot, they poofed into sparkles and vanished.

Everything on this plateau was under an enchantment. Nothing was what it seemed. "I'll be glad to get back to the real world," he said out loud.

The words were no sooner spoken than he saw the stream flowing in front of him. A large bass leapt out of the water to land at his feet. *"Dinner,"* the fish said, and winked at him.

Tor ignored it all as another bit of sorcery. "Into the water with you, my friend." He tossed the fish back. *It will have to be jerked beef tonight, and whatever roots are left in the saddlepacks.*

He looked up to plot the course of the sun. He'd been gone long enough. It was time to return. When he reached the silver rowan tree, Mouse was sitting almost exactly where he'd left her — but the stakes had been pulled up and the net lay sprawled over an empty nest. The phoenix was gone.

He walked over to her, his face set.

"I set it free," she told him defiantly.

"You were a fool," she added, "to leave me

alone with the phoenix. You should have known I would release it at the first opportunity!"

"Yes, I suppose I should have."

She'd released the bird, knowing that he would hate her for it. But where she'd expected anger, there was only coldness in his eyes. It chilled her to the bone.

Suddenly he squatted on his haunches beside the nest. "You are the fool, Rosaleen." He plunged his hand amid the silver leaves. When he pulled it out, something glowed through his fingers, showering the air with radiance.

Her face went white with shock. "The phoenix egg!" She hadn't seen it there, buried among the leaves. "Then . . . that part of the legend isn't true. It laid its egg and has flown away to die. But there is still only one phoenix. One egg."

Tor wrapped the egg in a handful of leaves and placed it in a leather bag attached to his belt, where it would stay safe and warm. "Come. There is no reason for us to tarry now. If that road cutting through to the south is not an illusion, we can reach the castle by nightfall."

Mouse stared out over the plateau to the final ridge of land. "I'll go my own way. There are other cities on the far side of the mountains where I can claim sanctuary."

Tor replied firmly, "You'll go with me, if I have to lead you all the way."

She was subdued and didn't protest as he saddled the horses. She tried to mount on her own, but her foot slipped out of the stirrup. "Help me up."

He came beside Mouse and put his hands on her waist, warm and strong. For a moment they stood close, their eyes locked. Her heart beat faster with the memory of his hands upon her bare flesh, the hot touch of his mouth. She could read nothing in his expression. He tossed her up into the saddle as if she were a sack of oats.

The moment she was in the saddle her demeanor changed. She nudged her horse and took off without warning, giving the cob its head. He gave a shout, but she was already urging the beast faster. If she had enough of a start, Tor wouldn't bother to pursue her, she was sure. Not now that he had the precious phoenix egg.

She'd read him wrong. Hoofbeats sounded behind her, gathering speed. He wasn't going to let her get away so easily. *If I can get past that mound in the distance, there will be only enough room for one horse between the rocks. He'll have to give up.*

Crouching low in the saddle, Mouse galloped across the plateau. He was gaining on her. The old cob was no match for his fiery steed. She felt her horse faltering.

Almost to the mound! She glanced over her shoulder and saw that he was almost at her flank. Suddenly the cob reared up, whinnying in fright. When it came down, one leg crumpled beneath it. In the moment before she was pitched over the horse's head, Mouse caught a glimpse of squat, gnarled bodies, heard the clash of tusk and metallic teeth. *Trolls!* She flew out of the saddle.

The trolls closed in on her, blood dripping from their serrated teeth. As she rolled into a protective ball, Tor galloped up, his sword flashing. She heard the ring of it on those fearsome teeth, the thud of it plunging through the troll bodies.

Tor leaned down from his saddle, scooped her up in front of him before she knew what was happening, and spurred his horse hard. She could only hang on tight and pray she wouldn't fall off.

Her ribs felt bruised from the strength of his arm against her. She tried to look back. "Don't!" he commanded.

They raced on. Small red birds flew up and lizards dashed for shelter. Tor didn't rein in until they reached the edge of the plateau. The horse was in a lather and

Mouse was trembling from head to toe.

"That was a foolish thing to do," he said grimly. "We might both have been killed!"

"You didn't have to follow me," she said, shaking with emotion.

Tor cupped her face in one hand. His finger traced the line of her mouth. "Didn't I?"

Mouse looked away. "I don't understand you. Every time I think I know you, you change."

His voice was hard. "I am the same man I always was. And now you must live with the consequences. Much as you loathe the sight of me, you have no choice of destination. You must ride with me — and I, fair Rosaleen, am going back to Airan."

She saw that there was nothing else to do. She lifted her chin. "I will go back for Elva's sake. And I will hold you to your word to see us safe."

He swung down and lifted her from the saddle. For a moment she was weightless in his arms. Then she was on the ground, her legs shaky.

Tor kept his arm around her until she got her balance. She was pale, her eyes wide and her mouth pink as a rose. He gritted his teeth. "By the gods, I should throttle you!"

"If you wished to be rid of me, you should have left me to the trolls."

His face darkened with anger. "Do you think me capable of such a thing?"

She bit her lip. "No." The admission was wrenched from her.

He opened the leather pouch to check the egg it held. As he unknotted the strings, light shone from it as before. She didn't know whether to be glad or sad.

They shared his water and what little cold food he had left. Everything she had was gone along with her poor, doomed horse. They remounted Tor's steed with Mouse riding behind. Mouse leaned her cheek against his broad back. It was awkward being so close to him, inhaling his masculine scent. His muscles rippled beneath his leather jerkin, and she could feel the power of him radiating through her.

They took the impossible shortcut and came out into a grassy meadow as the sun sank in the west. The sky turned orange and rose and gold, highlighting the familiar hills of Airan. If this wasn't another mirage, they would reach the castle before midnight.

The horse thundered on, its long legs eating up the miles. The moon rose, silver and full, to light their way. Mouse was too exhausted and heartsick to care. She had thought Tor different from other men, but he was just the same as all the rest. Power was all he cared about and winning the hand of the princess Camaris.

Her eyes were wet. *Tears for the beautiful phoenix,* she thought. *And a few for myself.*

At last the towers of Castle Airan rose up beside the river valley, ghostly white in the luminous light. Mouse closed her eyes. She wanted to disappear into the darkness before they reached the gates: The last place on earth she wanted to be was by Tor's side when he claimed Camaris for his bride.

15

The hour was past midnight when something awakened Elva. She went to the window that overlooked the river road and the distant hills beyond. The world was still dark, the only light that of the torches blazing on the castle's walls. Then she saw it: a glow coming up from the valley, white as the heart of pure flame. Her heart thumped with fear and hope. Gathering her cloak, she ran out of the cottage.

A group of men camping along the river road saw it, too. Broch gave them the signal. He'd been waiting for it, but never expected it this soon. "By the gods, he's done it!"

In the queen's bower at Castle Airan, Bryn awakened from a troubled sleep. Her skin prickled. She listened and heard shouts from the watchtower. She ran out of her chamber, scarcely stopping to snatch up a warm velvet cloak.

Gilmore was there in the corridor before

her, still wearing his coronet and his robes of justice. There had been a council meeting tonight, from which she'd been excluded by law. It always rankled her that she could rule Gilmore through her spells, but not his kingdom. Fortunate for him, she thought viciously.

"What is it?" she said. "Are we under attack?"

"No." Gilmore rubbed his forehead. "But it is something dire, no doubt. Why else would a lone horseman be abroad at such an hour?"

They went out onto the ramparts together. A few seconds later they noticed the glow. It was far too bright for a lantern. Gilmore was puzzled, but Bryn knew what it was, even before the rider swept around the curve to face the castle. *The phoenix egg!*

And Tor, the dark warrior, come to claim Camaris for his bride.

Her eyes sparkled with mingled joy and malice. *I will have youth and beauty, but you will never have my daughter. I will see to that!*

She touched her husband's arm. "You are tired, Gilmore. You can scarce keep your eyes open. You will seek your bed and fall into a deep sleep."

Frowning, he turned away. "I will wait to see what news this messenger brings to us."

Bryn made a small sign and murmured a word beneath her breath. "You will go to bed now, and you will remember nothing of this in the morning!"

Gilmore struggled, then turned stiffly and moved away like a sleepwalker. A moment later his door closed behind him.

Bryn stilled the rapid beating of her heart. She could not keep him in her power much longer. He was fighting off her spells, starting to remember things that were best forgotten. The woman Deirdre and her daughter among them.

That was unfortunate. He was a lusty lover and an able king, and she still wanted him, even if his passion for her had waned. But once he knew the truth of what she had done so long ago, the last link between them would be snapped.

The queen shrugged and hardened her heart. All things, no matter how pleasant, must come to an end. As for Tor of Far Islandia . . .

She smiled. Camaris was not for such as him. Camaris would marry the duke — no matter her tears and tantrums — and extend Bryn's power.

She sent for her new captain of the guard. "The barbarian from Far Islandia is approaching. You will escort him to the privy chamber immediately."

"Yes, Majesty."

"When he realizes that the king is not there, he may try to escape. If he does, your own life will be forfeit."

The captain felt a shiver up his spine. He recalled what had happened to his predecessor a week earlier, in the castle dungeon. "Yes, Majesty. It will be as you say."

"I hope so," she said with a tight little smile. "For your sake."

"There is someone riding pillion with him," the man added.

She hurried to the window just as Tor and Mouse came over the bridge to the castle.

Two birds with one stone!

"The man is accompanied by a young woman," she said. "You will bring her to the presence chamber with him. You will see that they are treated with all respect."

Her eyes shone like pieces of gold. "And you will also see to it that neither leaves the room alive."

16

The moment the gates opened and they rode beneath the portcullis, Mouse and Tor were almost surrounded by soldiers. His horse reared at his command, and they backed away from the flailing hooves. Mouse clung to him with all her strength.

"We mean you no harm," the captain of the queen's men said. "We are an honor guard, sent to escort you to the presence chamber."

Tor's sword swept a silver arc. "We need no escort."

Again his horse reared. "Stand back!"

The soldiers obeyed. Tor wheeled his mount and rode up the courtyard steps and into the great hall. Sleepy-eyed servants and guests rose from their pallets and scattered as he entered.

They clattered past the dais and Tor dismounted at the presence chamber, sword ready. Mouse slid down from her perch and darted behind him to open the door. The moment they were inside the chamber, she shut the door and slid the bolt across. Then she turned around and gasped. It wasn't King Gilmore, but Queen Bryn who stood before throne, flanked by her henchmen. Her golden eyes were filled with greed and eagerness.

"So, your quest has been successful."

"You must be the judge of that," Tor answered coolly. "It will hatch soon."

He took the pouch from inside his jerken. Light leaked from it, growing ever brighter as he opened it fully and removed the egg. The thick shell sparkled and glinted in his hand with increasing radiance.

Bryn's eyes opened wide when she saw it. *Youth and beauty will be mine once more!*

The magic she'd tried to conjure in their absence had failed her again. Now she was paying for the years she'd kept her youthful beauty through means of the Dark Arts. Her skin was increasingly furrowed, her eyes duller. She could feel herself aging minute by minute. And now, here was the chance to reverse the terrible process.

"Give me the egg," the queen commanded.

Tor closed his fingers around it. "And what will you give me in return?"

"Damn you for your impudence! Guard, seize the egg and bring it to me!"

One soldier tried to grab the egg from Tor's hand, then leapt back, howling and holding his hand aloft. The skin of his palm was singed and seared.

A hush fell over the chamber. "Perhaps you are as unaware of the legends surrounding the phoenix, as I was previously," Tor replied. "Rosaleen has related them to me. The egg cannot be taken from me. Only the person who has claimed the egg from the nest, can give it away."

He stepped closer and lowered his voice. "And now I repeat my question: If I do freely give the egg into your hands, Majesty, what shall you do with it? When the new phoenix bursts forth, will you keep it caged, a tame bird to sing within your bower?"

Her breath came rasping through cracked, dry lips, "There are caged songbirds enough to suit me already, and one is very like another."

Tor smiled grimly. "I am told that this egg is the last of its kind. The *only* one of its kind. Once it is gone, there will be no more. The phoenix, in all its unearthly beauty, will vanish forever from the world."

Bryn laughed harshly. "Why should the phoenix, with no more brains than the chickens scratching in the kitchen yard, have eternal youth and beauty? I am a queen, surely more worthy of such a gift." She threw her head back haughtily. "There are other birds in the forest. However, there is only one of *me*."

Her words echoed the ones Rosaleen had spoken to him earlier — but how different their meaning.

As he stepped closer to the queen, Mouse blocked his way. "Do not do it, I beg of you!" Her heart was a ball of hot lead inside her chest. Burning, burning.

"I have no choice," he said.

Mouse blinked away a hot sheen of tears. "We have traveled hard and long on our quest, Tor of Far Islandia. During that time I have seen your courage and knightly compassion. You risked your life for mine. And," she continued, "you risked that phoenix egg when you saved me from the trolls."

She clasped her hand upon his arm. "If actions speak louder than words, then I will use them for my guide. If you give the egg to the queen, you will destroy a creature that has done no harm to anyone, one that brings great pleasure to many with its beauty and song. And that would mean you are not the man I lo—"

She stopped and took a breath. "That you are not the man of honor and principle that I believe you to be."

His gaze was black and opaque as onyx. "You ask a great deal of me, Rosaleen. To give up the hand of a princess and half a kingdom. If I do what you ask of me, what do you offer me in return?"

Mouse shook her head sadly. "I have nothing to give you."

Tor looked down at her, his eyes dark as night. "You are wrong on two counts." His voice rose, sparked with passion. "You have much that I want, fair Rosaleen. But I am afraid that I am not the man you believe me to be."

He lifted his arm and held the egg out toward the queen.

17

Mouse stepped before him. "If that is all you'd wanted of me, you could have taken me that night, with my full will and passion. I thought you turned away from me that night, because you needed a virgin to lead you to the silver rowan tree. I was wrong. You are good and true, Tor of Islandia! You cannot betray the phoenix any more than you could betray me."

His gaze locked with hers. "You truly believe I will forfeit everything I have fought for, while you boldly state you can offer nothing in return?"

She threw pride and caution to the winds. "The reason I have nothing to bestow on you is this: You already own the one thing that is mine alone to give — my heart. It is yours, Tor, now and forever."

"Enough of this folly," Bryn cried out. "Give me the egg before it is too late!" Already her knuckles were thickening, her hands curling into claws.

The egg in Tor's hand jumped suddenly. It almost bounced from his palm. As his fingers closed on the shell, a thin crack opened around its perimeter. Light spilled out from it, ever brighter. It dimmed the light of the torches and the flames leaping in the hearth.

Brynn held out her hand imperiously, and the jewels at her wrists and fingers winked like stars. "Hurry. You must give the egg to me! Only think! The hand of the princess and half the kingdom."

Tor wrenched his gaze away from Mouse. He lifted the egg high, and its brilliance banished the shadows from the darkest corner of the old hall. "Is that all?" His voice rang out. "What if I want more?"

The queen's eyes were wild and tarnished, her gnarled fingers ready to snatch the precious phoenix egg. "Anything! Ask anything of me, and it is yours! Even the crown of Airan."

The curtains behind her parted and the king stepped out. "Generous of you, wife. But the crown of Airan is not yours to give!"

Gilmore dismissed the guards. When they were gone, he bolted the door again. "I will take the egg."

"No!" the queen cried. "Come, give the egg into my hand, and you shall have

Camaris to bed this very night. Only give me the egg!"

Tor held it just beyond her reach. It bounced again, and another crack opened. Suddenly Bryn could stand it no longer. She lunged and tried to grab the egg from his palm. Tor snatched it back. "How badly do you want it?"

He hurled the glimmering oval straight into the blazing fire that danced in the great hearth. The flames crackled up around it, erupting higher. Something cracked louder still. Zig-zag lines formed around the egg as it fractured and sizzled in the heat.

"No!" the queen shrieked in a blind fury. She dashed to the hearth, where she took up the fire tongs and she caught the egg, rolling it out onto the stone flags. An aura of light blossomed around it and the shell broke open in a dozen pieces.

Mouse threw herself at it, but Tor caught her in his arms. He pulled her hard against his chest and kept her pinioned there. "Do not look, for the love of God!"

Her face was buried against his shoulder, and she felt the strength of him, inhaled the warm, familiar scent of his body. Her body curved to fit his, supple as a willow. She felt the steady beat of his heart against her own.

Lightning filled the chamber, and the

pungent odor of sulphur. Flames leapt up in a mighty roar. Despite the turmoil around them, Mouse felt safe in the circle of his arms. Safe as she had never felt before in her life.

"Look in the mirror, not at the fire!" he said urgently to the king.

Mouse lifted her head and glanced into the looking glass that hung over a chest. The presence chamber was reflected there — the hearth with flames leaping up to the chimney, gold and orange and red, casting their lurid glow upon the queen's ivory gown and golden hair.

But something was different. Chillingly so. Mouse blinked in disbelief. Queen Bryn was frozen in place, one hand extended greedily. From the tip of her velvet slippers to the crown of her head, she had been turned to stone. Every line of her face, every fold of her silken gown, every pucker of scar tissue on her unveiled throat was precise, as if carved by a master sculptor.

There was a scrabble of scaled legs among the logs, and Mouse saw what the others had already noticed in the looking glass: It was not a phoenix hatched from the egg, but a fierce lizard, with gold and silver scales. Its wide neck-frill covered its sinewy shoulders, and gave the illusion of wings.

With a sharp hiss, the creature turned and ran back inside the huge hearth. It vanished up the chimney in a puff of glittering smoke.

"What wizardry is this!" the king exclaimed.

"No wizardry, Majesty" Tor said, "but the cold stare of the fire-born basilisk, which turns the unwary observer to stone."

Gilmore shook off the clinging webs of Bryn's spell and stared at what she had become. A lump of harmless stone.

Mouse blinked. "But how did you get the basilisk egg?"

Tor laughed. "I spied the basilisk on our way to the plateau, before we reached the silver rowan tree. When I went off 'fishing' I kept an eye out for it. When I returned to camp after you set the phoenix free, I brought the lizard's egg with me. By sleight of hand, I merely pretended to pull it from the phoenix nest and your nest I returned after leaving you alone."

Mouse smiled up at him, her face shining. "You *knew* I would release the phoenix!"

His mouth turned up wryly. "Yes, Rosaleen. I counted on it."

He turned to the king. Gilmore looked dazed like a man awakening from a long and dreadful nightmare.

"A great evil has been removed from

Airan. You have successfully concluded your quest, Tor of Far Islandia. I will stand by my word. You may claim the Princess Camaris and half my kingdom now, as is your right I will give you my blessing."

"I do not want the princess called the Flower of Airan. My desire for her was not love, but infatuation. Nor do I want half your kingdom. I ask instead for the hand of the Fairest Rose in all the world, my darling Rosaleen. It took only a few days in her company to know that she is my true heart's desire. *If,* that is, she will have me."

Tor turned to Mouse and took her face between his hands. "*Will* you have me, love?"

She threw her arms around his neck. "I will, with all my heart."

As they started to kiss, Gilmore cleared his throat loudly. "You cannot have her."

"What?" Mouse exclaimed.

"By the gods," Tor roared, "I will take her!"

"Only," the king said, "if you agree to half the kingdom as well. It goes with her, you know. And it might have been yours by right."

Gilmore saw the startlement in Tor's face. "Yes — I know who you are, grandson of the great Orgus. Your father was Loric. He was my friend. If the wars had gone differently, he might have sat upon the throne of Airan instead of I, so we have come full circle. I am weary of this crown. I will grant half my kingdom to the Princess Rosaleen, my first-born daughter. She will hold it in her own right. The other half I will convey to you, on the day you two are wed."

He took Mouse's hand in his and joined it with Tor's. "Together, you will rule wisely, and well."

"But what of the Princess Camaris?" Mouse stammered. "She is your daughter, too."

The king smiled. "I assure you that she will be perfectly happy. She has neither the ambition nor the wits to rule. Last evening, after the queen retired to her chambers, Camaris eloped with her handsome lordling. They sailed with the tide, and will be far at sea by now. I'll settle a fine dowry upon her, along with my personal estates in the Western Lands. All the rest I leave to you."

"I don't need your kingdom," Tor said. "I am heir to Orgus's holdings. I have a manor and a thousand acres in Far Islandia."

"Keep them, with my good blessings. But do not forsake Airan." Gilmore's smile went awry. "This I humbly beg, not as a king but as a father. Do not take my daughter from me now when she is finally restored to me."

"That is entirely up to her." Tor tipped

her chin up. "What do you say, my love?"

Mouse's heart was full, her joy complete. "I say that this is the happiest moment of my life!"

Tor drew her into his embrace. "Ah, love. This is only the beginning. There is so much more to come!"

Epilogue

Tor's bride lay against him in the darkness, her auburn hair spilling over his naked chest like skeins of silk. The bells of Airan that had rung out in celebration of their wedding day were stilled, the explosions of fireworks were long over.

He cupped her breast and kissed it. She sighed and moved against him, feeling him stir to life. "You are greedy," she whispered.

"No more so than you, fair Rosaleen. How many times do you expect me to make love to you?"

She laughed softly. "As many times as you can."

"Is that a challenge? If so, I am more than up to it."

"So I see, braggart!"

He rolled over, pinning her beneath him as his mouth ravaged hers. He touched her and she parted to him, and her sweet scent filled the air like perfume. "Slow or quick?"

571

he asked. "Rough or gentle?"

"I don't care, as long as it's thorough. And soon!"

Her teeth nipped his skin. Her legs wrapped around him and she pulled him deep inside. He took her with all the passion that was in him, urging her on to wild abandon. She arched against him, crying out his name. As she went spiraling up, her body filled with heat, with light. With him.

When it was over they lay spent and replete in each other's arms — but the light was still there. She could see it through her closed eyelids.

Mouse opened them. "Look!"

The phoenix had flown in their open casement and perched on the deep stone windowsill. Its eyes were filmed, its feathers bedraggled and dulled, but sparks flew from them, and its proud head was still lovely.

"What is it doing so far from its nesting grounds?" Tor murmured.

But Rosaleen knew. It had come to thank them. The phoenix cocked its head and gazed around the room. It spied her short cape of cloth of silver, which lay discarded on the floor along with her gown, her silk stockings, and velvet shoes.

It fluttered down to the cape and settled among the folds of cloth. Suddenly the bird's feathers took on a molten glow. Then the phoenix lifted its head and trilled a song so wondrous, so heartbreaking in its beauty, that Mouse's eyes filled with tears. As the highest note filled the bedchamber, there was a burst of bright white light too dazzling to watch.

Heads averted, eyes covered, the lovers waited until its glory dimmed. The light died away.

"Oh! Tor!" She clasped her hand to her heart.

Of the old phoenix, nothing was left but sparkles of glowing ash, but an egg lay among the folds of her cape. It was smaller than the basilisk egg, with none of that reptile's strange and coruscating light. It glimmered gold and silver, as elegant as the phoenix that had brought it forth.

While they watched, the shell cracked and a young phoenix rose from the jagged pieces. It gazed at them with eyes of glowing ruby, then sang a song so pure, so golden, that their hearts were filled with joy.

Tor's arm went around her shoulders. "Out of nothing, everything. Just like our love for one another." He drew her against him and kissed her. As their passion bloomed again, the reborn phoenix flew out the open window and was lost among the fire of the stars.